NATALIA GROMOVA

MOSCOW IN THE 1930s

A NOVEL FROM THE ARCHIVES

Translated by Christopher Culver

MOSCOW IN THE 1930s
A NOVEL FROM THE ARCHIVES

by Natalia Gromova

Translated by Christopher Culver

Book created by Max Mendor

Glagoslav Publications Ltd
88-90 Hatton Garden
EC1N 8PN London
United Kingdom

www.glagoslav.com

ISBN: 978-1-78437-971-1

Contents

Finding a guide

By subtititling her book *Moscow in the 1930s* "A novel from the archives", Gromova is perhaps not specifying the genre as much as she is putting a potential reader to the test. Will the reader be able to overcome the widespread aversion towards musty shelves? Will the reader follow the author into an alien world, one that is forgotten and has slipped away?

Perhaps the reader won't accept the challenge – but Gromova is not afraid of that, she's not chasing after mass appeal. But any reader who follows her, will be rewarded with the opening lines, a recollection from her childhood that, as is often the case with such memories, offer a prophetic reflection on her adult life:

…It was an enormous barn key. Heavy and decorated with a string. I found it in the thick dust of the road in the village of Khortitsa on the Dnieper. It was somewhere here that the Zaporozhian Cossacks had written their letter to the Turkish sultan. I picked up the key, and in that same moment it came to me that I would surely find a door that it would open.

Already on the next day I was sliding down a rope through a narrow opening into the cellar of the village school. We children knew that, during the war, the Germans had been headquartered here. It was scary, but I was completely convinced that now, right here, once I hit the floor

I would discover a secret door, I would find treasure or important papers [...] Of course, it had been strange to think that the key I found along the road would fit right into this cellar door.

But years later, as I was wandering through different cellars – people's recollections, archives, card catalogs – it would happen that the oddest things, things one could not imagine side by side, would come together in consecutive links and whole chains. And in the reality that I found myself in, the keys unexpectedly found their keyholes and opened the doors. Sometimes one needs a long time for this, but sometimes success comes quickly…

Gromova returned from these wanderings, which quite often involved hardship and difficulty, bearing books that set down the experiences of one person studying the literary life of the mid 20th century. Their titles – full of Acmeist conciseness and at the same time lit through with symbolism – are a legacy that she received from her informants, those who preserved the memory and maintained the culture of a vanished and remarkable time: *The Knot: Friendships and Ruptures between Poets from the late 1920s and 1930s* (2006) and *The Collapse: The Fate of the Soviet Critic in the 1940s and 1950s* (2009)…

The first of these titles was suggested by Maria Belkina, author of one of the most famous books in Russia, *The Intersection of Fates*, dedicated to the last years of Marina Tsvetaeva's life and the fate of her children. The second reconstructs the literary biography of Belkina's husband, the influential critic Anatoly Tarasenkov. It is this same Belkina who became one of the main characters in the first part of *Moscow in the 1930s*, along with Tatyana Yermolinskaya (the widow of the playwright

Sergei Yermolinsky) and Ludmila, daughter of the poet Vladimir Lugovskoy who was famous in these years. The second part of the book deals with the Dobrov family, or rather, the Dobrov *home,* which offered a refuge for Daniil Andreyev (the mystic and victim of Stalin's camps). We also learn of two women intimately linked with this home, namely Olga Bessarabova and Varvara Malakhieva-Mirovich, who kept fascinating diaries that bear witness to what befell to the Russian intelligentsia from the second decade of the 20th century through the 1950s.

Within the commentaries and notes that Belkina, Lugovskaya, and Bessarabova had once left behind and which pointed to the fates of great 20th-century poets, one finds woven plots very much like those of a novel. In Gromova's book, *secondary* things become *primary* ones: the author follows, as it were, Sir Walter Scott's take on the novel, where the main characters in the story recede into the depths of the plot's canvas, while in the foreground one finds ordinary participants in whatever is going on, who in this case are writers of memoirs. I daresay that this was undoubtedly a conscious choice by Gromova: as a senior fellow at the Marina Tsvetaeva house museum, and with unprecedented archival materials at her disposal, she nonetheless writes not about a lofty Olympus of poets, but rather about people who stood next to those well-known figures and remained always in the shadows:

It always seemed to me that background figures, people who are much more difficult to glimpse or learn anything about, offer the possibility of imagining the world of the past in a much fuller way. These unnoticed characters began to come out of the shadows of the Soviet underground in the Nineties, when we wanted to believe that the Soviet regime had ended for once and for all…

One recalls here the phrase "unsung heroes", a saying quite in tune with the living current of literature in the early 21st century. Certainly in recent years, one of the most heated topics of debate in the literary world is what "heroes", what a book's protagonist(s) should be today. It has been hashed out in thick issues of literary reviews, at events where writers have featured. People have sought a hero in the latest novels and are ready to see one in e.g. the mediocre businessman of Denis Gutsko's *Beta Male*, in the "office tadpole" of Olga Slavinokova's *Light-headed*, or in the free artist of Alexei Ivanov's acclaimed novel *Bluda i MUDO*... Ultimately people have become accustomed to a contemporary hero being something found only in the past, whether the Russian or Central Asian Middle Ages (Evgeny Vodolazkin's *Laurus*, Andrei Volos's *Return to Panjrud*) or back in the depths of the Soviet era (Zakhar Prilepin's *Abode*, Guzel Yakhina's *Zuleikha Opens her Eyes*). Gromova's *Moscow in the 1930s* stands alongside such literature. It is clearly a non-fiction book in terms of its content, and it is a truly contemporary Russian novel in the way it perceives both history and the place assigned to a person within this history.

The strong and unbreakable Maria Belkina, the bright Olga Bessarabova (sister of Boris Bessarabov, the very same "Communist" whom dedicated readers of Tsvetaeva will recognize from her poems "Side Streets" and "Yegorushka"), the wise and longsuffering Varvara Malakieva-Mirovich... Standing in the wings of history, away from the spotlight of researchers and readers, they vividly manifest what Marianna Ionova called, in her review of the novel, an "ethical design".[1] Indeed, we have grown used to the fact that in the case of great artists, it is difficult to apply the standards of conventional morality: how can

---

[1] Ionova's review appeared in *Novy Mir* 2015/1.

one judge Tsvetaeva, Pasternak, or Bulgarkov by them? Another matter is their contemporaries, the "people around them", whose fate is apparently unknown to all but the all-seeing eye of the state, and they provide examples of great deeds carried out quietly, of true heroism. Maria Belkina "left her one-year-old son with her parents and rushed to the front, secretly leaving Tashkent [...] She had no permission to do so, she had no papers, but she managed to reach Tarasenkov and they were together for some time at Lake Ladoga." Or take Varvara Malakhieva-Mirovich, who spent her whole life educating and caring for the children of others, including the children in the Dobrov–Andreyev home, and who appears in Gromova's book as a moral guide who stands out from surrounding (Soviet) life and reveals it for what it was.

Such indicative heroes solve a double task: on one hand, they uphold timeless ethical principles, which were so battered by the 20th century; on the other hand, they share various private events from literary history of the 1930s through the 1950s, shedding light on these matters in their diaries and reminiscences. The latter, however, is something that the reader might need more than the author does: Gromova understands readers' expectation and curiosity towards the little-known pages from the lives of Vladimir Lugovskoy and Daniil Andreev, but she turns her own attention to something else. She is interested not so much in people of action, but rather in those who preserved these stories, because those guardians with their "book-like" memory seemed on the surface to play the role of bearers of the *ancien regime,* but in fact they were upholding universal and timeless moral principles. As Gromova herself admitted during her speech at the ceremony held to award the annual Znamya prize, "I began to write my 'novel from the archives' precisely because I had an acute sense of the moral tension of the 20th century, which continues to affect our lives and our destinies…"[2]

This feeling of a "moral rupture", of the moral collapse of the era evokes the theme of Hamlet, key to the entire 20th century in Russia. Like Mandelstam, who asked already in 1922: "My era, my wild animal, who will ever look into your eyes, and with his own blood glue together the backbones of two centuries?", and like hundreds of her own predecessors and contemporaries, the author of *Moscow in the 1930s* acutely feels the need to reconnect the periods of history, to restore a sense of continuity:

> I felt that I had come into real contact with that era. I pulled on a chain in my time, and an answer came from that time.

> This is just a part of the chain. Sometimes I regret that I cannot see the whole picture. The thought has long tormented me that here is a person that we see at a certain time and place. Where does his past lie, his actions, his path in life? Perhaps some invisible body grows within him? A person sees only the fragment that lives for this particular moment in time. Where is the person as he was yesterday? He touched someone else's life and forgot about it. He crossed someone else's path and then disappeared. But the picture remains. The invisible world of human beings, their fates, look like a single circulatory system woven in the past and in the present day. It is for that reason that a person who strikes, humiliates, or insults another, will inevitably bring harm to himsself…

---

[2] Gromova's remarks were published in *Znamya* 2013/3.

Of course Gromova, as a professional woman of letters, has managed in her life to be "an editor at a publishing company, an author of encyclopedia articles, a budding playwright, and employed at a newspaper…" She knows about Sergei Bocharov's claim that "literature is like a circulatory system". However, in her case this single, organic system encompasses not so much literature as fleeting lives; the laws of literature, the very "intersection of fates" as in Pasternak, are clearly stated in Gromova's chapter "The Methodology of Miracles":

Gradually a new reality was revealed to me. I started seeing not only separate personal stories, but also the invisible map of the world of these people, who were joined, separated, lost and found, forming a distinctive landscape of entwined fates and intersections that resembled a panorama of aerial photography, or a book of anatomy with its networks of blood vessels. It should come as no surprise that precisely in these entwined fates a miraculous element appeared, which Pasternak wrote about so much in his novel *Doctor Zhivago*.

Miracles were part of life. When I noticed their presence, they were an additional compass guiding my journey.

A similar feeling, instilled in us all by the 20th century, often gives rise to other novels of our time – one need only look to Alexei Ivanov, who feels an extreme sensitivity to modernity and who carved out his novel *Bad Weather*, which describes in great detail the roaring Nineties and the critical time of the early millennium, as if he were using Pasternak's *Doctor Zhivago* as a model. Like Gromova's *Moscow in the 1930s*, Ivanov's *Bad Weather* attests that the "intersection of paths through life", inscribed in the atlas of people's fates, do exist, and the laws that are discovered by literature and affirmed by it, are set unchangeably in stone. Especially since these laws, just like anything else that makes up our lives, have their terrible dark sides:

> There has never been a subject that has arisen so frequently in conversations with different people. The entire Soviet world that some people sigh for with nostalgia, and others look back on with horror, is run through with eavesdropping, denouncing, or informing on people, binding each and every person with the shackles of slavery. This spiderweb wrought with human hands is clearly a creation of hell, because it can catch onto every life, every relationship between two people. This is a hellish reflection of the human circulatory system created by what lies above, granted to us by fate. This is most likely a distorted resemblance to the light golden net connecting all of us with our past...

This dark side, the "hellish reflection" of God-granted relationships, is also something that Gromova explores. One might say that the subject of her books is this very battle between shadows, fear, an element that is chthonic, infernal, and destructive – with an element of light; a battle waged in the heart of every human being. Thus *Moscow in the 1930s* starts with a story about Vladimir Lugovskoy's running away with the evacuation instead of to the front, and it continues with difficult reflections on the biography and tragedy of the "hopeless liar" Tarasenkov, so that it can then recognize the author's own secret, the story of her grandfather who worked for the state security... It seems as if the "dark side" proves victorious, that Man is held captive, but no, at the same time discreet worship services are held in the catacomb chapels of the "Last Moscow",

Daniil Andreyev writes his novel *Wanderers of Night*, and Varvara Malakhieva-Mirovich notes in her diary the prophetic words of her friend Lev Shestov: "If all people are children of God, then that means that one does not have to fear or regret anything."

Perhaps Gromova would describe herself as a writer with the words of Joseph Brodsky, who claimed that the main theme of his poetry was time and what it does to a human being. Does it break men, mangle them, or provoke a terrible "transformation" as in the case of Fadeyev and Lugovsky, or does it retreat, unable to disfigure the blessed image of the human being, as in the case of Belkina, Bessarabova, and Malakhieva-Mirovich? "I realized that I had to write a book about this Transformation," we read in Gromova. "I had to write about the 1930s using everything that had been revealed to me in the collections at Lavrushinsky Lane about Lugovskoy and his friends: Nikolai Tikhonov, Dmitri Petrovsky, Alexander Fadeyev, and others – about their gradual falling into the abyss. About how Tikhonov and Petrovsky were friends of Pasternak in the late 1920s and what this friendship was turned into in the late 1930s. About how Pasternak remained Pasternak, and how everyone knew it; and about how this caused annoyance, alarm, fear, or respect…"

Here is where the riddle lies. It might seem like we already know of this – how "the tectonic layers of history had shifted, and from the gap that now opened up, one could see the priests of the catacomb church, the children of dispossessed kulaks, the first female university students, prisoners in labor camps, followers of Vlasov, survivors of the siege of Leningrad and prisoners of war, emigrants and evacuees." We know these things from literature that has come back to Russia, from countless family sagas, among which one finds both untalented screeds and masterpieces; we know them from an abundance of historical investigations... But Gromova's book gives us something more. Why is it so fascinating to follow her down into the cellars of human memory and dusty archives? Perhaps it is because at each turning point of history, Gromova chooses the right key for it, a suitable way of bringing it to life, a special formula, backed up with facts – a shred of a document, a piece of paper, a shard of home furnishings,[3] and this detail that she came across by chance unexpectedly helps to form a mosaic that was held, in bits and pieces, in our memories.

In Moscow one can identify to this day the buildings where people lived in the Thirties, from the ramshackle doors with their peeling oil paint, from the stone spiderweb of walls, the crumbling window frames, from the rusty nails in fixtures, from the broken stairs in the staircases. The unevenly cut wooden boards, which were quickly installed to cover holes in the building entrances. Everything is twisted and slanted, the result of disorder and poverty.

---

3   A story that Gromvoa tells from her life at the museum, when she set up exhibits at the Marina Tsvetaeva museum, is illustrative: "I once created an exhibition devoted to the evacuation of writers and their children to Chistopol and Yelabuga. On the table I set a number of items that any family would have: they are scattered around people's dachas, stuffed into closets, we walk past them when they lie forlorn in a rubbish heap. Iron glass holders, aluminum spoons, thick tumblers, old and rusty irons... How surprised I was when I saw how interested the visitors were in each item, looking at it as if there were a treasure laid out before them. Some asked if they could touch the items, while others took photos, and still others copied down the words written on the labels..." Perhaps the reader today lacks precisely these evocations of mundane life?

The remains of 1930s life smell like mustiness [...] It was as if the Thirties wanted to disappear, evaporate, to turn to dust.

The most important thing in the Thirties, however, were the utterly Shakespearean scenes and emotions that never made it into literature. In my book dedicated to the Thirties, there were so many stories of this nature, they popped up again and again. The thing is, they could have only happened in that era...

Perhaps it is the way that every accidental detail comes together, the way that the smallest trifle fits into an overarching vision, that we find attractive in Gromova's book. Soviet history, seen in its fullness, continues to be bloody, of course, but suddenly "something else" shines through the blood, an "element of the miraculous", and by this light the writer guides us through the twists and turns of history. It goes without saying that with such a storekeeper as a guide, it is easier for us to enter into this history, as into an unfamiliar river with dangerous currents and whirlpools.

Elena Pogorelaya

Elena Pogorelaya is a literary critic, secretary of the review *Voprosy Literatury*, and a member of the jury for the 2013 Russian Booker Prize.

Part I. The Key

...It was an enormous barn key. Heavy and decorated with a string. I found it in the thick dust of the road in the village of Khortitsa on the Dnieper. It was somewhere here that the Zaporozhian Cossacks had written their letter to the Turkish sultan. I picked up the key, and in that same moment it came to me that I would surely find a door that it would open.

Already on the next day I was sliding down a rope through a narrow opening into the cellar of the village school. We children knew that, during the war, the Germans had been headquartered here. It was scary, but I was completely convinced that now, right here, once I hit the floor I would discover a secret door, I would find treasure or important papers. In reality, the cellar was empty, the door would not open at all, and it seemed like I would be stuck there forever. Of course, it had been strange to think that the key I found along the road would fit right into this cellar door.

But years later, as I was wandering through different cellars – people's recollections, archives, card catalogs – it would happen that the oddest things, things one could not imagine side by side, would come together in consecutive links and whole chains. And in the reality that I found myself in, the keys unexpectedly found their keyholes and opened the doors. Sometimes one needs a long time for this, but sometimes success comes quickly.

Chapter 1.
Lavrushinsky

Knock, and it shall
be opened unto you...

Scattered sheets of thin paper with tiny letters. A fragment of text with no beginning or end, where suddenly one could make out the phrase "And then Akhmatova said to me..." A letter whose author was unknown, a letter without an addressee. The torn edge from a notebook, with the date at the top – "1927" – and everyday notes. A manuscript with folds where the pencil mark had been completely wiped out. A notebook with three pages on which the events of August 1936 were described, and then everything else had been torn out. A grayish-yellow sheet where letters had been erased, words had become smudged, and the meaning was lost. An address. Initials. A last name. A number.

And what is more, myriad references – you pour over them and you start to see how this or that name that you need connects with the others, and they weave a thread that has remained invisible to everyone. The text of a letter reveals a fragment of a life without a beginning or end. It unknowingly enters into an invisible dialog with other letters and papers that had been discovered before. Before your eyes there unfolds a living ribbon of personal stories that are tightly interconnected, and you have the visceral feeling that this ribbon extends to you too. And you yourself are just a small whorl in an enormous fabric.

I was forty years old. Papers and other people's letters, smudged ink, that was all something I knew little of. I had been an editor at a publishing company, though, and I had authored articles in encyclopedias, some short stories, I was a budding playwright, and I had been employed at a newspaper. I had taught in school a subject they called "philosophy of literature". I had been picked up and swept along by the free winds of the 1990s, when a person could participate in, create, undertake anything at all. But I could not manage to find myself…

In childhood I had been tormented by the mystery of time. When I came home from school to our communal apartment, all alone, I would sit at the scratched writing desk and think for hours about how to enter into my own time, how to physically feel its presence. I came to one conclusion: to write a letter from this time, from the age of 11, to my own self at 13, with the aim of "here you go, the time will come when you will open this envelope and from the heights of your thirteen years you'll see me, an 11-year-old, and you'll see how you're smarter, taller, and better, but what's important is that you not forget what you were in the past." This letter was sealed with glue, and then wrapped into some fabric and sewn up, so that there would be no temptation to read it before its time. The acute interaction with time took place both when the letter was being written and when it was being read two years later. Within me there arose for an instant a feeling of things coming together: I was here and there at the same time.

I had the same feeling again many years later, when the 90-year-old writer Maria Iosifovna Belkina told me at her apartment in Lavrushinsky Lane about how Marina Tsvetaeva had visited her before the war at her house on Konyushkovsky Lane. I then clearly saw how I was standing before the balcony door of our apartment on the twelfth floor looking out at Prospekt Kalinina, now known as Novy Arbat. I was ten years old, and before me were the rows of the wooden village of Konyushkovsky, which would burn down in a few years and completely disappear from the face of the earth. All those houses and the little street I was hearing about at this moment, in my childhood I knew them almost by touch. Maria Iosifovna, who had grown up in Konyushkovsky Lane, knew these places in the very same way.

And suddenly I see how that girl standing on the balcony, is gazing out across the houses and alleyways right at me, now in the present day and listening to the story about Konyushkovsky Lane. Our gazes met.

We could start like this

Lyudmila Vladimirovna Golubkina, the daughter of the poet Vladimir Lugovskoy and my former mother-in-law, and I were leaning over some papers that had been rolled up and tied with a thin silk ribbon. When we unrolled them, we discovered some letters from which various passages had been carefully cut out with nail scissors. The letters had belonged to her late aunt Tatyana Alexandrovna Lugovskaya, a set designer in the theatre. They had been written in the late 1930s or 1940s. They were addressed to Leonid Antonovich Malyugin, a playwright and theatre critic in Saint-Petersburg, who in 1949 had suddenly been labeled a rootless cosmopolitan. These were not the originals of the letters, but rather a poor-quality transcription, and thus there was no beginning to them, and sometimes no end, but that did not get in the way of hearing the author's truly living voice. His voice resonated in a mocking, gentle, and charming fashion. And I thought – and it was probably no coincidence – that Malyugin's play about Chekhov and Lika Mizinova, which had a successful run at the Vakhtangov Theatre when I was a child, had been titled *My Mocking Happiness*. It had been written later, but the tone of the letters was destined for the play still to come. From the atmosphere of these letters one could see the ample Moscow of the late 1930s rise up: trams slid along their tracks, birds sang, rain come pouring down, and I could clearly hear the smell of lilac trees.

* * *

These letters became the beginning of my first book and the woven themes that set out from it. Already at that time some effort was called for in order to riddle out the secrets and things unsaid within them.

While I initially thought that it was I who would search, that it was I who would find them, as time went by it became clear: these are something that find you, they hurl themselves at you through space.

In the beginning they might greet you. Yes, indeed, they greet you, because across the boundaries of time you start to speak, hear, and meet with the person in question. Maria Iosifovna Belkina was a completely grounded and no-nonsense woman, who laughed at any hint of mysticism, and who had a very ironic relationship with faith. Once she said to me, "I never, *never* wanted to write about Tsvetaeva." Maria was talking about her book *The Intersection of Fates*. "Why do I need to do that? And who am I to write about her?"

"And how did you?", I asked with some amazement and wariness.

"She herself wanted it!" Maria said, and then she calmly added, "Tsvetaeva tossed letters at me. She made me bump into the right people. I tried to avoid it for a long time, but I suddenly felt that she herself wanted this."

When Maria Iosifovna said this, I felt that it was the truth, but I was still unaware of the bar in the secret mechanism – I had only just started to look at it in detail. The key word here is *greet*.

Everything started with letters

Ludmila Vladimirovna, editor and scriptwriter, moved after her dear aunt's passing to an apartment near the metro station Aeroport, where Tatyana Alexandrovna was living with her husband, the playwright Sergei Alexandrovich Yermolinsky. Ludmila Vladimirovna was gradually looking through a large amount of remaining papers. I had visited here when Tatyana Alexandrovna was alive, and now, when I had time, I looked at the notebooks, some recipes, on the backs of which one could make out reminiscences that were abandoned in their second paragraphs. For years this had become part of our life together. I loved to hear the story of "Malyugin's letters."

At the end of the 1980s Ludmila Vladimirovna, weighed down with groceries that she had managed to find, opened her door with her key and saw her aunt sitting on the bed, bent over some scraps of paper spread before her. Tatyana Alexandrovna had carefully cut something out of them with nail scissors.

"What are you doing?" she asked with great surprise.

Her aunt had likely decided to put her past in order and thought that the right time for this had come.

"I want to destroy my letters to Malyugin," she calmly replied.

They had once carried on a great and friendly correspondence, which was fated to break off. Tatyana Alexandrovna demanded the letters back. He said nothing and only six months later did he sent her a package with the letters she had sent him. She then, without thinking long about the matter, destroyed them. Then the gloomy postwar years came, and Malyugin together with a group of critics were declared "cosmopolitans", they lost their jobs and they stopped putting on plays. It was here that Tatyana Alexandrovna forgot about any offense taken and completely restored their old friendship. It went on like that until the end of Malyugin's days. When he died, it turned out that he had not left any kind of personal archive, that he had destroyed all his papers, letters, and drafts. Nothing was left of his past but a small packet. Malyugin had no wife or children, and it was his sister who brought the letters to Tatyana Alexandrovna. When she opened the package, she found her letters to Malyugin that she had long ago destroyed. He had copied them out and saved them for as long as he lived.

And here she was now, cutting out from them passages (already once destroyed) that made her upset. Something was not going right, and he said that she would cut them up, burn them, and then throw them out again.

But for some reason she left them alone.

When they maintained a correspondence she was only 27 years old. She was working in the theatre, putting in a lot of hours and a lot of effort. He was 30 then and a successful theatre critic. He had still not written a single play, and he was clearly being eaten by the feeling known to everyone that life is passing one by. Not a single one of his letters to her has been preserved. Leonid Malyugin is only reflected by these messages from Moscow to Leningrad.

"…Lenya, it came to pass that I get on well with you, and that is why I want to scold you a little bit. It seems to me that you don't have enough of a certain quality necessary for life, which we can provisionally call persistence. You have a poor grasp on life. This is visible in everything. In your personal relationships with people, in your work, and in you in general. You are a terribly fragile person. It's so easy to offend you, upset you, or make you change your wants and decisions. If you ask me, if something doesn't work out for you, you just shrug your shoulders. You just don't care. (There are many such examples.) When a person does not have this solid core, he or she begins to be afraid of resembling a proofreader or a clerk at a counter. Essentially, nothing ever happens smoothly. But all of this mess made up of pleasant and unpleasant things is called life, to which we cling so strongly and which we 'love so gently'…"

"…I want to do nothing at all, just put on some new coat that I don't have and go for a walk through Moscow and buy flowers, as the streets are already so full of them. And I want to go into a bookshop and buy some books. And into a stationer's for some paints. And I want to go to a cafe and buy some coffee, and something that would fire me up a little more. Just walk through this magical city and marvel at the houses that have sprung up over the winter and what wonderful dark blue shadows they cast."

"…We have had a terrible frost here. I just weep from the cold outside. I feel sorry for Chkalov. I remember it well – I was in a taxi on the 16th, after having waited for it for half an hour and almost frozen to death. I had to go a long way, to Meshchanskaya Street. A ZiS car stopped for me, there were a lot of places into it, it was spacious, like an empty train carriage. I tucked my legs under myself and thought about my mixed-up life. The terrible cold was coming in from the outside. In the air, foggy with the cold, small groups of people were moving with funeral banners. There was not a single living soul around at the time, except for the driver with his back towards me. It was very sad. And then the driver turned on the radio, and suddenly there was music. Beethoven was playing. The whole car was filled with this music. Some kind of unusual clarity arose. (I realize that there's no point to me writing this.) It's just that, you know, when I came back to the car from the house I was delivering a package to, I hoped that I would still have that melody, but the happy moment had already come to an end, and an ordinary everyday voice was trying to convince me that Chkalov is a hero, but I already knew that. T. L., Moscow, December 18, 1938."

Of course, Malyugin could not give these letters to Tatyana Alexandrovna, not only because he had a quiet and unrequited love for her, but rather because there was the very fabric of life in them, and as a playwright, he felt this very well. Her ironic tone seeped out of these letters and got into Chekhov's correspondence with Lika. It could not have been any other way.

But nevertheless

I met Tatyana Alexandrovna when I was 20 years old and she was seventy. Never before or after that time have I met such a strange person, except maybe in Dickens. The first character that comes to mind is Betsey Trotwood in *David Copperfield*. Just like David Copperfield's grandmother, she was tall, with an absolutely rigid spine, every statement she made could not be contradicted, and she carefully followed your reaction, and in spite of her gaze that seemed so impenetrable, somewhere in the very depths of her eyes was a merry devilishness. When I sensed these depths of joy, I stopped being afraid of her and I began to be able to talk with her without any problems. Being someone from the theatre, she dressed in a very sophisticated way for these drab years of the Soviet Union. At home she would walk around in a long silk robe with tassels at the end of the belt and wide sleeves, under which one could see a white lace blouse.

"My dear!" she would say in her low voice, made husky from smoking, when I humbly sat down before her in her kitchen under its large lampshade. Everything around me was unusual: the long multicolored beads hung on the wall, delicately knitted tablecloth, the woven napkins on the table. This was something completely un-Soviet: the kitchen was like a small, cozy room to entertain guests, and in the study of this standard Soviet home, an enormous antique table and bookshelves from an old Moscow house had sailed in.

At this time she was carefully examining how I was dressed and how my hair was done.

"Well, tell me, what poets do you like?"

I was attempting to hold my own ground, but at the same time I aggressively answered, "I love Mandelstam!"

Her face showed a clear disappointment, but deep down inside she seemed to nod in agreement. I again said, aggressively, "You don't like Mandelstam?" If I was in this game now, then I should play to win.

She answered with a contrary air, "He was so unpleasant. He would come on too strong, he always had busy hands."

She saw how I was seething inside and she took the initiative:

"Now, Gumilev, he was a real poet, he was something else entirely."

I however needed to vent my indignation. How could she throw all this into one pile? Busy hands?! I unleashed a barrage.

"Well, your Gumilev dedicated a poem to Blumkin, that scoundrel who shot Mirbach!" (I had learned that only the same day when I was in the metro, when I saw the latest issue of *Novy Mir* out of the corner of my eye.

The face of this elderly woman began to change color, showing looks of surprise, mistrust, and perturbation.

Oh, how I would curse myself years later for my foolishness, the eternal foolishness of youth! I should have asked her to tell me how and where Mandelstam had courted her. But I had wanted instead to express my own feelings.

But when it came to Mayakovsky, she would tell stories of him with great pleasure. They had met by chance not long before he took his own life, in a stationer's shop where she was buying paints, and he told her tenderly of how much he loved to paint. He asked her out somewhere, but she was embarrassed and said that while they would have to get together sometime later, she was presently occupied.

How often have I read stories by different beautiful young women whom Mayakovsky asked out, and each one of them added, oh, if I had known, I would have gone anywhere with him, just so that he wouldn't have died. But I wouldn't have gone, like Tatyana Alexandrovna, because just then the hands of fate brought something important.

Once in Peredelkino, when her husband Sergei Alexandrovich Yermolinsky was still alive, she said to me in a tone of great importance, "You know, all the ladies of Peredelkino are totally bald. They wear wigs."

I froze in astonishment.

"Really, Natasha," she said emphatically and firmly. "You must look out for this when we go to have lunch."

As she spoke, I was looking at the curls in her thin hair. Sergei Alexandrovich was sitting in a wicker chair with a blanket around his shoulders and a smirk on his thin lips, but not taking his eyes from his book.

"What are you smiling for, Sergei? What I'm saying is true!"

At the age of seventy, Tatyana Alexandrovna wrote a remarkable book about her childhood before and after the October Revolution, entitled *I Remember*. The narrator was a teenage girl with an ironic style, who analyzed everything in great depth and had a great admiration for her father Alexander Fyodorovich Lugovskoy, a teacher of literature at the 1st Moscow Gymnasium. As a matter of fact, the book ended with her father's burial at Moscow's Alexeyevsky cemetery, where she too now rests. This account was so stunning talented that Tatyana Alexandrovna was immediately accepted into the Union of Writers at the end of the 1970s. When we embarked on reissuing the book twenty years later, we had to put back bits of the text that had been cut out by the censors. I thought a lot about Alexander Fyodorovich then, he was an extraordinary personality who was a teacher to many great writers and scholars. After the revolution, he saved his pupils from hunger by creating a colony in Sergiev Posad where children grew vegetables and learned different subjects at the same time. He was a classic example of the Russian intelligentsia, the kind that arose in Russia in the mid 19th century. He humbly carried the torch of enlightenment and didn't understand the current political situation very well, or simply didn't want to understand it. This particularly distressed me.

Here is a picture of Alexander Fyodorovich's funeral. It shows Sokolniki in 1925. His loving pupils crowded around the grave. The priest is uttering the funeral rites, but Alexander Fyodorovich's son won't let the priest finish his recitation: he pushes the priest away with his shoulder and begins to read over the grave a poem by Alexander Blok, whom his father had greatly admired. Everyone is listening in amazement, including Tatyana Alexandrovna. The mother, a singer, sings something majestic.

His son Vladimir Lugovskoy, the future poet, was born at the very start of the century. The revolution swept him up like an adventure novel, a story in which he found himself a role to play all the way to the war.

Alexander Fyodorovich served Russian literature like a priest: literature had completely replaced religion for his generation. But neither literature nor culture, as it became clear later, could save them from the chaos of the revolution and then all the ugly realities of Soviet life. Many of these high-born gymnasium teachers and university professors looked at the complex issues of society and politics with disgust, and the consequences of this naturally fell on the heads of their children, who were swept into the maelstrom of history.

At the end of her life, Tatyana Alexandrovna felt a cosmic sense of cold, which blew from a crack in space where there was no God. One day after Sergei Alexandrovich had died, she said to me, "What if I never meet him there," she pointed a finger upwards. "What if I'm not worthy?"

The only thing I could tell her is that love brings people together. She listened to me attentively, not because I was telling her anything new, but just because she needed someone to tell her precisely this.

When I had arrived at their home, Sergei Alexandrovich was still alive. I was twenty years old and I was adrift and thinking frantically about my future. I felt that something important was going to happen, and I was very afraid of missing the sound of the curtain being drawn back. It was already the bleak year of 1980. There was a feeling that the seasons of the year no longer changed, as if November and December would last forever. The stagnation was in its darkest stage, and it seemed like it would go on for eternity. But precisely for this reason, people would shine brighter. Human relationships became more interesting, people would talk for hours on end, taking the greatest pleasure in discussing this or that person.

Sergei Alexandrovich was a real elderly gentleman, the kind I had only seen in foreign films. He was thin and upright, with a handsome rugged face, large eyeglasses, and a gaze that seemed mainly directed inward. However, it did not bother him to look upon the others who came before him with happiness and a gentle irony. It is hard to imagine that years later, I would be left with his past, his entangled life, which had it all: a major Moscow celebrity – Bulgakov, the basements of the Lubyanka prison, and denunciations. Caressed by the love of his dear wife during his life, after his death this man would stand face to face with an enormous army of haters. Why? It looked like I would be able to dig and find the answer to this question, but for that I would need experience and an understand of how lives were intertwined. Life rolls on like a ball, lifting up its heroes on high and then dropping them to the bottom. This ball keeps rolling even after the person passes away, it continues to act on his fate in the same way as when he was among us. How many times have I had to witness the strange reflections or distortions of a person's life in their posthumous existence!

Sergei Alexandrovich appeared in Tatyana Alexandrovich's life shortly after Malyugin's letters, and more importantly, after Tashkent.

"I'd really like to write about Tashkent, the *balakhana*, Akhmatova," she said. "That is the most important thing I should manage to do."

Later, after she had passed away and when no such book was found, Ludmila Vladimirovna also frequently uttered the word "Tashkent", the place where Akhmatova, Nadezhda Mandelstam, and Elena Sergeevna Bulgakova spent time. In Lugovskaya's apartment near the Aeroport metro station, where Ludmila Vladimirovna would settle, all the text snippets that were found, all of the pages torn from somewhere were collected together in a file. Ludmila Vladimirovna took out a register containing entries made about Tatyana Alexandrovna. A slip of paper fell out with "Necklace" written on it, followed by a list: Akhmatova, Tyshler, Tatlin, Melnikov.

It was a yellow, ragged piece of paper. A portable typewriter with small letters. "Akhmatova came down with scarlet fever…"

It was at the same time that they began to transcribe the fragments of the letters to Malyugin. A whole world that had been lost rose up again.

When the war broke out, Lugovskaya's mother became seriously ill and could no longer move. On October 14, the day before the "surrender of Moscow" which everyone saw as inevitable, Fadeyev telephoned and said that they, her and her brother, and their ill mother should immediately leave for Tashkent. The authorities were evacuating the country's "gold reserves": the directors, actors, writers, and scientists. There were crowds of people at the Kazan railway station, shouts, dirt, stampedes, parcels, bundles wrapped up in cloth, and among them colorful patches of foreign suitcases. The mother was carried onto the train on a stretcher. In her half-supine position, she smiled to everyone and gave a little bow. Their good friend Elena Sergeevna Bulgakova was on the same train...

From a letter to Malyugin, Tashkent, beginning of 1942:

Dear Lenya, it is very difficult now to write letters, difficult to find the right tone to hide behind. And then you have to describe a lot of things, how you're getting by, what you're eating, about yourself and other people. The case is clear: another foolish thing has been done, and I (you know how easy it is for me to move somewhere else) found myself in Tashkent. A city where even the water smells of dust and disinfectant, where water boils in the sun in summer, and in winter there is dirt that is like nothing else on earth (it is more like fast-setting wood glue). A city where dolled-up women have come together and where all of the grief of the Soviet Union has come together, where camels and asses move along the streets instead of trams, where people address you as *aga* for some reason, where they refer to your native Leningrad and Moscow land as "Russia" (!), where coffins are one of the goods in shortest supply. This is the city, one founded for dying, that I have ended up in. Why and how, I just can't fathom.

I live like in a dream. I remember snow like I would a delicious treat, and the sirens of Moscow, and everything else I look back on as meaningful events in my life. I am living someone else's life now. I am scared of this city. I think that I will be stuck here for the rest of my life. Lenya, promise me that, when the war is over and if we both survive, you will come to me and take me out of this wretched city. Okay?

The book that Tatyana Alexandrovna never wrote, suddenly began to write itself. It seemed as if one just needed to put everything that one found in the right order… The feeling was deceptive, however: the letters remained letters, and whatever happened between them remained a vacuum, a set of questions to which there were no answers.

It was particularly then that my life abruptly changed. The career of a playwright that I imagined, the theatre that I would dream of, were wiped away like the trace of pencil on a sheet of paper. I initially resisted this, I sought my own niche, but then I felt that this road in life, which I had walked for ten years, was leading nowhere. Another era in my life began. A voice from another world got ever louder and clearer.

A confession

I was only slightly familiar with the poet Lugovskoy. Sometime during my adolescence I heard his poetry on the radio and I thought that I really must look through his poems someday, but I forgot about him, swept away by Pasternak, Akhmatova, Zabolotsky, Tsvetaeva. In the family I happened to enter, as the wife of his grandson, no one told me anything in particular about being related to him. So, he resided only on the periphery of my consciousness.

Granted, several times I attended some unusual annual event called "Vladimir Lugovskoy's Birthday". It was organized in the apartment in Lavrushinsky by his window, Maya

Lugovskaya (her real name was Elena Leonidovna Bykova). A group of ladies, already advanced in years, gathered around the big table. Maya, a lady with ashen gray hair that fell over her eyes, would announce, "These are all of the women that the poet fell in love with, let each of them tell a story about Lugovskoy." I remember the gray-haired Yevgeniya Laskina, and Olga Grudtsova was there too. The most wonderful of all was one beauty who, after a third shot of vodka, told of how the poets who were her husbands had beat her. All of this frankly shocked me, and Ludmila Vladimirovna too. Tatyana Alexandrovna couldn't stand Maya, she considered Maya a vulgar person, who had also added something to the publication of Lugovskoy's last poems. At these gatherings there was also Yevgeny Rein, who adored Maya, and a great deal of her friends. Of course, this didn't make me feel any closer to the poet, but rather evoked repulsion.

There was one more thing. When I worked in the team for literature at the *Soviet Encyclopedia*, our editor (and subsequently editor-in-chief) K. M. Cherny, whenever he saw me and was in good spirits, would recite, "Take me as you wish and then throw me away with a crash!" Honestly, I didn't quite understand what he meant, I just smiled stupidly, hoping that it would all become clear someday. Later, it became clear that these were Lugovskoy's lines of repentance written after the disbanding of the Russian Association of Proletarian Writers, a poem where he offered his services for the remaking of his nation under any circumstances.

The team in which I was working, was not fond of anything Soviet. The compendium of author biographies, which (not coincidentally) was a reference on 19th-century writers and only slightly dipped into the 20th century, cleverly ended with the year 1917. When I came to my elderly colleagues with the question of what came next, what lives would the poets who were chopped off, like Pasternak, Akhmatova, and Mandelstam, go on to live, they gave me a sly smile and explained that for those whom a heavy fate had brought into the Soviet era, a formula had been thought up, almost like a tongue twister. (That is, one had to quickly, with great haste, list in a telegraphic style what happened in their lives and work after 1917.) In that way, we could avoid the great headache of selecting writers, deciding how much space each of them should take up, and dealing with their made-up Soviet biographies.

Working with biographies, mastering the secrets of how to search through the archives, passed before my eyes, and I studied this art every day. Discoveries, the intertwining of fates, being immersed in these lives like in reality, made these years some of the happiest for me. And again the stagnation of those years made our work on the dictionary even more of a pleasure, as the world seemed stable for us, it consisted of our investigations, debates, and meetings. The Soviet world lived outside the bounds of our office, we would joke about it. Lying to the censors was approved of, as was getting around any obstacles in our way. Only several years later did I understand that for most of the editors, working on the encyclopedia felt like a sort of prison sentence.

In those days the editing staff was led by Mikhail Nikolayevich Khitrov, a stocky man with a kind and open face, who was at the same time the secretary of the encyclopedia's Party organization. How surprised I was to later discover that he had long served as secretary for Tvardovsky's literary magazine *Novy Mir* and that Solzhenitsyn had painted a dark portrait of him in the short story *The Oak and the Calf*. At the very beginning of perestroika I read that story in the metro and, when I got out at Kirov station, I happened to run into Khitrov. By that time he was already working for the publisher's general staff. But since he never bore himself too proudly and he could always give fatherly advice about any everyday problems, I asked him as we were walking together, right to his face, what he thought about Solzhenitsyn's portrait of him. Khitrov was taken aback, he hadn't expected anything like that at all. It even seemed as if he went completely into his shell. I regretted this impertinence of mine a bit, but my curiosity was stronger.

After a pause, Khitrov said, "You know, he's a great writer of course, that's true, but just between you and me. He was a jailbird and remains a jailbird. Tvardovsky always understood that."

I answered with something, waving my hands in disagreement. Khitrov just gave a wry smile and remained silent. He didn't say anything more, but somewhere on the margins of my consciousness a light came on, that he was not only my former boss, but he had long been someone that was part of my literary process, and Khitrov knew that too.

This double vision, this effect of two things coming together when a character from diaries, memoirs, or prose works appeared before me in real life, has become a lens I could focus when observing people.

After I had already learned how to search for facts and compile them together, I came across a remarkable thing. At that time I was reading Bulgakov deeply and was even writing something under the influence of Bakhtin about space and time in the novel *The Master and Margarita*. Suddenly, when I had taken a volume of Lugovskoy in the "Poet's Library" series from the shelf, I stumbled upon his poem "A Tale of a Dream". The poem was an enigma from beginning to end. Two loves, the end of the world, an enormous house on the Moscow River, the roar of airplanes, sirens, the last farewell before the characters' death. But strangely, for the entire length of their rendezvous, these lovers were being watched by a cat wearing cuffs on soft paws.

I couldn't shake off the feeling that through this text, another one known to everyone shone through. The most fantastical thing of all was that the poem was dedicated to "E. S. B.". I quickly wrote Elena Sergeevna Bulgakova under these initials, but the meaning of the dedication became no clearer to me. I hurried to Ludmila Vladmirovna with a barrage of questions, but she just looked at me with surprise. It was clear that she knew nothing of this. I honestly thought that my writing about Bulgakov was driving me mad. A week later, however, Ludmila Vladimirovna came from aunt Tatyana Alexandrovna and, with downcast eyes, said, "It's true."

She then said that Tatyana Alexandrovna was very surprised by my detective work. The affair between Lugovskoy and Elena Sergeevna Bulgakova was confirmed, and from that moment I forgot about it for some fifteen years.

So, they fled from Moscow, with the Germans at the door, to Tashkent. The whole way, Lugovskoy sat by the window, talking with Zoshchenko. He would gaze sadly on the countryside passing by and discuss the possibilities for retreat, the execution of the field marshals, and Stalin's unprofessional command. Tatyana Alexandrovna caught bits of this, shuddering with fear and hoping that the sound of the train's wheels would cover up what they were saying.

At the end of her difficult but unforgettable Tashkent life, Tatyana Alexandrovna wrote to Malyugin:

"…But nevertheless, I waited for you for so long. To be frank, I stopped waiting for you only three days ago. Well, fine, you don't have to come. Don't, please. You won't see

Tashkent. You won't see the streets lined with poplars; the vast spaces covered in dust; the camels whether singly or entire caravans of them; the starry sky that covers the earth like half of a sphere; our little yard laid with stone; our tomcat Yashka who so recently was as fat as I was in Plyos; and you won't see me, I who have become as thin as that cat Yashka looks when he's taken out of water; you won't see the shower with its broken roof and the aqueduct feeding it, and many more aqueducts, and the thrifty and angry Polya (actually, she has become much more quiet recently, after she had her purse stolen with her passport and with all our cards and passes); tomatoes as large as a child's head; Lugovskoy on a binge; our harridan neighbor; Uzbeks wearing burkas; the Alay bazaar; the "Old Town"; my drawings; the sun so hot you could light your cigarettes from it; the hops growing at our windows; the park bench on which I write these letters to you; the braziers that release smoke during the day and look magical in the evenings; the mosquitoes and flies as large as a thimble; the moon which looks like it was taken right out of a bad theatre play; the scorpions; the donkeys; twenty different varieties of grapes (granted, they are very expensive, but lovely); a white dog named Tedka that bites postmen and whose brows someone carefully and completely deliberately dyes with black paint; the cool, quiet Tashkent morning; the telegraph office I sent telegrams from; the pink walls and light-blue shadows in the alleyways; goats on every street; the botanical garden and zoo, where there are three expired crocodiles, a lot of goats, even more chickens, even more young naturalists, even more flowers and silence and one small bear cub (my friend); Pushkin Street; the black-market traders;

the pickpockets; the women who sell baked apples and garlic; the tomcats of Tashkent; the houses; the samovars; my friend Nadya; Sasha Tyshler; Babanova; melons the size of a laundry basket; raisins; walnuts in the trees and at the bazaars; my brothers' poem, twenty-two pencils, fifteen notebooks and a little Buddha, all of which are on his splendidly adorned desk; my pupils and my anger; my red umbrella; the house known as the Rookery; the girls Zukhra and Vasilya who sell yogurt; the people sleeping outside; the golden flowers on the windows; the kitchen with its sunken floor; the lines for rations, Karl Marx Street and Spring Street, Beshagan and Urda; the stone steps and the grass growing on the roof of our house; our cozy quarters and the mess here; an old broom; a coal shovel; the paper lampshades and the lamp made from a child's toy; the clay pitchers; the furniture I painted myself; the sofa I have poured more than a few tears out onto; the cigarette sellers on the corner of Zhukovsky Street; the Tashkent trams that are impossible to make one's way onto; the bright blue sky; the white acacias and the Paulownia trees; the grills over the windows to keep thieves out; the lady who sweeps the street; the train station; the yellow drapes over my windows, which are hung on billiard cues; the cooking range at the end of the room; saxaul trees; a Bible; a broken electric plug; three different chairs and the round black heating stove in our room; the playing cards that I made myself; my suitors, including the groundskeeper Larion; the ladder going up to the *balakhana*; Akhmatova who is like a woman chained; the bell at the gate and the baker's at the corner that resembles a rat's hole – you won't see all this…"

I would continually turn over this fragment of the letter in my mind. Tedka, the dog whose eyebrows someone had painted, was running along, while an emaciated Nadya Mandelstam, who resembled a Baba Yaga, was whistling something on the balcony, Lugovskoy's notebooks were scattered around the room, the curtain over the window fluttered in the wind, and Akhmatova with her great burden sat by the window and looked out on the street.

Lavrushinsky Lane, apartment 95

Then one day something was heard from deep inside the old grandfather clock, an old spring squeaked, it came to life, and the large hands, reluctantly obeying the great pendulum, began to turn. I think it was in that time that the clock had been repaired in the apartment near the Aeroport metro. It was around this time that Mukha came into the house. She heralded the time of Lavrushinsky Lane for me.

Mukha ("Fly"), as Maria Vladimirovna Sedova was affectionately called, was Ludmila Vladimirovna's sister. They were both the daughters of Vladimir Lugovskoy, but they were born to different mothers. Mukha was a famous archaeologist, she had received a PhD and was named an honorary citizen of the city of Suzdal. She was short in stature and glamorous, with the manners of a lady who had been brought up well. She had thin hair tied in a bun, which made for a combination of a lady already advanced in years and a naughty child. This combination appeared even more in her manner of speaking.

"Why should I busy myself with scholarship when I would rather look through the family archives, just like you!" As she said this, she drew the words out contrarily. She spoke as if we could stop her from doing anything.

As an inheritance from Maya Lugovskaya, who died in 1993, she received her father's apartment in Lavrushinsky Lane and was confronted with an enormous heap of his manuscripts and letters.

At that time Ludmila Vladimirovna and I were finishing up a book about Tatyana Alexandrovna. We had putting the story she had written back together again, her letters, her reminiscences, we had found a publisher, and we were waiting for it to come out. Maria Vladimirovna looked upon us, who were busy in our little "sandbox", with envy. She got all excited like a child and offered us the opportunity to look at Lugovskoy's archives.

Initially, I didn't even known how one could "look at" someone's archives. But these would eventually become for me a house with myriad rooms, the doors to which were either locked or wide open. I understood that behind the archives there was a distinct design. They were not a random collection of papers but a story about an era. That's why one had to pay great attention to tickets, receipts, documents, drawings, and even the labels on matchboxes. The most important thing is that I learned to distinguish whose handwriting it was on the letters and manuscripts.

I would ardently tell Maria Vladimirovna everything that I found out about the history of Tashkent, and consequently she set before me the most precious thing that I was searching for. These were the letters of Elena Sergeevna Bulgakova to Lugovskoy after she had already left Tashkent and began writing to him from Moscow. There were some twenty letters in the collection. They were humorous, tender, and highly-strung. These were answers to his letters, a clarification of their relationship, discussions about problems that they both faced. But I had no letters in the opposite direction!

The world of these Tashkent exiles grew as ever more details emerged. I sensed how important this period of life was for Tatyana Alexandrovna, Malyugin, Lugovskoy, Elena Sergeevna, and even Akhmatova. Curiosity continued to gnaw at me, but I just couldn't understand how to approach this story.

More and more questions were piling up, but there was no one that I could pose them to. And then I started posing them to Lugovskoy. I would walk along the lane from the Polyana metro station without seeing anything around me, and I would ask him what had happened to him. What was he running away from in Tashkent? What strange thoughts were driving him? Why did a woman who was ten years older, Bulgakov's widow, need him?

Sometimes weeks would go by, and suddenly in a heap of papers a draft of a letter would appear, without any beginning or end to it, in which he explained to someone how they would live together after the war, and that she would eventually have to move on from Bulgakov, from his famous name, and finally stop being his widow. It turned out that this was a draft of a letter to Elena Sergeevna, where Lugovskoy seemed to be answering just what I was asking. It was then that I felt for the first time how the person on the other end of the line wasn't silent, but rather he simply didn't answer right away. However, this only the beginning of my journey.

To get to the house on Lavrushinsky, one had to walk along the narrow Tolmachevsky Lane, past a church. Tolmachevsky would end at a housing block for writers hanging over the Tretyakov Gallery like some gray mass. Located among the narrow streets along the Moscow River, the writers' house was cramped and uncomfortable, and it had clearly long been taking up the space of something else, but with time it took on an air of its own. Soviet writers would walk up and down its staircases, go down its elevators, take out the rubbish bins, and – thanks to the design of the housing block with its horseshoe shape – often peek into each other's windows. The seven-story Stalin-era building with its marble entrance facing the Tretyakov Gallery could vie with the gallery itself: behind the doors of its apartments stories, dramas, tragedies, and farces would play out, some of which were set down, but more often they remain unknown.

Usually I would walk from the Polyanka metro station past the church of St. Gregory Thaumaturgus. The chiming of the small round clock on its bell tower could be heard from far away, and then one came to a view of the Bolshoy Kamenny bridge packed with cars. This is the start of the Zamoskvorechye district. I would turn right and walk along Spasonalivkovsky Lane until it came to a small estate (which probably dated from before the fire of 1812) that resembled a little theatre set piece. Each time I expected an empty lot to loom before me, but the shingles on the sides of the manor would always appear in a pitiful manner, and the holes in the ramshackle roof would gape mournfully. Then the house was covered in a transparent green netting and it started to look like an old broken piece of furniture that one tries to hide under a sheet. I had a dreary premonition that this sad old piece of furniture would soon be thrown out, and under the netting another dashing monstrosity wrought from glass and concrete would rise in its place.

In the apartment on Lavrushinsky everything was put neatly in its place, it was a sort of Lugovskoy Museum. The walls of the enormous study were decked with books, many of which were turning to dust before one's eyes (they had been printed on newsprint in the Twenties and Thirties). A carpet, already greatly worn, hung on the wall, along with a wealth of unusual objects, and trinkets from every part of the globe crowded the empty spaces on the bookshelves. It was said that the walls of the study had previously been adorned with a mighty collection of swords, but it had long since been sold off, and only dark stains remained.

Maria Vladimirovna didn't live in the apartment – she was looking through the papers which Lugovskoy's widow Maya wanted to turn into an expanded complete works. Her plans came to naught, however, due to the onset of perestroika and old age.

Maria Vladimirovna, who approved of my investigations, in the course of events solved her own personal needs that she had never told me about. On one hand, she laboriously sought after a way to house the archives that had fallen onto her shoulders. On the other hand, studying the letters and papers became for her a sort of dialog with the dead: with Tatyana Alexandrovna, whom she accused of arrogance and insufficient love for her mother; with her father, who (as she saw it) had offended her mother at the end of the 1920s; and with Maya Lugovskaya, who had handled her father's archives inappropriately. Each new sheet of paper was weighed in the scales of her own judgment and was examined from this perspective.

She had mastered an amazingly vivid and detailed way of telling stories.

"My grandmother's maiden name was Oleynichenko." I would listen to her words strung together and feel bad that I couldn't commit any of it to memory. I felt like I was sleeping with my eyes open, listening again and again to her stream of wonderful Russian speech, which was enchanting and flowed like a winding river, without any particular theme and thus passing from my mind in an instant.

Or:

"Once my father came to me and said that we should go for a walk. This was before the war. It was spring or autumn. We walked to the Novodevichye cemetery. We went up to Nadezhda Alliluyeva's grave. My father said that when Stalin came here to visit his wife's grave, the cemetery would be closed. Then we went further inside the cemetery, and we saw a woman sitting on a bench, sitting in front of one particular grave. My father told me that this was an acquaintance of his, Elena Sergeevna Bulgakova. She greeted me. The three of us left the cemetery, I was shy and walked in front of them silently, and they were talking about something behind me. This is probably the reason why papa would send me greetings from her in the letters from Tashkent, remembering our meeting."

Or like this:

"I remember how – this was already in 1944 – I was walking to Furmanov Lane alongside the Arbat, I walked up the stairs and rang the doorbell. A woman in a Chinese silk robe opened the door. Her face was covered with cream. She asked me to wait while she said goodbye to her beautician and washed the cream off. I remember the room. Then I understood that this was Bulgakov's study. We headed along Lavrushinsky Lane to my father's apartment. Glass was scattered everywhere – someone had broken the windows. Elena Sergeevna got a bucket and a cloth and started to clean the mess up and wash the floor. She was readying the study for my father's arrival from Tashkent."

For three years I would go to Lavrushinsky Lane like going to the office, solving the riddle by putting documents and letters together. Somehow I sensed that I was allowed little time for this, that they would either send me away from the house, or give everything away to some big archives, or something else would happen. Then the saddest thing happened: Mukha, Maria Vladimirovna, unexpectedly died. The door of the house was closed to me. But by then it already seemed that I had succeeded in discovering and doing the most important things.

"Do you want me to introduce you to Maria Iosifovna Belkina?" Maya asked, literally pulling me away from the papers.

"The one who wrote that book about Tsvetaeva, *The Intersection of Fates*? Is she really still alive?"

The words "intersection of fates" were always bound up with the book that I had read at the beginning of perestroika. We would read it in one sitting. The book talked not only about Tsvetaeva when she was still alive in the prewar era and about her children, but also off of its pages there blew in a wind of private life in the Thirties, Forties, and Fifties, which we knew very little about in those days. The book put a spell on readers with its multitude of stories. Names popped up that one would have liked to know more about. The inimitable voice of its author rang out on every page, a voice that was clear and sincere. We would remember it for ever.

"Maria Iosifovna lives right below us. She invited us to tea."

We walked down the flight of stairs. At the time I could not imagine that a few dozen steps would change my life completely.

Lavrushinsky Lane, apartment 96

The stern and gray-haired lady that met us at the door didn't awaken any desire in me to ask questions. She too was clearly not disposed to any such discussion and saw it as a burden.

A book had appeared for the one-hundredth anniversary of Vladimir's (Lugovskoy's) birth, that's all very very good. Yes, Tatyana and I were friends. She said all this as she poured tea into elegant little cups. On little exquisite plates there was marmalade and German cookies with cinnamon.

A respectful distance came between us, which was softened by polite talk. Mukha twittered in a jolly mood without being aware of the awkwardness hanging over us. I nonetheless decided to ask Maria Iosifovna about Tashkent.

"Tatyana, Vladimir and I were evacuated in the same train carriage," Maria Iosifovna said plainly. "From each train stop I would send Tarasenkov letters. Tarasenkov was my husband." As she spoke, she strained to look at me. She was already partly blind – she was 88 years old and it was obvious how hard it was for her to follow the reactions of the person she was talking to. I only knew the famous bibliographic reference by Tarasenkov, which the editing staff for the *Russian Writers* project had used so much it had fallen apart.

"Yes, that's his book," she said, and her tone seemed to become warmer.

She opened an enormous cupboard with glass doors and took out a packet of letters bound with string.

"I was carrying my newborn son. Tarasenkov was very worried about us, he had barely escaped the German invasion of Tallinn… It was like hell on earth there. Then he lived through the siege of Leningrad. And his friend Vladimir Lugovskoy went off in the opposite direction, away from the front." She said these last words with great emphasis.

I felt then that this was the reason she was so tense. Lugovskoy's daughter was sitting in front of her, and it was extremely unpleasant to recall this whole story.

But all this was barely noticed. The important thing for me was that I had encountered a person who could tell me what was behind the letters. From that time on, I stopped being afraid of her strained voice, her stern face and manners.

She knew things that I absolutely had to understand. At some point I started feeling I could see an event in its entirety, to turn it around and look at it from different angles, and this made my head spin. In the mosaic made up from different accounts, I could create an entire picture of the era.

I constantly had to deal with the fact that my understanding about this point in history, about the war events were being turned upside down. The Soviet writers in Tashkent for the first year could not believe in the possibility of victory, and they spoke of how their evacuation would soon become an emigration. Everyone was preparing for Uzbekistan to become an English colony and they had to learn the language. Alexei Tolstoy had already thought up a name for Tashkent: "a poor man's Istanbul". No one believed a single thing that the government said. How could anyone believe when they had all participated in the lies of state propaganda?

From that day on I started spending time at her home. First she studied me carefully, she would give me various papers and letters and watch what I would do with them. After some time had passed, she confessed that she had initially taken me for some kind of journalist who had nothing better to do than visit apartments in Lavrushinsky Lane.

The train

We didn't start talking right away about the Tashkent-bound train that Maria Iosifovna traveled on together with the rest.

For some time we would skirt the subject. She would describe it with pictures. Here's Eisenstein sitting in a train carriage and drawing some amusing and obscene caricatures. Here's Lyubov Orlova talking with the engineers at every station so that the train would not stop for long. Trains with weapons were going in the opposite direction, with soldiers huddling together on the completely exposed train beds. There were fur coats, hats, and colorful suitcases with foreign labels. How annoyed Maria Iosifovna was by all this! She wanted to rush back to Moscow and defend the city from the Germans! But she had a two-month-old baby in her arms that needed her, and her husband's cry over every front, "Save our son!" In almost every letter he added, "Don't greet that coward and deserter Lugovskoy."

Lugovskoy appeared in Moscow at the beginning of July. He had a limp and was leaning on a cane. He always walked in a military uniform with dust-covered boots. When Maria Iosifovna encountered him looking like this for the third time, she couldn't stand it any more and she screamed, "Vladimir! Take off those boots already!"

His story could have been described as tragicomic if it weren't for the war. He had long since tried on the mask of the warrior poet. Gumilev, whose works had been banned, had been his idol since he was young. His poetic inspiration was fueled by wild raids across the borders of Central Asia, hunting for Basmachi, or pseudo-liberation trips through the Baltic countries and Western Ukraine. This was all a never-ending adventure, and it turned into the drums of war expressed in poetry that his students repeated in turn: Simonov, Dolmato-vsky, Margarita Aliger. For them, he was an example of man-liness and courage. On June 24 he faithfully set off to serve in the place the Union of Writers had assigned him: the editing staff of the frontline newspaper in Pskov. The place had already been shaken by bombing, the Germans had seized the western districts. What appeared before his eyes was completely opposed to what he had imagined war to be, namely fleeing troops and heaps of twisted iron, the bodies of women and children. And the continual bombings, from which there was no escape.

Maria Iosifovna remembered how he always wanted to talk to her on the train. She claimed that because of Tarasenkov – who had been Lugovskoy's old friend from when they worked for the magazine *Znamya*, in the first days of the war at the front – Lugovskoy was always ashamed in front of her. He frequently returned to the story of his "flight". He kept trying to explain to her that the catastrophe he had witnessed was not a war, it was hell itself, and it had changed him completely. He didn't know what he should do now, how he could live with himself the way he was now. But now there was no theatricality in his words. Here one must add, to his defense, that he had been discharged for reasons of health.

Years later, the story of Lugovskoy in the first days of the war would continue in an incredible way.

Once in the Tsvetaeva Museum, where I worked for several years, someone brought in a cardboard box that had been thrown away. The people who found it, believed that the handwritten pages with poems by Marina Tsvetaeva they found within were the poet's own, and they decided to sell them to the museum. But it was someone else's hand, someone had copied the poems by this poet who had been banned. The box remains in the museum, cast aside like an abandoned puppy. These were the papers of a journalist from *Pravda* that everyone had forgotten, Rudolf Bershadsky: notebooks, letters, diaries, photographs. There were diaries, all tied up with string, of the siege and his sister's letters from the camps.

I knew that these papers held no promise, and I absentmindedly went through the small notebooks filled with round and easily legible letters.

And suddenly on the very first page I saw: "Pskov, July 2. I met Lugovskoy yesterday." It was Bershadsky writing. "He turned forty yesterday. He was scruffy, sweaty (in big drops), and he smelled of valerian drops from a mile away. He told me that on the day that war was declared, he had bragged to the recruiters, 'From this day forth, I'm a healthy man.' But in general, 'I physically cannot withstand being under bombardment.'" Bershadsky wrote several more lines about him with disgust and wariness. Lugovskoy would have to live with the same attitude from frontline soldiers for the rest of the war years and feel pangs of guilt until the day he died.

These notes by Bershadsky, like the focusing ring on a pair of binoculars, added contrast and clarity to the picture.

I was struck by this, of course. But it wasn't even by seeing Lugovskoy with drops of sweat rolling off him, justifying himself to his acquaintance by saying he had gone to the front ill. I was rather struck by the way things had happened.

Some people threw out a collection that should have faded away. But other people had crawled into a waste container, gone through it, and thought that there was something valuable there. They made an effort and brought everything to the museum. I opened the diary and read something destined just for me.

Who is listening to us? How? Bershadsky's account appeared when the book about Tashkent had already been published, it made no difference for eternity.

And there's more. I was especially struck by the sentence, "He turned forty yesterday.", for another forty years on

Lugovskoy was no longer among the living, but my son had been born, whom I called Vladimir at the request of Lugovskoy's widow, Maya Lugovskaya. My son was born on the very same day and at the very same hour as his great-grandfather, and he will resemble him, though only outwardly. When Maria Iosifovna saw him, she would say to me, "It's good that he's different, he's not my Vladimir." All the relatives looked for features in common, but she looked for differences.

I went down to her from the upstairs apartment after working with Lugovskoy's collection. It became clear that events took on a deeper meaning if you could also hear a voice from "beyond".

Lugovskoy along with his sister and dying mother settled down in Tashkent on Zhukovsky Street, on the *balakhana*, and above them lived Elena Sergeevna Bulgakova with her thirteen-year-old son. Their mother died in terrible pain; Lugovskoy turned to heavy drinking for a time and would sit like a beggar in the Alay bazaar, collecting alms and reciting poems from behind a glass of vodka. The local Uzbeks respectfully called him the "Russian dervish". Only after some time did Elena Sergeevna make peace with Lugovskoy after their lengthy argument and they began living as one family.

Maria Iosifovna and I talked a lot about fear and its nature. As I listened to her, I understood very clearly that in order to save himself from his fear, Lugovskoy had to overcome an even greater fear. He read *The Master and Margarita* in Tashkent again and again, the manuscript of the novel that Elena Sergeevna had brought with her, and the book said the same thing: "cowardice is the greatest of flaws". Then he started writing his own book, a collection of poems called *The Middle of the Century*. He wrote the best he could, completely honestly, but most importantly, totally revealing himself. Elena Sergeevna typed it up, and she saw that he was saving himself, and she was no longer so worried about him.

When Maria Iosifovna and I started talking about these things, we did not yet know that we would have to start from an essentially private matter and eventually come to a great general Fear that tormented and killed her husband Tarasenkov. In the meantime Maria Iosifovna had left her one-year-old son with her parents and rushed to the front, secretly leaving Tashkent in the plane of a friend's husband, Ivan Spirin. They landed right in Moscow. She had no permission to do so, she had no papers, but she managed to reach Tarasenkov and they were together for some time at Lake Ladoga.

Her correspondence with Tarasenkov – he writing from besieged Leningrad and her from Tashkent – was an entire drama of her unruliness and his devotion and love. Whether teasing me or being serious, she said, "I wanted to burn it all. Who needs our private correspondence?"

"You know," she said, months later, asking me to sit down in her kitchen. (I had to wait while she turned on her "ear", the hearing aid that she didn't like to wear, but without which it would have been impossible to talk with her. As she was putting it on, she would say terrible things about herself: "Maria the old hag" and so on.) "You know, the book, if you are going to write it, can only be built around a character that is interesting to follow. A character should have a distinct personality. All you've got is Lugovskoy. Vladimir is wonderful and kind. But is he really a hero in a story? He can only be the protagonist of a love story. And his poems! Those silly rhymes."

She told me funny stories about Lugovskoy and the last of his wives, whom she had lived near for the last several years.

"Being neighbors with them really annoyed me. Girls in love with him would always hammer on my door, since they had the address wrong. I sent them upstairs, and there Mayka (his wife Maya Lugovskoy) would open the door and yell at them. But she was nobody's fool. She was always having a good time, she would live it up to the point of collapse. That was already after Vladimir. Once she played the piano all night and brought so much noise down on me. She was composing the libretto to an opera with some composer. I called her and said that if she didn't stop, I would call the police. But she was generally an interesting lady. After Tarasenkov's death in 1956 I got over my grief by endlessly walking at night along the Moscow River. In 1957, after Vladimir's death, she also started to wander the streets to overcome her sadness. I often met her and talked with her. She was an interesting and special woman."

Maria Iosifovna did not read the works of her poet friends. In her eyes there was only Pasternak, Tsvetaeva, and – years later – Brodsky. It was with some amazement that she discovered that Lugovskoy had written *The Middle of the Century* in Tashkent. I told her that the first printing of that collection began with poems entitled "1937", which was later heavily revised and became "Up and Down".

Tashkent: the story continues

In Tashkent, the city that Maria Iosifovna had flown out of in Ivan Spirin's small plane (hidden under his great cloak), the life of its famous and non-famous refugees continued. For me the book imperceptibly became more a history of a flight, of the exodus of great crowds of people, who made a new life in Tashkent in a remarkable way, although some found their deaths there. The story unwound of its own accord, taking on ever more characters and themes.

As I was going through Lugovskoy's papers, and then after I found myself sitting next to Maria Iosifovna, I had not forgotten Tatyana Alexandrovna and her letters to Malyugin, but that was only a window in which I could see the scorching sun in the east, Elena Sergeevna Bulgakova, Akhmatova, the *balakhana*, Uzbek women in burkas, old dresses made into curtains, and ramshackle sheds.

Elena Sergeevna lived in a wing of the house for writers (at 54 Zhukov Street) on the *balakhana* (an additional story added to an Uzbek house) with her young son Sergei, and downstairs, in the two small rooms beneath them, the Lugovskoys: Vladimir, Tatyana, and – for a very short time – their mother, who would soon die. One day Elena Sergeevna hurried to Tatyana Lugovskaya. She had unexpectedly received a letter from an old friend of Bulgakov, Sergei Yermolinsky. At the end of 1940, several months after Bulgakov's death, Yermolinsky had suddenly disappeared from Moscow, and only later did it become clear that he had been arrested. At the secret police headquarters in Lubyanka Square they had tried to concoct a "Bulgakov case". Yermolinsky refused to cooperate with the investigation and refused to make any confession that would tarnish the good name of the deceased writer. However, at that time the circumstances of his arrest and the course of the investigation were still unknown.

From the letter that she had received, Elena Sergeev discovered that Sergei Alexandrovich had already been freed from prison, but that he had been sentenced to exile somewhere nearby, in Kazakhstan. It turned out that he was starving, he had no money, but he could receive things that were sent.

They made up a package together. "And suddenly – joy!" Yermolinsky wrote. "A little package from Elena in Tashkent. Little sausage-shaped pouches, neatly sewn, into which groats, sugar, tea, and low-quality shag tobacco had been poured, with a piece of lard put in too, and all this wrapped up in Bulgakov's striped pajamas, the very same ones which I wore when I was talking care of him in his dying days. This gnawing feeling of abandonment blew away, replaced by warmth, love, affection, and home…"

Thus Tatyana Alexandrovna Lugovskaya first learned of Sergei Alexandrovich Yermolinsky. But he did not know anything of Tatyana Alexandrovna yet, for it would take a long time for them to meet.

In July 1943 Elena Sergeev Bulgakov and her son left Tashkent. She had been invited by the Moscow Art Theatre to revive Bulgakov's play about Pushkin. When she got to Moscow and went through the papers, letters, and her diaries from the Thirties, she had a clear realization that she was Bulgakov's widow, and she decided to change nothing of her fate as a woman. She wrote about this in a clear and concise manner to Lugovskoy, who had been hoping to bring her back and marry her.

In November the Lugovskoys returned to Moscow from Tashkent. For Sergei Alexandrovich, however, the road to the capital was closed. His friends helped him move to Georgia. Nonetheless, he secretly arrived in Moscow to put on a play he had written in his exile about Griboyedov.

Then they met for the first time. His was 47 years old and she was 38. And they had everything still ahead of them.

After the death of Sergei Alexandrovich, Tatyana Alexandrovna tried to write a book about him.

I remember, for example, how I first met you. You remember, in 1947 I came to Fradkina's home to hear *Griboyedov* and someone got up from the sofa to greet me, a tall (it seemed so to me), light-haired and very pale man with glasses, very thin and sickly, and he had thin and slender hands. That was you.

Fradkina had invited some more directors in the hope that they would take up your play. You were reading the script and were clearly shaken, so I couldn't hear the play well, it was bothering me… They praised the play, but no one was ready to stage it.

You tore a little turquoise ring from my hand and said that it would bring you luck. Then everyone walked out. Outside I ended up between you and Gushansky. You were both staggering drunk. When we got to Nikitskie Vorota, I asked here you were staying, and I received the answer, "I'm going to spend the night on the boulevard." "I won't allow it. Come spend the night at my place."

Gushansky, drunk, demonstratively staggered to the side, pulled his hat over his forehead, and showed with his whole body how unacceptable my offer was. In the middle of the night, a woman was asking a person she had just met for the first time to spend the night at her place.

We stumbled into Starokonyushenny Lane. There was a light in my window. To my husband's credit, I must tell you that he received us with pleasure. "Sergei, how did you get here?" Really, how? They had known each other for years.

A fifth of vodka that had been stashed away appeared and was gladly accepted. I laid down to sleep in the small room. They whiled the night away in the big room.

I was awoken the next morning by a phone call. You were calling Elena Bulgakova: "I'm at the home of Tatyana Alexandrovna Lugovskaya. That's how it turned out. I was drunk, but she brought me to her home." And that was how we met for the first time.

Yermolinsky returned to Tbilisi to live out the exile he had been sentenced to forever. He lived in a small Creative House for writers in Saguramo. There followed endless autumn days of solitude and melancholy, and Sergei Alexandrovich had to check in every week at the NKVD office. There was no answer from Moscow about the fate of the play. He was completely desperate. One day he readied a rope and found a hook to throw it over in the shed. At that moment someone knocked at the gate. The knocking was insistent and could not be refused. He went to open the gate. The postman had brought a letter from Tatyana Lugovskaya. In it, she announced that never in her life had she been the first to write to a man, but in this case something had compelled her to. She wrote that she was constantly thinking about him, and she begged him not to lose hope because of the play, to hold on, and to hope for a meeting between them. And that is how he went on living.

"...Your letter moved me so much," Yermolinsky wrote, "that I felt an unbearable need to immediately commit some kind of great deed. If I were a pilot, then I would have looped the loop. If I were a soldier, then I would have, maybe, taken some kind of unassailable fortress. If I were Pushkin, then I would have written some great masterpiece about sadness and love, one that centuries from now would bring our unknown descendants to tears. But since I am none of these things, the only thing I can do after dreaming about such deeds, is to comfort myself with the thought that God has granted me this contemplative life and nothing more. Bless you that you exist in this world! And I kiss you with great esteem for the words 'I miss you'."

The play was staged at the Stanislavsky Theatre, and Sergei Alexandrovich was invited to Moscow. A very difficult and, at the same time, a very happy affair began. They were divided by his exile and her marriage.

"…How many calls were made to the KGB, how many lies to his sister and refusals to register him; how many times I had to hide him from the police at my place, and they would come to his aunt's to try to chase him out of Moscow; how his hands would tremble if we walked by policemen in the street, how many summons were made by night to a secret apartment in the Arbat where a detective sat, how many nasty tricks were played by his former 'friends'."

Their life together as a family began in the cabins of various riverboats. Only there could they be together with the damned need to register with the police. One ship, a second, a third. The river established the unhurried, measured course of days where there was a place for a calm conversation, and for remembrances, and for joking, and for everything that filled their life together.

When they got their own house, Elena Sergeevna Bulgakov came to visit them and wrote them letters. As Yermolinsky recalled:

She was already over seventy, but she was attractive like she always was, like she had been before and, without any exaggeration, I will say: young!

When her life had fantastically changed, she was already living not on Furmanov Street, but rather in a new, very comfortable apartment on Suvorovsky Boulevard near Nikitskie Vorota. There was an enormous portrait of Bulgakov in an oval frame, which had been painted from a photograph and only vaguely resembled his real appearance, but that appearance came to life in the stories she would tell. She would bring to life his sense of humour, his tone of voice. She would still remain the same Elena, but she would open up to an extraordinary degree. His death was a truly overwhelming grief for her. It wasn't a loss, it wasn't the mourning that a widow shows. It was a real grief. But it was so strong that it didn't destroy her. On the contrary, it awoke the life inside of her!

On the day of Sergei Alexandrovich's death, February 18, Tatyana Alexandrovna gathered their friends.

"The time has come to constantly think about you, Yermolinsky. Before I was afraid, but now it's already time for me to die." It appears that this was the only time that she addressed him in Russian with informal language.

In 1994 their friends also gathered, but this time it was not at the abundantly covered table around which everyone would meet year after year. The guests sat in the kitchen, and she was already lying unconscious in her room. She would pass away the next day. Everyone said their goodbyes to her.

Once he wrote to her when he was in the Creative House, where he was working on another one of his scripts: "I feel lonely without you. I love you so much. You are the one love of my life. That burdens you, forgive me for that."

And Malyugin? He remained in her life as a friend and a recipient of wonderful letters, the kind of letters that she no longer wrote to anyone else, whether to her loved ones or even her beloved husband.

Malyugin and Yermolinsky had been acquainted since they were young. They became friends. At the end of his short life Malyugin became seriously ill. He spent the last New Year's at their place in his hospital gown after he had secretly escaped from his hospital room.

The last meeting

I saw Tatyana Alexandrovna in February 1994, literally two weeks before she passed away. I knew that this was time to say goodbye. She was lying on the sofa among pillows, and a loud asthmatic wheeze came from her lungs. It seemed like I should come in for just a minute and then leave, to spare her the torment. Shortly before our meeting I returned from the hospital after I had literally been on the brink of death, and I was extremely weak.

"How are you?" she wheezed and touched my hand.

I said that I had survived something unusual.

"Tell me, please. I really need to know."

She held me by the arm, but her eyes were fixed on the ceiling.

It had happened to me when I was unconscious. I saw an enormous golden sphere shining with an incredible warmth. All people were parts of it, like little pieces, and they were dissolved in its light. I was a little piece myself, and the only thing that worried me was that I could not recognize myself. Everything else only brought me joy. Suddenly I could see the meaning of words: words were said, and I examined every word, its essence, which shone with a special light, and I was amazed at how easy it was to understand everything. In that world stability and clarity reigned. But suddenly I looked somewhere down below, at the earth. It was raining there, leaves were falling, and I was lying there in a hospital room. I was amazed that there was a flat earth under me – it resembled a cardboard cutout, completely lacking any volume and (it is terrible to say) primitive, but at the same time something dear and close to me. A terrible feeling of pity for our world came over me, and right then I began to return to the earth. I was literally flying down from high above. When I came to my senses, I continued to repeat, "Who am I?"

I told Tatyana Alexandrovna all this. She asked me to repeat the part about the golden sphere once more and then, thanking me, she said:

"You can't imagine how wonderful it is that you told me that story."

As I left her, I had the strange feeling that my otherworldly journey had been granted to me for her sake as well.

The book about Tashkent was written, printed, and had been bound in a rather childish yellow cover – the editor-in-chief of the publisher thought that it was the right color for that oriental city. I couldn't argue with him – it was my first book. I was still unaware that it would act as a kind of magnet attracting the stories that followed.

Lavrushinsky Lane, apartment 74

This happened almost right away. I made the acquaintance of Anastasia Kovalenkova, the granddaughter of Margarita Aliger. It turned out that characters I had not expected to see walked right into the Tashkent book. In the Lugovskoy archive, among the letters from Fadeyev, there was one from 1942 that had been sent to Tashkent:

When I was ill with flu, Aliger and I agreed that when I got better, we would go together to Sokolniki: I needed to find out where the family of my younger brother had been evacuated to (he had been gravely wounded and now lies in hospital in Pyatigorsk), and Aliger had to visit the family of her husband, who had been killed on the front. From the ring we went on foot along the fifth radial street. And suddenly I was again at the dacha that many things in my life had been connected with, and where you were my guest during the winter more than once, and where we would take walks in the summer. The fence had been used for firewood, the forest around it had been heavily cut down. Nonetheless, this was still the same wonderful Sokolniki like when we were young. Then we reached the places where once I drank a wonderful kagor wine with you straight from the barrel, and later it turned out that Aliger's relatives live in the very same prefab buildings on the field that you and I had walked past when we visited your father's grave. We walked through the same field to the church at the cemetery, only now it was snow-covered.

The day had been cloudy from early morning, but the wind had picked up. The church was standing there so beautiful, so old, rising upwards, with its Russian-style porches. For a long time I trudged through the snow and I fell waist-deep on several occasions – I wanted to find your father's grave. But a lot of the crosses were entirely buried in the snow (that winter was a particularly snowy one), and it was impossible to reach many places because of the snow. So, I couldn't find the grave. When we reached the church itself, we heard that a service was being held – it was Sunday. At the main entrance these sounds could be heard especially well – it was a service held without singing, just the voice of the priest clearly resounding from the empty and cold church. In the entrance some beggars were standing on crutches, and this whole thing was so unusual in our modern Moscow! It's just amazing how many things our Russia holds within herself!

In Fadeyev's letters one can hear a tone of true friendship, without any empty formalities, just the affection between friends. The walk with Margarita Aliger through snow-covered Sokolniki, the search for the grave of Lugovskoy's father in the cold wartime Moscow had happened against the background of the affection that had arisen between them, an affection which Fadeyev did not write a word about. However, there was one allusion to it.

For a long time I was wandering around Moscow without an apartment. Our house in Komsomolsky was taken over by some military department. They haven't actually used it, but the house isn't being kept heated, and my things were taken out by my friends and relatives. Finally I found a place for myself on Bolshoy Levshinsky Lane at Pavik Antokolsky's. Here I live in a tiny little study, next to shelves full of great books, on the sofa, which as a bed is just a bit too short for me (so at night I have to rest my feet on the French poets). Pavlik and I became friends more or less in Kazan. I've respected him for a long time. There is something noble and sincere in him, without ostentatiousness – he is very shy, which Irakli Andronikov imitates in a very talented way, he's smart and emotional, talented, and he loves poetry. Zoya is very sweet and kind. Their apartment is warm and especially cozy. It turns out that I feel good there.

Pavlik Antokolsky was a dear friend of Margarita Aliger, who often came to his place, and the homes of Lugovskoy, and Belkina, and Tarasenkov. His welcoming home received everyone for many years.

Before the war, Margarita Aliger had a husband who was as young as she was. His name was Konstantin Makarov. He was a composer, known and loved by Shostakovich (I learned this from the letters), and he could have had a great future ahead of him, but he was killed on the front in the first months of the war. But when he was still alive, the young couple would argue and then make up. In the evening friends would spend hours laughing and playing cards, but Margarita would stand up and say, "Guys, it's time for sleep. Tomorrow morning there's a Komsomol meeting."

Then a son was born to them, but it seems that he lived less than a year. Margarita suffered greatly, she wanted a child, and just before the war their daughter Tanya was born. The war broke out. Margarita took her baby girl and her mother to Chistopol and then Naberezhnye Chelny, ultimately returning to Moscow where she wrote patriotic poems. After learning of the actions of Zoya Kosmodemyanskaya she collected materials about the young partisan and visited the village of Petrischevo. Later she said that when she was writing her poem, she felt like it was her who had been executed.

Then the funerals came. Konstantin was killed. Maria Iosifovna told of how she was the last to see him. They had met while standing in line for their pay at the Khudozhestvennaya Literatura publishing house. He was dressed in a military tunic and dirty with stubble on his face. She rushed to kiss him, but he couldn't control himself, he reminded her how much she hated unshaven men. She laughed and then burst into tears. No one saw him after that.

Margarita often left her lonely and chilly home to visit Pavlik Antokolsky's warm apartment on Bolshoi Levshinsky Lane. There she met Fadeyev, who was living with the poet and recovering from an inflammation of the lungs, forgetting for a time his life as a bureaucrat. Thus their affair began. And then in the cold and dismal year of 1943 their daughter Masha was born with Alexander Fadeyev's eyes. In this story each event was the cause of the next, driven by some invisible mechanism whose workings were still not known to all participants in the tragedy, especially not to Aliger's daughter Tanya, who was still living in Chistopol and unaware of the loss of her father and the birth of a sister.

Some fragments of this story found their way into the book. For that reason I visited the apartment of Margarita Aliger, where Anastasia let me look at her grandmother's notebooks, diaries, and letters. Their apartment was on the top floor, facing the courtyard. From the windows one could easily see Maria Iosifovna's kitchen on the fifth floor, Lugovskoy's balcony with its peeling wood, and to the side the narrow little windows of Pasternak's apartment. This building became for me ever more of a book with pages that had not yet been read.

When Maria Belkina married Tarasenkov in 1938, she entered among his young and literary friends. He was the secretary of the literary magazine *Znamya* ("The Banner") and surrounded by young band of Komsomol members and poetry lovers. Margarita Aliger had just graduated from the Literature Institute at that time. One day they showed up to the newlyweds' home (Maria and Anatoly) at Konyushkovsky Lane with friends – Yevgeny (Dolmatovsky), Daniil (Danin), and Konstantin (Makarov). I read about this evening in Margarita Aliger's diary. She was angered by the Belkin's bourgeois house, the fine dishes on the table, the mahogany furniture, and a servant.

When I read these pages from 1938 to Maria Iosifovna, she laughed until tears came out of her eyes.

"Her father was an artist. He loved beautiful things and would sometimes buy items at second-hand markets. The mahogany furniture was left over from an undertaker named Belkin (not her real grandfather), and the servant was a woman from the countryside, a housekeeper, like they all had back then."

But these comments were made only in a brief outburst. Soon Maria Belkina and Margarita Aliger became friends. Friends were staying at their place at the same time that Marina Tsvetaeva and her son Mur came to visit. However, their paths did not cross.

Once, already in the 1990s, Maria Iosifovna was coming home and suddenly felt weak in her heart. She sank to the stairs in front of the entrance. By this time Anastasia was following the story. Anastasia saw an elderly woman with an aristocratic face who had turned very pale. It was clear that something was wrong with her. Anastasia offered to help her to the door. The woman agreed and they walked to her apartment. Anastasia asked Maria Iosifovna if she should call an ambulance, but the latter snapped, "Call if you want, but I'm not going anywhere!" A doctor came, gave Maria Iosifovna an injection, and left. Anastasia stayed with Maria Iosifovna, waiting for her to feel better. The lady seemed to her to be very stern. They talked for a while. And now Maria Iosifovna understood that Margarita Aliger's granddaughter was sitting before her; she was deeply struck by this. She remembered the little girl who had been orphaned early on, who had been passed around in the family from one person to another.

Thus they became friends.

As Anastasia told me: "My grandma didn't like my mother." The main child in the family was Maria. There was only a small difference in age between Tanya Makarova and Masha, Fadeyev's daughter, but they didn't get along. Masha was loved, well-treated, she did well in school, and until some point she was a very obedient child. Tanya was a problem child, she played hooky from classes, she started smoking early, and she eventually dropped out of school. They would say that Masha had a big future ahead of her, but when it came to Tanya they simply shook their heads. Tanya secretly – but very sincerely – adored her mother, she wrote poems and stories, and she wanted more than anything that her mother would pay attention to her. She ran away from home, she married several times. When it comes to her poems and stories, Chukovsky said that she wrote better than her mother, but that made Margarita furious.

Masha grew up. She was a beautiful woman, but cold. She had become accustomed to being loved, but she never learned herself to love. Tanya, on the other hand, was warm, passionate, sensitive and also very beautiful. But she ended up in a mental hospital on several occasions. Maria Iosifovna told me that the first crack in her own relationship with Margarita happened because of Tanya.

"I couldn't bear to see them love one child and not the other. I told her that straight out."

Once she went to the clinic to visit her friend Yevgeniya Taratuta, who after being interrogated in Lubyanka and beaten over the head, was now tormented by headaches. Suddenly in the corridor Tanya rushed towards her crying, "Auntie Maria!"

"My heart sank," Maria Iosifovna said softly.

Tanya had a biblical kind of beauty. She died at the age of thirty-three from blood cancer. Little Anastasia was left behind. She had a difficult upbringing, going from one grandmother to the other. She would walk into the house and take her coat off.

"Am I staying at your place tonight?"

Margarita took the death of her eldest daughter hard. She became aware of all the guilt before her. A small and fragile woman, already advanced in years, she married Chernoutsan, who chaired the culture division of the Central Committee. At that time Masha had left with her poet husband for England. They soon divorced, but Masha received a substantial sum. However, she did not find happiness. She hated her mother for getting married again, and especially to a Party bureaucrat. When she visited Moscow, she stayed with acquaintances, avoiding her mother and thus tormenting her. She could not understand why no one needed her any more, why the swiftly changing Moscow had ceased to be interested in her. In 1991, on the day before her mother's birthday, she hung herself in her home. Anastasia went to the funeral. When she came back, her grandmother told her:

"Tell Masha not to be so foolish, I love her all the same."

Anastasia was aghast – she had brought things, the death certificate.

Margarita did not give the impression of being a madwoman, she was calm and collected, but when Anastasia began to talk about Masha, she said:

"I understand that she wants to hide from me, but I love her all the same."

A year later in Peredelkino, as Margarita was leaving her little dacha to visit a neighbor after dusk, she stumbled and fell into a ditch. She died instantly, but as it was already dark, they found her only several hours later. Thus Anastasia remained among the ruins of her family, where the grief was neverending.

I met Anastasia just after the death of her father, the artist Sergei Kovalenkov.

Once she told me:

"Every spring I feel like I'm dying. I fall seriously ill for a long period. I recently realized why that is. It was exactly at that time of the year when my mother was four months pregnant and the doctors decided to perform an abortion. My mother jumped right out of her chair and ran from the doctor's office in bare feet with blood streaming. Something had really got to her, and she saved me. But I will always remember that horrible month when they wanted to take a knife to me."

From my diary, September 6, 2003

It's funny, Maria Iosifovna decided to introduce herself after we have already know each other for three years. That is, she had heard that my second husband, whom I met when we were both teaching in a school, has the same last name as her – Belkin. She realized that they were from the same family. After that she began to tell me about her ancestry.

"My aunt told me that my maternal uncle was a priest. A big fire had broken out in the city of Syzran, and the bishop told my uncle to put all of the priceless church vestments into a chest and take them away from the city. He placed all of the church vestments into a chest, put his wife in a boat, and rowed to an island in the Volga. He stayed there for quite some time, though, and the boat got carried away by the river current. They managed to put out the flames in the city, but they couldn't find the priest anywhere, and rumors began to fly that he had run away. And eventually he managed to get back, and he even received a medal from the bishop."

The story of the Belkins

In Moscow the Belkins rented rooms in Konyushkovsky Lane in the home of an undertaker called Belkin – by some incredible coincidence he had the same last name as them. The undertaker had no family, and he was very fond of his tenants.

When she was a little girl, Maria Iosifovna would get up in her little bed on her knees and pray to the Virgin Mary that her parents would not fight and would not separate. Her artist father had already left the house once and even managed to escape from Russia to Istanbul with the White Army. He was in love with a young nurse, who died from typhoid after they had left the country. Her father returned to his homeland and to his family, but her parents' relationship remained tense. Maria had a little sister and they came down with scarlet fever at the same time. Her sister's condition did not improve and, when her sister was already close to death, her mother came to her, the elder daughter, and insisted that she pray to God to save her younger sister. Maria Iosifovna said that she thought her mother wanted her to ask God to take her instead of her sister. Right at her sister's graveside, her mother cursed God and then fainted. Her mother also demanded that her surviving daughter forget about God. When the girl went to confession and communion with the porter of the house, who was also the caretaker of the Church of the Nine Martyrs, her mother frowned and said:

"Just don't kiss the icons. You'll catch some disease."

With old man Belkin, little Maria went to the Smolensky market to sell buttons and other small items, which the old man carried in a wheelbarrow. Once the wheelbarrow broke, and the handle struck old man Belkin in the stomach and gave him a hernia, soon after which he died. The house in Konyushky Lane was inherited by the new Belkins. Maria's father learned to be a painter. He mixed paints, helped make shop signs in Saint Petersburg, and painted the apartments of the wealthy. In the Twenties he worked in the theatre and painted the walls of clubs. He hated the Bolsheviks and was utterly convinced that they would not be around for long. He intended to wait out their regime. Maria also said about her father, that he told her that he was a Jew only when she turned seventeen. Indeed, her father had converted to Orthodox Christianity in order to marry her mother.

He forbid his daughter from attending a Soviet school. He hired a tutor to home-school her until she was in the tenth grade. In her last year she was forced to go to a school so that she could subsequently enter an institute.

Maria Iosifovna grew up to be completely different from Soviet girls. Although she was introverted, she was an independent thinker. The only thing that she regretted was that she had never learned to speak in public, and she thought that this was a skill that she needed to have to protect her friends from attacks.

In the Literature Institute she studied in the translation department in the late 1930s. She was a tall woman, with long blond hair, and she liked sports. She would play tennis on the court at the Writers' Club. It was there that she met Tarasenkov. He was then leaving one in a series of wives. He would speak only of books, of poetry. That decided everything. They got married. Maria Iosifovna's father liked Tarasenkov very much. Tarasenkov brought his things to Konyushky Lane and began calling her father "dad".

Maria Iosifovna often talked about herself in the third person: "Maria is old, Maria needs to eat."

Or: "Refined people died long ago. Only I am left."

Usually our meetings began with ringing the doorbell. A long silence would follow. And suddenly a loud voice would come from deep within the apartment: "I'm coming!" The sound of the door opening, and then her face, lovely even when she was in her nineties, narrow, very pale, with straight features. She held her head high, her hair was gathered in a large hair clip. Pants and a blouse. She looked very modern – a real elderly lady from the West.

While I waited at the door, I would look out the window in the staircase, which was decorated with geraniums and begonias. Behind them one could see the dome of the Kremlin. Soon the view would change greatly: the river embankment and the Kremlin palace was obscured by another new building.

Maria Iosifovna always spoke clearly, enunciating her words well. She had a youthful and booming voice. She would laugh and tell of how, when people spoke to her on the telephone, they did not understand that she was the ninety-year-old lady. She purposely called herself an old lady, although she understood that she wasn't one. She would fall ill, have aches and pains, and eventually lose her sight and hearing, but she held herself tall.

The very fact that she was born in 1912 was something fantastical for me. Her mother and father looked out at me from a photograph: she was wearing a long dress and he was dressed in a suit and was holding a cane. When the terrorist attacks happened, she told me, "My childhood was the Caucasus, horsecarts carrying the slain. The carts were covered with sackcloth, and the feet of the dead would stick out from under it. And here we are in a new era, and it's all happening again. Why did I end up in the twenty-first century? What's the point of this?"

She would make jokes about herself and her condition, although from time to time she would emphasize that she still found it great (in spite of her blindness, deafness, and poor feet) to be alive. I told her about the internet and blogs, about Khodorkovsky and everything that had happened of late. She never grumbled about how things were better in the past. She saw the world changing before her eyes and she kept up a lively interest in everything around her. I have seen many times people carrying their past like a shell on their backs, feeding only on this, and they buckle under the weight. Such people do not know how to live in the present.

At the same time, however, Maria Iosifovna never forgot about her old life. She would let the eras of history pass through her and she again and again tried to riddle out what she was witnessing before her. Furthermore, when she talked about things from the past, she had the ability to depict them vividly like in films, or as she said, "in the pictures."

She paid close attention to what Fate intended for her; or at least in the second half of her life she tried very had to discern this.

In her personal relationships she kept the bar so high that, to come up to her height, one had to physically stretch to reach her. She could be wonderfully tender in her words and comfort others, but she lacked any physical expression of tenderness: she would never allow anyone to kiss her in greeting or farewell, or even touch her. Her bearing seemed even solemn. Some people thought of her as proud and unassailable, but this was most likely caused by her introverted nature. She would suddenly, speaking in the third person, mock herself, her own clothes and habits. She was afraid of being stuck in a certain role – a writer, a wise elderly lady. She was very lively, and therefore she would always find some comedic formula for herself, so that I could laugh at her together with her. A readiness to respond to her extended to her cleaning woman, her neighbors, and to the nineteen-year-old young man who ran errands for her. They were all happy, delighted even, to carry out her every request. There was something aristocratic in her, in the best sense of the word.

Her ability to look at herself from the outside, to laugh at herself, saved her life. It happened that, after she was left all alone (her son, daughter-in-law, and granddaughter emigrated from the USSR in 1977), she decided to end her life, as she thought that she would never see her loved ones again. Then she went up to the top floor of the building in Lavrushinsky, intending to throw herself from the window. However, the window was too high, and as she was standing on the staircase, she thought of how she would have to go down to her apartment and get a stool, and then she would have to struggle to get from the stool onto the windowsill and open all the latches over the window. This image seemed comedic and, looking at herself objectively, very silly. She went back to her apartment, closed the door, and decided to start her life all over again. She took all her notes and sketches, left for the Nikitsky Garden in Yalta, and began to write her book about Tsvetaeva, *The Intersection of Fates.*

The methodology of miracles

In 1940, Marina Tsvetaeva came to the house on Konyushky Lane. She came not as a guest, but rather with a mission: to use Tarasenkov's home library of poetry, which contained a collection of her verse. Tsvetaeva looked old and haggard, but her way of speaking, her face, her manners, and her questions and answers were so different, so outside the general pattern of Soviet life, that Maria Belkina fell under her spell without even noticing. She would later judge many things in life according to Tsvetaeva's standards.

These meetings and talks with Maria Iosifovna changed something inside of me.

I came face to face with someone who had been transformed by Tsvetaeva and who had drawn from her an extreme frankness and severity. Maria Iosifovna never developed confidence in herself. Sometimes she would say that she didn't know who she was, but nevertheless she would always claim that she would write about herself in time. This self-flattery disturbed me: I knew for a fact that she didn't have any time left, no days and hours left to write about herself. My heart would be pierced by a sharp sense of compassion for her. But she would tell the stories that she intended to write in such a vivid way, that I was quite uneasy trying to listen to and memorize them – they were meant for *her* book. She told me:

I went ice-skating at the rink on Petrovka Street. There were always actors there performing in Bulgakov's *Days of the Turbins*. I loved that play so much that I learned it by heart, I went to every performance. At the skating rink I met Tarasova, who was still quite young. I fell down skating, and she fell down too, and that is how we met. I said that I liked their play. We talked for a while. She told me about her father, who had been in Stanislavsky's acting classes, later worked as a set designer in the theatre, and now painted in clubs. "Come to the rink at six o'clock tomorrow," she said. "I want to introduce you to Lariosik and the others." But the next time I went to the rink, I wasn't brave enough to get onto the ice and go up to them. A young man came on to me, he looked like a worker. I fell down several times, he helped me up and said, "Listen, I like you, let's get married. I'm getting a room in the workers' dormitory and a card. I'm a hard worker with a writer's calling. They chose me at a meeting, Stavsky himself is supervising my novel. Are you literate?" I said that I had graduated from the tenth grade, and he was very happy to hear this and said that I could help him correct his mistakes. After that I stopped going to the rink.

I clearly understood then that it was impossible to immerse oneself in a different era that one hadn't lived in. It's impossible to pass through the sea of common words and preconceptions.

One day she was coming from lectures with Konstantin Simonov, a colleague from the Literature Institute. She was going to Konyushky Lane, and it was on his way. They spoke freely about all kinds of things. He would always dress very stylishly and take great care of his appearance. He visited hard-currency shops and looked for imported clothes. He said to her:

"I'll have it all, Maria, a car and a dacha."

She stopped in astonishment – people didn't speak like that in their circles. It was bad form to talk about material things. Simonov was different, though. He could greet you at the door of his apartment in a long robe. As Margarita Aliger later wrote with bafflement in her diary: "Konstantin walks around his home in a robe and drinks black coffee. He's an everyday guy, but he's a very talented and intelligent person. That's how it often is.".

When you listen, when you feel how the space of the usual history warps and you literally fall through a sort of crack, an opening where new details are revealed to you, then you can see and convey to others something unusual, which will depict the time in a sharper way.

The first day of the war. In the Union of Writers a meeting was held. When it finished, a few people for some reason headed to the German embassy on Leontyevsky Lane. It was a two-story red building, and in front of it there was a car with the engine running. Through the window a figure could be seen running around and burning papers. People stood looking at the building. They had come here on their own in an unorganized fashion. A policeman stood guarding the embassy. He was short-statured and looked like a teenager. He ran back and forth in front of the gathering crowd and repeatedly moaned, "Citizens, don't destroy anything! Citizens, don't destroy anything!". Then some old lady said, "What a short little guy. He could drop to the ground and a bullet wouldn't hit him.". Maria Belkina was amazed that no one shouted or uttered curses. Everyone stood and watched in silence.

Moscow at war, the beginning of October. The bombardment, the lines outside shops, the men and women in military uniforms with khaki backpacks. All of this has been shown many times on screens, and heard, and read in books. But here is a little-known detail: the Kremlin was covered with a vast fabric, which had multicolored pictures of houses drawn on it. This was meant to fool German bombers. Thick ash in the streets would leave traces on the hands and faces of the Muscovites. The ash blew in from documents, papers, and archives being burned en masse.

Maria Iosifovna was never a Soviet kind of person. However, she embraced the war as a demand that could not be refused: to rush to the defense of the Motherland. Her patriotism was absolute. When she found herself in 1945 in Germany and under bombardment from Soviet planes, she jumped into a bomb shelter, where a young German woman the same age as her was also sitting. Maria Iosifovna began to berate her about the death camps. The German woman was frightened and answered that she knew nothing about any death camps, that she had not heard anything like that. Maria Iosifovna said that her heart was pierced by the German woman's words and thought, "Well, we don't know anything, we have no information about our own camps. How am I any better than that frightened German woman?"

I have found that in the maelstrom of events people would meet here and there, the things they needed to know would pass between them, and they learned the truth that they were so desperate top discover.

Gradually a new reality was revealed to me. I started seeing not only separate personal stories, but also the invisible map of the world of these people, who were joined, separated, lost and found, forming a distinctive landscape of entwined fates and intersections that resembled a panorama of aerial photography, or a book of anatomy with its networks of blood vessels. It should come as no surprise that precisely in these entwined fates a miraculous element appeared, which Pasternak wrote about so much in his novel *Doctor Zhivago*.

Once a woman already advanced in years told of her childhood experience of fearlessness through the story of her slain uncle.

She was nine years old during the war. Her father went off to fight and her mother died. She managed to escape being placed in an orphanage and she lived on her own. She learned to hunt down things that she could get with a ration card, and when they asked her at school where her parents were, she answered that her father would come back from the front soon and would be with her. She walked alone down unlit streets, she went into dark entryways, wandered around in search of wood to heat her frozen apartment, and through all this she was not afraid. During bombing raids she didn't rush for shelter but calmly walked down the street under the bombardment. Her father had been in prison before the war. Her uncle was the administrator of a tuberculosis ward at Stromynka Street where many people had been saved, but in 1952 he was imprisoned in the so-called Doctors' Plot. They beat him severely during interrogation, and just when he was freed after Stalin's death, he died. Years later this woman was recuperating in a health resort and glimpsed an elderly

Jewish man. She herself couldn't understand why she decided to ask him about her uncle. To her great surprise, it turned out that he was a "co-conspirator" of her uncle, they had been interrogated for the same thing, and they were both asked to identify the other. He could only answer her questions with bitter tears. He had also been a doctor at a tuberculosis ward. They were imprisoned because they allegedly intended to infect the Russian people with tuberculosis. When her uncle was taken away after the other was forced to identify him, her uncle managed to shout, "Solomon, I didn't sign anything."

Almost every such story, regardless of the darkness it contained, revealed some element of the miraculous, like in this story of the meeting at the health resort.

Miracles were part of life. When I noticed their presence, they were an additional compass guiding my journey.

A change of trains: 1930

After the book about Tashkent, after the story of Margarita Aliger and her circle, I started thinking about the friendship that poets in the Twenties maintained: Mayakovsky – Aseev – Pasternak, Selvinsky – Zelinsky – Lugovskoy – Tikhonov – Antokolsky, Pasternak – Tikhonov. New connections between people were beaded onto the string, but many of them were cut or became hostile, and some quietly grew into a mutual relationship that would last many years. The main thing that distinguished the Soviet era from others was that the state interfered with these connections with all its might, and nearly everyone involved came face to face with his or her own tragic fate.

Of course, almost everyone knows that a Soviet-era person, especially a Soviet-era writer, was tragedically and sometimes absurdly split in two; he lived with two, or sometimes more faces at the same time. It was no consolation to think that in the person's private life he was a real person, while in public life he was an artificial person. Life showed that at times when society wasp going through some cataclysm, everything would be confused. Sometimes people who were close one day would become enemies the next, wives betrayed their husbands, and children their fathers.

For example, Mayakovsky didn't know how to live with a split personality at all. That's why he put a bullet through his heart. Stavsky, Vishnevsky, Bezymensky and many others were fierce and zealous in their single personality, but they were not interesting for it, though one encountered them everywhere.

Private life swelled, was turned upside down, lost its personal and intimate quality. The further one went, the less was left of oneself. Of course, a great deal depended on a given person's nature. But friendships and close relationships were still present at the end of the Twenties with their men's world and code of honor, their arguments and rifts. The unions, groups, and circles of poets and writers were not only literary organizations: creative figures could come together or be sundered according to their temperaments, according to whether they liked each other, and according to many other things besides literature.

No one became a Soviet poet or writer right away. At the end of the 1920s everyone was still very different from each other. They still had no idea that they would be confronting their former peers at constant meetings in the late 1930s and offering their own services as executioner. It took some time before they reached this state. As I was going through the papers in Lugovskoy's home, I came across documents that shocked me: a long letter of repentance from the poet Petrovsky to the Party committee at the Writers' Union, letters from Lugovskoy that were full of trepidation and an increasing sense of horror.

I went to the archives for literature and art and started to select, consciously and deliberately, the collections of literary figures known to me from a certain period: the mid to late 1930s. I was blown away.

The diary of the poet and later – because it was no longer possible to write poems – translator Alexander Romm (the older brother of the well-known film director) struck me by how openly he was destroying his own talent. He increasingly sought to keep up with the times, and he increasingly tripped up and complained about how it was impossible to remain in the same ranks as the leading Soviet poets.

A diaristic novel by Grigori Gauzner also made a powerful impression due to the sincerity of how the author changed himself within and his active desire to be a man of his time. He wrote the novel based on his own life under the telling title *The Transformation* about how he killed the member of the intelligentsia within himself and became the kind of writer that "the people needed".

I realized that I had to write a book about this "Transformation". I had to write about the 1930s using everything that had been revealed to me in the collections at Lavrushinsky Lane about Lugovskoy and his friends: Nikolai Tikhonov, Dmitri Petrovsky, Alexander Fadeyev, and others – about their gradual falling into the abyss. About how Tikhonov and Petrovsky were friends of Pasternak in the late 1920s and what this friendship was turned into in the late 1930s. About how Pasternak remained Pasternak, and how everyone knew it; and about how this caused annoyance, alarm, fear, or respect.

Maria Iosifovna did not believe that such a book was possible, but I had a vision of it.

I felt that I had come into real contact with that era. I pulled on a chain in my time, and an answer came from that time.

From the diary

This is just a part of the chain. Sometimes I regret that I cannot see the whole picture. The thought has long tormented me that here is a person that we see at a certain time and place. Where does his past lie, his actions, his path in life? Perhaps some invisible body grows within him? A person sees only the fragment that lives for this particular moment in time. Where is the person as he was yesterday? He touched someone else's life and forgot about it. He crossed someone else's path and then disappeared. But the picture remains. The invisible world of human beings, their fates, look like a single circulatory system woven in the past and in the present day. It is for that reason that a person who strikes, humiliates, or insults another, will inevitably bring harm to himself.

In the 20th century in Europe and in Russia, some people incessantly destroyed the lives of others. In Europe there was a spiritual crisis, while in Russia people lost the will to live.

Lidia Borisovna
Libedinskaya, apartment 37

I decided to enter the Thirties through a door that had long been nailed up, that of the Russian Association of Proletarian Writers (RAPP). What was interesting about this new generation of writers is the fact that they tried to combine the role of writers and of propagandists within themselves. They were the first to fall on a battlefield where they themselves had dug the trenches and fought with the enemy. Many of them met a terrible fate. Probably even when they were brought in to be shot, they still did not understand how this had all happened, and why it should happen to them, the most faithful and proven warriors, who were now liquidated en masse.

I decided to visit Lidia Borisovna Libedinskaya. Though she was only ten years old when RAPP flourished, some years later she became the wife of one of the first leaders of RAPP, Yuri Libedinsky.

For some reason, it was a long time before I decided to call her. Maria Iosifovna said:

"Don't worry, Lidia is a very nice lady. Granted, she can't pull herself away from the television, but it doesn't affect her."

I called her and introduced myself.

"Why haven't you come yet? I've been waiting for you for a long time now."

I was stunned.

"Yes, I read your book about Tashkent. I liked it a lot."

Libedinskaya's enormous apartment, filled with things, was the complete opposite of Maria Iosifovna's ascetic and bare-walled home. Here everything jumped out at you: the painted wood cutting boards which covered all the walls in the kitchen; the paintings, pictures, and photos; heaps of souvenirs; and little china plates. My warm and smiling hostess blended perfectly with all this. While things were always difficult with Maria Iosifovna – slowly entering into her life, listening carefully to her way of speaking, and gradually becoming someone important to her – in this home everything was the opposite. Just a few hours later I already felt like I had come here a hundred times before, I had sat in the corner in the kitchen and talked with her about everything under the sun.

It immediately became obvious that Lidia Borisovna combined in herself the irreconcilable. She loved her late husband, she was devoted to the memory of his friend Fadeyev, and she had been friends for many years with Margarita Aliger who was Soviet to the bone, while Libedinskaya hated the Soviet regime.

Yuri Nikolayevich was persecuted himself, he barely survived the purges in 1937. If it had not been for Fadeyev, I don't know what would have happened. Yes, he was a Soviet person, he hoped that everyone would be happy, but what could you do? Such were the times.

Libedinskaya's story left me unsatisfied. It was a very common and bleak one. Libedinsky was obscured behind generalities that she constantly repeatedly. It was different when it came to the others.

She told me with zeal about Boris Levin, who had described the members of RAPP in his novel *Youth* (*Yunosha*) in 1933 and mentioned Averbakh, Dinamov, and Fadeyev. His contemporaries quickly guessed who they were, and the novel completely disappeared from literary history.

Libedinskaya spoke about Fadeyev willingly and in great depth. In her eyes, he was undoubtedly a victim. He had simply been mistaken, he suffered a lot, and he hated Beria. He could not handle the burden that had fallen on him, the burden of undeserved criticism, and he took his own life. I realized that Lidia Borisovna had set her opinion as if in stone. I viscerally felt that she had repeated her stories many times, and I sought a crack in these stories through which I could enter into the truth.

The subject of suicide turned out to be one such crack. She had accompanied Fadeyev all his life. That was something to think about. There had been a beautiful woman – Olga Lyashko, the daughter of a proletariat writer. She had been the secretary at the literary magazine *Krasnaya Nov* ("Red Virgin Soil"), where Fadeyev was also working along with his wife, the proletarian writer Valeria Gerasimova. Once Fadeyev and Olga Lyashko went for a cruise on a steamship, and Valeria Gerasimova took an enormous dose of sleeping pills. Her sister Marianna brought her back to life with great effort. Fadeyev rushed to the hospital, and years later Gersimova recalled with what tenderness he nursed her. These were the happiest days of her life, though she would say that it would have been better if she had died back then, so that she wouldn't have experienced such grief later on. Fadeyev stopped seeing Olga. Soon afterwards she committed suicide along with the writer Viktor Dimitriev, who had fallen in love with her. All Moscow was talking about this terrible event, which happened after Mayakovsky's suicide, though I found out these details myself. Lidia Borisovna claimed that all this was only a coincidence, but Fadeyev had been constantly haunted by these circumstances.

He had a short affair with Inna Belenkaya, an intelligence agent, a beautiful woman, and the sister of the Deputy People's Commissar for the food industry, Mark Belenky (who was later shot). She worked in Spain, and in 1937 Alexander Fadeyev went to an anti-fascist congress there. He met Inna in the street and embraced her, and thus he unknowingly blew her cover.

Inna was immediately summoned to Moscow. As soon as she got back to the capital, she went up to the roof of Nirnzee House and threw herself off of it. Several years later Marianna Gerasimova – Valeria's sister and someone very close to Fadeyev – took her own life after she had just returned from a labor camp.

Of course, everything surrounding the general secretary of the Writer's Union was pure gloom.

Lidia Borisovna told me that she had heard from Libedinsky, that the only person that Fadeyev wanted to leave his wife for was Margarita Aliger. Libedinsky went together with Margarita to Fadeyev's funeral service at the church on Pyatnitskaya Street. At the cemetery, every year on the anniversary of Fadeyev's death, they would meet Maria Petrovykh.

Margarita was unhappy, she said that she only loved her daughter Tanya, and she felt truly guilty concerning her. She was in love with Kazakevich when they were working at *Literaturnaya Moskva*… When she was told about his terrible diagnosis, she cried, "Why has this happened to me?! Why?!" He treated her very carelessly. He would make comments about her that all Peredelkino would be repeating. She however was steadfast as if made of stone. After the death of Stalin, she said that she had never felt so bad as when the nation had lost its dear leader. It took her a long time to get used to the new circumstances.

The suicides that surrounded Fadeyev and his own suicide gradually developed, without anyone noticing, into a metaphor. When I read the emotionally moving correspondence between Fadeyev and Aliger from 1943–1944, I couldn't help feeling sorry for this man crushed by fate, someone who was lost and could find no way back to his main vocation – writing. That is what his cries and pain were about. But the regime could not let him go, and he too could not break with the regime. This is how the most terrible things began in the postwar period, when he attacked his former friends who had instantly become "cosmopolitans", and monstrous Party meetings were held, where they would distinguish between writers according to their nationality and then send them to be executed. He hid behind the words that he had once told Tarasenkov, "You have to understand that it's much better if we beat up each other, than if they start beating us from up there at the top!"

Suddenly a parallel and previously unknown reality was revealed to me, which I had little inkling of. Although collections of documentation about Soviet literature had been published, from which vague members of the *nomenklatura* emerged without names or distinct personalities, and there were a large number of polished memoirs that had remained from the Soviet era, there was also an oral history, which had now almost disappeared: in the last decade it vanished before one's very eyes.

Nearly all the writers working back then sooner or later fell into the net. Many of them would die before the eyes of their fellow writers who, themselves dying from fear, watched them be executed. Some of them helped to tighten the noose around their fellows' throats so that they would not get away, but the next day, everything would change, and they themselves would find themselves defeated, lost, and waiting for death.

For a while, however, I had to set aside my wanderings through the 1930s.

Chapter 2.
Borisoglebsky

Because

I was hired at the Tsvetaeva museum. In this, Maria Iosifovna played a role, as well as the fact that in the Tashkent book, I wrote about Mur, Tsvetaeva's son. No, so many circumstances came together here – it cannot be explained all at once.

And so, the building was located on Borisoglebsky Lane. It is a three-story yellow cube with nice, old-fashioned windows, with the main entrance under a wrought iron awning. It had always been on my left whenever I walked from Nikitskaya Street to Novy Arbat.

I never wanted to go into the museum, I just rushed past it time and time again. This was linked to the silly grudge I held in my younger days against the museum's founder, Nadezhda Ivanovna Kataeva-Lytkina. In the 1990s I was writing a small guidebook entitled *Marina Tsvetaeva's Moscow*, and when I called the museum and asked them to check the book to ensure there were no errors, Kataeva-Lytkina answered, "My dear, first try washing the floors here for three years, and after that I'll take a look at what you've written."

I understood what she was getting at, but I still didn't like this exchange. I set the guidebook aside unfinished.

Now times had changed and I opened the heavy wooden door and went up the winding stone stairs. This wasn't quite a museum, it was a home. This home entered into my life without any of the boring quality of a museum, without any field trips or solemn commemoration of someone. I simply settled into it, delighted by its spiral nature, the tiny room just under the roof. I lived on its sofas and I found objects that were appropriate for it. During my wanderings through different places, meeting different people, I came across items that had belonged to Tsvetaeva herself. The owners of some of these agreed to donate them to the museum.

When I got to the museum, I realized that I would inevitably have to write a sequel to the Tashkent book about the evacuation, about Marina Tsvetaeva and Mur's last journey to Yelabuga, which was logically connected to the story of the writers' colony in Chistopol. The atmosphere of Tashkent appeared in a different way elsewhere. It was enough to utter the names: Tsvetaeva – Yelabuga – Chistopol, and history would come to life. It turned out that Lidia Borisovna as a twenty-year-old woman together with the painter Lev Bruni saw Tsvetaeva off at the river port on the way to Yelabuga. Pasternak was there too, as was Viktor Bokov and many others, but most of all Lidia Borisovna remembered how Tsvetaeva was standing on the bank, nervously tugging at a pillowcase filled with rice and saying, "Lev, the rice is going to finish, and what then? The rice is going to finish."

When saying her farewell, Tsvetaeva kissed the young and stout Lidia Tolstoya (as she wasp then known) and said:

"It's a pity that you aren't coming with us."

I realized later that Tsvetaeva hadn't said that out of mere politeness. What place could there be for good manners among the shouts, chaos, bundles, suitcases, faces distorted by tragic emotions, tears, and women weeping hysterically? Rather, it was simply that such an enormous toughness, a life energy, emerged from this young woman, and Tsvetaeva could distinguish it and wanted to wrap herself around someone strong and reliable, like a knot around an anchor. Life was being pulled out from right under her feet and she floated, just like their overloaded boat, to another shore, to the Non-living.

Lidia Borisovna and I started to look for the last photograph where everyone was in it – Lidia, Kruchenykh, Tsvetaeva, and Mur – on June 18 in Kuskovo. However, it wasn't that photo that we discovered. Instead we found old women in hoop-skirts and dark-eyed young ladies from Tbilisi in soft and light dresses looking into the camera with a questioning glance. Here was Libedinsky embracing Marianna Gerasimova and Libedinsky and Fadeyev bearing Mayakovsky's coffin.

"Look," Libedinskaya pointed out to me in a sarcastic tone. "Everyone said that the members of RAPP didn't go to Mayakovsky's funeral. There they are, the members of RAPP!"

Then, suddenly there was a couple, him and her. Nice-looking and happy. Dezik Samoylov with his first wife. A beautiful woman with an enormous braid in her hair and clear and tranquil eyes, was looking out of the photograph. Next to her a handsome young man with curly hair was sitting. It was hard to recognize him as David Samoylov.

Exactly one week later, in a kitchen near the Aeroport metro station, I was sitting with Gedda Shor and her sister, and the very same photography of Samoylov with the beautiful woman appeared in front of me.

I had found myself sitting next to Shor in a completely unexpected way. A discussion began about Gedda's memoirs of Chistopol that had been published, and these memoirs were very different from what I read before. Gedda was already a very old woman, short in stature, with a shrunken face but with bright and lively eyes. Her sister was the same.

These Shor sisters, Agda and Gedda (named after two of Ibsen's characters) were the daughters of the forgotten writer of children's poetry Margarita Shor-Ivensen and Alexander Shor, who at the beginning of the century had launched courses of music, opera, drama and dance taught by various famous people. The Shors had a huge number of eminent relatives, from the musician David Shor to Olga Shor, the personal secretary of Vyacheslav Ivanov. Granted, their connection with their relatives was not very strong, but they talked about their younger days with passion and many interesting details. They made the acquaintance of Dezik Samoylov through a close friend, the very beauty in the photo. Gedda had peculiar talents: first of all, she was an expert whistler, and secondly, she could imitate the mannerisms of anyone. She always gave these brief performances wherever a lively group of people came together. Samoylov referred to this as "Gedda doing an Irakli", from the name of Irakli Andronikov. Each time he would beg her, "Gedda, please do an Irakli", and she would start to do her act to much laughter or astonishment. Once, during such a home performance, she turned pale and then fainted. After this, she completely lost her ability to imitate people. She said that every time she had done such an act, she felt that her soul would leave her body for a while and something else would take its place. On the day when she fainted, she felt that her soul had left her body forever. However, her life came back to her.

When Gedda took out the photograph of Samoylov (as we were searching for photos from Chistopol taken during the war), I was stunned and I said that I had seen it in the Libedinsky home. They looked at me sternly and said that the photo had probably been taken again at their place. This was followed by the story of the tragic fate of their female friend, ill treatment, and lies. More stories about ill treatment then followed. About the museum at which I had just started working (earlier, under another director, there were caged parrots which Gedda and her sister had made from papier-mache, and now they knew for sure that the birds had been taken away). They underestimated their mother and them as well.

I heard for the first time that Maria Iosifovna had written her book *The Intersection of Fates* to clear her husband Tarasenkov's name. I expressed my surprise at this, but the sisters waved their hands. They told me that they understood the real motives of various people, but I was new to this world, and that is why I didn't understand anything. I started to lose the thread. The story of Gedda "doing an Irakli" dwindled, the details disappeared, as well as the smell of the time. Everything was covered by a sad layer of them being angry with their life.

I realized then with some surprise that in four years of talking with Maria Iosifovna, I had never heard something like that from her. She told me a lot of cruel things about people, about the past, about herself, but she never judged anyone. It would be impossible to imagine her as someone trying to guess at things. She would simply cross someone out, and that was that. The Tsvetaeva museum, which was headed by the Shor sisters' friend Kataeva-Lytkina, ceased to exist for her, as well as for many other people. This was probably the reason why.

Everything was happening for the first time for me, both wonderful things and difficult ones. People revealed the most varied sides to me, citing long-dead witnesses, piecing together their own histories, casting blame on whomever, crying, and making confessions.

Could I have ever imagined this when I was reading the letters of Tatyana Alexandrovna to Malyugin and thinking of the hot Tashkent sun?

Anyone frequenting the Tsvetaeva museum would inevitably end up in Yelabuga sooner or later. It was a kind of initiation.

From the diary:
at the end of the world

Yelabuga. On the anniversary of Tsvetaeva's death. The cemetery. At the entrance one immediately finds an enormous stone engraving with the name "Marina Tsvetaeva" and her birth and death dates chiseled out. Around the four sides of the engraving there was a fence designed to resemble chains. This was an official memorial. People brought flowers, but everyone knew that this wasn't the real grave. They had simply agreed on this. It was a ritual. We came quietly in the evening when everyone had left. We came to the grave from the left side, people would point it out in a low tone. The little fence. The letters "M. Ts." could be made out.

The grave was covered with wild strawberry leaves. The neighboring grave, and then another one, also showed the letters "M. Ts." Almost all of the mounds were covered with wild strawberries. On a bench next to the little fence, a beautiful woman sat drawing something in a notebook. I said:

"Do you think that this is her grave?"

"Of course, according to Kropotkin's testimony."

Wait a moment. I didn't know who Kropotkin was. An anarchist? A building superintendent or paramedic? This woman seemed to be mentally sound, however. It was just that everyone here is caught up in a kind of whirlpool of names, citations, testimonies, and confessions. This afternoon a beautiful woman with gray hair, and with the foreboding name of Lilith, was throwing out a whole bunch of names along with statements by witnesses involved in the matter of this cemetery. Devastated by her grief, this mother would sit daily on the little bench next to the grave of her daughter, who had died before her time, and watch how strange funeral ceremonies were carried out literally just one grave over. The woman's daughter had died on August 20 and a funeral was happening every day, including on the 2nd. That is, the grave was nearby. Lilith had gathered all this information already four decades before. Why should I believe her account? Why shouldn't I? The questions multiplied. There was one more issue, which should not be ignored. The NKVD and later the KGB forbid the witnesses from saying anything, they shut them up. Through the joint efforts of individuals, a legend was created, something resembling the truth, but not the whole truth. But what was there to hide? She took her own life, that's a fact. She was buried, that's a fact. But did the authorities need, many years later, veneration of a mad poetess? The confusion over the graves looks like the authorities' trademark. Let there be as many graves as possible. It is strange that in a bureaucratic system, which kept track of everything and everyone, where so many papers were demanded from Tsvetaeva herself, suddenly there was nothing: no death certificate, no investigation. Furthermore, it is obvious that the graves were dug chronologically, so there would be one date and then a later one. This is why the grave was "on this side of the cemetery", as it was written on the cross set up here by Anastasia Tsvetaeva.

We didn't believe in the grave claimed by that Kropotkin (the cemetery caretaker), and our guide lead us to a different one, next to that of a girl named Mateeva. For some reason, we immediately believed in this one, though there was the same fence with the letters "M. Ts.", but instead of a mound, there was a concave depression with wild strawberry leaves and rowanberry.

On August 17, 1941 a strange pair, a woman and a teenage boy, stepped off a steamboat onto the pier and changed the fate of a small provincial town. They didn't much care for it. On the route from Paris to Moscow and then Chistopol, Yelabuga seemed like the end of the world.

As they went into the town, they said to each other, "Where's the town?" Delapidated shacks stood along the bumpy, dusty road. The fences were slanted and drab. This is what sadness looks like. The entire town turned out to consist of a single street on a hill with three churches, a row of former merchants' homes that, under the Soviet regime, held the city council, the library, the NKVD office, the community center, and so on. Where else would they be?

Now there is a museum here to the painter Shishkin. A museum for the cavalry maiden Durova. A small square with a gazebo overlooking the Kama River with a monument to the painter, and among all this grandeur, right under the windows with their frilly curtains, a few cows nibble at the grass. How nice it was to watch cows walking along the town's streets! Did Tsvetaeva know about Shishkin, about the cavalry maiden, did she meet cows everywhere like we did now?

The symbol of the city is the "Devil's Fort". It was left on the high bank of the Kama River by the Volga Bulgars. An awkward structure of flat stones looks out at three churches standing on the other bank. Our guide whispers, "The devil on one side of the river and God on the other." Thus Tsvetaeva came here and saw both of them, and thus she departed. The street along which she spent her last days was presided over by the now-destroyed Pokrovsky cathedral. In front of the house in which she and her son rented a corner there was a dusty street with open sewers. Now little white bridges stand over the ditches along the road, like Manezh Square in Moscow when Luzhkov was mayor. Now the beginning of the street (first known as Voroshilov Street, then Zhdanov, but it was really Pokrovsky Street) is presided over by a wondrous monument: an antique portico, and inside it a bust of a Komsomol heroine or someone stands on a column with "Tsvetaeva" written on it. As one clever local woman told me, this was a monument to what the authorities imagine poets to look like. Well, let them be. Tsvetaeva, who was not inclined to humor, would have laughed at this freak of nature. Napoleon, Rilke, Pasternak, Goncharova, Pushkin… But really, why did this forgotten town end up in the whirlwind of such poems? Just this moment they recited into the microphone words and rhymes with such energy that it became embarrassing for the people looking from behind the fences, looking from behind the gates, and for the cows which could not chew the grass in peace with these annoying poems.

From the diary: September 4, 2004

After I returned from Chistopol and Yelabuga, I visited Maria Iosifovna. We had already discussed that strange town on the phone, its prominent people, who had visited her and recorded her on video.

The country was going through horrible times. There was a terrorist attack on the school in Beslan. We spoke about bombings during the war and in our time.

Maria Iosifovna had almost not changed in three months. As always, she was dressed elegantly with her hair arranged. The table was set with everything for tea.

I asked about Sikorskaya, the one who traveled together with Tsvetaeva on the steamboat.

"I visited her home once. She was an old and haggard woman sitting by the window. She would talk about Tsvetaeva only grudgingly and with visible discomfort. Go and get the photo on the table. Here they are meeting with Ada Shkodina. They are all together: Sikorskaya, Bolotin and Alya. Tatyana and Bolotin would visit warships and perform popular songs. Tatyana had a soft, wide face and she had a nervous tick in her right eye. Her husband, on the other hand, had a nervous tick in his left eye. They would read poems together and people always gave them a lot of applause, thinking that they were doing it for laughs. One of them would have that tick in their eye and then the other. The toilets (they used the naval term "heads") were shared ones, so when she had to go, a sailor would stand guard outside. Once a lieutenant came. The sailor saluted and said, 'Comrade lieutenant, lieutenant third-class Sikorskaya is pissing!' This saying eventually made its way through the entire navy."

I discovered that seventy-four letters from Adriana Efron to Sikorskaya's relative by marriage Alla Belyakova had survived.

"This is how it started. Sikorskaya carried on a correspondence with Adriana. But someone in the Writers' Union found out and accused Sikorskaya, saying that she was writing to an emigrant and a person who had been imprisoned. Sikorskaya was a member of the Party and she stopped writing. Then Alla Belyakova joined this exchange of letters. She was a plump girl with blue eyes, very sweet but not very deep. She busied herself with painting and writing. Adriana asked her for brushes and paints. They wrote to each other all the time, but when Adriana came back from the labor camp, she abruptly ended her friendship with Alla. The latter was extremely upset, especially as Adriana had completely restored her friendship with Sikorskaya. Alla told me in Maleevka that she would destroy all the letters, because she deeply disliked Adriana. I begged her not to do that. I think that Adriana simply didn't want to talk to her any more, because she had realized that Alla was too shallow."

Then Maria Iosifovna said, "Berta is still alive, you should go visit her."

Berta

Berta Gorelik traveled on the same steamboat as Tsvetaeva. She was a famous doctor working for the Literary Fund and she had once treated Tatyana Alexandrovna Lugovskaya. I remembered her a little bit. She lived in the writers' home near the Aeroport metro station. She was ninety-one years. Her neighbors addressed her affectionately as Bertochka. She was small, hunched, and slightly deaf, and she was happy to answer anything I asked her. She read a great deal.

"Thank God, I'm still alive."

The war came when she was a twenty-six-year-old woman. She was mobilized as a doctor.

My husband wasn't a member of the Writers' Union. He was a reporter, a journalist. He started working for the newspaper *Izvestiya* when Nikolai Bukharin was the editor-in-chief there, I knew him. Bukharin introduced me to his young wife, "Young lady, you haven't met my wife yet? She's a charming woman." He was sharp-witted and a jolly fellow. In those days, the tango and foxtrot had just come into fashion. Once he joked, "I thought that people do that only at night, and it seems that they do it during the day too."

Everyone was being sent to prison. My husband came to me and said, "You know, there are meetings going on every day at the office, and everyone is apologizing, but I have nothing to blame myself for."

We lived in a dacha between Udelnaya and Otdykh, in a little set of houses belonging to *Izvestiya*. Every day someone would be arrested at one house or another… I came to my husband once and asked, "Should I be afraid?"

At the beginning of the war, her son was sent along with the rest of the kindergarten to Bersut, and he cried bitterly when saying goodbye. Berta could not find a place for herself and two weeks later she rushed to join him. It was only possible to get there on a steamboat, and she ended up on the *Sovetskaya Chuvashia*, where Tsvetaeva was traveling with her son.

"Tsvetaeva was pale, gray. Her hair was colorless, already with gray streaks, and there was such sadness in her eyes.

I didn't know that her husband had been shot, that her daughter was in a labor camp, and I didn't know that they were not allowed to live in Moscow. I didn't know any of that. When we got to Chistopol, the poet Obradovich came to the gangway of the steamboat and said, 'Only Vsevolod Ivanov's mother-in-law and wives of Writers' Union members can come ashore.' What was she to do?!"

She couldn't tell me very much about Tsvetaeva herself. The most surprising things were her other stories. How she lived in Chistopol first and helped out at a clinic. About writers' wives with their manicures and high heels, who didn't understand very well where they had ended up. How she moved to Kazan with her son and began working at a hospital. They rented a corner in the home of a terrible landlady, who wouldn't let her son in after he came home from school, and he would sit freezing on the stoop with his knapsack. Until one day the head of the hospital where Berta worked came and scolded the landlady so much that she got scared. The landlady knew that Berta and her son were Jews. She would continually say that the Germans were coming, and that she would immediately give them up so that the Germans could take care of them. Because this war was happening because of the Jews, who should be driven out. I remembered that the "Tashkent people" would write the same things, because the local people there also talked at the beginning of the war about how the Jews were "guilty", and that they all had to be gotten rid of.

How patient one had to be when hearing this day after day, avoiding the temptation to hit the landlady in the face with the frying pan. But bad things never happen singly. The most tragic thing is that Berta was summoned to the NKVD and asked to inform on the doctors and the nurses who assisted her during operations. They threatened that they would arrest her if she refused.

"Can you imagine? What was I supposed to do? Eavesdrop and spy on people that you work with in the operating room from morning till night? It's unthinkable. I would have killed myself, but I had a little boy. They gave me three days to think it over. I couldn't sleep at night and I kept thinking what I should do. I came up with an idea… I told them that I talk in my sleep, and because I often slept at the hospital, everyone would find out about their secret. The NKVD agent was immediately dejected and lost interest in me. Of course, I signed some paper about confidentiality."

A journey in chains

I am perfectly aware what or whom the title of this section alludes to; the words "chains" (Russian *puty*) and "journey" (Russian *put'*) will now always rhyme with our era. Therefore, it is so incredible that these words lead us where they should, since now I would like to talk about the security agencies recruiting people to inform on others.

There has never been a subject that has arisen so frequently in conversations with different people. The entire Soviet world that some people sigh for with nostalgia, and others look back on with horror, is run through with eavesdropping, denouncing, or informing on people, binding each and every person with the shackles of slavery. This spiderweb wrought with human hands is clearly a creation of hell, because it can catch onto every life, every relationship between two people. This is a hellish reflection of the human circulatory system created by what lies above, granted to us by fate. This is most likely a distorted resemblance to the light golden net connecting all of us with our past. Instead of an invisible lace net, there are a multitude of nooses, one of which Marina Tsvetaeva entangled herself in.

Nearly all of my conversations with people about the past ended up sooner or later with stories about attempts to recruit them as informants. Gradually I came to the awful conclusion that there was not a *single person* who had not been approached with such a proposal. People were under constant surveillance whether they were inside, that is, in prisons or labor camps, or outside.

Maria Iosifovna talked to me at first about her father. It was him who managed to escape with the White Army to Constantinople during the Civil War, and then after he came back, he was under surveillance. They summoned him to an apartment on Povarskaya Street for "chats". However, these chats did not last for very long, as her father had no steady job. He did interior design jobs for cultural centers, and they couldn't get anything out of him. However, her father had a very dim view of the system. When Maria Iosifovna's cousin, the secretary to Nikolai Ezhov, started inviting her to literary salons (which were held at the home of Yevgeniya Khayutina, the wife of Nikolai Ezhov), where different writers including Babel would visit, her father told her flat out that she could never get close to those affiliated with the regime. She accepted this, although she was unhappy and considered his worries silly. Time proved him right. Several years later, none of the attendees of these literary salons remained alive, including her cousin.

I have kept a photo of Maria Iosifovna from when she was a child, where she is standing in the yard with a charming little girl with very sad eyes. This is her very cousin.

From the diary: November 24, 2004

We might have never talked about it, but when she was sorting through papers, she came across a note that she had left in the event of her death, asking Daniil Danin and Vershigora to take care of her son.

This happened several months after Tarasenkov died. Late 1956. She had begun traveling around as a magazine reporter. She would often choose the most remote places, somewhere close to the border. She flew once in a small plane. There were only a few passengers, and a well-dressed man came up to her. She noticed his navy-blue suit for some reason (the thought came to her mind that it was similar to the one Tarasenkov was buried in), and the man bore some resemblance to her husband. This was very unpleasant for her. They starting talking, mostly about literature, and he gave her a collection of poems by Omar Khayyam. For some reason she noticed the library stamp: Library No. 6. Later, by coincidence, they were traveling on the same train. He didn't have money and she loaned him fifty rubles. He took her phone number so that he could repay the debt. In Moscow she felt that something was wrong, and she realized that this wasn't merely a fellow passenger, that he had been watching her.

So, she started following him. She saw him once getting into a car, and she went after him in a taxi. He turned into the driveway of a building at Kuznetsky Bridge. There was almost no doubt. She asked a well-known bookseller, a friend of Tarasenkov, where she could find Library No. 6.

He answered almost at once, without even thinking, "On Lubyanka."

Soon unknown men came to her and introduced themselves as officials from Lubyanka. They told her that they wanted to offer her the role of a socialite patroness, who would organize salons in her apartment in Lavrushinsky for people they would specify, and they would eavesdrop on them. If necessary, they would even find her a suitable husband.

Obviously they had an image of her there as a socialite who could be used for their own purposes. She tried to think who could have said something like that about her, and she concluded that it had been Yevgeny Dolmatovsky: he told everyone right after Tarasenkov's death that she would get married again. Or it was the well-dressed gentleman whom she had met while traveling. In any event, she felt disgust and horror.

She told the men that besides her, her sickly mother and son lived in the apartment. Then they tried to persuade her to meet foreigners at the Hotel National. They gave her time to make up her mind. She wrote a suicide note and went off on a long business trip. She had to cross a river on a small steamboat. On a lower deck there was a small door with a metal bar, which opened easily. One could take a step overboard and fall under the spinning propeller. When the sailors left the deck, she lifted the metal bar and lifted her leg over the threshold. At the very moment she felt strong hands grabbing her waist.

"Hey, lady, have you lost your mind?!" the sailor cried as he managed to lift her up under her arms and drag her away from the brink.

When she had returned to Moscow, they came to her again, this time even more rude and unceremonious.

One of them said that she shouldn't be so stubborn, that they had just visited her neighbor on Lavrushinsky Lane and he agreed to cooperate with them. She didn't ask who it was, she only looked at the long, white dog fur stuck to the trousers of one of the men. She knew who the only person was who walked such a dog. I asked her who it was. She said that she wouldn't tell me – what if there was even a one-percent chance of error?

Then, exhausted by their insistence, she asked them why they had come specifically to her. One of them smiled and answered, "You have already helped us once."

"When?" she asked, aghast.

He took a report dated 1943 from her file, a report drawn up at the Sovinformbyuro. She looked at it and recalled how this document came to be. The writer James Aldridge, a great friend of the Soviet Union, and his wife came to Moscow. Maria Iosifovna and Tarasenkov were sent to meet them in the Moskva Hotel, where the visitors were staying. The evening proved very boring and snooty. Then her superior at the Sovinformbyuro summoned her and asked her to write a report about the evening.

Maria Iosifovna answered that Tarasenkov had already written one.

"No," Lozovsky said. "Each person has to write one, especially since you spoke with them in English."

She wrote up something without particularly thinking anything of it. Now this paper, which had reached the place it should, was in the hands of the agent trying to recruit her. They threatened her that Tarasenkov's book wouldn't be published, and they said that they could help her. She said that it was all the same to her, that whatever happened would happen.

Then she told Vershigora, her closest friend, about everything. He, as a serious player in the partisan movement, knew this organization pretty well, and though he feared it like everyone, he had his connections there. Some time later, he told her that the people over there were overhauling their staff, and that is why they were recruiting new people. That he would call them and demand that they leave her alone. They went away, and she thought that she had got rid of them. They came to her a second time in the Seventies, but this time the recruiters were so naive that she quickly got rid of them. The nasty feeling remained with her for the rest of her life.

From the diary: July 26, 2004

I'm reading about the trials, about Stalin. Can the human soul withstand again and again this "cracking of bones on the wheel"? But if you do not mourn every one of the victims, there is no future.

I understand now what happened in the case of my father. He had a breakdown. I remember his happy, joyful lightheartedness of youth, his being at peace with himself.

And with what horror he took *The Gulag Archipelago* from me in 1983 and how he gave it back! He said that he didn't believe a single line, and if this all was true, there was no point living. It all turned out to be true, and he began to attack my grandfather, his father. I know that he visited him on holidays and, after they had had a few shots of vodka, he harangued him. He tried to restrain himself, but he couldn't do it. And then he burned up and died inside. In his place there stood a feigned cynic:

"It's all the same to me!"

My 1937

It is no accident that I am calling this section thus. The elated "My Pushkin" could not help but be replaced with the terrifying "My year 1937", marking the central split of the 20th century. The biggest nail in the body of the populace was hammered in, and this wound came to resemble a huge black hole which one would look into again and again, and which sucked one in. I constantly felt the gaze of this abyss on my back, although there were times when it seemed like I forgot about its existence. I was busy with my own things, I studied, I worked, but subconsciously I knew that I would have to face it again.

Our family's past was always connected with mystery. This concerned my grandfather. The adults would mysteriously smile at my childhood questions about who he was, what he did. They would look away or change the subject. It was as if they had drawn a circle within themselves beyond which they could not pass. Everyone accepted the rules of the game except me. I was persistent. On May 9th he would take a bunch of medals out of his drawer and start pinning them on his black jacket. You could see with what pleasure he did this, looking forward to his upcoming meeting with his comrades. For some reason, he always went alone to these meetings, no one ever saw his friends and fellow veterans, I never walked hand-in-hand in him, holding a bouquet of carnations. There was no table that had been laid out for everyone.

Once, when I was six years old, I asked my grandfather; he was standing in front of a long mirror and looking himself over with great scrutiny, and I studied him carefully:

"Grandpa, why do you have only medals and not even one big award?"

This question followed from the detailed stories from my father's youth about the war and the decorations that had been handed out in wartime. It taught me to recognize what decorations were given for what, and how they were different from each other. Now I saw my grandfather as a living textbook. I asked him just like that, out of my abundance of recently-learned information. My grandfather reacted very strangely. To this day I remember how his face turned red and he began explaining how his medals were no less important than a major decoration.

After that he went to the kitchen and confronted my mother and my father. This surprising turn has remained in my memory forever. When my grandfather left home later that day, my father put on an unnatural smile and started to ask me about what I had said. I didn't like the expression on his face at all, I didn't like his unnatural way of speaking, and so I only gave him one-word answers. Ordinarily my father seemed to be a completely honest and forthright person, but in my grandfather's presence he would completely change.

Our building was built by German prisoners of war. I remember the stories of how my father and his fellow youths brought them bread, keeping it a secret from the adults. How they felt sorry for them. The place where we lived had the strange name of Butyrsky Khutor, although it was in Moscow. Actually, the street was named Rustaveli, but everyone said, "I'm going to Butyrsky Khutor" or "It happened in Butyrsky Khutor". Not far away from us the Butyrsky prison was located, which I had no idea about at the age of five, until fate decided to bring it to my attention. And so, our building wasn't like all the others. It was built after the war according to a special design: three stories, with little towers, and a fountain in the courtyard. Everyone living there called it the "Green House".

The first thing that I clearly remember from my childhood was my rabbit, Tyopa. I was around two then.

We sat together until the table. Tyopa looked at me in a cold and indifferent way. I was squatting on the floor, holding my knees under my chin, and I was looking intensely at Tyopa. As soon as an adult appeared under the table with the words "Here you are!", the rabbit's face immediately took on a silly animal appearance. It wagged its ears and pretended that it was chewing something. As it seemed to me, it tried as hard as it could to pretend that it liked when it was poked in the nose or scratched behind his ears, or when people raved about its soft fur, paws, and tail. I knew that he was fooling everyone, except me. He wasn't ashamed in front of me, because I was just as mute as he was.

The rabbit waited until everyone left the kitchen. It studied the legs walking around the table – indeed, it even seemed to count them. It sniffed, and then it lazily closed its eyes. When the kitchen was quiet, it suddenly perked up and, without paying any attention to me, it went out from under the table. Then something unbelievable happened: the rabbit put its front paws on the table and drew a piece of sausage to itself in a very methodical way. It then returned to its place under the table, and I watched with growing amazement how it devoured the sausage. The adults came back into the kitchen.

My grandmother got upset and shouted, "Look at that girl! You were told not to touch the sausage before dinner!"

However, I still could not speak in an intelligible way, in complete sentences. I could only see and hear. The rabbit knew that, and it looked at me triumphantly. It knew that I wouldn't say anything about its sneakiness. No one treated my babbling like human speech.

The rabbit seemed to me like an adult that knew the secrets of life while I did not.

Every day, when I would go for a walk outside, I would descend from the third floor along the twisting staircase and be sucked down to the bottom of its spiral shape. For some reason, it was right there that I first started thinking about death, and about how one day I might no longer exist.

One day I went down the stairs and went to my sandbox to make mud pies. Around me some boys around twelve years old were playing their boy games, they chased one another and shot their toy guns. One of them ran to the little yellow building that housed the utilities. Suddenly, I heard a terrible scream and the boy, covered with blood, jumped out from behind a corner. His mother heard him scream, rushed outside, and ran around the yard holding her son's hand and shouting. Then the ambulance came and they took him away. I was squatting on the ground, frozen with my little shovel, and everything I saw has left a trace in my consciousness, as if I had a little camera inside of me. Then I went back up to our apartment, where my grandmother was standing at the stove and cooking something like always. She somehow had already learned about what had happened outside. She answered my questions by saying that police and detectives lived in our building, and crooks were taking their revenge on their children. I couldn't help but ask if the same fate from these crooks awaited me. My grandmother gave me a vague answer that no, I didn't have to worry, because while my grandfather had once worked – here she made a long pause – in the police, he didn't any more.

This story continued with a series of strange riddles. My grandfather went away, and the word "Magadan" was now constantly heard in the house. In Magadan he was supposed to end his service, so that he could then retire and draw his pension. One year of working in Magadan was counted as two years, so he could leave his job. Why did he want to leave it? Because of Krushchev. Krushchev was destroying the army and navy, he cared only about growing more corn, and everyone was telling jokes about him.

Years later I discovered that according to an order from the Komsomol, the rural youth were sent after the fourth grade of a church-run school to serve in the police and security services, immediately after the great purges of 1937–1938. My grandfather was serving together with Sudoplatov in intelligence, he was working on a partisan movement, though he then served as the deputy for the head of a labor camp, already in 1951–1956.

My father, and consequently I as well, was not supposed to be born. He came into the world in 1937. My grandmother had filled the bath with extremely hot water after she had decided to get rid of her unwanted pregnancy. For some reason, my grandfather came home from work early that day, he started banging on the door and shouting, "Don't kill my son!" His son therefore remained among the living. Later, when my grandfather had already become an important person and everyone would hide in the corner of the home so that he wouldn't see them after he came from work, my father committed what my grandfather considered a terrible crime. My father had the best grades and was a secretary of his school's Komsomol, but he stood with his class, which was supporting a girl whom the teacher had slapped in the face for some reason I cannot recall. The class wouldn't come to this teacher's lessons. Of course, the school called a meeting with the parents, and my grandfather was there. As he came home from the meeting, he started shouted at his son, demanding that he tell him who the instigator of the class boycott was. When my father answered that he would not betray anyone, my grandfather yelled back that he had got many people to talk, and he beat my father mercilessly.

The story ended with my father leaving home and entering a military school instead of pursuing a glorious education in Moscow. Fate brought everything together so that in the army town of Manzovka in the Russian Far East he met my mother, and I was born.

Here one cannot fail to be again and again amazed by the twists and turns of fate: had this chain of events not happened, from a slap in the face to my father's leaving home, I would not have come into the world and would not be writing these lines.

I was always troubled by the world of adults, it seemed to me to be hidden behind a screen of omissions, evasions, and subterfuges. I realized early on that I could find answers in books. And I loved books so much that it made my head spin. From the time I was a child, in any home I would sneak over to the bookcase and begin to run my fingers over each book and examine it. The adults obviously thought I was like Gogol's Petrushka and they could not understand why I was devouring so many books one after the other. I myself did not understand what was happening in my head, which was gradually filled by books for children and for adults: atheist pamphlets, dictionaries, books about biology and physics, philosophy, and literary theory.

Scoring a few points too low to get into the History and Archives Institute, I found myself entering a real heaven of books. It was the book deposit of the Historical Library. My work consisted of running around with a bunch of request slips sent to me through a pneumatic tube. The capsules would fly out of the tube and land in a metal box next to the table at which the retrieval personnel were sitting. These fetchers were usually young people who didn't get into a university or who went to night school or were doing distance education. Between the time that the capsule landed and the required item was sent back, they would obsessively read books or copy love poetry into their notebooks. You then had to run as fast as you could to the stacks with their shelves weighed down by books. The stacks could be move back and forth on rails by turning a big wheel. The main pastime for the guys doing "cart duty" was to squeeze the girls retrieving items between the stacks. Usually the girl would let out a piercing scream, after which the poor victim would be set free.

The books were arranged according to their classification numbers, and finding the right one by memory required the greatest skill. I think it was there that I developed a "photographic" memory for which book was located where, which proved extremely useful later when I had to read through a sea of documents and absorb any information that could come in handy.

In the beginning, I read everything that fell into my hands. Most of all, I was excited by books held in a certain locked case made out of ordinary wood. These book weren't *spetskhran* (limited-access collections of ideologically dangerous material) but rather they were simply books that people would line up for. For example, under this lock and key was Mikhail Gershenzon's work about Chaadayev, which sparked my imagination. I loved Chaadayev so much that I even dreamed of writing about him. In the same place, books by Tsvetaeva and Khodasevich, Berdyaev and Florensky were kept, they stood on the same shelf with Golon's *Angelique* and Maurice Druon.

They were loaned out with the approval of the director, as they were in such high demand and there were waiting lists for them. Nevertheless, these books were stolen without mercy.

As a library employee, I had the right to check anything out first and I read everything there was. Later, however, I discovered magazine stacks that were many kilometers long, where I once came across an issue of *Novy Mir* from 1926. It was so thin, and as it turned out, Boris Pilnyak's novel *The Tale of the Unextinguished Moon* had been torn out of it. On the first page of the issue there was a note by the editor Alexander Voronsky stating that Boris Pilnyak describes in his novel the death of general Mikhail Frunze on the operating table as Stalin's expressly ordered elimination of his political opponent. However, the editor-in-chief could not agree with this and had therefore removed the novel from the issue. Obviously, he was forced to remove it after the issue had already been printed. I sat for a long time opening and closing this magazine that had been made so scrawny, and I couldn't come to my senses. My misfortune was that I had no inkling of many things and treated every such discovery as something unbelievable.

I couldn't see the whole picture, I couldn't understand what had happened in my country long before I was born. The history we were taught in school contained so many inconsistencies and absurdities that I had long since stopped believing any of it. The past seemed like a stage in a theatre where the light had gone out; you could see the silhouettes of figures moving, someone whispered or shouted, and sometimes there was a rumbling, but you couldn't make any sense of it.

I cannot remember what brought me to the newspaper room on the fifth floor. However, it proved a difficult trial. There exists a distance in time between a book or magazine and the reader, but a newspaper, because of its ephemeral nature, is like a blow to one's head, it has a very direct effect. I never thought that paper could convey such a sense of hate, such a misanthropic energy. I would read for hours the court transcripts of the trials and I could not believe that everything written there had really been said, that those people making such condemnations and admonishments, nailing the enemies of the people to a pillar of shame, were actually real, flesh and blood and some mother's child just like us.

Soon, however, something happened to me which completely turned my thoughts upside down. I had already got married and I had a little boy. It was summer, and my son was living together with my mother-in-law next to the Creative House in Bolshevo. Once I came to her home so that she would be free to attend to her things. In the evening, a very beautiful elderly woman came down the stairs. She would visit my mother-in-law to drink tea and talk about the grandchildren. I think her name was Lidia Alexeevna. She had a light-blue silk robe. She was very slim and beautiful. As it later turned out, she had been a ballerina when she was young. We calmly drank tea. The children were in bed, it was June and the sun would set late. The bright evening put one in a tranquil mood. My neighbor talked about Leningrad before the war, about the theatres and famous people. To tell the truth, I wasn't paying close attention to what she was saying, but the mention of Leningrad always made me think about the war and the siege of the city. I quickly asked her:

"Were you also in Leningrad during the war?"

"During the siege I wasn't in Leningrad," she said nearly syllable by syllable and then fell silent. The silence went on for so long that I started fidgeting in my chair and didn't know how to get out of this awkward situation. I could see that the woman with whom I was speaking was now so far away from me, that I wasn't sure if she would ever come back to this kitchen.

"During the siege – and before it, starting in 1939 – I was in a labor camp for wives of enemies of the people, the Alzhir camp it was called." She said that as if listening within to her own words.

I was persistent and I said, "How many years were you inside it?"

"Eight years."

"Why?"

"I came to the Big House to ask about what happened to my husband, who had been arrested. He was a physicist. They immediately arrested me too."

At that moment time ceased to flow, it came to a stop. When I came to my senses, it was bright out: as it turned out, the sun was now rising.

The place was in the empty plains of Kazakhstan, where today the city of Tselinograd stands. The wives of diplomats and writers, marshals and military commanders, pianists and singers, actresses, ballerinas, and housewives, all of them were sent to plow the hard earth in the steppes. They were beautiful, intelligent, and educated. Mirra Freud (Sigmund Freud's niece), Kira Pilnyak (the wife of the writer), Gaidar's first wife, Tukhachevsky's sister. In the evening, after twenty hours of labor and breaking the ice open to drink, wiping the frost off each other's clothes, and exhausted from the hard work, they would nevertheless sit in a circle and organize evenings of literature and music. They would hum or play with a comb and a piece of paper famous symphonies and operas. Chopin, Vivaldi, Beethoven performed by the best pianist in the country! They would recite from memory entire chapters of books or whole novels, someone even knew *Anna Karenina*, and they would listen page by page one evening after another. Lidia Alexeevna herself recited by heart Grin's *Scarlet Sails* (*Alye Parusa*).

"That terrible camp became my university. I made friends there for life. There was a great deal of grief. Not to mention the children who had been taken away, the husbands who had been shot, and the relatives who had disappeared. But we tried to remain human beings. The head of this camp, Barinov, was a remarkable man. First of all, our women taught his children foreign languages, and he felt sorry for us. When the war broke out, trains full of criminals started to come. These were the most terrible times; the criminals considered themselves 'pure' and they considered it just to defile and torment women who were imprisoned for political reasons. Once Barinov gathered the criminals together and said to them, 'There are honest mothers and honest women imprisoned here. If a single hair falls from their heads, you'll be dealing with me.' The criminals calmed down."

After her sentence was up, her mother came and led her home. But the people she had met would remain with her forever.

She told me many other things, and the more she spoke, the more I felt a terrible darkness in my soul. It was as if I was guilty of her fate, as if I had done something wrong. I shook my hand and remembered that that wasn't the case, that I was here in 1986 and I had nothing to do with that life.

This bitter feeling did not go away, however. I felt like the character in Ibsen's *Ghosts*, who was forced to pay for the sins of his fathers.

The sins of the fathers

Our lives begin long before we are born. I realized this while I was heading home on the regional train from Bolshevo. Between this woman, whose sufferings I felt with every nerve, and my grandfather, an invisible thread was woven, one that passed through my heart.

"Why don't you write down everything that you said to me tonight?" I asked her.

"I belong to an age which fears documented proof," she answered.

My grandfather, who stood on the opposite site of the barbed wire, was much more afraid than this woman who had spent her youth in the camps. He never admitted to his grandchildren where he had worked, he would highlight and cut out from political directories articles about people who were declared enemies. He never told any stories about his friends or his life.

Still, there was one event that particularly struck me. I did not understand anything of it, but I felt it emotionally. It was 1974, during the spring holidays, and I was in the apartment on Varshavskoe Highway where my grandfather and grandmother lived. I was alone with my grandfather. In the kitchen, where he was sitting, the radio was on, and I was reading something. Suddenly he jumped up, red with fury, and with a terrible grin that distorted his wide face. He cried as if to some invisible other, "Finally, they kicked that bastard out! How much more could he lie, lie, lie!" He crowed these last words again and again, unable to stop. Then, he turned to me for some reason and said, "I was an inspector in the camps. No one died there from hunger and they didn't pour cold water over anyone."

I looked at him with astonishment and I couldn't understand anything. The only thing that was clear to me, was that what he had heard on the radio in the kitchen had made him furious. Of course, years later I understood that we were dealing with Solzhenitsyn, his book *One Day in the Life of Ivan Denisovich*, and the fact that at the end of my grandfather's career, when he worked for the directorate of labor camps, he would make inspection visits. How did this sole person who managed to write about the camps awake such a hatred? Because his words caused my grandfather sporadic attacks of fear.

The fear which so tormented my grandfather destroyed all his large family. I never saw and never got to know any of our relatives from his side of the family. There should have been a great number of them, as he was born into a large rural family. However, the jobs, the lifestyles, and the marriages of his brothers and sisters cast a shadow over him, and he broke all ties with them.

Still, some of our relatives came already in the Seventies, when he was playing at "searching for his roots" and he told his grandchildren how important it was to preserve the memory of the past, to know the story of one's ancestors.

Later our own family began to unravel. It was held together due to my grandmother's efforts, but she fell seriously ill, and they brought her home from the hospital. This was several days after he had been yelling about lies. The three of us were together in the room. My grandfather acted strangely: he constantly sniffed and talked with her in a compassionate and unnatural voice. He had never talked that way with anyone before. For some reason my grandmother turned to me and said, "He should leave." When he threw his coat around himself and literally ran out of the house, she said distantly, "I can't look at him, he's taken the life out of me."

To my eyes, their roles abruptly changed. He understood that she was dying and became sentimental in a way that was uncharacteristic of him, while she managed to become independent from him before she died and stand up for herself.

The most terrible thing happened at dinner after her funeral, several months after the events I've just described. My grandfather began to give a speech and turned towards the portrait of her that stood on the end table. He started scolding his children one after the other, and then read out my grandmother's last will. He said that she was commanding them from the grave to respect and obey only him. He was saying this to what were now completely adult people in their forties, whose ears he had boxed for many years. Everyone knew that he was putting on a role in a comedy known only to himself, but this time something came clattering down. While my grandmother was alive, his children could endure everything for the sake of some common good, but now, when the pain of her passing was so sharp, when he was using her death for his own ends, it was unbearable. A mutiny broke out. I remember how the adults started to shout, to interrupt each other in telling him everything that had built up inside them during their life together. The younger ones looked at this with eyes wide in shock.

My grandfather was riled up and – it seemed to me – he was listening to these shouts with great pleasure, because he knew what he wanted. Suddenly he lifted himself up on the table and shouted, "Get out! Damn you all, get out of my sight!"

We gathered our things and left. I no longer had a grandfather. One grandfather I had never met at all, because he died in the war at the age of twenty-six, and I felt terribly sorry for him. The other grandfather left us of his own accord. Well, decades later I visited him and his youngish wife. She was a pudgy and short woman, who called him by an unnaturally childish name and fawned on him, something which seemed to make him very happy. Maybe she was the reason that he kicked us all out of his life. She was already in the picture before my grandmother died, and he saw no other way to bring her into his home.

He lived for a long time, but we did not meet. The children would only visit him on his birthday and then quickly leave. He lived until the Soviet Union collapsed, until Solzhenitsyn came back to Russia and a great deal of books about the camps appeared. I am convinced that he remained afraid until his last days. Afraid that they would come and make him pay for what had happened.

Once my aunt told me that she had dreamed about him – this was already after he died. He was standing in some lifeless, cosmic landscape and endlessly repeating that he was freezing, that he was terribly cold and could not get warm. I shivered – I had a vision of Dante's icy lake of Cocytus in the ninth circle of hell.

A hole in time

I was grateful to Lugovskoy. He gave me a key, a key to the hole in time. His strange collection, consisting of myriad documents that seemed irrelevant, but which were in fact an invitation to a journey. He had thought about the future, he thought about the person who would follow him into the Thirties. To keep such an archive required either an especial courage or a certain carelessness and recklessness.

Furthermore, he had to have a strange inclination, to preserve seemingly useless things. In school notebooks filled with neat children's handwriting, in letters from him and letters sent to him – his wives, his lovers, his mother, and his sister – there existed something that represented his personal, inner lifetime. Newspaper cuttings looked out from folders and drawers, containing lines of poetry, agendas, doctors' prescriptions, drawings, notes. The routine of his days.

I learned a great deal from him. The living, unsettling words of his notebooks and the first draft of his poetry collection *The Middle of the Century* was shocking in how one could see the development, the movement of both one man and the entire community of writers. The polished, censored, and self-censored flow of literature from that time stood in sharp contrast with the bitter course of life revealed in these letters and diaries.

In this, a Soviet poet tried all his life, whether openly or in secret, to catch Time in the butterfly net of his poetry. He repeated the formulas of his time, he watched how the time changed, he collected its traces and impacts, in the hope that a generation would come who would find all this useful.

I would look for a long time at photographs of people from the Thirties. They are very different from others. Here it was completely clear that neither the men nor the women had a single item of new clothing. Perhaps only the military tunics looked clean and fresh. In all of the winter and autumn photos, people were wearing old, threadbare clothing – worn since before the Revolution – that badly fit people's figures and were found or bought second-hand. In the summer, one found only clothes of a blindingly white color: white dresses, white trousers, white caps, white twilled cotton slippers, white hats, and white headscarves. The white color attested to a lack of dyes, the lack of a chemical industry.

The world of these photo shoots reflected the harsh black-and-white quality of life. It appalled André Gide on his visit to the USSR. To some this seemed an angelic, incorporeal whiteness: these sickly faces which had rejected the material world, and with a hysterical concentration sought to look to a future that would never come.

This fierce battle with the bourgeoisie, with everyday life, with the ordinary man, with things is found in Mayakovsky, and in Olesha, and in Lugovskoy. There was no doubt that everyday life was advancing like an offensive in war and people were forced to comply with it. Mandelstam, Akhmatova, and Tsvetaeva never fought against mundane things. They didn't feel the need, and they clearly weren't tempted by it. Nevertheless, there was some hidden meaning to this tortuous escape – probably sensing some deep danger for the human spirit, in approaching the death of the soul, the breeze that they felt acutely in the period of the NEP.

People not only wore clothes until they wore out, they did the same with the literature and art from the beginning of the century, as well as philosophy and the natural sciences. From that past, Andrei Bely and Mikhail Bulgakov, Max Voloshin and Vsevolod Meyerhold remained alive, but everyone who lived alongside them understood well that they represented only fragments, not the whole. There was a fear of falling behind the times, to be relegated to the margins. Time was flying by. The "Classicists" and "Neo-Classicists" died like flowers in the field. Voloshin, Parnok, and Bely could not survive in this new world.

When the Thirties came and Stalin began to eliminate the kulaks, the geologists, philologists, biologists, naturalists, and old Bolsheviks, he sought like a pagan god to wipe out not just them but their era as well. In this he was partially successful. People from the war years and the years following the war bore absolutely no resemblance to people just a decade apart from them. Even those who survived and made it into the next era, tried to forget the Thirties and wash away its traces. Only shadows remained from the Thirties.

In Moscow one can identify to this day the buildings where people lived in the Thirties, from the ramshackle doors with their peeling oil paint, from the stone spiderweb of walls, from the crumbling window frames, from the rusty nails in fixtures, from the broken stairs in the staircases. The unevenly cut wooden boards, which were quickly installed to cover holes in the building entrances. Everything is twisted and slanted, the result of disorder and poverty. The remains of 1930s life smells like mustiness, but one cannot say that about the marble staircases and windowsills, as well as the heavy front doors from the late 19th and early 20th centuries. All it took was a clean cloth, and the fine look of the wood or marble would instantly be restored. It was as if the Thirties wanted to disappear, evaporate, to turn to dust.

The most important thing in the Thirties, however, were the utterly Shakespearean scenes and emotions that never made it into literature. In my book dedicated to the Thirties, there were so many stories of this nature, they popped up again and again. The thing is, they could have only happened in that era. One of those stories was about Alexander Afinogenov, the author of the play *Mashenka* that drew such buzz before the war.

A young and talented playwright, Afinogenov was a lucky fellow. He was adopted by Gorky, and he was a Party member from the age of twenty-two. Together with Krishon and Averbakh he led RAPP. His wife was a beautiful American woman, he lived with her in a dacha in Peredelkino, from which he would travel to Moscow in his own car – back then, such cars could be counted on the fingers of one hand. He was a very sincere and naive person, including when it came to writing.

He wrote a play entitled *Fear* about how the intelligentsia, for some reason, had a terrible fear of the authorities. The play was staged and somehow found great success. One of the characters in 1931 said from the stage, "We live in a time of great fear." Both Erdman and Bulgakov could sign their names to these words. But in fact, Afinogenov simply didn't know what he was doing.

Then he wrote a play called *The Lie* about how lower-ranking members of the Party were hiding the truth from their superiors, and how the whole system of Soviet industry was increasingly built on lies. Stalin sat down and personally edited the play, and then he spat and banned it. Gorky, for whom Afinogenov was like a son, tried to support him in a letter, saying that a play like that needed to be shown privately among vetted Party functionaries. In August 1936 a series of meetings began that were dedicated to the Trotsky and Zinoviev trials, and at the meeting held by Moscow literary figures, Afinogenov declared that he was personally prepared to shoot Kamenev, Zinoviev, and others. He was refused this great honor, however.

In early 1937 he and a group of his former comrades became enemies themselves. Everyone with whom he led RAPP were put in prison. He himself was turned away wherever he went. He sat in his dacha in Peredelkino and day after day he awaited his own arrest. Everyone shunned him, his neighbors tried to avoid him. His acquaintances crossed to the other side of the street when they saw him trudging towards a shop. But for some reason, they never took him away. Then, he started to write a speech in the hope that they would suddenly let him speak at a meeting again.

But what happened then? This is what happened. They took a peaceable guy, a playwright, who thought of nothing else besides writing another dozen good plays for the benefit of his country and the Party. And then they made a laughingstock out of this person, an object of shame and ridicule. They rolled him in the vilest filth, hung him out to dry in the sun, and shouted to passersby, "This is the one, the agent and bad guy. Hey kids, look at him, how thin and pale he is, how everyone despises him."

And all the townspeople walked past him and ridiculed him, and all the children walked past him and turned their heads away, because the appearance of the fifth that covered me was truly terrible. Lumps of this dirt were hanging off me like scabs, and they couldn't see my face or my eyes – I was like a heap of manure.

He went on:

Why did they roll me up in filth and push me down the stairs? For what reason are they torturing me, asking me questions and not believing the answers, demanding the truth although there is no other truth in this world than what I have already told them? What is the purpose of all this? It is only because I have known Yagoda for several years, and I considered it an honour to be acquainted with him. I tried to look up to the people I saw there, and I was utterly convinced that right there, in Yagoda's house, there was no one who could betray me in a political or any other sense. …And who, who would have rejected the honor of being a guest at Yagoda's? The Pharisees and liars are the ones who now shout "Crucify him!", the ones who are laughing at me, at my sincere doubts and words. …Can people here really judge a man and condemn him because he didn't know the true face of the commissar of internal affairs, the fear of all the Chekists, a person who knew everything about everyone? …Do you really have to crucify me because I knew Averbakh without being aware of his true nature, and shout at me that I got my bad and tasteless plays staged?

During the days when he wrote these tragic lines, he continued to live quietly at his dacha, reading Dostoyevsky and Shakespeare, thinking about how all things shall pass. Unexpectedly, in his diaries one starts to find passages about how happy he was at this persecution, because he could finally think, read, and ponder life.

Almost every day Pasternak, a neighbor of his at the dacha, would visit him. They would talk for hours. Afinogenov discovered an entirely different world: outside meetings, slander, and rumor-mongering, there was only artistic creation.

My conversations with Pasternak will always remain in my heart. He comes in and immediately starts talking about great, interesting, and true things. ...When you visit him, he will immediately set aside all trifles and barrage one with various topics, opinions, conclusions, and everything that he says seems important and real. He doesn't read newspapers – this is strange for me, for I cannot go a day without reading the news... Whether he lives in a palace or on a bunk in a prison cell, he will always manage to keep himself busy.

His mention of a prison cell with regard to Pasternak was no mere figure of speech. Everyone knew that Pasternak was surely bound to be arrested soon. Suddenly he came up with a insane idea: to write a novel about Pasternak.

But fate took a new turn just in time. In early 1938 his Party membership card was returned to him, and then his membership in the Writers' Union was restored. All of his fellows had already been shot by that time. In 1941, his play *Mashenka* was premiered to incredible success. The main role was played by Vera Maretskaya. The war broke out. On September 9, 1941 he was appointed director of Sovinformbyuro, and on October 29 he died in downtown Moscow in the Central Committee building on Staraya Square in a Nazi bombing raid. The enigma here is that he was never arrested, never shot, and he was granted three or four years for making sense of his own life, a short period of success.

While I was writing about the Thirties, a thought troubled me the whole time.

If an evil is done for some period of time and is destructive to the human race, this evil will surely leave its mark on the way people subsequently live. Generations will follow that will lack strength and inspiration. They will look at everything around them with apathy and indifference. Their spirits will be burned out, they will grow tired long before they are even born. This is how today the 20th century casts a shadow over the 21st.

The lives never lived by those who were shot, tortured, and murdered could not vanish. It is likely that their era silently flows alongside ours. To save the generations following after, one will have to see and hear these lives, to let every lost soul, every person who died in vain, reappear now in our time.

Space is a moral category. It is no accident that people would spend such a long time to choose a site for a monastery or a church. Builders would try to listen for the whisper of a certain place, to find out what had happened there long before their own time.

I believe that an invisible map exists, the intersection of unlived time and the uncreated space of those who were so easily robbed of their lives only because they were born in a dark period of history. I keep poring over this map, which will eventually become clear to all, and I feel an unending guilt and a pity that I cannot express.

What relationship do I have to the fact that before I came along, people fought, murdered, lied, and destroyed their own humanity? Why should I answer for the terrible 20th century? But is this what really matters? Unnoticeably, strange creatures are arising here and now with dead hearts and cold gazes. They tell us something from the pages of newspapers, on the television and radio, they fulfill some orders given them, and they preside over something.

The era that was built on bones continues today.

A meeting with an elf

The further in time I went, the more my manuscript was filled in by new documents and rare photographs of those times, I found the houses in which my subjects lived.

I wanted others to feel the same sense of plunging into history that I did, but there was no publisher that would turn my thoughts into reality. And then, one day, he appeared.

It happened on the evening organized in memory of the writer of children's poetry Berestov, where I was to say a few words about his life in Tashkent, about how he and his friends lived there almost as if they were going to school, learning English from Nadezhda Mandelstam, visiting Akhmatova at her *balakhana*, and learning to paint from Tatyana Lugovskaya. I sat waiting my turn to speak in a rather nervous state, because friends and contemporaries of Berestov were giving speeches, and because my position at this evening event seemed a rather doubtful one.

He was sitting not far from me with his wife – he was a elderly elf straight out of a fairy tale, one whom I recognized immediately. For me he was a completely different kind of being, a legendary and famous one. I didn't even know if I had read his collections of poetry long before; perhaps I didn't read them, I simply heard them recited. It seemed like he had lived across every literary epoch, he knew everything, he was a friend to everyone, everyone loved him, and he loved everyone. His presence was no surprise. When he came up to speak, or rather, when his wife led him up, because he was nearly blind, he spoke with an incredible fire about a friend who was dear to him, and then with great enthusiasm he sang – without an ear for music or ability to carry a tune – Berestov's song "Live, Live, Love", and finally, he coughed and sat back down in his place. Now they called me up. Of course, it was hard to speak in his presence, but I nonetheless talked of Tashkent, about the atmosphere of the war years, about how the evacuated writers felt there, and about how Berestov was transformed by Chukovsky, A. Tolstoy, and Akhmatova from a starving wunderkind into a writer with broad horizons.

When I finished speaking and sat down, I saw out of the corner of my eye that the elf out of a fairy tale was moving several seats down towards me. He felt my hand like a real blind man and introduced himself, "I'm Korzhavin." I meekly answered, "I know."

He and his wife invited me to the apartment where they stayed in Moscow. At that time, he managed to visit from Boston for one or two months each year.

Our conversation moved almost immediately to the Thirties and books, his and mine. We talked, going from one thing to another and never stopping for a single minute. From the moment we met, I was utterly sure that he was a part of this life, a part of the subject of my book. In fact, he felt the same. He asked me for the manuscript in a business-like manner. I was amazed that he wanted to read it, for he could hardly see anything. To this he answered that he still had a little peripheral vision and he felt certain that he should read my book. Indeed, this blind elf read the book in just a few days. It turned out that he was deeply moved, even tormented, by the same things that I was. He had published around this time huge memoirs about that bloody era, he read me his poems about Stalin, which he considered rather embarrassing, but they contained some striking passages: "There, though visible to everyone, and yet / One who personified the cruel age appeared / A hard and cruel man / Who didn't grasp Pasternak."

He constantly told stories about fear. About Lugovskoy. How he came to Lugovskoy's seminar, and the latter thought him an agent provocateur, because Emka Mandel (Naum Korzhavin) would say everything that came to mind. Lugovskoy shook him off. He said that there were times when he himself had been afraid, and when he hadn't been. But if someone puts a gun to your head, then you put your hands up, but a person cannot live with his hands up all the time, and drawing any pleasure from that is perverse.

He told of how he had come to Akhmatova and asked her to listen to some poems by Chukhontsev that he liked very much. She however said that she would not meet him and Chukhontsev at the same time, because if they were arrested and interrogated, then two witnesses would produce enough evidence against her. This conversation took place in the Sixties. He practically worshiped Pasternak, like everyone of his generation, but when he went to visit him, he found Pasternak to resemble a spoiled wunderkind.

He took my manuscript and immediately started thinking about what he might do with it. The most important thing, however, is that he wrote the afterword to it. Thus his magical appearance left its mark both on my life and on the book.

Maria Iosifovna was delighted by my story about Korzhavin. She knew him a little from a Tsvetaeva conference that had been organized in the United States in the 1990s. He was there with Anna Saakyant. He wouldn't let her be, he called every other day, talked and talked, and then vanished completely.

"The same will happen with you. Poets are inconstant," she added ironically.

Indeed it happened thus. He was present in my life for three years, calls every week, conversations and conversations, arguments, poems, and again arguments. And then it broke off… At first I was baffled, but then I realized that he had come and gone exactly when he needed to. The fact that he had done everything he could for me and then disappeared, was in perfect accordance with the world of fairy tales from which he had materialized to meet me.

In the end

When the manuscript was ready, Maria Iosifovna said that she had had a dream in which she was holding my new book in her hands, and on the cover was written "The Knot". The word was alive, it pulsated with a red-orange color. But I hadn't yet come up with my own title. "The Knot" was the name of a publishing cooperative that had published slim, light-blue books of poems with engravings by Favorsky; I had written a little book about the firm, and I described how in 1926, the publisher brought vastly different poets together. I thought that if this name were used again, it would be too obtrusive. Maria Iosifovna wouldn't budge, however.

"The title expresses what happened to people. They were bound with a knot, and then… You yourself wrote what happened next."

She gave me an entire lecture about what should appear on the cover of my book. It would be best if there were one or two catchy words, which get straight to the point, which chime and echo in people's memory. The most surprising thing of all is that the word "knot" began attracting other words to it.

Sergei Durylin wrote in his diary that, with time, the knot of personal relationships had become a noose, or even a garrote. These words became the epigraph for the book.

But every burst of energy, every effort she made took more and more from her.

"Can you imagine, I have only six years left before I turn a hundred. And Mashka has a whole hundred years ahead of her."

She let out a huge laugh.

Our meetings became less frequent. She had less and less energy, and she was saving it for arranging her personal archives neatly into folders and accompanying them with pages of stories about what document was what. She practically wrote an enormous commentary on the life of Tarasenkov and on her own. Her words were transcribed by a neighbor, who would patiently visit her almost every evening and with great zeal and neat handwriting take her dictation. The neighbor lived with her sister in the apartment opposite, they treated Maria Iosifovna with incredible respect. They would inquire about how she was getting on every day, and they would bring her nice things to eat. Maria Iosifovna would protest at this, but they would quietly leave the plate full of food in the kitchen.

These notes taken down by the simple and kind-hearted neighbor, with their large, child-like handwriting, were, as I later discovered, made for me too. Maria Iosifovna arranged fragments of life according to different-colored folders. There was a folder from Tarasenkov's youth, when he wrote bold articles for RAPP, when he was bringing new collections of poetry from the market and first called on his poetic idol, Pasternak. He was writing some notes about Pasternak for a literary encyclopedia.

Here is a folder about Tvardovsky, whom Tarasenkov had dragged from Moscow to Smolensk when Tvardovsky was being scrutinized at meetings and labeled a supporter of kulaks. And here are folders with his "ideologically correct" articles about Zabolotsky, Mandelstam, Pasternak, and others. Here he is climbing ever higher in the ranks and becoming the vice editor-in-chief for the magazine *Znamya* ("The Banner"). And now we're in the Thirties! Here there are more and more notes from writers' meetings.

She had plunged into the depths of time. You could hear it in her voice, which became grim, hopeless, and filled with a century of fatigue. She again told me that she wanted to "finish with Tarasenkov" and, finally, if she couldn't write something about herself, then she wanted to at least dictate it.

"You see, for a writer, to become blind is unbearable. I need to be able to see how one word follows on another, how they lie alongside one another on the page. Only in that way does a text come to be. But I am blind. My time has run out."

We talked about the nature of fear. About how many times their generation died in the war. How Tarasenkov fled out of hell on a ship leaving the Tallinn port, under a hail of shooting, both from his own side and the enemy, and how the sea – filled to the brim with the dying – raged. How he was dying of starvation under the siege, how he worked as a frontline correspondent at Lake Ladoga. About why they suffered so much during the war, how they saved their comrades, how they charged at the enemy and carried out reconnaissance, but several years later they turned their backs on their friends and even on themselves.

Maybe it was because dying in combat seemed glorious and honorable? But in peacetime living outside of society, living as one branded an enemy of the people and traitor, was worse than death. These thoughts couldn't help but arise as I read about prominent commanders and heroes of the Civil War. Why did they so eagerly give in to their interrogators and betray their comrades? Where was their own sense of courage?

Maria Iosifovna told me, "In the beginning I didn't read his articles at all. They didn't seem interesting. We talked about poetry, he recited thousands of poems to me. Now I know everything about him. But it's completely clear to me that without Tarasenkov, I would never have met Tsvetaeva, I would have never got to know Pasternak or Tvardovsky. He gave me very many things. I cannot deny that, I cannot forget it or be ungrateful. My life would have been different without him. You see, it wasn't Tarasenkov that I wanted to write about – I was supposed to write about that period that broke and shattered people's lives. I wanted to call my book *And He Denied It Again*: about Pasternak, about our entire generation's love for him and his poetry, about betrayal, about denial. I wanted to write these things, but I couldn't. I could have never imagined how unbearable it would be to live through that period, through the Forties, a second time."

She told me this time and time again. The more intimate we became, the more often she would start on this subject.

"Hundreds of times I have gone over in my mind the day when Samuil Galkin was arrested. I went to Maleevka; it was already widely known that Kvitko had been arrested. I knew that Galkin was waiting for the news, that he had just suffered a heart attack, and the paramedics had only left his place that morning. I didn't want to tell him about Kvitko. But when I was going down the hallway to the shower, he waited for me and took me by the hand: 'Kvitko?' I nodded. 'Now they're going to take me too,' he said with hopelessness. 'But why you?' I exclaimed. 'Why Kvitko?' he answered, looking at me with grief in his eyes. They took him that very night from the Creative House. I can never forget his face, how he was standing in front of me with a sense of doom in his eyes. How can I write that? How can I live through that horror a second time? There is nothing more terrible than the postwar years!"

As I listened to her, I thought that if the Thirties with all their horror were years of societal blindness, where people gave speeches, shouted, wrote letters, and could not come to their senses, then in the postwar years almost the whole intelligentsia understood that they were part of a lie, condemning Akhmatova and Zoshchenko and taking part in absurd vigils concerning the "cosmopolitans". The contrast and tension between the two decades was enormous.

Once I told her, not caring a whit for the consequences, that I had already written about the Thirties and the war, and so I needed to write now about the postwar years, so that I might understand what happened to the characters of the previous books, and how literature deteriorated along with the deterioration of Stalin's own personality. She listened and kept silent.

When *The Knot* came out, Maria Iosifovna suddenly told me, "You can already start writing the third part. What do you think?"

"Yes, I could."

"You said that you were going to write more."

"Yes."

"I'm prepared to give you everything connected with Tarasenkov."

Her proposal was an interesting one: the folders held a sea of undiscovered material and I was driven by curiosity, but a sadness weighed on my heart. Tarasenkov! What am I going to do with him? Take up a figure whose writings made me grimace?

I received from Maria Iosifovna an enormous bound collection of the *Kultura i zhizn* ("Culture and Life") newspaper from 1946 to 1951. How many names did people back then have for it! "Aleksandovsky Central" from the name of its editor-in-chief, or "Culture and Death". I don't know who in their right mind would have read this newspaper. Maria Iosifovna confessed that she had tried, but she got so depressed that she threw the issues under her bed and tried never to pick them up again.

I started reading. The newspaper was expressly launched with the aim of preaching, catechizing, and condemning. Tarasenkov was a member of this cohort and wrote, "A disregard for Russia, its culture, and its great ideas was typical of that Jesuit Bukharin and of the outlaw 'cosmopolitan' Trotsky. These are frightful reminiscences. They show what the worship of Western bourgeois culture and civilization in contemporary politics is linked to, what it serves…"

And right here in the folder containing postwar documents, his striking account for future generations is preserved, of how he threw off Polikarpov, he didn't agree to his monstrous criticisms, how he made accusations to the Central Committee that his superior had mistreated writers, how he had proposed Pasternak for the Stalin Prize. And then he left *Znamya* with his head held high and again started writing his book, now under the publishing house of the Soviet Writer's Union.

But when the steamroller of arrests and verdicts began to crush everyone around him, Fadeyev denied his comrade in a letter from 1948 to Zhdanov and Suslov regarding a collection of Pasternak's poems: "…the collection begins with an ideologically dangerous 'preface', and it ends with a tasteless poem in Akhmatova's style entitled 'A Candle is Burning'. This poem, dated 1946 and completing the collection, sounds in the contemporary literary atmosphere like mockery.

For this reason, the secretariat decided not to release the collection."

After Tarasenkov's death, Fadeyev called Maria Iosifovna – this was a year before his suicide – and he told her that the two men were "products of their time". How terribly this sounded coming from a writer, calling himself and his peer "products". How unpleasant it was to write about this! As Pasternak bitterly noted after Tarasenkov's early death from a heart attack, "His heart was tired of lying." It was not just tired, it was shattered into a million pieces.

Maria Iosifovna looked inside me with her now almost sightless gaze, and I was afraid that she would sense what I was really feeling. She could see the torment I was experiencing perfectly.

Things were as they always were: archives, stories. I found some striking things in Tarasenkov's correspondence stored at the Russian State Archive of Literature and Art. On the backs of the letters that he had received from Fadeyev, he wrote down everything connected to each letter. He was drawing up a history of Soviet literature as seen from all sides, although he himself looked unsightly within it. He loved history, but… this was the reason that Maria Iosifovna and I had our first and last quarrel.

For a time I was troubled, not knowing how I should begin the book, how I should lay out the plot so that it presented how literature in general fared in those days, and not only Tarasenkov.

Finally all the pieces came together. Maria Iosifovna would give me documents, letters, her own recollections. Among the papers was a letter that she herself had sent to Tarasenkov, which shocked not only me but her, too, in spite of the fact that she had written it. In this letter, written in late 1939, just six months since they had married, she wrote that she was surprised to hear him complain about the difficult fate of Soviet critics, because there was no one more dishonest and without scruples than him and his fellows, and in fifty years' time Tarasenkov's own works would be utterly forgotten, and they could all expect a terrible, inglorious end. The letter was not simply written in a sharp tone, it summed up quarrels and debates that she had long forgotten. But this was the year when Tarasenkov renewed his friendship with Pasternak, who in turn brought Tsvetaeva to him. Thus he and Maria Iosifovna could overcome the consequences of this crisis of ideas, and this letter didn't lead to a break in their relationship, though a line was now drawn between the two.

It may be that at the end of the Thirties when Tarasenkov renewed his friendship with Pasternak, who had been recently pardoned after his first condemnation, he mainly wanted to show his young wife that while he did not come out looking good in the pages of newspapers, with Pasternak he was different. This could not fail to make an impression. He wanted to have some effect on her, at least in this way.

I placed this letter at the beginning of my life of Tarasenkov – it seemed to be something symbolic and prophetic.

A month after her neighbor had loudly and clearly read my first chapter to her, Maria Iosifovna called me. Her voice sounded distant and hard, even metallic. She said that for me, they (that is, the people I was writing about) were just chess pieces that I placed on the board, and I had no regard for them whatsoever. She said that she didn't like how her letter sounded within the text. It was as if I destroyed Tarasenkov using her own words, and he was a much more complex personality than I had depicted him.

I answered that I could remove the letter if it caused such hard feelings. We ended our conversation.

I sat down with a hopeless sense of resignation and an empty heart, telling myself repeatedly that I wouldn't write the book, that it had been terribly foolish to intrude into the lives of others. If she herself could not decide whether to write her story, and I had stumbled across her path and something inevitable had happened, then I needed to exit her life.

Several days passed, and again the phone rang. At first Maria Iosifovna just said meaningless pleasantries. I understood that she was desperate for a truce, but she didn't know how to throw me a line – too much had happened in the past days. Then, she suddenly said:

"I'm calling to ask for your forgiveness. I said silly things, it wasn't true. You are the author of the book and you're free to do whatever you feel necessary. I don't have the right to interfere with your work. I think about you constantly. Forgive me."

I naturally forgave her. Not only that, I was struck yet again by her impartiality and fairness when it came to her herself. She looked at me like an equal and forced herself to accept a different truth, perhaps one unpleasant for her.

My mother passes away

I was in a hurry. And then something happened that I could have never have foreseen. My mother, who was still at an age where she could have been Maria Iosifovna's daughter, left this world so quickly and unexpectedly that I didn't even realize what was happening.

She died as we were walking down the stairs. She had felt poorly before this, and I decided to bring her back to her home in a taxi. Suddenly she slumped and died right in my arms. Ten minutes before we had argued about some everyday things, and now she was no longer there. My life after her passing took on a completely different rhythm. Everything around me started to happen in slow motion. I could not even imagine that in the suddenness of her passing, in everything that followed, so much meaning was contained. For the first hours and days I searched for her above, around me. I couldn't believe the emptiness, the gap that had formed in space. At the same time I felt that right next to me a black abyss opened, from which a cold draft was blowing, and it began to suck me in like a whirlpool. I was overwhelmed by despair. It was long and drawn out, and it just would not transform into something else. The question "where?" was the central one in those days.

After some time I started to notice other people like me, children who had grown up and then lost their parents. I heard stories that showed me life from its most painful side, as if this could console me. Things got more difficult, but the world got wider, and it became inhabited by the memory of the suffering that had been experienced.

Maria Iosifovna stayed by me for those days, weeks, months, although we only spoke on the phone. She said once that when her father, whom she loved very dearly, died of tuberculosis, she saw when she went outside that the light from the streetlights was completely different. She kept saying that something unreal had happened to me. But I started to fall ill, it was hard for me to accept everything…

Then another thing happened. On the day that was so tragic for me, Lidia Borisovna Libedinskaya called, and when I told her in a zombie-like voice what had happened, she answered, "How I wish I could die in the same way. How great it would be!"

She flew to Sicily for a week or ten days with a theatre company. When she came back, she lay down to sleep, and in the morning she didn't wake up.

When Maria Iosifovna heard this, she couldn't contain herself and she said, "I always felt that Lidia knew how to do things."

Thus Lidia Borisovna passed away ten days after my mother.

They departed

I almost could not write at all, I just kept thinking and thinking. If when a loved one dies, it is like one's inner world shakes, and things are much harder afterward, then with the murder *en masse* of people linked by myriad threads, what effect does *that* have on us? That hellish machine keeps exploding within our souls.

I was ill for around two years. I still did some things, wrote some things, read some things, but my depressive state dragged me down. Maria Iosifovna was very worried about me, and I felt that she was keeping watch over me, that her heart was full of pity, but she didn't know what she could do for me.

Then she started to tell me, "Forgot about the book. It's not worth your strength, your life."

Several times I decided not to go back to the manuscript any more. It had suddenly come to seem as if I were ill because of it. My mind was filled with these thoughts of resignation. For hours I would lie in bed and look at the ceiling. I couldn't see a single argument in favor of continuing to write. In general, maybe it is something I should have never started on? Why have I taken up writing about the lives of others? Who needs it? No, someone out there needs it. There are scholars, they write, they keep a distance from their characters, from the time described, but I took some desperate and dangerous route, where one begins to experience time and events as if they were one's own. I recalled how harrowing it was for Maria Iosifovna and I to forge a path through every episode, every subject of her life. I felt as if we were trying to move enormous rocks – it was that hard to go back into the past, to break through the fog of those years and get to the details. It was like going underwater, when you don't have enough air to breathe, your ears pop, and your head spins. This journey into the past was far more painful and difficult than the wonderful process of creating a future for oneself. I recalled how happy I was leaving my classes with Semyon Lvovich Lungin (he analyzed my plays and helped me bring them to life).

Here everything was different. I knew that after our meeting, Maria Iosifovna wouldn't get out of her bed for almost an entire day. I myself found my strength drained from my time with her. Our work became the sum of our individual energy, and we could feel this physically.

I got used to her being there, and it started to almost seem like she would always be there, though she was ninety-six years old. In my head I understood that a day would come when she wasn't there any more, when I would get a call and someone would tell me that she's gone. This day finally came. Her son, who had come to visit her for several days, told me that she had died. Doctors came and tried to do something for her, they wanted to take her to the hospital, but she categorically refused. She passed away before dawn. It was late January.

This came as a great shock for me. It seemed very unfair that she left me all alone in this world. She was too great to leave just like that.

She had completely readied her personal archives... and then she died, leaving me alone with the book that I hadn't written, with the manuscripts, and questions that only multiplied. Her time on earth had come to an end. On the day after her funeral, I felt that I was getting better, for as she went out into the universe, she had left me her energy.

The universe

Around a year before Maria Iosifovna passed away, we were sitting together in a room that was slowly filling with dusk. Suddenly, she said:

"Now, in my old age I feel how I am connected with the universe." She pointed to the dark frame of the enormous window.

For eight years now, I haven't been outside. If I'm ninety-five now, then the last time I went outside was, I think, at the age of eighty-seven. I might not be able to see what's happening outside the window, I feel everything that happens in the air in such an incredibly strong way. My whole body shivers from any changes in the weather, solar flares, the movement of atmospheric fronts. I feel how clouds gather in the sky and how the sun bursts through them. I don't need to see it, my own body tells me everything. Why wasn't it like this before?

It is certainly because a person comes from the universe and returns to it. It's my time now to understand that. You think that if I'm almost blind and almost deaf, I can't read or write, then I'm not happy at each new day. I know you won't say that out loud, but you look at me with pity. I can't make out your eyes, but I can see the sad look on your face. You see, here on the wall, I see an incredible play of shadows every day, which changes color and shape, and slowly crawls along the wall's surface.

In the morning they resemble long drawings of people and have a soft golden color. I recognize images of my childhood in them. As the day goes by, they change shape, and I see the most varied pictures. Ever since my sight started to go bad, strange and colorful visions have appeared before me. I'm afraid to tell people about that, they might think I've lost my mind. A strange world of color was revealed to me. I can tell you that I see certain words, and I see them as if they were full of different colors. In the evening, the paint on the wall turns into something different, and then a whole new spectacle begins.

It's interesting to be alive, even when you are as old as I am. You know, I'll try to hold on a while longer.

Every time I picked up the phone and said, "Hello?", a resounding and seemingly young voice would answer, "Hello, dear!" or "My dear!" I would almost always ask, "How are you doing?" She would say, "I'm still here. And you thought that maybe I was already soaring high above?" Since January 26, 2008, that is where she is.

Standing before the door

And so, everything now came into my hands. The archives, letters, reminiscences, and excerpts from memoirs. I put them together and made a single text out of them, but for some reason it sounded flat. So, there once lived a Soviet critic and he secretly loved poetry. So what? I made a space within my personal biography of Tarasenkov and inserted the main threads of his time, but I still felt that it wasn't right. I remembered Maria Iosifovna's words that I treated people like chess pieces on a board, and a voice within me whispered that she was probably right, I shouldn't be writing this book. I had a feeling as if I were standing in front of a locked door with a heavy keyring, trying one key after another, but in vain. The door wouldn't open.

Then I saw her in a dream. Maria Iosifovna was much younger. She was walking through the apartment, opening and closing the doors of cupboards. She stopped, sat down in a chair, raised her head and began to examine me closely. In the dream, I could see that I wasn't in the apartment, that she was completely alone, but nonetheless I felt her bright and penetrating gaze.

I remembered her story of how she had first visited Tarasenkov in cramped bachelor's room in an attic. The windows were open, and this entire space under the roof was filled with white doves: the birds were walking around the writing desk, the bed, and the windowsill. She stood in the doorway, astounded at this wondrous thing. The carpet of white doves resembled the outspread wings of an angel.

Then in the evening he saw her to Konyushkovsky Lane. Since they knew Moscow inside and out, they went along sheds, through gardens and orchards, where tired Muscovites were snoring on camp beds as if they were in their country houses. They laughed when they stumbled into yet another hammock hung from an apple tree and set the man swinging. They ran on to the house where they would soon be living together. To the house under a poplar tree where Marina Tsvetaeva and Boris Pasternak would visit. The house in Konyushkovsky Lane, which would burn down with its neighboring houses in the Seventies and vanish from the face of the earth.

Then I suddenly knew what kind of book it should be. It should be a book about compassion and sacrifice. By laying bare the tragic story of her husband, whose mauled conscience killed him, Maria Iosifovna had done a deed of love. She had created an altar and burned incense on it for the man so dear to her. That is something a great deal easier than trying to understand and relate the most painful aspects of the life of a loved one.

By telling of the things that tormented him, his falls, his hopes, and his death, she saved his own soul. No one has ever looked truth in the eye so bravely and in so merciless a fashion. I have encountered many children and women who have rewritten, who have recast the past of their loved ones. But to reveal a person's greatest flaws, like Maria Iosifovna did, is a mighty challenge. Her understanding of her husband evolved gradually. After he died, she first gathered all of his note cards and had them typed up on a typewriter. From this huge typescript, a bibliographic index of 20th-century Russian poets arose. Then, she wrote *The Intersection of Fates*, a book which she could not hope to publish. It was printed on thin paper and sent abroad. Although *The Intersection of Fates* contained a huge number of pages devoted to the era, Maria

Iosifovna nevertheless understood that the figure of Marina Tsvetaeva loomed over everything, including Tarasenkov, his friends, and even the horrors of their time. Other laws acted on Tsvetaeva, just as on Mozart, Pushkin, and Tolstoy. A genius slices any era with the knife of his or her talent, and then blood flows from the person's own wounds.

Perestroika came, and Maria Iosifovna's book went through several printings. It was translated into dozens of languages, there were talks, travels, conferences, but after it was all over, the time came to think and write about the most bitter theme in the world: about her own generation, about Tarasenkov. But she could only write the truth, everything as it was.

After she realized that she could not write the book as it should be written, she wanted to place her story in the archives, hoping that it would all be examined again one day, and then I appeared on the scene.

Once she said to me – this was already a year or two before her death, "How wonderful it is that you came into my life. It's as if you were sent."

Obviously, it wasn't just Tashkent that brought me into her home, it wasn't just the stories, or letters, or even the book about the 1930s. Rather, it was because the task for which she had gradually prepared me had to be done.

As soon as I could convince myself of this, a door opened without any need for a key, and the book began to take shape.

I gave it the short and foreboding title *The Collapse*. It referred to the last days of that gloomy era when living speech, living souls were shattered to pieces and decomposed, but at the same time, like any end, it contained within itself the seeds of something new, which immediately sprung out of the ash-heap, out of the paved-over field of Soviet literature after Stalin's death. Tarasenkov himself did a great deal for it to sprout when he collected the writings of Bunin and Tsvetae-va, when he promoted the works of Nekraskov, Panova, and Grossman. In his life, everything was ambiguous and contra-dictory – that is what Maria Iosifovna wanted most of all to convey to me, to everyone.

And now I understood the metaphor of her fate. When feeling compassion for the weak, the humiliated, for people devastated by their own lies and the lies of others, one must open the door of one's own past, whether noble or lowly. The past may hide great deeds or cowardice and betrayal. This holds for both the fate of individuals as well as of an entire nation.

Only then will the handwoven threads which bind all of our pasts, with their tentacles reaching to the present day, be torn asunder. Only then will the heavenly pattern that connects all of us together be cleansed and shine brightly.

Though she was not a believer in the usual sense, Maria Iosifovna was undoubtedly a virtuous pagan, like the best of people in Antiquity. In Dante, she would live in Limbo, in the first circle, home to wise men and philosophers, the main fate of whom is painless sorrow. I think that she's there.

Part II. The Last Moscow

When did I come to realize that the past does not exist?

Perhaps it all started after the fire at the Historical Library, when I was going through burnt books kept in storage at the former Vladimir church in Starye Sady. I felt then that I was a link in a common chain and that the current of departed lives now flowed through me, too.

Or when a blue volume of diary entries appeared before me, written by a forgotten girl who died young and published before the revolution. For some reason, I felt a strong connection to her. I found the story of her brother, who wanted to spite his family and so published his sister's diary, which described the dramas of their household just before the revolution. He was a director, and I wrote a play about him…

It always seemed to me that background figures, people who are much more difficult to glimpse or learn anything about, offer the possibility of imagining the world of the past in a much fuller way.

These unnoticed characters began to come out of the shadows of the Soviet underground in the Nineties, when we wanted to believe that the Soviet regime had ended for once and for all.

The tectonic layers of history had shifted, and from the gap that now opened up, one could see the priests of the catacomb church, the children of dispossessed kulaks, the first female university students, prisoners in labor camps, followers of

Vlasov, survivors of the siege of Leningrad and prisoners of war, emigrants and evacuees. Before this time, their voices had been little distinguished.

And it is no accident that the Tsvetaeva museum, which I worked at, opened in 1992. It arose from the same historical upheavals. What had been lost now began to return: boxes came from Paris with the collections of emigrants. New books, memoirs, and exhibitions began to push aside not only the prior era but also a great deal of the present, as if time had been made to go backwards. Granted, this only lasted for a brief time, as the general interest in these matters was satisfied fairly quickly. But the little stream has never dried up since, and one finds more and more stories of people who, as one of my heroines called them, were "unknown and silent martyrs of History."

Chapter 3.
The Diary of Olga Bessarabova

Borisoglebsky Lane,
Marina Tsvetaeva House

I had been working in the Tsvetaeva House museum for several years already, but the more the times changed, the more distant I felt her house to be. At first I thought that this had something to do with Marina Tsvetaeva herself. I felt uneasy serving her without at all feeling the fanatical worship I often saw in those attending evenings in memory of her. They would read Tsvetaeva's poems aloud, playing with the intonation of their voices, and aggressively stressing words that already had enough explosive force.

Marina Tsvetaeva's portrait was always adorned with a rowan branch, it seemed to present her like a Venus emerging from the sea foam. Tsvetaeva so risked falling into kitsch that one sometimes wanted to lock her poetry away from certain easily excitable readers.

I myself would only become greatly sentimental when I had to defend her, usually from particularly "well-informed ladies": "She killed her daughter Irina", "She married that spineless man Efron", "She shacked up with every guy she met",

"She hated Adriana once she had grown up", "She hung herself because the NKVD was after her".

At the same time I was aware that Tsvetaeva herself had given her readers the right to say whatever they pleased about her. She hid nothing from anyone.

In the 1920s she had written about herself and her lost daughter: "It would have been easy to save Irina from dying, but there was no one who could do it. The same thing will happen to me."

Indeed, in those August days of 1941, when she found herself between life and death, no one intervened.

There is no point trying to defend Niagara Falls. It roars and carries away everything in its path, but it is nonetheless great and beautiful.

Ariana Efron was deovted to her mother and sealed Tsvetaeva's archives until the 21st century. The set period eventually passed, however. The year 2000 arrived. (Perhaps her daughter did not believe that the new century would ever come?). The notebooks, the diaries – everything was published, and Tsvetaeva stood revealed before her readers just as she was in the past.

The Tsvetaeva House starts at number 6 Borisoglebsky Lane, near the Arbat in the heart of Moscow. It was the same back when she was searching for a new home. In front of it is Sobachya Square, and behind it the Ss. Boris and Gleb church. Two old poplars stand outside its windows. From the street, the house looks like it has two floors, but from the side or from the back, it seems to have three or four. Such a house could only be found in old Moscow.

Thus it is hard to tell how many floors it has, how many rooms, how many unknown little closets, which open like secret drawers. The house resembles a sturdy yellow jewelry box with doors, smaller doors, and even tinier doors. A person can get lost and confused in it. One walks up the "Jacob's ladder" to the luxurious attic, into its owner's favorite room (like a ship cabin), and looks out the window, squinting to see only the roofs of the tenements, and not the forest of ugly and drab highrise buildings on Novy Arbat, which stand in the half-destroyed street of Bolshaya Molchanovka.

The "magical house" for its unusually young family, where the husband was a student who never finished his studies, the wife was a young poet, and they had a beautiful daughter who needed a fairytale house – Tsvetaeva first conceived it in her head and only then found it. The family had only a few good months of peace, but their life together proved to be far from easy. Sergei Efron was soon put on a army train to the front as a stretcher-bearer, and later he became a junior office who was forced to participate in the defense of the Kremlin in October 1917 and hide from the Bolsheviks who were then seizing Moscow. He subsequently retreated with the Volunteer Army, and then there was the Ice March, Perekop, Constantinople, and Prague...

The house increasingly turned into a collection of uncomfortable rooms, gloomy and freezing, where Tsvetaeva was confronted with the hungry eyes of her children, and where all the pots and pans were covered with black soot; to get water she had to go outside, and at night she could only press her face into her pillow and weep for yet another hopeless love affair, for being left alone, and pray to God that her husband, who had disappeared in the chaos of the war, would finally return to her.

As a result, the house was abandoned, and Tsvetaeva and her daughter left to start a new life.

Twenty years later, in 1942 during the Second World War, a twenty-year-old female surgeon settled here after she had been assigned two rooms in the communal apartment, rooms that she claimed the hospital had given her for her good work. She had been told about Tsvetaeva's connection to the house by an actress of the Moscow Art Theatre, who also gave the female surgeon a collection of Tsvetaeva's poems published while the poet was still alive, *"The Magic Lantern" (Volshebny fonar)*. Nadezhda Ivanova Lytkina – as the young doctor was called – lived in that house for several decades, never allowing it to be demolished. She campaigned for the house's famous owner among Moscow society, and in 1992 she became the founder of the museum.

It turned out that Marina Tsvetaeva home's, which from the outside looked like a cozy old Moscow detached house, was in fact bursting with explosive stories, which fully reflected the character of its famous inhabitant.

A museum is a sort of stall with antiques. As needed, one brings items here that more or less correspond to whatever existed here once.

But in a country where square meters became the most precious dream for ordinary people, where large houses were turned into a collection of living spaces divided up with partitions, no one wants to talk about preserving the history of the 20th century. Items have survived only by accident, or in homes where they are left over from the previous owners, or in the apartments of important officials.

The museum tried to arrange the old items as if its former inhabitant had set them out herself. Tsvetaeva's contemporaries and relatives made an effort to remember what stood where: sofas, chairs, and desks were put in their original places. The things could no longer be shifted from room to room, they were now frozen in the places they were when their owner left the house. The people at the museum stopped at the happy time when Tsvetaeva had not yet burned the bookshelves in the stove to keep warm, the building caretaker had not yet nailed boards over the windows to ward off the cold autumn and winter in 1919–1920. The objects stood as if the hands on the clock had ceased to move in 1915–1916, and Russia had never seen a revolution nor a civil war, and no one had ever left the country.

I liked the strange theatricality of the items in the museum. I once created an exhibition devoted to the evacuation of writers and their children to Chistopol and Yelabuga. On the table I set a number of items that any family would have: they are scattered around people's dachas, stuffed into closets, we walk past them when they lie forlorn in a rubbish heap. Iron glass holders, aluminum spoons, thick tumblers, old and rusty irons… How surprised I was when I saw how interested the visitors were in each item, looking at it as if there were a treasure laid out before them. Some asked if they could touch the items, while others took photos, and still others copied down the words written on the labels. The museum space itself seemed to cast a spell on the objects and give them a special significance. Through the combination of these old irons, spoons, and glass holders, one could feel the draft of history blowing in, one could hear the clickety-clack of the train or a conversation over tea in the carriage.

The sense of frozen time, however, became increasingly painful. I apparently lacked a flow of fresh air that could turn our usual conception of the past upside down, dislodge these firmly-rooted museum artifacts and make them spin.

This impression, which came to me as I was reading diaries, documents, and letters, became ever sharper. One day I had the feeling that there was nothing more that connected me with the museum, and our time together had come to an end.

This feeling came to me once and for all at the end of December 2008.

A journey to Peredelkino

On that memorable Sunday, I went to Peredelkino, to Pasternak's house, together with Anna, a younger colleague from the museum. The weather was typical of the week before Christmas. It was certainly over such days and hours that Dickens' Mr. Scrooge had come up with cruel measures to save money on his poor clerks, and the spirits of Christmas past, present, and future were already preparing their terrible lesson. These spirits were apparently sitting behind us in the local train and listening to our story of how the museum part of my life had now ended. Even now I am utterly sure that they were really there – the events that followed this day evinced their supernatural presence.

Anna was responsible for the archival material held at the museum. She was still quite young, very lively and not at all a museum sort of girl. Rather, she could have been the owner of a hotel. She came to the museum by accident, and she eagerly began putting the museum in order as if it were her own holding.

Anna had a sincere attachment to me, and although she treated my undertakings like strange whims, she listened to my stories as if they were fairytales, and sometimes she was even moved.

In the winter cold, the train was half-empty. We arrived in Peredelkino. It was snowy and freezing. The road turned at the cemetery, and then it went past a field now covered by houses that resembled the squat metro stations of the 1930s. It was impossible to imagine that people could live in them. The asphalt ribbon going past the old dachas finally led us to Pasternak's house.

We were met by an employee of the museum, Tatyana Neshumova, who usually led tours of Pasternak's house that now stood empty. She immediately commented on this house and how it was different from Chukovsky's house. Chukovsky's was full of things, but Pasternak's contained little, and the visitors said that everything must have been hauled off.

Tatyana invited us to sit on the large and well-lit veranda and have tea. When I told Tatyana what the green-eyed beauty was doing in our museum, she looked at Anna with a scrutinizing gaze.

"You've got a lot of letters in the museum archives that I need," Tatyana said, and the casual tone she had greeted us with now disappeared. She continually bored into my companion, but Anna was nonetheless unfazed.

I must say that Tatyana had, for several years of her life, been occupied with a particular forgotten poet and translator who – in spite of his talents – choose the fate of a Keeper. He was a real background figure that no one would have ever heard of were it not for Tatyana's superhuman efforts.

In his poems and letters one could make out how doomed his generation was, a generation that died under the weight of their past culture, unable to pass it down to anyone or even merely preserve it until happier times. Nevertheless, as the whirlwind of history went by him, this poet tried to rescue the pages of letters, poems, and memoirs that were flying off, although it seemed impossible to hold on to them. Tatyana gathered everything that he had managed to save. Thus she became the Keeper's Keeper. When she published a book two years later, its title came from a line of one of his poems: *We Have Almost Died Out.*

I especially liked how she chose a painting by a forgotten painter for the book cover. This painting had been used in 1937 for a postcard with an image of Sobachya Square.

Winter twilight in Moscow. Snow quietly falls. In Khomyakov's house several windows are lit. The fountain is covered in snow. Two lovers walk towards one another.

This book was published only later, however, and meanwhile…

The lovely woman that accompanied me was full of pride and a sense of peacefulness. She answered Tatyana like a senior authority who didn't like any fuss and kept everything locked away deep behind other locks.

A collection? Yes, they had one. However, it still hadn't been organized, and she doubted that she would be able to find someone to take care of it anytime soon. So she explained as she sipped her tea.

On one hand, I was surprised by her unflappability – she was hardly older than twenty. On the other hand, I felt a spirit of researchers' camaraderie. I realized that I wouldn't give her any peace.

On the following day, we were already looking for the letters. Fortunately, they turned up very quickly. Tatyana started to come by and go over them. Soon the spirits of Christmas past, present, and future changed her life, and she left Peredelkino to work with us in the Tsvetaeva museum.

On the day when we were looking for the letters, however, my dashing colleague suddenly said to me, "Here in the collection there are unlabeled notebooks, someone's diaries. Do you want to see them?"

Of course. I started looking through them.

Thus in one of the museum's secret drawers something that I had never expected to find turned up: some unknown diaries.

They were notebooks of different sizes and shapes, and there were many of them. Some had been made into the covers of old books, while others consisted of pages sewn together. On certain pages postcards had been pasted with city scenes and reproductions of paintings. Besides the diary entries, here and there letters were inserted, their four corners placed into incisions in the page like in old photograph albums. When I started to flip through the pages of these notebooks, photos started to fall out. From them eyes that were young and full of life looked out at me.

On each notebook cover there was an inscription made in neat and round handwriting: "Olga Bessarabova".

I gradually realized that these were not simply diary entries. Within the author's own writing there were transcribed letters and fragments from the diaries of other people.

The handwriting was completely legible, and therefore I began to make out names on the pages: Leonid Andreyev, Nina Balmont, Alla Tarasova, and other famous people. At first I thought that it was just a young lady recording what she had been reading, her visits to the theatre, and so forth. But no, it was about people who were still alive, who came to visit her family, drink tea, and talk.

They lived an ordinary, everyday life which, in a way that I couldn't quite understand, revolved around the Dobrov home.

Moscow ark

The more I read, the more colorful a picture I got of an old Moscow home. There were more than enough of these in the past. To a degree, these Moscow homes were literary figures in themselves: from the Rostovs' happy home on Povarskaya Street in *War and Peace* to the home of the Gromeko family on the Arbat in *Doctor Zhivago*. Here the doors were always wide open, the house would teem with guests, a number of relatives would be resident, and holidays would be regularly celebrated, with Christmas festivities for children and adults.

In her diary, Olga Bessarabova described the Dobrov home in the same way. Although the house was known from memoirs and oral accounts, on the pages of her notebooks it was revealed in a different light, in its everyday existence, in the unhurried flow of everyday life before the revolution.

Moscow was revealed. The city, as if it were founded for the warm coming together of family and friends, and covered in lanes and wide boulevards. The city, turned inwards in a spiral like a seashell, ringing with church bells and shaking with the wheels of horsecarts on the cobblestone streets.

This house was the standard for the best of old, cozy Moscow intelligentsia life at the beginning of the 20th century. It drew people to itself and gave them a roof over their heads.

The head of the household was Filipp Alexandrovich Dobrov. He had been born into a family where the fate of the eldest son was to be a doctor. His father's patients called him not Dobrov but *Doktor Dobry*, "Dr. Good". Filipp Alexandrovich also lived up to his family's legacy – for fifty years he worked at the First Municipal Hospital in Moscow.

His wife Elizaveta Mikhailovna belonged to the venerable Veligorsky family, which could trace its paternal line back to the old Polish aristocracy. Together with them in the house lived Elizaveta Mikhailovna's mother, the domineering Yefrosinia Varfolomeevna, who was the grandniece of Taras Shevchenko. The future writer Leonid Andreyev studied with one of her sons in the Oryol gymnasium.

Thanks to the Veligorsky brothers, Andreyev came to the Dobrovs' house, and later he wrote, "…if these Dobrovs didn't exist, I would now be either in the Khitrov marketplace [a haunt for criminals and the unemployed] or the hereafter, and in no case would I have ended up working in literature."

He found here a combination of great friendship, inspiration, and passion, and a hope for a happy future.

It was in this home that a 27-year-old Leonid Andreyev began courting the fifteen-year-old Shurochka Veligorskaya, another daughter of Yefrosinia Varfolomeevna. The budding writer initially fell in love with her older sister Elizaveta Mikhailovna, the wife of his friend Dr. Dobrov, and only later did his attentions turn to the young Shurochka. Although the young lady reciprocated his feelings, she was frightened by Leonid Andreyev's demands for how his future wife should be, essentially a passive slave of her husband. Shurochka Veligorskaya didn't think she was ready for such a role. Leonid Andreyev began to have thoughts of suicide, especially since Yefrosinia Varfolomeevna was categorically opposed to her daughter marrying a little-known writer who went out drinking.

For a time, Andreyev even separated from Shurochka, thinking that he would spend his life with another woman instead. Nothing came of this, however. By early 1900 his fame in the world of literature was growing, and he was again on the doorstep of the Dobrov home – by that time major literary celebrities sought his friendship, from Gorky to

Chekhov. Leonid Andreyev's views of marriage even began to change.

Dr. Dobrov was not only a friend and confidant, he was also the first to read Leonid Andreyev's stories. His affection for his friend and, perhaps, the writer's growing fame played their role: Shurochka agreed to marry Andreyev.

They married in 1902, with the wedding at the St. Nicholas Yavlenny church on the Arbat. At the end of the same year, their son Vadim was born.

Vadim, too, had a deep love for the home of Filipp Alexandrovich Dobrov, and years later he would write in his memoirs, "…Uncle Filip was in every facet of his being a typical member of the Russian intelligentsia – with guests who would stay up until after midnight with arguments about revolution, God, and humanity. His warmth and kindness was combined with an almost puritanical rigor and reserve. His spacious office with its bookshelves and plush sofas, with its large Bechstein piano – Filipp Alexandrovich was an excellent pianist – did not at all resemble a doctor's practice. The waiting room next to his office, after all the sick had left, turned into an utterly ordinary room, where in the evenings I would prepare for my lessons. In the dining room, which was separated from his office by curtains made from thick cloth, a portrait of my father that he himself had painted hung on the wall. My father's well-defined profile with a bare and hard chin was depicted, as if on a medal, in front of a coal-black background – it was Leonid Andreyev from a time when he was known under the pseudonym James Lynch, columnist of the Moscow newspaper *The Courier*. There was a great deal of furniture in the house: huge chests of drawers, gigantic wardrobes, bookcases. In the room in which I lived together with Daniil, an entire corner was adorned with old icons – no one had touched them after the death of my grandmother Yefrosinia Varfolomeevna. In the house, especially in its rooms set off from visitors, a trace of her invisible presence remained. I thought that I once saw her figure – tall, straight, and authoritative – slowly walking down a half-lit hallway, in a long dress that trailed behind her on the floor."

In 1906, immediately after the birth of their second son Daniil, Shurochka died. Leonid Andreyev considered the four years of their marriage the happiest time of his life. It was not by chance that rumors arose that his second son Daniil was for him a tragic reminder of the loss of his beloved wife and that he did not even want to see him. This was not the case, but fate decreed that the brothers were separated: the elder son Vadim with his father and his new family ended up abroad, while Daniil remained behind in the Dobrov home in Moscow.

Daniil was initially raised by his grandmother, whom the grandsons called "Busenka". Her bad feelings about her daughter's marriage had ultimately been justified, her Shurochka had died at a very young age, and she placed all of her bitter love into little Daniil. When her grandson was six years old, she died after she caught scarlet fever from him.

Thus, for Daniil Andreyev, Elizaveta Mikhailovna became "mama Lila", and Filipp Alexandrovich became a father to him.

Elizaveta Mikhailovna and Dr. Dobrov had two children of their own. This family had the tradition of naming their children either Filipp or Alexander. When the Dobrovs had a daughter, she was named Alexandra, thinking that they would never have a son. Nonetheless, a boy was born, too, and he was also named Alexander.

This was always the target of laughter from their many friends.

Dr. Dobrov's house was located between Prichestenka Street and the Arbat, in Maly Levshinsky Lane. The neighborhood was mainly inhabited by scholars, doctors, and professors. When Olga Bessarabova arrived in the house as a nurse to little Daniil, everything looked like in an old Moscow play.

The first floor. A copper plate on the door inscribed, "Doctor Dobrov". A doorbell outside.

The head of the household Filipp Alexandrovich, in spite of his title of medical doctor, was a humanities man: a fine musician, and a passionate lover of classic literature. Besides the medical school of Moscow University, he had also graduated from the conservatory in the piano department. He would be completely transformed behind the piano, playing each evening alone, or four-hands with his friend, the pianist Igumnov. Dr. Dobrov was around forty years old then, a tall and overweight man who tended to slouch a little, and he wore a Van Dyke beard with an effusive mustache. He spoke in a voice that was low and pleasant to the ear, a baritone. He enjoyed singing and would accompany himself on the piano. His thick brow and eyelashes underlined his grayish-blue, deep-set eyes. His laughter was infectious and resounding, and he would laugh loudly, but always with a sense of moderation, never too excessively or annoyingly.

To visit his patients he would travel all over Moscow. During these journeys, undertaken mainly by tram, he studied several European languages and would read books in the original.

Elizaveta Mikhailovna, his wife, had once completed a nursing school. She was a very kind woman, always ready to help. She was the lady of an enormous home, where they not only received guests, but even had some people settle down and live there.

Their daughter Shurochka Dobrova, a beautiful woman, dreamed of becoming an actress, but her stage fright would not allow her a theatrical career.

Their son Alexander Dobrov was trained as an architect and became an artist and designer. He was handsome and full of life, but he was a spiritually weak man, suffering from drug addiction and drinking frequently.

Daniil Andreyev, living with their family, was surrounded by the love of the older members of the household and from childhood he wrote poems and stories about fairytale worlds.

In early 1917, Esfir (Kira) Pines arrived here, a devilish and enigmatic woman, who shaved her head, wore men's clothing, and – like in any authentic drama – played the villainous role.

The Christmastide story
of Olga Bessarabova

And so I followed Olga Bessarabova into this Moscow home…

The most interesting events in her diaries began in 1915, when World War I had already broken out. Then seventeen years old, Olga came to Moscow from Voronezh to study and she settled into the Dobrov home. In the summer, she went with them to their dacha in Butovo, where she taught little Daniil Andreyev to read and write. It was there that she met Leonid Andreyev.

"Leonid Nikolaievich has a beautiful mind," Olga wrote when they were all staying together at the dacha. "And what surprising things he says and what stories he tells. It's the first time that I've ever heard such bright and sparkling stories. You can see how he feels at ease in the Dobrov family, as if these were the people with whom he feels the greatest friendship, intimacy, and kinship, but they are more festive than his own family. There is a complete freedom and a simplicity to their relationship, together with the joy one finds in loved ones who have not seen each other for a long time. In addition, how tired, gloomy, and irritated he is, neurotic – as if he were surrounded and already caught, I don't know by what, perhaps by fate."

"Caught by fate" here refers to Leonid Andreyev. I started to dwell on such descriptions in the diary. This young lady had glimpsed something important in people and each time she would accurately capture their essence.

Olga wrote in a completely open way about everything that she saw around her, and at the same time with a sense of pity: about Alexandra Dobrov's cocaine use, and about how her dear Shurochka Dobrova was carrying on a strange relationship with Esfir Pines. From Olga's accounts, one had the feeling that the order of even this warm and friendly Moscow home was breaking down, that it existed in some strange way with Turgenevian maidens and noble young people out of books.

"In general, everyone here in Moscow seems tired, worn out, and high-strung," Olga Bessarabova wrote to her mother in late 1916. "It is enough to touch them in a careless way, and they go boing like a spring in a clock when you turn the key. I don't know why I'm saying this about the people here, the Muscovites. At home in Voronezh things are better, people can breathe more freely."

And here, to the Dobrovs' home, came Olga Bessarabova's distant relative and mentor, the poet and critic Varvara Malakhieva-Mirovich. Since the beginning of the 20th century the Dobrovs had been her close friends, and so it was their pleasure to accept her young friend Olga Bessarabova into their home.

Varvara Grigoryevna took the young lady to the lessons organized by her friend Lev Shestov, to the showings at the Moscow Art Theater, and she organized philosophical and theatrical circles.

When I began reading these diaries, I couldn't have imagined what role Varvara Grigoryevna would play, not only in Olga Bessarabova's life but in mine as well.

Then, suddenly, Olga fell ill in early 1916 with an unknown disease. She grew thinner each day and was tormented by never-ending pains. She soon lost all hope of recovery.

I read pages where my chronicle writer made her farewell to life, and I gazed on the last notebooks.

"No, she can't die!" I said to myself. "After all, someone has filled the rest of the pages with entries." I was deeply touched by her farewell to life. At nineteen years old, Olga could be totally convinced of both life and death. When she got up from her bed before a dangerous operation, she first went to a photographer to be captured on film for the last time. Her lush chestnut hair, her pale skin, and her special beauty impressed the photographer, and he displayed the photos in the window of his studio on Nikitskaya Street.

Olga Bessarabova looked forward to the future with joy. Regardless, we might add, of what kind of future it might be.

"It is good to live, and not terrible to die," she wrote to her older friend Varvara Grigoryevna Mirovich, whom she called "Vava".

As Varvara Grigoryevna advised her on the eve of the operation, "One shouldn't wish something hard on a loved one. But someone whose lot it is to face these things, is a chosen one... You sought from life, as its first and greatest gift, knowledge. Life responded to you in a well-disposed way by revealing an exceedingly short path that leads through a narrow gate, a path of pain and suffering... I believe that your path will lead you high and far, and that this gate was not opened to you in vain. I embrace you with love. Christ be with you. V."

Her older friend was describing to her a path that she had probably walked herself – gaining a knowledge of life through pain and suffering. But how could one write such words to a young lady who stood then between life and death?

It was probably because the two of them, Olga and Varvara Grigoryevna, could speak to each other in their own private language about the most difficult matters in the world.

Olga Bessarabova survived. The year 1916 came to an end.

Like a boat, the Dobrov home was gently rocking in the waves of History, and it seemed as if nothing unfortunate would happen for its passengers and crew.

In early 1917, Olga Bessarabova visited the circle called "Joy" (she herself had given it its name) that Varvara Grigoryevna organized for the daughters of her friends from Moscow and Kiev. It drew Alla Tarasova (a future actress at the Moscow Art Theatre), Anna Polievktova (the future wife of Nikolai Bruni), Nina Balmont (the wife of Lev Bruni), Lidia Sluchevskaya (a relative of the poet), Tatyana Berezovskaya-Shestova (daughter of the philosopher Lev Shestov), Olga Ilyinskaya (sister of the future actor Igor Ilyinsky), and other young ladies.

What did they spend hours there talking about? About abstract affairs remote from life, deeply literary and fantastical. For example, they talked about the character of Don Juan, about being happy at another's misfortune, about the villainous Iago, about Pechorin and his ironical *Schadenfreude*.

There were many debates about the feminine soul, about walking paths of solitude, pain, and suffering.

For each of the young women, however, as the future shows, this experience in reasoning became a series of spiritual exercises for the trials still to come. Some of them would leave Russia in several years, some would stay and accept everything that happened: hunger, cold, the arrest of their husbands – and still others would find success and recognition, but without it bringing them happiness.

Each of the young women would look back on that table where, in the first months of 1917, they came together to discuss how the world and the human spirit worked.

The last days of February went by. Spring was near.

"On the threshold of the door where Vava lives, I said something without meaning to: 'I feel that time has come full circle today.' I was embarrassed to think out loud like that, but Vava was surprised and said to me, 'Strange, I have the exact same feeling myself.'" So Olga Bessarabova wrote after another meeting of the Joy group.

Moscow: time comes full circle

I think that time, as Olga Bessarabova told Varvara Grigoryevna on that February day in 1917, has begun to come full circle only now, almost a hundred years later.

They found themselves at the beginning of a catastrophe that was to be the long-lasting stage of Soviet history. I, in turn, could clearly see the dying of that era: first its most acute stage in 1991 and 1993, and now a slow extinguishing.

The world created by that era has been dying for decades, but it still believes that it continues to live. Images of what came before go past its dimming eyes, accompanied by the sounds of the old (and new) anthem. The life force of that era has long since disappeared, but the shape of things remains. The more people try to resuscitate it, the uglier they become.

On February 28, 1917 the Duma was dissolved.

"Since the morning there has not been a single policeman around," Olga Bessarabova wrote in her diary. "Without the trams running, the city is unusually quiet, the coachmen are charging seven times the normal price. All day long there have not been any rumors of clashes or shootings. What will happen tomorrow? From Moscow, among the crowds themselves, one gets the feeling of a holiday like has never happened before. That is time coming full circle for you! Today on Myasnitskaya Street near our Union[1] (near Lubyanka, the former Sibirskaya hotel) some people destroyed a tram and started to strike at the rails with a sledgehammer. The crowd, whistling and laughing, drove the troublemakers away: 'So you want to be vandals? Go get rid of the provocateurs and idiots. What are you vandalizing that for, and who are you out to hurt?'"

It was a happy city. Everyone was wearing a ribbon on their lapel, and people talked in the squares. Olga was part of the happy spirit of the times.

"People are laughing, shouting, expressing their joy. Many people don't even know what they are doing it for, they have simply been caught up in the whole wave, just like me. Everyone is part of my family, everyone here are my kin, everyone is my people and I am the people. This is a very good

---

1   The Archives at the All-Russian Zemstvo Union for Aid to Sick and Wounded Troops, founded in Moscow on June 30, 1914. A week later a similar "Union of Towns" was created. Soon these unions merged under the single name of Zemgor.

thing. The sun is shining bright and the snow crunches and sparkles."

Several days later, however, on March 3, Olga acutely sensed a change in peoples' attitudes. Something else was creeping in.

"Later, towards evening, the crowd in the streets became unbearable and truly horrible. I could no longer recognize this city, these people. This is not Moscow. There's no celebratory atmosphere that embraced everything and everyone like during the day. Rather, there was idleness and a heady daze. People were no longer smiling the same smiles, but now they smiled in such a way that one did not want to see their faces. They were out only because there were a lot of people in the streets. Some of them had the faces of criminals, or rather, criminals must have faces like that: they don't just look, they look out. A word came into my mind and I could't shake it off: 'lecherous'. I even started feeling sick and miserable. Those faces were nasty, ugly, when policemen walked by. The policemen themselves had unpleasant faces, but they were frightened in a human manner, and the crowd had jeering faces. All that jeering, the evil grimaces, the obscene comments. And it was disgusting to see the faces of women when they talked about the former tsarina. The men's faces were simply angry, severe, even malignant, and I found this repugnant. And the footsteps of the crowd were different too: they were no longer floating through the streets. Rather, now they were trudging. Oh, if only everything could soon be as it was before! Get to work, get to work! Otherwise the whole miracle of these last days will blow away in the wind. We cannot stand idle like this, not even for a minute. Or maybe it's me who has got tired? I started feeling nauseous, like from the smell of blood in a butcher's shop, or maybe this is how it smells at a slaughterhouse. I can't describe it; I'm not talking about the smell but about something similar to it in a moral sense, from the general sensation and impression of the crowd."

Those snide, mad, lecherous faces soon displaced the ones from the first days of the revolution. Thus in a flash the people were replaced with an underground that had hitherto been dormant, with the gutter and dark alleyways. Now the mob ruled the streets triumphantly. The tissue of time was being torn apart ever more and there was no power that could put its parts back together. Summer gave way to autumn. In October, after the coup, utterly bizarre people came into the streets, as if they had crawled out from hell. They had narrow slits instead of eyes and empty holes instead of mouths. Olga had the impression that they were made of clay. There were machine guns on roofs, and here and there one could hear their awful rat-tat-tat. Rumors flew: "Three thousand killed!" After a month had passed, in a dark and gloomy November, Olga Bessarabova came to the director of the archives where she worked, the famous historian Stepan Borisovich Veselovsky, with the unusual question of what was going to happen with the country. She wanted to understand how she was supposed to live. Was there any point studying?

He thinks that the events are only starting. That such a breakdown and upheaval has begun that it's enough for some fifteen years ahead, such turmoil and profound change that we cannot even imagine. And if in ten or fifteen years we are still alive, we might not be able to recognize either the world around us or one another – the changes will have been that profound. They would have taken place regardless, but they would have taken a very long time, maybe a hundred years or a hundred and fifty. But now the pace is going to be dizzying.

While something new is emerging, it's going to be such a destructive process, perhaps a historical precedent (in its scale and significance). There will be storms so great that many will physically vanish. From among all the people we know today, in ten years or so only a few will survive, by accident. Stepan Borisovich smiled in response to my silent interjections:

"I'm speaking as a historian."

"But can the country avoid too bloody an upheaval?"

"Yes, but at a very heavy price. Maybe they could stop us from destroying each other, but they would turn us into a big labor camp. That would be even worse."

The civil war had not even started yet, but Veselovsky could already see the consequences. Although his reply to Olga shocks readers for its farsightedness, at the same time I understood how already then the dichotomy was emerging: it will either be the people destroying one another, or "they" will turn the whole country into a camp, "this is even worse".

Worse than ten million killed?

And Russian people would end up scattered around the world regardless. His estimations were evidence that the image of the Great and Indivisible Russia muddled the thinking of the most bright and educated people of the time. After all, these stereotypes would lead a part of the intelligentsia into a readiness to forgive Stalin many things, precisely for the sake of preserving the empire. Nevertheless, Veselovsky (who would become a member of the academy) as a historian and as a private individual, while the great leader was alive, at the end of the Forties, would dissociate himself in his diaries from the Stalinist era of history.

The years of 1991 and 1993 bore a strange resemblance to that February and October of 1917.

I remember how on October 3, 1993 Moscow fell silent, it was petrified. Rare cars darted about, and then there was a strange silence, so unusual for the city. I could see how the thick, dark crowd poured through the Garden Ring from the Krymsky Bridge towards the New Arbat. The crowd appeared here and there on the TV screen; the mouths that seemed to rip the lower part of the head asunder were pursed, distorted with a grimace or wide open. In the house on Smolensky Boulevard where I lived at that time, I could physically sense the approach of that crowd. The evening before, I had gone out to the Arbat to get some milk, and then I saw for the first time how a few people were overturning cars and setting them on fire right next to the building of the Ministry of Foreign Affairs. It was as if these people had come out of the sewer: they had dark, weather-beaten faces and black caps were covering their heads. I ran, coughing from the smoke that was belching from the burning tires. For several days the city was left for them to tear to pieces. There were no police or soldiers in the city. The day before I had stood at the mayor's office. We were a small bunch of people who tried to shout down the singing that was coming from the loudspeakers of the White House – one could hear the gloomy lines "Arise, great country…" The people surrounding the White House were singing along or shouting curses at us who had gathered at the mayor's office. We were divided by barbed wire. There were different faces and a different city in 1991. After the three days that it had survived, it opened again and became completely sweet to us. The crowd (which could no longer be called a mob) shone with happiness. The streets, the squares, the boulevards were open to everyone. We walked in hundreds of thousands through Red Square, Staraya Square, and Lubyanka and there was not a single policeman anywhere, but there were no incidents either. Except for bringing down the statue of Iron Felix, which was deeply auspicious and meaningful.

The end of the diary

The historian Stepan Borisovich Veselovsky, who had told the young lady what awaited Russia in the years to follow, set her on a different course in life than the one she had imagined before the revolution. At the end of 1917 she returned to her hometown of Voronezh. At the same time, her brother Boris left for the front.

"The Whites are in the city," Olga Bessarabova wrote in her diary. "Hunger, cold, looting, murder, death, panic, betrayal. A city that has to endure people hung in one of its squares (apparently in Kruglye Ryady) and comes to look at them with their wives and children. One of the hung people is a woman, a Chekist."

The vengeful cruelty of the Whites proved enough to sway students from good families to the Bolsheviks' side. Thus the machinery of brother killing brother was set in motion, and it tilted the scales in favor of a side that could not bring Russia any more good than the other.

The city was ravaged by a typhoid epidemic. Olga fell ill. Her mother looked after her, became infected too, and died. Some time later, after Olga had recovered, she went to work as a nurse in a cholera ward, tending to the sick that had been abandoned without any proper care. Due to the lack of proper nurses, even local prostitutes and railway workers were brought in to help.

Only when the epidemic was coming to an end did she decide to visit Varvara Grigoryevna Malakhieva-Mirovich in Sergiev Posad. Here at the Lavra monastery in 1920–1921 gathered scholars, priests, former princes, and aristocrats – everyone who had decided not to leave Russia. They fought to save the Lavra from total destruction and set up a local history museum in it.

Among them was Fr. Pavel Florensky with his family, the orphaned family of Vasily Rozanov, the artist Vladimir Favorsky, princes from the Golitsyn, Komarovsky, and Shakhovskoy families… Only a handful of them would survive. Everything happened as the historian Veselovsky had foretold.

Olga Bessarabova called this wonderful but brief moment of her life "The Saint-Germain of Sergei Posad". In Sergiev Posad all of the youngsters were under the enormous influence of Fr. Pavel Florensky's sermons. He won the hearts of his parishioners with his incredible mind and his exceptional ministry, which became the center of their little world.

Meanwhile the Dobrov house in Moscow was celebrating. Their daughter Shurochka was getting married to the dazzlingly handsome young man Alexander Kovalensky. He was the second cousin of Alexander Blok, and himself an exceptional poet whom everyone expected to have a great future. That spring, Kovalensky (he lived nearby at house number 3) had come to Shurochka's window, and it happened that their talks led eventually to a wedding.

"Behind closed doors at the church on Maly Levshinsky Lane there were only the witnesses, the best man, and Elizaveta

Mikhailovna with Filipp Alexandrovich," Olga Bessarabova wrote in 1922. "On the threshold of their home they set out a fur coat. They met Shurochka and her husband with an icon painted in gold, bread, and salt. They showered them with hops and rye grains. This is not a religious ritual, just an old custom, but here the stern, luminous faces of Shurochka and Alexander made the hops and rye look downright blessed."

This year was a happy one for her as well. At Sergiev Posad she met and fell in love with a remarkable man, a sculptor, painter, and dollmaker that was twice her age. She put all that she had into her love for him. As Varvara recalled, "Olga had long, lush, and golden-red braids at the time and dark-brown eyes. Sometimes they were full of *joie de vivre*, like the sun sparkling on the surface of a river. At other times, her gaze turned inwards, stern and mournful… She had a rare gift, a wish to be happy."

But Olga could not and did not want to take the man she loved away from his wife, also an artist, and someone to whom he was deeply linked.

Once she had a dream: huge scissors in the sky were snipping threads that were leading somewhere high above. One end of the threads were coming down to earth and touching her and her loved ones. She saw how the blades of the scissors were coming close to her, and with the power of her gaze she was pushing the scissors away.

Soon after this dream, at the end of 1924, Olga Bessarabova was taken to the hospital. Her friends gathered by her.

People lay dying on the beds neighboring hers, and around her hopelessness and desperation reigned.

The diary breaks off in 1925.

When I had finished reading, a new year had been ushered in, 2009. I was doing something in real life, but everything felt as if in a dream. Time for me had shifted to back then. Years were passing by there, dramatic events were taking place, people met and parted. All this had, in a way I couldn't understand at all, fit into just six days for me. It was similar to the experience one feels in childhood, when one disappears into the life of the book. With age, the same feeling of being lost to the present started to come from historical documents and diaries, in the reconstruction of the past.

What was I supposed to do with the world that had been revealed to me? I had an almost physical sense of its presence. I was tormented by this interrupted novel, whose ending was suspended in midair.

Only one thing consoled me: that together with the diary in the archive, the papers of Olga's brother were held – Boris Bessarabov.

These notes were an attempt to write a personal account of the Civil War, about Marina Tsvetaeva, the Dobrov home, and about Boris himself. It was thanks to Boris's notes that the Bessarabovs' collection had found its way to the Tsvetaeva museum. They revealed to me a further page from the life of the Dobrovs' house.

The main plot of Bessarabov's account came down to how, during the Russian New Year (i.e. the eve of January 13, 1921) Marina Tsvetaeva came to the Dobrovs' with a female friend. In Shurochka Dobrova's room she recited her poems; Boris, who knew Tsvetaeva's "Poems about Moscow" by heart, surprised her with his understanding of her work.

Bessarabov claimed that Mayakovsky was lying right there on the carpet, occasionally sniffing some white powder, and near him Lilya Brik sat. For Tsvetaeva, Boris Bessarabov, who had recently returned from the front, was a representative of the new regime – a Bolshevik, a Communist. She wanted to take a closer look at him.

In fact, it was only an illusion. Boris Bessarabov, who had recently finished the gymnasium, was a typical young man of the early 20th century. He merely tried to resemble the "new people" by copying their coarse manners and loud speech.

On that winter night, the Russian New Year's Eve, Boris Bessarabov left to accompany Marina Tsvetaeva and her friend from the Dobrovs' to Borisoglebsky, going through Nikolopeskovsky Lane. They stood talking for a long time. Tsvetaeva did not just like the young man, she saw in him a hero for a poem she would write, "Yegorushka", meant as a counterpart for the poem "The Tsar-Maiden" which she had just finished. As they were saying goodbye, Tsvetaeva asked Boris to help her friend Tatyana Skryabina – the widow of the composer Alexander Scriabin – to help with some logs of firewood that the city authorities had rationed out. Bessarabov agreed, as he had already done so for other friends. From neighbors he acquired some wedges, splitting mauls, a sledgehammer, and a saw, and he broke those unmanageable trunks down into smaller pieces.

Boris turned out to be an extremely emotional youth with a worldview and an understanding of people and life that had not yet crystallized. Nonetheless, he was endowed with an understanding of the new art. He dreamed of becoming a painter. Bessarabov followed after Marina Tsvetaeva like a calf led by a rope. This, incidentally, eventually found its reflection in the poem "Side Streets" (*Pereulochki*). There, the sorceress Marinka turns the hero into an auroch. Tsvetaeva deeply amazed and delighted Boris. For her, he was ready to do anything she might ask.

Thus Boris Bessarabov started spending nearly every day in Borisoglebsky Lane. At first their friendship was strong. He sat by her day and night, copying out "The Tsar-Maiden" in his fine hand.

He told his sister Olga Bessarabova about everything in letters to her: with pathos and affliction he wrote about how much he liked Marina Tsvetaeva, about what a wonderful daughter she had, and how great the house in Borisoglebsky Lane was. About how he dreamed that two women for whom he had such great love would get to meet each other.

He had come to Moscow immediately after being at the front and in a hospital, and he naturally settled in the Dobrovs' home. He was assigned to a military railway organization with the awkward name of TsUPVASO.

It is important to note here that for the Dobrovs, it didn't matter whether their guests were Reds or Whites. It happened that people who had been on different sides of the front, who might have even been shooting at each other a short while ago, met at one table. Under their roof, the Dobrov family did not want to divide Russia into "us" and "them".

Soon Boris would leave the hospitable Dobrov home and move to Tsvetaeva's, in Borisglebsky Lane.

"All the material benefits given for the month and a half of my assignment – my rations, bread, sugar, meat – I left them under Marina's name," he wrote to his sister in 1912. "I gave her the right to collect my salary payment, reimbursements, firewood, and so on and so forth. This will make Marinochka very happy."

A few months later, Marina would turn cold to Bessarabov. Now she saw him as a savage and the incarnation of ignorance. That is why the poem "Yegorushka" became something unpleasant, and she never finished it.

Olga Bessarabova went to take her brother's letters and things from the house in Borisglebsky Lane. She found Tsvetaeva unpleasant, haughty, and unkind. The two women looked at each other from different worlds. True, Olga Bessarabova recognized Tsvetaeva's enormous talent, but Boris, who had longed for the two to meet, was too optimistic.

The Dobrovs' and the Skryabins': Tatyana Skryabina and Marina Tsvetaeva

The pages of Olga Bessarabova's diaries, which acted as a crossroads for the Dobrov home and the Skryabins', helped to explain a few mysterious aspects of Tsvetaeva's life.

Thus, as already mentioned, on the snowy winter night of January 13, 1921 which Boris Bessarabov recalled, Tatyana Skryabina and Marina Tsvetaeva went to the Dobrovs' to celebrate the Russian New Year.

"I went with Skryabina," Tsvetaeva wrote in one of her notebooks. "She in her seal-fur coat, on heels that were as narrow as pins. I walked as smoothly as a tiger with my felt boots, but she kept falling down. It wasn't a long way to go, but in that winter everyone was afraid of 'jumpers'. It was in any case the winter of the 'jumpers' – exceedingly tall creatures wrapped in white sheets, who would jump out from behind white snowdrifts and attack single women wearing fur coats, and sometimes even take the suits men wore under their fur coats. After that, the person out walking, now running late, would be covered in white, and the enormously tall person, who now seemed suddenly shorter, would be wearing the fur coat." Thus the two of them walked, looking at the houses with boarded-up windows and going past building entrances whose doors swung in the wind. They were walking from Skryabina's cold house to the warm home of the Dobrovs'. The fire in the Dobrovs' stove was what attracted them and gladdened their hearts. The Dobrovs got firewood from people as payment for Dr. Dobrov's medical care, and thus it was warm at their place, just like in the days before the revolution.

It is known for sure, that it was Skryabina who brought Tsvetaeva as a guest to the Dobrov home. But how did Skryabina know its inhabitants?

A year and a half before, she had been in a safe place for refugees in Kiev – friends and acquaintances had settled in the home of the millionaire owner of a sugar factory. Tatyana Skryabina (with her three children, mother, and brother) found refuge there from the chaos and hunger ravaging Moscow. She experienced a great tragedy there. Her son Julian Skryabin, a young composer only eleven year old, drowned in a small bay of the Dnieper River when she was away from the city.

Varvara Malakhieva-Mirovich lived in Kiev in the same house as the Skryabin family and offered enormous moral support, as Tatyana Fyodorovna suffered from a deep depression that would lead to illness and then her death in little more than two years. Varvara Grigoryevna stood by her side; they would walk together to her son's grave, and to services in the church and at the Kiev Lavra.

On August 3, 1919 Varvara Grigoryevna Malakhieva-Mirovich wrote to Tatyana Skryabina, "That I loved you unintentionally, strongly and forever, you know that. That in your great sorrow I find reflections of an unearthly, incredible joy, you must know that too. But I also want to tell you that the weapon that has pierced your soul had been created from your sacrificial blood by such wonderful flowers in the spiritual world, that one cannot stop marveling at their beauty, and their meaning is an angelic secret."

"Varvarushka, my dear sister," Skryabina wrote back to her. "God bless you for your kind words, I needed them so much, especially today… I feel like my soul is plunging into some depths of suffering, it's falling further and further down, and though it still hasn't hit the bottom, it will soon, and then I will begin to rise again towards the light – I wish it were so. But I'm still on the downward fall, and I need to go through all of this alone."

By the spring of 1920, when the Civil War had ended in most of Russian territory, Tatyana Fyodorovna returned to Moscow with her Belgian-born mother and her two daughters (Adriana and Marina). They settled in the house of her late husband on the Arbat, which the Soviet authorities had turned into a Skryabin museum. She became the first head of this museum, but only on paper. Skryabina hardly had the strength to struggle with the difficulties of life in Moscow at the time. It was at this time that Boris Bessarabov, at the request of Marina Tsvetaeva, chopped firewood for her, and Skryabina thanked him by playing the piano for him and telling him stories about Alexander Scriabin.

At almost the same time, Varvara Grigoryevna also came to Moscow, to the Dobrovs'. She arrived at a house where one could now meet a large number of people that had moved through a country torn apart by civil war. Varvara Grigoryevna most likely met Tatyana Skryabina at the Dobrovs', especially since Skryabina constantly required the doctor's care.

Marina Tsvetaeva, however, was not fond of the Dobrovs'. All of Tsvetaeva's indirect mentions of the house are either condescending or mean-spirited. She found there a kind of "priestery", spiritualism, mysticism. She did not care for Skryabina's friends, though she soon led her "calf" Boris Bessarabov away from there.

Tsvetaeva, who herself had experienced all kinds of misfortunes, thought a great deal in early 1921 about her own inner path, rejecting the new state of affairs that she found detestable, with the "old world vanished without a trace" and the former honor and nobility gone. Against the civilization that had disappeared forever she erected a world of creativity and craftsmanship. It became a parallel reality, but at the same time the main one for her, a kind of magical reality. Thus, in a psychological sense, the closeness between her and Skryabina did her good during this difficult period in her life.

"I feel a tenderness for T.F. Skryabina," Tsvetaeva wrote as soon as she had met her. "It's as if she comes from some other land where everyone speaks quietly and experiences gentle feelings. She not only doesn't seem Russian, she doesn't seem from this earth. She speaks as if she barely touches the words, so gently."

Furthermore, Tsvetaeva found in herself some strange affinity with her: "T. F. Skryabina… has beautiful eyes. Yesterday we almost completely threw ourselves somewhere, me tired of the day, and her tired of life. We get on well when we're together, we have a strong sympathy in both body and mind: a love for snowstorms, for stunningly heavy drinking, for smoking, for floating away into nothingness." One might conjecture that this "sympathy in body and mind" also included memories about their deceased children, the widowhood of one and the orphanhood and semi-widowhood of the other. In the poem "Insomnia", written in May 1921, Tsvetaeva recreates in an almost documentary fashion her and Skryabina's common affinity for stunningly heavy drinking with "floating away" into nothingness.

Insomnia! My friend!
Again I meet your hand
With an outstretched glass
In the soundlessly jingling night.
…
Oh, my friend! Don't shy away!
Join me!
Drink this glass!
Of all desires
The most desirable, of all deaths
The most tender… From these two hands
Of mine: join me, drink!

For Skryabina, her headaches and insomnia really did become an excruciating torment before her death. The Dobrovs' home was part of her life after she had fallen ill with typhoid, as was Esfir Pines who was nursing her (and who had already been rejected by the Dobrov family), and Skryabina repeatedly called for Dr. Dobrov from Maly Levshinsky Lane. Skryabina's daughter Adriana with her friend Elena Zhdanko would also rush there to get beer yeast for the ailing Skryabina, as it was a recommended treatment for attacks of neurasthenia.

According to Elena's account, Esfir Pines had an enormous power over Skryabina and would not let any of her loved ones come near her.

Olga Bessarabova once met Esfir while walking past the Skryabin home. She knew Esfir well and, after she had chatted with her, recorded her thoughts in her diary.

"The 'dealings' that Esfir is involved in include: theft, blackmail, money, lies, brazen trickery, dark connections, cocaine, and so forth."

Olga never fell into Esfir's net herself, and she was always amazed at how Esfir managed to fool everyone around her.

If Tsvetaeva visited the ailing Skryabina at all in those months, it was for a very short time.

As Elena Zhdanko wrote, "When winter came and T. F.'s health worsened, and it became more difficult to heat the apartment, the ill woman was moved into the living room. There I saw T. F. Skryabina for the first time. She was already a seriously ill person, half undone by her disease. 'Suffering Job' is how she described herself. She could neither lift herself nor turn over to the other side without someone else's help, and she would let out a moan if anyone touched her. At all other times she would lie quietly, without saying a word, and bear her affliction with a rare acceptance and patience. She was capable of hardly any conversation in her state... Later Tatyana Fyodorovna told me about how she had taken part in fortune-telling at New Year's. She had drawn a Bible passage about 'Job on the dungheap'. T. F. believed that her illness was the fulfillment of this prophecy."

This was undoubtedly linked to a pastime of Varvara Grigoryevna Malakhieva-Mirovich, who had organized fortune-telling for her friends and loved ones at Christmas. She wrote out words from the Bible, lines from spiritual verses, and everyone drew a slip of paper out that told their future. These prophecies often came to pass, and many of her friends would remember later in life the words directed to them personally.

In the spring, on March 22, 1922, Tatyana Skryabina died.

As Tsvetaeva wrote from Berlin, recalling the recent funeral, "And the grave: a white one without any wreaths. Already close by is the consoling arch of the Devichy monastery: a blessed place… I think about T[atyana] F[yodorovna], her last days on earth. And then, bam, a feeling of *interruptedness*."

Varvara Grigoryevna was most likely one of the people who came to say goodbye. Marina Tsvetaeva and her must have nodded to one another. And there was certainly someone there from the Dobrov home. Thus the paths of Varvara Malakhieva-Mirovich and Marina Tsvetaeva, that had once crossed due to Skryabina, were now going in separate directions. On April 29th of the same year, Olga Bessarabova came to Tsvetaeva's home in Borisoglebsky Lane to take her brother's things, as Boris had left to Voronezh.

It was then that she wrote in her diary, in a harsh tone uncharacteristic of her, about Marina Tsvetaeva.

"Even if she's talented and intelligent, people say very bad things about her, evil things, especially in connection with the poor departed Skryabina. They feel sorry for Skryabina, and they talk about Marina Tsvetaeva and Esfir with reluctance and disgust. I remembered what someone said about Tatyana Fyodorovna, that she 'burned in those witches' cauldron.'"

From these words of Olga Bessarabova, one can hear the voices and disputes of the Dobrov household. Tsvetaeva's expressiveness, the revolutionary features of her poems could hardly help a sickly woman, one prone to neurosis, headaches, and depression. Tsvetaeva herself made this sorcery and fortune-telling the main theme of her poetry during that period, the time of the collection *Craft* (*Remeslo*). She recited these poems publicly, shocking people who were already weary from the Civil War and the loss of their loved ones, people who were desperate for consolation from religion, art, and life. But there was never any consolation in Tsvetaeva's poetry.

"Yes, a woman, because she is a witch, and because she is a poet," Tsvetaeva wrote in February 1922. She was leaving the Moscow that she had stirred up like an anthill, saying goodbye to Russia, and departing with her husband who had miraculously turned up in Prague, Sergei Efron.

The Arbat:
enigmas of the Skryabin home

In the sketch for Tsvetaeva's "The House at Old Pimen", dedicated to an "adopted" grandfather, the historian Dmitri Ilovaysky, I always dwelt with amazement on the passage where the old man is being held by the secret police. A certain woman from the police told Tsvetaeva what he had said there and how he behaved.

As Tsvetaeva wrote, "My informant (a former investigator of the Cheka) was shocked by the fearlessness she found in this old man and many other people not as old as him who were awaiting trial. This investigator gradually realized that the Whites were also people, and she soon found employment at a handicraft museum, in the toys section. The Whites had killed her husband. She had a son with a large and shaven head, he was four years old and very hungry."

Who could this have been? Where in Tsvetaeva's circle could she have met a female investigator from the Cheka?

At the Skryabin house, a certain Lenochka often visited and even stayed the night.

Arianda's friend recalled, "Elena Usievich (I never learned her patronymic, the people around her just called her Lenochka) was living then with her young son in the second House of the Soviets in the building of the Metropol hotel. Lenochka was always merry and full of *joie de vivre*, and she had a positive effect on the ailing woman. She would occasionally spend a long while with her. Her little boy was jealous of his mother's long absences and once said, 'I got unlucky with my mother.'"

This was Elena Feliksovna Usievich (daughter of the revolutionary Feliks Kon, exiled to Siberia, and wife of the Bolshevik Grigori Usievich, who had been killed in 1918). In late 1928 she became a famous Soviet literary critic.

She often would take trips to faraway places with Esfir in order to exchange clothes for food.

It was probably after her brief period working in the Cheka that Usievich was forced to recuperate from bad nerves in a sanatorium, something that often happened at that time to Communists who had a conscience. Adriana Skryabina went to visit her, an event that she recounted in a stunning letter to Varvara Grigoryevna. She wrote that when she came to Lenochka, she found her literally with a noose around her neck, which she had tied because of Esfir Pines.

Much has been written about Adriana Skryabina's life after her emigration, but in Olga Bessarabova's diaries new and unusual details emerge that are linked to her whimsical character and talent. She was not at all an ordinary young lady.

"Adriana Skryabin is sixteen years old," Olga Bessarabova wrote. "She is writing a passion play that ends with the death of all the characters, a real death in a bonfire on Red Square. She wants to go to the Patriarch of Russia and ask him to bless her for this passion play and death – a voluntary sacrifice and redemption for all the terrible and evil things that reigned in the world, in Russia, on the Volga, everywhere. And in the West, in Europe and especially with us. She's very lovely."

After emigrating she had a spiritual conversion and adopted the Jewish name of Sara. During the war she was a heroine of the French Resistance and was shot by the Fascists in 1944.

Daniil Andreyev was just one year younger than she was. Over a brief two years (1920–1921) they became close friends. Perhaps it was because these teenagers shared some particular quality, they sensed the imminent upheavals of the age.

A story of sacrifice and redemption, similar to the one Adriana Skryabin wrote in her mystery play, was included in Daniil Andreyev's novel *Wanders of Night*. Who knows, maybe years afterward Daniil recalled the story of the mystery play that his friend wrote in her youth.

Olga Bessarabova's wish for happiness

...And there were gentle hands
That caressed the heart so tenderly,
That all terrible torments abated
And all nightmares flew away...

—Varvara Malakhieva-Mirovich

A young lady with dark brown eyes looked out at me from the photograph. She no longer had long braids, they had been cut when she was ill with typhoid. Now her hair was gathered in a bun at the back of her head. She is not smiling, her gaze is searching and sad.

Before I stumbled across Olga Bessarabova's notebooks, I had read a few diaries by women. Take, for example, the one by Elizaveta Dyakonova from Yaroslavl, who had fallen in love with a French doctor, mysteriously died in the Altai mountains, and was from a completely different era; or the diary of Olga Bergholz, madonna of the siege of Leningrad, with entries that are merciless with regard to herself and her contemporaries.

Olga Bessarabova's notebooks, on the other hand, were like nothing I had ever read before.

It is no coincidence that she called her philosophical and literary circle "Joy". Like her older friend had once said, the basic trait of the young lady's character was a "wish for hapiness".

Olga Bessarabova was directed not inward at herself, but at the world and people around her. The main quality of her spirit was something unbelievable, almost impossible for those years: love for other people. This love was difficult, for it underwent constant trials of hunger, cold, deception, thievery, death, and violence. At that time such love was almost a miracle.

In late 1917, then a twenty-year-old woman, she had to leave Moscow for Voronezh to be with her family. In the still-empty carriage she settled on an upper bunk with a small valise. But when the train had left the city, it suddenly filled with soldiers fleeing from the front, who were eating, drinking, spitting, and smoking poor-quality tobacco. The presence among them of a young lady with enormous red braids and dark-brown eyes did not leave them indifferent.

"At night among the snoring, in the darkness half-lit with the glowing ends of cigarettes, I felt that all this was a hell. I couldn't tell where the sinners were and where the devils were. It was all martyrs."

She got down and hid behind the backs of the sleeping soldiers, taking refuge from the dangerous neighbor on the upper bunk opposite, who harassed her the whole night. "The man on the neighboring bunk, an engineer, watched me carefully, but I was no longer afraid, I was totally calm. I felt that all the soldiers around me were my friends. This is something that is difficult to explain, but I knew it for certain. I closed my eyes and nearly fell asleep." With the same trust in fate, Olga could tell a robber who had climbed onto a balcony in Sergiev Posad to go away, because what he aimed to do was not good. He hesitated and then left.

Once Olga's close friend Shurochka Dobrova told her about herself, "I'm really struck by your purity, Olga. It's not due to naivete, you have excellent intuition and can really grasp the essence of things you are unfamiliar with. Well, I don't know if one can call the naivete of unknowingness purity, but for you it's purity, real purity."

"But Shurochka, what is purity? And what is impurity? Everything can become dirty, soiled. And everything in this world can be cleansed and remade. If only there were enough love and creative activity. As soon as something stops, it gets grown over with weeds. It can even start to rot."

This deep faith in the purifying power of life apparently allowed her to pass through unbearable trials – to save cholera patients in the ward near Voronezh, when the entire medical staff were doing nothing, and even prostitutes had to be recruited to help.

She really never was naive, she knew how to immediately see another human being as a whole, to embrace and forgive everyone whom she encountered.

"He's slow, gentle at the very first sight. It's even as if he were quickly hewn from wood, with a beard in the style of the countryside," she wrote about the artist and woodcut illustrator Vladimir Favorsky. "Later it is difficult to even recall this first impression. This man, this creature is made from the most precious material, a very fine piece of craftsmanship. He has great hands, they are small and graceful. He has a wonderful face."

And she wrote unexpectedly harsh lines about Maya Kudasheva, the future wife of the writer Romain Rolland: "She is a very interesting woman to talk to, but today I unexpectedly realized that she's really just a horrible lizard who has taken on the appearance of a woman."

In Sergiev Posad she fell, like many other people, under the great influence of Fr. Pavel Florensky's sermons. She was tormented most of all by the unpleasant idea that earthy life was sinful, as she found it marvelous in spite of all its catastrophes. One has to note that her reflections on this theme took place in the hunger-plagued Twenties. With remarkable innocence and lightness she talked about this with the church historian Mansurov:

Sergei Pavlovich thinks that I'm talking about the world as if it were already transfigured, like paradise, but one cannot jump up into heaven just like that. It is granted (achieved, won) at the great price of overcoming the world, transforming the flesh.

"And perhaps also love for this world and the flesh, Sergei Pavlovich," I asked.

Mansurov thought about that. Only after we had walked past three houses, he answered, "There are realities that are of a higher value than the realities of this world."

"I think that Florensky knows both, that world and ours, and he lives on a very narrow line between the two."

"Yes, that may be so."

With the same questions in mind, she went to the famous elder of the Optina monastery, who was serving in the 1920s in Zosimova Pustyn.

"I told the elder about my 'absence' from the church, about the mistaken surges and reactions I felt, about how there was no way I could understand and believe that everything in this world was sinful and evil, and how I was even angry because of that and that I love everything of this world. He looked fixedly and quietly into my eyes. 'Talk, talk. I think that this is the most important thing. Listen to your heart, my child.' He put his hand on my forehead and made a slight motion, looking again into my eyes. I did not understand, I thought that he was leaning towards me and I wanted to kiss him, grateful and happy that he wasn't angry at me, that he was very kind. 'No, my child, don't do that, you can't kiss a monk. Don't be afraid of anything or anyone. Listen to your heart. You have a clean and bright heart. May God bless you.' Then he blessed me and gave me an icon of the archangel Michael. 'He will drive away anything dark if it tries to approach you. And don't fear anything or anyone.' I said, 'I have never been afraid of anyone' 'I can see that.' And he blessed me again tenderly and let me kiss his hand." Olga was most likely saved from an inevitable death in the various zigzags of fate precisely by this love of life, which was meant to lead her to her true destiny.

When I learned from the documentation attached to the diaries that they had been donated to the museum by Anna

Stepanovna Veselovskaya, some vague suspicions about Olga Bessarabova's future sneaked into my heart.

I would soon meet that very Anna Stepanovna, and she would tell me about an unusual turn in Olga Bessarabova's life – essentially, about a new stage in her life, which began literally a year after the diary breaks off.

Once Olga was walking along a Moscow street and met her old acquaintance Stepan Borisovich Veselovsky, the historian under whom she had worked in the archive before the revolution. He was already old, and by that time he had left his large family, with five adult sons living their own lives. They talked for a while and then parted. Several days later, she got a letter from him in which he asked to meet. She went to their appointment, where he proposed to her right away. To her friends' general surprise, Olga Bessarabova immediately agreed to be his wife. A year before her decision she had written, "I am possessed by my work well and good… Either a convent or a family, that is what I would like to see at the crossroads of my life."

In a sense, she disappeared. She became Olga Veselovskaya, with a different history and a different fate.

A metaphysical design:
in the enchanted wood

What happened to the generation of young men and women who were born in the 1890s, is something we generally don't know. If they lived through the Civil War, if they didn't emigrate, and if they weren't arrested, then their lives mainly passed into libraries, archives, museums, and laboratories. Some of them were even happy to see the arrival of the Soviet regime, but the late 1930s proved a sobering experience.

The deeper I plunged into those lives and that world, however, the more I was seized by a feeling of perplexity. How much I had already read about the pre- and post-revolutionary years; they seemed even closer to me than the Soviet years of the 1930s–1950s. It seemed as if everything were already known down to the smallest details: the terrible premonitions before the revolution; the sweeping nightmare of the war and the revolution; and the pain, and the horror, and the hunger, and the trains weighed down with people.

But in her entries there was no talk about Russia dying, there was no railing at the terrible conditions that were ushered in after the October Revolution.

There was also no fear for the future, though her life and the lives of her entire generation were overwhelmed by catastrophic events.

Nevertheless, Olga recorded a general state of hopeless- ness–a feeling of being at an abyss. As she wrote in 1923, "I was briefly at the Dobrovs'… We talked about all of us, about the general weariness and gloom, the heavy weight on people's spirits. We all stand on some kind of edge, at a cliff or at a hole in the ice. We must not look back at the enchanted wood of life, otherwise we will turn to stone, or monsters will tear us apart if we look back at them."

They did not rebel, protest, or weep over their fate. Life in Russia had been too complex before. They took Russia's fate as their own. Sometimes it seemed that these were characters out of Chekhov continuing their tragic journey after the playwright's death. This was how Uncle Vanya and Astrov would live in Soviet Russia, and Chekhov's three sisters would be teaching in a Soviet school or working in a library. Everyone was simply extremely tired, young and old alike.

In the same way Yuri Zhivago was tired of the revolution and the war, of the smell of blood, when he returned on foot from the Urals to dust-filled Moscow. He walked for several years and experienced the rift of time on the road. He arrived in Soviet Moscow as a different person.

Spring of 1923. Sergiev Posad. Three young women stand in the photograph, leaning against a wooden fence. At the gate Olga Bessarabova is standing with a wide scarf over her shoulders.

How drab their faces look from never having enough to eat! These people went starving throughout the entire Stalin era. The lines for bread began in World War I, and the lines for food lasted the entire 1930s, and then there were ration cards during World War II, and then the famine of 1946, and then the ration cards were abolished, but you could only buy the bare necessities.

Although their faces are smiling, they are pale in a certain way, and in their eyes one can see the experience of sickness and death.

Their coats are draped over these young women like bags. They wore clothing – mended and re-mended – that had been made before the revolution. The clothes hung on them with awkward bulges, which were easily visible in photographs. Bigger men would walk in Tolstoy shirts, sandals, and pea-ked caps. The former upper classes had suit jackets that had been mended. Girls walked in berets and almost formless dresses.

One could "end it all" easily and with dignity, and that would have been a solution for many, but… If only it weren't for the children and other loved ones. This was the hardest part.

Some of them wanted to forget the past. "Don't look back at the enchanted wood of life." To forget the names of their grandparents, who they were and how they lived, how they prayed, and where they kept their sacred books. Forgetting meant dissolving into the general life of society. Olga Bessarabova however could not forget and could not dissolve, although her diaries suddenly show pages thickly written over with ink. This meant that at some point, fear had nevertheless come into her life, and the elder's advice and protection ceased to be effective. This most likely started later on, but when?

What kind of people were they? They were neither Soviet nor anti-Soviet, but something different. I didn't know them and could not get a sense of them. In a strange way they didn't dissolve into Soviet society, they did not adopt its language and style. They silently bore in themselves a special quality, which could be seen in lines for bread, in prison cells, in the classroom, and when they came to teach. This special quality was distinguished by an ineradicable sense of one's own dignity… and also by the fact that they did not seek anything better for themselves.

I went through the notebooks again and again. It was clear how conscientiously Olga Bessarabova had assembled a mosaic from the letters and diary entries of her and her friends: postcards, letters from the front in World War I – everything was gathered together, copied out, and pasted into these notebooks thick and thin, so that *we* could read them and learn.

Nearly ninety years had passed since that time.

Olga Bessarabova's diary was one of the links in the chain of history that was interrupted, never becoming part of our culture even though it long since could have.

And I think that, behind all those dark images of the present, behind all the negative things you see around you – from the holes in the asphalt to the dirt along the streets – one finds the broken threads of the lives of people who didn't have enough time or didn't know how to change those lives for the better. Every time I am outraged about something, when I get upset at this unfairness, I suddenly see the link that fell out of the chain of history, and I understand that someone didn't manage to live long enough, to say what they had to say, to reach what they sought.

I had to find her descendants. I had to write a book from the diaries. Furthermore, I understood very well that these entries could easily be divided into bits that scholars of Daniil Andreyev, Pavel Florensky, Vladimir Favorsky, and other figures could use in their investigations. But then the entire fabric of life would disappear, be lost forever. That is how it always happens.

The daughter of Olga Bessarabova

At long last I found the telephone number for Olga's daughter, Anna Stepanovna Veselovskaya.

I dialed the number. The phone rang for a long time. I had already lost hope when suddenly someone answered. It was her, Veselovskaya herself. Her voice sounded so quiet and unclear; it felt like I was talking to a shadow and it was whispering something to me in reply.

Nevertheless, I was besides myself with joy. I jumped from one word to another and mixed up the questions I had, all the while expressing my great surprise. I asked if I might come and talk with her. It was as if she didn't even hear my request. She couldn't hear my enthusiasm and my desire to publish the diaries. And she wasn't happy about my call. However, it was clear that she wanted to give the impression that it pleased her. The voice continued to sound as if it was coming through a curtain.

I started asking her what had happened to each of the figures in the diaries. What course their lives took later. I was afraid that I wouldn't find the last pages of the story, that the conversation was going to be interrupted, and the ending would escape me. No, she answered. Calmly, clearly, but completely colorless and joyless.

Yes, Olga kept diaries all her life. She died in 1968, she had heart disease. She was generally occupied with the affairs of her husband, the historian and academician Veselovsky. The diaries of the second half of her life deal only with her family, and Anna Stepanova did not intend for them to be published. Boris Bessarabov, her uncle, worked for the rest of his life as a painter and designer, fulfilling commissions.

With regard to Daniil Andreyev and his wife Alla, Anna Stepanova knew them very well, and she barely avoided being caught in the "Andreyev affair". Andreyev had showed her and an acquaintance of hers the novel *Wanderers of Night*, which he was keeping hidden under the floorboards. He said that as soon as someone else finished copying out the manuscript, he would give them the copy. He didn't manage to do this, however. They arrested him. If they had read it, they would have been arrested as well.

"After all, you know that they arrested everyone who had read *Wanderers of Night* or heard it read aloud. That was right after the war."

Shurochka Dobrova and her brother died in the camps. They were all accused in connection with the same affair.

When I asked about Varvara Grigoryevna Malakhieva-Mirovich, I sudden heard a fresh tone in her voice. The dullness disappeared, replaced by a different color.

Yes, her mother was a friend of Varvara Grigoryevna Mirovich, who lived until 1954, and died at the age of almost eighty-five. Varvara Grigoryevna also kept a diary, which her mother came into possession of after Varvara's death. Olga herself was making notes from them until the end of her life, and then she gave them to Dmitri Mikhailovich Shakhovskoy, Varvara Grigoryevna's godson. The Shakhovskoys were a large family. Anna Stepanovna Veselovskaya gave me his telephone number.

When I met Anna Stepanovna, it was already spring. She lived at the beginning of Leninsky Prospekt, in an enormous home for academicians that was built in the Stalin era.

I entered the apartment and stepped from the corridor into a tiny room like a shoebox. Of course, I tried to find in Anna Stepanovna some similarity with her mother whom, frankly, I couldn't imagine as an adult, let alone an elderly woman. Before me sat a thin and energetic woman, already advanced in years, who resembled – as I saw at once – her academician father. Her bright blue eyes, the color of a forget-me-not, gleamed just like on her childhood portrait "Girl with a Teddy Bear", which hung here in the room.

We sat on the simple bed covered with an old bed cover.

She spoke very nicely and answered all of my questions that she could. She showed me some works by her uncle Boris Bessarabov that were quite good. She was a different person than the one I had heard for the first time on the telephone. However, from what she was telling me, I began to understand the center of her life had always been her father, the academician Veselovsky.

I looked around and saw various things lying around, and I noticed that time in this home had stopped at some point. A box of sweets with photos could have come from my own childhood. Old erasers, quills, and inkwells.

When I walked out into the corridor, six identical fluffy cats came, one after the other, from the opposite door through a hole cut out just above the floor. They stood and looked at me dumbstruck. It seemed that it was the cats who were the real owners of the apartment and I was unceremoniously trespassing on their property. I shivered under their scrutinizing gaze, quickly said goodbye, and left the house.

Olga Bessarabova's diary could not stand as a book by itself, it needed the "help" of Marina Tsvetaeva. I decided almost at once that the documentary story of how Boris Bessarabov appeared in Borisoglebsky Lane and the collection of his letters to his sister in which he talked about Tsvetaeva would be a kind of a locomotive that would pull Olga's diaries up.

From Sobachye Square to Novy Arbat: a virtual layout of Moscow in the 1920s

I was actually working in the part of Moscow where my people had lived. As I followed Boris Bessarabov, I walked the same road that he had so often, from Borisglebsky Lane to Maly Levshinsky and back.

But however much I tried to see at the end of Borisoglebsky Lane the Sobachye Square that everyone walked across in visiting each other, nothing happened. I turned the houses I was imagining around in my head, but they wouldn't line up around the little square with its fountain. The picture with

Khomyakov's house on the book cover refused to fit in anywhere.

It seemed as if nowhere else on earth did the stumps of streets and little lanes stick out so much. The broken-off Bolshaya Molchanovka with a few houses that by some miracle had been saved, was bent and violently thrust out next to Povarskaya Street. Trubnikovsky Lane lived a double life, with one part utterly separate from the other. In Krechetnikovsky Lane, there was once a house where Tsvetaeva's friends, the Gertsyk sisters lived, and where philosophers and poets would gather. The lane is suspended in midair, however. It doesn't exist any more.

Once, on the eve of the revolution, the philosophers gathered in this house decided as a joke to publish their own journal entitled *Boulevards and Lanes*. Yevgeniya Gertsyk wrote about this in her reminiscences: "By the end of 1916, there was a split in people's relationship to the war and events within Russia itself… Vyacheslav Ivanov querulously asked, 'How will you overcome the individualism of the intelligentsia and join with the spirit of the masses in your lanes and back streets?' Berdyaev parried with, 'Do you think that the spirit of the masses lives on the wide boulevards?' We learned at once that all of the people who were for the wellbeing of the nation, all the optimists – Ivanov, Bulgakov, Ern – really were living on the wide boulevards, and people who foretold a catastrophe, who felt the symptoms of one coming – Shestov, Berdyaev, Gershenzon – were living in those crooked lanes where people rarely passed through… We laughed and cracked jokes about this phenomenon, and we came up with the idea of a self-published journal entitled *Boulevards and Lanes*."

Krechetnikovsky was itself a link between the boulevard (one end of it started from Novinsky) and the lane. Nowadays, however, there is no trace of it. Now Novy Arbat lavishly spreads over it.

Now where do today's optimists live?

I looked at a photo of the demolished, semi-detached, pseudo-Gothic house of Mizulin in Sobachye Square. Once the Union of Composers was based there, and it closely resembled another pseudo-Gothic house, the former Grauermann maternity hospital where half of Moscow was born, that had miraculously survived.

The spiderweb of vanished streets refused to reappear over Novy Arbat. It fluttered and swelled in my mind like a sail.

With great effort I recalled how, as a child, I had walked past the half-wooden Moscow buildings with low windows. Between the window frames people had put cotton balls and Christmas tree ornaments. These windows were low enough for me, so little at the time, to see. There were flowers on the windowsills. Fences. Wooden doors with the paint peeling off them. Nevertheless, I couldn't remember the streets themselves.

Now a city that has been humiliated and torn asunder by the Novy Arbat stands before me.

Then I suddenly realized that Prospekt Kalinina, which chopped through the living flesh of the old city, was nothing other than the route the emperors took from the Kremlin out towards their estates near Moscow: first through the Old Arbat into Matveevskoe to their dachas, and later to Barvikha, to the Rublevka. The road had been laid according to the same principle as Roman triumphs, whose celebrants cleared a path regardless of what stood in the way.

Every time I went to work at the Tsvetaeva museum, clouds of polished cars would whiz past me with sirens blaring, and the largest would have a squad of men with machine guns pointed right at me. It feels as if Soviet and post-Soviet history *is* Novy Arbat, which cut through everything that was dear to us in the past, everything that was connected with Pushkin, and Tsvetaeva, and Khomyakov, and Chaadayev. It went through the lives of the living and the departed, leaving us with fragments and ends of history scattered as if after an explosion.

Nevertheless, I am walking from the house in Borisoglebsky through the imagined Sobachye Square to the Dobrovs' house in Maly Levshinsky Lane. In the dense cluster of buildings on the other side of the avenue, there is a hatch, a little hole, that leads to Nikolopeskovsky Lane. There, at the beginning, stands a two-story home where Balmont once lived.

"Tomorrow the Joy circle is meeting at the Balmonts," Olga wrote. "They live in an old-fashioned house in one of the lanes of the Arbat, but with a vaulted ceiling. It's spacious and very lovely. The hallways are extravagantly spacious like in olden times, the walls are incredibly thick and the window niches deep."

The Balmont family moved out in 1920. Marina Tsvetaeva and little Alla saw them abroad. Right next door was the Skryabins' house. It was then, it seemed, that Marina Tsvetaeva even met the composer's widow Tatyana Fyodorovna.

After walking past the Arbat lanes and around the restored church restored in Bolshoy Levshinsky, I enter Maly Levshinsky lane.

The Dobrovs' home, which stood here at number five, no longer exists. It was demolished two decades ago. The only thing that has survived is the building that stood next to it and once faced its windows. The shades that once walked here – Boris Zaitsev, Andrei Bely, Leonid and Daniil

Andreyev, Marina Tsvetaeva, and even Mayakovsky – have scattered. The floorboards under which Daniil Andreyev had hid the manuscript of his novel *Wanderers of Night* has also disappeared.

The lace of history continued to be woven, however, and the Dobrov family's home lives on in stories, oral accounts, and diaries. The same is true for Sobachye Square and Krechetnikovsky Lane, which come to life again whenever people's thoughts turn to them.

And the Dobrov home warmed the hearts of all with its light. It attracted a number of people and served as one of the central points where the fates of many met.

Protochny Lane:
the inside of the Arbat

When I was a child, I lived not far from these places, next to Protochny Lane, which was a sort of inner side to the Arbat. It connected the Garden Ring at the level of Kompositorsky Lane (which led to Skryabin's house) with the Moscow River embankment. In Protochny Lane the lowest classes of the city had lived since time immemorial. They say that in Protochny Lane, not only did stolen goods disappear, but so did the people who were stolen from. Rumor had it that, when they demolished one of the homes, they found several human skeletons in its basement.

Here, on Protochny Lane, one feels an especial curvature of Moscow space. From each end of the lane one could see two different faces of the city: a darker one, closer to the river, and a tamer one around the lanes of the Arbat.

The windows of our communal apartment looked out from one side on "Protochka" (as the lane was known) and the Moscow River embankment, and from the other side there was a view of Prospekt Kalinina going towards the Kremlin. I lived in a large twelve-story building which was called "The Generals'", though in my time there were no generals living in the building – there were simply communal apartments for officers. I would walk to school through Protochka. Parts were often being demolished, and when we were coming home, we would walk through ruins of brickwork. Once plaintive singing could be heard from one of the basements that remained, and in the light of a streetlamp hanging from a wire some men were playing cards, while cursing drifted from one of the basement windows at street level. Another time, after we had seen a few idle young ladies shuffling from foot to foot, some dark figures started to usher us towards their lair, and we ran away in fear.

In my class there were some children from the slums bordering on the Protochka. For the first time in my life, I saw not a floor but a heap of compressed earth over which unstable floorboards were laid. The most surprising thing of all was that nearby, literally just a few meters away, were the lights of the grand avenue with white high-rises that were then brand-new, and the colored glass sparkled on the SEV building that resembled an open book.

Now on the site of the former Protochka stand luxurious high-rises that have completely annihilated the former shape of the city. They head further and further towards Smolensky Boulevard. Here, near the metro, the demolished buildings lay bare the ribs and bones of the Moscow of yesteryear, which had been squeezed into ungraceful inner courtyards deep within the lane, while an impressive facade looked over the boulevard. Now all that space has been destroyed, laid to waste, and in the gap that appeared, suddenly one had a view of the river, which could never be seen from here before.

In the lanes of the Arbat: the Dobrov home in the 1920s

How we have survived and how much we have dwindled!

—Dmitri Usov

From Olga Bessarabova's diary, new stories of post-revolutionary Moscow life would pour forth. Sometimes one had to fill in some of the gaps oneself, and sometimes everything would appear in full. These stories were unknown to all. The most important thing, however, is that they contained the living fabric of that era.

Something new was emerging in those lanes. In waves, a portion of their inhabitants would move away. Now the Zaitsev family left, while the Balmonts had already been gone for a long time. The Skryabin house was emptied, Tsvetaeva left. Not long before, Berdyaev – before his emigration – had led his Tuesday meetings in his home at 14 Vlasyevsky Lane, meetings which Olga Bessarabova attended:

Yesterday at Berdyaev's we heard a chapter from a forthcoming book by Florensky. ...There were two candles lit, many people listening, an old oval portrait and an oval mirror. The cups were of old porcelain (probably Gardner, which still has such a rich blue color and medallions with flowers). The bright lamps annoyed me, it would have been better if only those two candles were burning.

…When the reading and the following discussion had ended, people tried to leave quickly. They had still not managed to put their coats on when Florensky came in the door. People barred his way… "May I have the honor", "It's a pleasure", "When can I find you at home", "Where are you staying in Moscow", "I'm so happy to see you".

No one could even imagine what awaited them all in the future.

The New Economic Policy was introduced and it brought a huge amount of new people to Moscow.

The lights unexpectedly came on in shop windows, new stores opened that grew bigger and bigger. Again variety shows, casinos, and fine restaurants popped up, as if from underground. Movement returned to the streets: daredevil cab drivers, open carriages. Advertisements. Well-dressed men appeared from somewhere in capes and hats and holding canes. And the ladies: in the summer they carried parasols and wore dresses, and in the winter they walked in manteaus.

The inhabitants of the Dobrov house were still trying to survive on the ship rocking from side to side on the waves, but living conditions were being made tighter. People came in from the street and drove them out of their own kitchen. They divided part of Filipp Alexandrovich's office. As Olga wrote, "Tiny rooms with shadowy chimeras, divided from one another by Filipp Alexandrovich's bookcases. The dining room is divided from all these hovels, which seem like paradise to their inhabitants, by a heavy blue curtain hung on rings."

The Dobrovs themselves took in and fed the old Prince Urusov, who had neither a corner to live in nor a piece of bread to eat. Soon another dramatic event occurred: Elizaveta Mikhailovna Dobrova met at church a priest who had come from Siberia; on the way he had lost his wife – she died of typhoid – and for several days he had been living with his eight children under one of the bridges over the Moscow River. They had given him the opportunity to serve in the church on Levshinsky Lane. Elizaveta Dobrova invited him to their place for tea. He lay down on the sofa to rest and died. He too had been excruciatingly worn out, like many in those days. The Dobrovs managed to place his children in various foster homes, and the eldest daughter Serafima lived with them.

The lanes of the Arbat are still home to doctors and university professors. The employees of the State Academy of Arts, which had opened at the initiative of Lunacharsky in the former Polivanov gymnasium on Prechistenka Street, would meet at each other's homes, trying to escape all of their torments by seeking refuge in science and art, in service for the sake of culture and learning.

For the Dobrovs, there was no problem of choice: they continued, like they had done before, to live in accordance with their views on what was good and right.

Olga Bessarabova, meanwhile, was enormously impressed by Alexander Kovalensky. Every time he entered the house, she heard something new from him:

"Alexander Viktorovich is writing something about the Lemurians, about Lucifer, about Lilith, and about the Fall. He is the last in his line, and his ancestors go back seven centuries. His family has included cardinals and all kinds of remarkable people. There are even ghosts – everything in their home is as it should be! At night, it sounds like someone is walking around the house. Sometimes it is something bad, and sometimes it is good. They sometimes organize exorcisms and sprinkle the rooms with holy water. But as long as Alexander Viktorovich's manuscripts are there in the house, all kinds of apparitions are inevitable. He won't destroy them. For defending against evil forces, one can use prayer and a cross, but one shouldn't disturb the forces of light."

Alexander Kovalensky was a mystic, perhaps even a secret knight of some order. It is thought that he was a great influence on Daniil Andreyev.

Daniil experienced a special epiphany that he described years later in *The Rose of the World*:

"It happened in August 1921. It took place in Moscow, at the end of the day, when I had still not turned fifteen years old, and at the Christ the Saviour church. It was clearly already seven clock, because the churches were calling people to vespers... The experience that was revealed before me, or rather above me, was a raging, blinding, incomprehensible world that merged the historical reality of Russia into a strange oneness with something immeasurably larger above it. For many years afterward, my inner self was nourished by the images and ideas that gradually floated within the range of my consciousness."

At this time, mystical visions, which were experienced to excess by many people in the last years of the revolution and war, became for people like Kovalensky a personal "Faustian" path in search of Truth.

The spiritual longings of the intelligentsia, which partly fermented and produced the revolution, could not be satisfied by the socialist and communist idea. The new church life, with the persecution of Patriarch Tikhon and the appearance of "renewers", failed to convince many people. The small circles that arose in Moscow around priests like Fr. Alexei Mechev and several others, would be mercilessly persecuted, and the priests themselves would be exiled or shot.

Mystical societies, which had been popular even before the revolution, now became widespread among the intelligentsia, who were searching for new truths.

The rift in the fabric of time revealed an abyss, and sometimes from it various "knights and Rosacrucians" would appear, such as the improvisatory poet Boris Zubakin who was famous in Moscow, as well as followers of Roerich with their search for Shambhala. There were also various groups for fans of occult teachings, which drew many actors, directors, historians, and art critics. Sadly, out from this same abyss crawled people from the Joint State Political Directorate, who either joined these mystical associations themselves or recruited some of their members, and thus undid any spiritual movements that might emerge.

Later, nearly all members of these societies would be arrested.

A.A.S.

One of those "mystics" found mention in Olga Bessarabova's diary under the initials A.A.S. I long wracked my brains trying to determine who this might be. Olga wrote that her female friends in the Joy circle, the former pupils of Varvara

Grigoryevna, had come under the influence of mystical ideas. As she recorded in a diary entry:

Tanya and Zhenya finally introduced me to A.A.S. They both recommend me. When I went to see him, I was expecting impressed. However, I had a vaguely unpleasant feeling – I don't even know where, what, or why. My soul could not accept him. I don't even know what it would not accept.

I didn't like his hands. They were crooked, and the tips of the fingers were wide and flat. It was not the shape but rather some unpleasant gesture, predatory or something even worse. And his empty but eerily gleaming eyes. And then – I cannot explain this completely, I don't even understand it myself – I got scared (I didn't get scared, I felt ill at ease) by something looming and dark. I felt that I wanted to take my dear friends by the hand and lead them away from this cellar, this underground place with its rats and spiders. The room itself was ordinary and even well-lit. The whole time, I wanted to get out as soon as possible…

…I was staying at the Dobrovs', but late at night, after midnight, Tanya came and took me to her place. We talked for half an hour about things that could completely change my life and hers. Zhenya had apparently already lost her mind. …I told Tanya straight out about my vague, unpleasant feeling and even about the "looming and dark" thing. …Then we both laughed for some reason, and I showed her the gesture he had made with his hand, and I imitated his empty but eerily gleaming eyes, two or three ways in which he spoke, and two or three ways he had moved his head. …And then Tanya was shocked and told me that my caricatures of A.A.S. were awfully close to the truth.

The diary contained a note written later in the margin:

"1942. This man – the one in search of a New God, no matter what good he has done and so on – turned out to be an agent provocateur who caught and ruined a whole circle of young people. Tanya didn't fall into his web, and Zhenya was saved by a nervous breakdown, otherwise she would have perished, too."

Through various indirect suggestions, I found the name of this man in the book *Poetry and Prose by the Russian Knights Templar*.

He turned out to be a famous art historian, a professor at Moscow State University, who was never arrested and who lived until 1977. His name was Alexei Alexeyevich Sidorov.

It was claimed that this man had been sworn in as a mason and became a member of the Order even before the revolution. In 1927 he was sent to work at museums in Austria and Germany, and at the same time the purges began at the State Academy of the Study of Arts where he worked. He amassed an enormous collection of books, manuscripts, and drawings related to mysticism and esoteric teachings. He also had an enormous collection of erotic drawings. He was surrounded by young people, especially by impressed girls, who flew into his net like moths towards a flame.

He had a remarkable brother, Fr. Sergei Sidorov, who had been arrested four times and in 1937 was shot at Butovsky Polygon. This had no effect on Alexei Sidorov's fate, however.

A relative of his recalled, "the war years: dark streets, boarded-up windows, cold, feet freezing in worn shoes, a neverending feeling of hunger… I was a student then at the Moscow Mining Institute. With frozen hands I rang at the apartment in Bolshoi Afanasyevsky Lane where Alexei Alexeyevich lived in the 1940s. His wife opened the door in an extravagant robe, with red cheeks, brown eyes that shone, with a full and proud figure. After expressing her pleasant surprise, she led me into a room where, among the wardrobes and bookshelves up to the ceiling, there was a table covered with an embroidered tablecloth, a tall lamp shone under a golden silk lampshade, and everything had an air of prosperity… I was hiding my terrible feet in my wet and torn shoes under the chair, and I was offered tea and croissants with sausage like I had never seen in shops. A pleasant conversation about new books and poetry began… I was hungry as a wolf, but I tried to eat with good manners, and I never asked them for any help. Other people, my fellow students first of all, had helped me get through the institute, but Alexei Alexeyevich never gave me a single ruble all these years."

A.A.S. came to own Vladimir Solovyev's library and a complete set of Blavatsky's books. His engagement with mysticism gave him no peace, however. When his brother, the persecuted priest, came to visit him between periods of imprisonment, he felt sorry for the successful and assertive Alexei Alexeyevich, because he understood very well what the price for such success was.

At the end of the Thirties A.A.S. officially denied his priest brother.

Later in life, A.A.S. himself experienced hardships. His wife fell ill and died, and when he (nearly in old age) married again, suddenly his third wife died. Thus he left this life sick and alone.

This history harks back to the story of Cain and Abel.

The rift in the fabric of time, the break between eras produced stories that sounded like a biblical parable.

The non-commemorators

The brother of A.A.S., Fr. Sergei Sidorov, was the type of ordinary youth who, before the revolution, led the life of the enlightened intelligentsia, who studied at university, went to the theatre and concerts, and discussed the books they had read. The new times unexpectedly took people like him and made martyrs out of them like the first Christians. How could such a thing happen?

The same happened to his close friend, Mikhail Vladimirovich Shik. He was Fr. Mikhail, a man who was spiritually close to Olga Bessarabova and a good friend of hers, as well as of Varvara Grigoryevna Malakhieva-Mirovich.

Mikhail Vladimirovich Shik appears in Olga Bessarabova's diary as early as 1915–1916. At that time, she was lying in the hospital, and Shik together with Varvara Grigoryevna Malakhieva-Mirovich were visiting her.

Olga wrote that Mikhail gave off a feeling of goodness and understanding. Varvara Grigoryevna was once the governess to his sister. They lived in an enormous apartment in the Arbat. When he was still a student at the gymnasium he fell in love with Varvara Grigoryevna, who was eighteen years his elder. Mikhail's young love lasted almost a decade. After a series of disappointments and crises, Varvara Grigoryevna accepted this love – for her it became a real anchor. They even spent some time together.

Mikhail Vladimirovich belonged to a venerable old Jewish family. His father was an honorary citizen of the city of Moscow. Shik studied in the 5th Moscow Gymnasium along with Georgi Vernadsky, thanks to whom he met Natalya Shakhovskaya. Natalya loved him from a distance for all these years.

Olga Bessarabova wrote that when she saw Natalya Shakhovskaya for the first time, she understood immediately that her distinct personality, goodness, and self-denial made her similar to the Princess Mary in Tolstoy's *War and Peace*.

During the war Mikhail Vladimirovich served in the army and exchanged letters with Natalya Shakhovskaya. With time, he realized that they should never be apart. Before he married her, however, he decided to be baptized.

Varvara Grigoryevna served as his godmother, which meant a complete change in their relationship. His godfather was a close friend, Vladimir Favorsky. After his baptism, Natalya and Mikhail were married. Both of them decided that Varvara Grigoryevna was a part of their lives and should certainly be nearby. For the wedding, Varvara Grigoryevna gave Natalya her ring, which bore the inscription "The light of happiness. The light of Love. The light of transformation". Mikhail Shik had two rings on his hand: one for Natalya, and the other for Varvara. This gesture meant a sort of triple alliance, the union of three hearts.

I wasn't surprised at all by this story: neither the young man's attachment to an older woman, nor the decision of the young couple to not be apart from her. The great affection between these three people was so obvious that it was simply taken as a given.

In 1920 they settled in Sergiev Posad.

However, it soon became clear that their idealistic aspirations were untenable. A family was still just two, a husband and wife. Varvara was saved by the birth of Mikhail and Natalya's firstborn, Sergei. She took to him as her own son, and from this time everyone in the family called her "*baba* Vava"

In July 1925 Mikhail was ordained a deacon, but soon after this he was arrested. He was held in prison for half a year, and then he was exiled to Central Asia. By that time, Natalya Dmitrievna and him already had three children.

When he returned home in early 1928, Fr. Mikhail first served at the Ss. Peter and Paul church in Sergiev Posad, where Sergei Sidorov was the head priest. The last place he served was the St. Nicholas in the Straw Gate-house church in Moscow. Here, he and another priest were barred from service for their refusal to commemo-rate the metropolitan Sergei. Thus Fr. Mikhail became a "non-commemorator".

In the early 1930s the Shik-Shakhovskaya family managed to buy a house in Maloyaroslavl and move there, though now without Varvara. They built a secret house church in that house. Fr. Mikhail served there in secret, accepting his spiri-tual children that had come from Moscow. Among them were Tatyana Rozanova (the daughter of V. V. Rozanov), E. V. Men-zhinskaya (the daughter of Vyacheslav Menzhinsky, the Peo-ple's Commissar for the Joint State Political Directorate), and many others. The pianist Maria Yudina was also his spiritual daughter.

In early 1937 he was arrested again, and several months later, along with other priests including his friend Fr. Sergei Sidorov, he was shot at Butovsky Polygon.

During the war, the tuberculosis that Natalya Shakhovs-kaya, now a mother of five, had suffered since youth got wor-se. Doctors had categorically forbidden Shakhovskaya from having children, believing that it would kill her. However, her illness became worse from the hunger and incredible burdens of that terrible winter in wartime.

With the hope that her husband would nevertheless come out of prison someday, she wrote him a farewell letter before she died:

My dear, my precious friend, now my last spring has already passed. And what about you? Your fate is still a riddle and a mystery. A tiny hope remains that you will come back some day, but we won't meet, though I wanted to wait for you so much. There's no need to feel sorry, though. If you had come back, it would be even harder to part, and now my time has come…

Your name is sacred for the children. Praying for you is the deepest thing that binds them together. Sometimes I tell them some story so that for them, your spiritual image won't be erased. Mikhail, what great children we have! This terrible year of war has developed many qualities in them, it has made them brave, and it apparently hasn't done them harm.

Natalya Dmitrievna died at the Moscow Tuberculosis Institute on July 20, 1942. Varvara Grigoryevna Malakhieva-Mirovich was by her side.

I was shocked to find out that the five children of the shot priest Fr. Mikhail Shik and the princess Shakhovskaya had lived to our time.

After Olga Bessarabova's death in 1968, Varvara Grigoryevna's diaries were passed down to her godson, Dmitri Mikhailovich Shakhovskoy. He was the son of Mikhail Vladimirovich Shik and a sculptor. The diaries were kept in his workshop.

The missing link

If I had earlier first come across people and then archival materials, and I could get a feeling for an era through a particular person, now I was going in the opposite direction. First there were diaries that filled the space of life with their stories, and only later did I find the relatives of the characters within.

Something similar was described in Kaverin's book *The Two Captains*, when Sanya Grigoryev finds a bag of letters, the postman dead, and takes them to heart, hoping to later find the people the letters were addressed to. This was a very strange feeling, when you already know somebody quite well, you are used to them, and suddenly a relative of theirs comes along, and you are suddenly plunged into a different reality, one completely different from the one you imagined.

The diaries had gradually been gathered, commented on, and turned into a planned book with the efforts of various people who felt a sympathy for Olga Bessarabova. Now I needed the diaries of Varvara Grigoryevna Malakhieva-Mirovich. I had already seen some notes that Olga had written about them. The atmosphere of Moscow in the Thirties came to life in them, with the demolished churches, hungry people thronging the streets, the funerals of writer friends, and many other things. They could serve as a compass in my journey, which I realized could not simply end in 1925.

Soon I was talking with Dmitri Mikhailovich Shakhovskoy about meeting him at his home. I thought that when he saw how many important things had been revealed in Olga's diaries (he remembered them), he would immediately light up and give the diaries of Varvara Grigoryevna Malakhieva-Mirovich to a museum.

I took the trolleybus from the metro station to Nagornaya Street. Behind an iron fence in a small garden there stood a lovely two-story home, and on either side of the door there were two memorial plaques: one for Favorsky, and the other one for Yefimov, the very same painter of animal scenes and dollmaker who had once fallen in love with Olga Bessarabova in Sergiev Posad.

On the eve of the war, the painters had settled in this house built to their own design on a plot of land received from the Mossovet. Here they set up a workshop and a place to live. Dmitri Mikhailovich was the godson of not only Varvara Grigoryevna Malakhieva-Mirovich but also of his teacher Vladimir Favorsky. He later married Favorsky's daughter Maria.

Shakhovskoy met me at the gate. It was autumn, the garden was bare, without any leaves. Dogs running free, but who seemed to be well-fed, barked energetically. We walked up the old wooden stairs.

The house had been a workshop for several artists at the same time. The apartment, as well as Anna Stepanovna's room, again surprised me with a sense of time standing still. It seemed like this place too had frozen in the mid-1950s. Clearly everything had remained the same as in Favorsky's time. The house smelled just like my grandparents' apartment when I was little. I didn't see anything from our time. The room belonging to Dmitri Mikhailovich Shakhovskoy was austere, ascetic. A wooden table, a trestle bed with a faded bed cover, photographs of his father, mother, aunt hung on the wall, and pictures drawn by his grandchildren.

I figured that for the inhabitants of the house, this freezing of time must have meant something. It seemed like the clock of these peoples' lives had stopped or only measured the distance dividing them from the past.

I started to show Dmitri Mikhailovich typed-up pages from Olga's diary, passages that dealt with his parents. At first, it was the ones about his father who had come in 1916 with Varvara to visit Olga in the hospital, and then the wonderful remarks about his mother, Natalya Dmitrievna Shakhovskoy, who was similar to Maria in *War and Peace*. And then, the passages about Sergiev Posad.

However, our conversation didn't click. What had occupied me in the past years – literary life in the Soviet era, the tragedies and dramas of Soviet writers – did not interest him.

I thought he would understand, that I was not just acting here on my own. That everything that had happened to me of late, and especially the appearance of Olga's diary, connected us all at some point that was still not clear to me.

I looked at the books with Varvara Grigoryevna's diaries. They stood right there in the corner. To all of my attempts to persuade him to give them to a museum, so that they could be combined with Olga's diaries, Dmitri Mikhailovich responded that he should read them all again himself. He didn't refuse, he just gently held his own ground, and I lost hope that I would ever read these diaries.

Month after month, I would call and try to persuade him of how important it was to hear the voices from back then, from the past. About how so little had remained from that time.

Dmitri Mikhailovich either remained firmly silent or answered, that Varvara Grigoryevna was a person who would fantasize and make up stories, and no one should believe what she wrote in her diary. When I would talk of how the entries that Olga had written, had made a great impression on me, he responded that, the way he saw it, the diaries could not be published at all. My references to Tolstoy did not help. I could see that he heard what I was saying, but Varvara's time had not yet come.

Chapter 4.
The Moscow of
the Wanderers of the Night

Moscow in the Thirties:
the Dobrov home

Tiring splashes of a human wave,
A whirring chain of trams,
The brazen and harsh screams of cars,
A red star on a dark house...

A street-seller begging passers-by
To buy golden-brown pears "for cheap".
People without faces, deaf and mute,
Hurry to finish weaving the fabric of the day.

—Varvara Malakhieva-Mirovich

Olga Bessarabova had written bitterly about how the Dobrovs' home was divided up. "This house is a living piece of old Moscow in Maly Levshinsky Lane off Prechistenka Street. This house still holds on with the earnings of the father of the family, Dr. Dobrov. The place is stuffed with people off the street like a tram, but it still manages to keep breathing, it hasn't collapsed yet. By some miracle it is still in the hands of the fragile, elderly, and sickly lady of the house, Elizaveta Mikhailovna Dobrova."

The Thirties inevitably came, bringing with them grief and terror. In the passages from Varvara's diaries there were pictures with emaciated people filling the future Kievsky railway station. "The Bryansky railway station is crowded with the families of Ukrainians who have come looking for bread. The faces of starving Indians, without any Indian modesty. In their eyes are dark flames of envy and malice. In the eyes of the women feeding their tiny, scrawny newborns one sees pain, grief, and desperation."

The world of the Arbat lanes was fundamentally changing. Soon the Smolensky market would disappear along with its men bringing heavy loads on carts (these huge men could bend horseshoes with their hands). The B tram would no longer go through crowds of buyers and sellers.

Here are some of the street scenes that Olga Bessarabova copied out from the diaries of Varvara Grigoryevna Malakhieva-Mirovich:

Why are you pushing? – You're the one pushing. – Idiot – You're the idiot. Ow, you stepped on my foot. – Your foot? So what? – Someone pressed up against my chest! – You're an old lady, who cares about your chest? – What, you think you're so special? – Where are you going with that bag? – And where you are going with that kerosene?

Yes, these are the times we live in. The tram, Moscow. You off the tram here on this corner. Why are the ones over there walking their path of suffering. And the people here with their "someone pressed up against my chest!" and pushing and shoving. And how vulgar the cinema is.

And the rats in the cheap eateries ("on the plate of one of the people dining there," says the newspaper).

The poor peasants in the streets, in bast shoes and homespun clothes, stand outside bakeries and ask not for money but for bread. How did the people who so prolifically penned those happy Soviet poems and songs not see all this?

And they are not accepting packages with food at the post office.

In 1933 kerosene suddenly disappeared from the shops. "They started giving kerosene out according to a quota for every person present… A three-digit number was written with a marker on people's palms."

With bitter irony Varvara Grigoryevna noted, "The poet Kovalensky is making toys (he was forced to take this up) – skiers, airplanes, and dragonflies. There are no earnings from literature. Lyrics are flourishing, though, they flow freely. The poet Daniil Andreyev is drawing diagrams. The poet Iris is correcting articles about soil. And yet this doesn't stop lyrics from flourishing. 'Are the high priests now sweeping the streets?' Yes, it so happens that they are. Old Mirovch (as Varvara Grigoryevna sometimes referred to herself) is sweeping the floors (literally), and there's nothing wrong with this."

Poems were still being written, everyone worked as they were accustomed to, but in the Dobrov home they were taking in people who had nowhere in Moscow to live, including Varvara Grigoryevna.

The house, that little ship was now tilting and its timbers were squeaking.

Once Varvara Grigoryevna thought about how amazingly Dobrov corresponded to his own surname, which came from the word *dobro* "good". Besides hospitality, another strong quality of their home was the tradition of friendship and understanding, along with total selflessness. Although all of the members of the family had their own griefs and shattered nerves, everyone who came here left cured and with a heart-warming feeling.

A person in the Soviet Union needed to be long-suffering more than anything else.

Alexander Kovalensky was long-suffering. He lived with back problems, he wrote poems that no one seemed to need, and he made toys to earn a living. Daniil was long-suffering, he also wrote poems that no one seemed to need, and to earn a living he drew graphs, charts, and took other odd design work. Shurochka was long-suffering, she adored her husband, but she was unable to help him.

All of them were forced to get by in large part from the earnings of Dr. Dobrov, who was already getting on in years. The house had long since been without an office where he could receive patients. Instead, only a corner remained behind a curtain, where his old and worn sofa stood, and where he would lie down with a volume of classical poetry when he came home tired from work.

From Zubovsky Boulevard to the Arbat: secrets of the Moscow home churches

Another city lived on in the lanes, however, one hidden from view. From diaries and other documents, I discovered a secret layer of Moscow life, which only involuntarily vibrated and almost didn't even reveal its presence. It remained known from oral accounts, vague references to names and surnames which started to make sense only when one put various facts together, and mentions of lost memoirs – all of this together led to hitherto unknown images of the hidden City which held on and refused to die.

It is from this combination of the secret City and the visible City that Daniil Andreyev wove his novel *Wanderers of Night*.

These were secret Moscow home churches that arose in the place of the Renovationist Church. One of them was located in the home of a former classmate of Daniil. Her name was Zoya Kiseleva, and her apartment had a so-called "Kiseleva" chapel.

One of Zoya's contemporaries wrote about her, "I came into the apartment… I met a girl with an indescribable beauty: the classical lines of her face, shining with a Byzantine spirit; her strict profile and the perfect oval of her wide face, with its delicately glowing cheeks; her chestnut-colored braids were twice woven around her head; her thick brows with a sad downward tilt; her gray eyes that shone with an inner light; lips of a classical shape as if drawn with a brush. She was above the average height, with a slim figure, and full of youth and good health. She was wearing a simple summer dress without any jewelry or accessories. I find myself looking at her involuntarily and cannot turn my eyes away."

Zoya and her mother lived in an apartment reached through the inner courtyard of an old building on Zubovsky Boulevard. The box-shaped building of the Progress publishing house would soon rise up here. In this building there was a secret house church that Daniil Andreyev attended along with some other members of the Dobrov family.

There was a spacious living room here with a leather sofa and armchairs. A mystical picture hung on the wall that depicted the demolition of the old cathedral at the Sretensky monastery. A door led from the living room to another room, the walls of which were completely covered with icons. For confession, people would go into a small closet next to the kitchen that held an old crucifix wrought in silver. It is simply amazing that in spite of the arrests and exile, this secret community as well as several others existed in Moscow. Peculiar elders came from far away, but their names were never uttered aloud. People served here and helped each other. They communicated in a secret language understood only to each other and almost never let outsiders in.

As the painter Semper-Sokolova, who had made the Kiselevs acquaintance at a dacha, recalled, "...I was at their place in Moscow on Zubovsky Boulevard a couple of times (the boulevard was famous for its linden trees and the dandelions in the thick grass). At the end of the courtyard, a tiny detached house abutted the wall of the neighboring building. There were three little steps, a vestibule, and a door leading right into the dining room. On the dining-room table there was a heap of little bags, packages, and bundles. The chairs held plywood boxes for sending parcels... They were sending eleven parcels to Ukraine. As a result of the forced collectivization and the merciless hoarding of grain, a nightmarish famine had broken out. The state took utterly everything from the farmers, people died by the thousands, their bodies rotted in their huts and in the village streets... Such a thing can neither be understood, nor forgiven, nor forgotten. I stood there for a while, looking, but I felt that I didn't belong there and I soon left. I was subconsciously embarrassed by their moral superiority."

Zoya Kiseleva herself was under the enormous religious influence of Nadezhda Stroganova, who had a secret house church in one of the lanes of the Arbat.

The house church was located in two small rooms side by side. In the first room lay a priest who was nearly a hundred years old; women from the house church took turns in attending to him. They had made forged documents for him. In the other room, the walls of which were covered with icons, secret meetings took place. The uniqueness of this community also lay in the fact that it had its own rescue service for people facing persecution from the Bolsheviks. They would bring in their own doctors, who could forge a diagnosis and place these persecuted figures in a hospital as if they were ill, and they would give them passports that had formerly belonged to the deceased. There was one former White officer who would occasionally spend half a year in a psychiatric clinic, pretending to be mentally ill and living under a pseudonym. This was a very conspiratorial church underground. Items for serving the liturgy would be brought in through the back door: golden crosses, cups, golden coins from the tsar's time. People trusted Stroganova completely. These golden items were melted down, and they used the gold to support the poor, those hunted by the state, the ill, and the persecuted priests and their families.

"Nadezhda Alexandrovna Stroganova," the painter wrote, "was the wife of a scholar… She was a woman in her sixties, with a sharp wit and irascible temperament. Her appearance is of an antique type that I was fortunate to find in a living person: a dry, dark face, burning black eyes that go right through you… Her hair was put back, but carelessly pinned, her dark-gray locks stuck out from her old-fashioned hairdo… She wore a loose black dress without a belt that extended from her neck to the floor, with narrow sleeves reaching to her fingers. The dress hung over her thin, energetic frame."

In the early 1930s, Zoya Kiseleva fell in love with the painter Sergei Ivashov-Musatov. Their feelings were mutual, but he was married and he and his wife had had a church wedding. Nevertheless, he decided to get a divorce. The young lady tried to fight her feelings, but she couldn't hold it any longer, and she agreed to a civil marriage. However, Stroganova had an enormous influence on Kiseleva and strongly opposed her decision. In her opinion, Zoya was meant to be the soul of the house church, that is, a nun living in the world, and the young lady heeded her. The painter wanted to take his own life. They say that it was Daniil Andreyev who convinced his close friend not to take this mad step. When the painter came to his senses, he divorced his wife and three years later proposed to another painter, the young Alla Bruzhes. She lived with him for seven years, and then she left him for Daniil Andreyev, whose wife she became. Thus a shattered love gave birth to another marriage, the consequences of which are hard to overestimate.

Fate took one other turn. Alexander Kovalensky had become a repressed person in the "Andreyev affair" and had buried his beloved Shurochka Dobrova after she had died in a labor camp in Mordovia. When Kovalensky returned from the gulag, he started going to the Kiselevs. He had known Zoya already before the war. He didn't have a place of his own to stay at, and the Dobrovs' home no longer existed. The Kiselevs fed him, and for a while he thought that he could marry Zoya. She liked him very much, too, but this time their relatives stood in the way. In the end, Kovalensky was taken in by another former classmate of Daniil Andreyev, a woman who had been in love with him since they were young.

After the destruction of the community around the priest Fr. Mechev, which nourished most of the Moscow intelligentsia, some followers of the catacomb church began to attend the church of Ilya Obydenny. Some still hid in secret house churches, but only such close-knit communities could survive in Moscow who had been proven for years and who believed that they lived in the USSR under conditions of occupation.

This secret world hidden from view could have been revealed to us by Daniil Andreyev's *Wanderers of Night*.

The wanderers of night

The title of Andreyev's novel Wanderers of Night refers to all of us who remained in Russia to live and die here.

—From the memoirs of the painter Alexei Smirnov

Moscow in a haze of blood

—From the diary of V. G. Malakhieva-Mirovich

At the entrance to Dr. Dobrov's apartment, there was a staircase with seven steps, the sort that were often found in old Moscow apartments. Along the sides of this staircase there were banisters, and on the left, under some clothes worn in the house, if you lifted a wooden board, a niche would be revealed that hid Daniil Andreyev's *Wanderers of Night* about life in Moscow in 1937.

The novel disappeared into the depths of the MGB, the staircase disappeared, too, as did the house where the Dobrov family lived, and the writer and mystic Daniil Andreyev had grown up. Only Maly Levshinsky Lane was left.

I knew that the novel had disappeared. However, it lived on in paraphrases by Daniil Andreyev's wife Alla and his friends.

When Andreyev returned in the summer of 1937 from Sudak, where he had spent several months resting, he found an everyday life that had been abruptly transformed: many friends and relatives had disappeared, Moscow by night became a city where arrests constantly took place, the car tires would squeal towards dark entrances to buildings, and door-bells rang in the dead silence of the apartments. The novel *Wanderers of Night*, which he started writing in the same year, begins with precisely these things.

The main character Alexander Gorbov (it is understood that this is an allusion to the surname Dobrov) has returned from an archaeological excavation, and he finds out that his native city has swallowed up a portion of its inhabitants. The darkness of totalitarianism has turned the hours of sleep and rest into a horrible time of death. One of the first chapters was entitled "Martyrology"; in this chapter, the protagonist's mother lists all of the people known to her, friends and relatives, who had been arrested in recent months.

The novel's action takes place at night and has two poles: the intelligentsia, which is trying to find a way to save Russia, and the all-seeing Eye of Lubyanka, the black pit which is filled with an increasing number of victims.

In an attic in Yakimanka, a group of people meet as dusk falls. They ensure their neighbor is away at the time by buying him a ticket to the Bolshoi Theatre.

The scholar Glinksy, an indologist, is involved in one of the novel's main plot lines. He has gathered in his apartment those who reject communism, socialism, and atheism. During this evening and night, he tells his friends of how one epoch is constantly replaced by another in Russia, the red and the blue.

"The essence of Glinsky's theory," Alla Andreyeva recalled, "lies in the alternation of red and blue epochs in the history of Russia as he saw it. In a red epoch, material values dominate, while a blue one is marked by spiritual values. Each historical era has two layers: the color of the aspirations of the dominant part of society is ascendant, and in each epoch there is always an underground movement of the opposite color. Later, after it has matured and gathered strength, this underground becomes the dominant color and is linked to the authorities of the next epoch, while the power and currents that were formerly on top retreat to the underground. As historical time progresses, the alternation of the two epochs becomes increasingly faster, and their colors burn brighter. In the depths of history, any material aspiration has never lost its spiritual tinge, while any spiritual one has never broken its connection with the world. What is relevant here is the structure of government, and not an ascetic act – that is something else. However, often this ascetic deed, as if it were detached from this world, is undertaken not for saving oneself but for the salvation of the whole world."

This conception finds an echo in Varvara Grigoryevna Malakhieva-Mirovich's diaries from 1937. She had probably read Andreyev's novels, and perhaps it was under the novel's influence that she wrote, "On Ostozhenka Street, gray crowds of demonstrators trail on and on, holding red banners drooping from the humidity. When will they be replaced with another color? I don't want to see anything that reminds me of blood. I imagine our nation's flag after the revolutionary period as green and blue."

The two of them, close in spirit, wanted a future of a different color.

During that evening meeting, Glinsky was a real spy who had entered into a group of friends.

Alla Andreyeva wrote that according to the author's conception, Glinsky was linked to a foreign intelligence agency and was member of a real anti-Soviet organization. He was involved in planning terrorist attacks and waiting for the opportunity to finally take action. This character clearly came to Andreyev from the Soviet anti-espionage propaganda of the time.

"Alexei Yuryevich Serpukhovskoy is an economist. He is a bitter and sarcastic fellow, with the elegance and upright bearing of an officer. He possesses clear thinking and a sharp mind. In his report at the meeting, he unleashes a torrent of criticism concerning the Soviet economy. He lays out the economic basis of life and society as it should be in the free Russia of the future."

He was counting on young people and the possibility that they might protest. However, during this evening he is disappointed, he feels that the youth is incapable of changing anything. He returns home on foot across Moscow by night. He passes Lubyanka: the huge building has lights in every window while the rest of the city is plunged in darkness – this was due to the nighttime interrogations going on in its offices.

One of the people arrested in the "Andreyev affair" recalled, "When he (Andreyev) was sent to the front, he dug a hole at his aunt's dacha and hid the manuscript in it. After the war, he dug it up. The traces of ink on the manuscript had been greatly effaced... This novel was actually not about Stalin's cult of personality, but rather about the anti-Soviet sentiments of the Moscow intelligentsia during the Soviet era. There were no revolutionaries in the novel, but one of the characters had 'terrorist sympathies' (the other characters did not suspect anything). Curiously, the people who were arrested were asked under interrogation about this character as if he were a real, living person."

Eventually, when the novel itself had been arrested, the investigators treated it like a factual document. They started to seriously hunt for the Serpukhovskoy group, questioning all kinds of people about it. This character was a real find for the investigators of the MGB; the novel featured the foreign agent they had long been waiting for. The only thing the investigators had to do was to create a real person from the character in the novel, while the other characters' thoughts about the future of Russia did not interest them much.

The three Gorbov brothers have roles in the novel: Sasha (again a name popular in the Dobrovs' home) is an archaeologist, while Oleg is a painter and sign-writer, who in his appearance and personality resembles the author. The third brother is the most unusual of the three, for Adrian is an astronomer who is studying the Andromeda galaxy. Adrian was based on Alexander Viktorovich Kovalensky, the husband of Shurochka Dobrova. Shurochka herself is present in the novel in the form of Irina Glinskaya, a young lady in love with Adrian. Her fiance in the novel is Oleg Gorbov.

The couple agree to swear themselves to celibacy after the wedding that was to take place soon in the Ivan Voin church on Yakimanka Street.

Adrian Gorbov combines two ideas within himself.

On one hand, he studies the cosmos and dreams of a universal symbol of Good that he sees incarnated in the Andromeda galaxy. The metaphor for cosmic harmony is a bouquet of bird-cherry, little flowers that resemble constellations. The bouquet stands in Adrian's room with its window that looks out at the wall of another building.

At the same time, the "The Demon Seated" by Vrubel hangs on the wall of the room. Lucifer, whom Adrian's prototype Alexander Kovalensky wrote poems about and sometimes considered himself the acolyte of, would come to life in Adrian Gorbov's thoughts, as he thought that the powers of evil were triumphant on Earth, and Christ had not succeeded in defeating them.

The character decides to repeat the act of Christ: to die and then be resurrected in order to renew the world and make it free of evil.

In *The Rose of the World*, the "Demon Seated" by Vrubel would be referred to as an infernal portrait, "the icon of Lucifer".

At the end of the novel, Adrian shakes off his mad thought. He is saved by the love of Irina Glinskaya.

The novel no longer exists, but a poem by Daniil Andreyev from 1937 does survive:

Morning. Drizzle. Damp bitterness.
Away from the gates of the heaven grown dim
Day and hunger with their cruel scourges
Drive us into concrete cages.

By night, soothsayers and magicians,
During the day we hunch over a pile of papers,
We scurry between plywood sheets –
Us, bookkeepers and engineers.

We polish the dormant volcano,
We march to the accompaniment

                           of the heavy pestle,

Following the incessant orders
We grind our mind.

The rings get smaller and smaller,
And about the truth of the holy night,
Walking with little steps around an even circle,
We do not dare to whisper to one another.

We unite in an energizing anthem,
We gasp... Help us,
Break the concrete apart at least for a second,
Almighty!

In the novel Glinsky ends up being arrested. After another interrogation, he is thrown into a packed jail cell. Unconsciously, without even knowing how or why, he begins to pray. His prayer is taken up by an Orthodox priest and then by a mullah. Thus they all pray together. The next day, at another interrogation, Glinsky says everything that he thinks about the authorities, about Stalin, and about his fallen country. At the end of this impassioned speech, blood begins to issue from his throat and he dies.

It should not be forgotten that all of this was written in 1937. Years later, Daniil Andreyev told his wife how everything he had written had horribly come true: being arrested, taken to Lubyanka, marched down its corridors, and the interrogations.

In the shadows of the Arbat lanes: Daniil Andreyev and Nikolai Stefanovich

Well, this isn't so terrible, is it?

—Nikolai Stefanovich

Other figures literally wandered through nighttime Moscow at the end of the Thirties. Besides Daniil Andreyev and his friends, who quickly ducked into secret house churches, and corners where the un-Soviet youth gathered and where unofficial poems were read – strange people walked the city streets. One of them admitted that he did not see his reflection in mirrors. His name was Nikolai Stefanovich.

On July 24, 1941, during the bombardment of Moscow, a bomb hit the Vakhtangov Theatre. The theatre's leading actor Vasily Kuza was killed. The inhabitants of the Arbat long remembered how bits of theatre sets were scattered all along the street.

Nikolai Stefanovich, an actor and poet who was working at the theatre at the time, miraculously survived, but he was injured and became handicapped. He lived nearly the theatre at the intersection of the lanes Starokonyushenny and Kaloshin. He played episodic roles, but the main task of his life was poetry. He was a poet in secret, however, and he tried to preserve and carry on in his verse the Silver Age tradition of Russian poetry that had been destroyed.

He walked the same streets and little lanes as Daniil Andreyev. Stefanovich's lines are literally oversaturated with the features of Moscow in the 1930s and 1940s.

Three-story buildings, puddles, ropes hung with laundry, attics with tin roofs, the filthy and spit-spattered boulevard, cigarette butts and leftovers of food, wet benches – all of this was only the background against which the central figure of his poems lived.

This sleepwalker, this self-contained person who carefully reconstructs images from childhood, as poets often do, had experienced an unrequited love – in a strong and talented fashion – and then would suddenly be distracted by some other obsessive topic. Although this figure really exists – he rides trams and walks down the street – he is in fact dead. He constantly keeps slipping down in the grave that lies in wait at every step. The poet depicts himself not as a dead man among the people, as Blok did, but rather as a veritable corpse, a decomposing cadaver.

"I fall into pieces / And damp mold covers me…" Or: "The itchiness of decomposition comes over me, / The hiccuping of the soul from the grave…"

The most characteristic theme for Nikolai Stepanovich, however, is the story of Judas's betrayal.

Everyone was struck dumb by fright, / They looked down, perplexed, / When Judas hung himself on the tree. / The apostle wordlessly swung / With his chin flung downward… / This is not difficult, it's simple, / Well, this isn't so terrible, is it?

It remains unclear what the last lines mean, "This is not difficult, it's simple.". Is he referring to suicide? Or betrayal? Or both of them at once?

Nikolai Stefanovich returned from the evacuation; he had known Daniil Andreyev since May 1941 and now, after the war, he again began to visiting him at the Dobrovs' home. These two men resembled one another in a strange way. They had both studied at the Literary Courses, and both secretly traced their creative roots back to the Silver Age.

When, years later, Alla Andreyeva wrote about his arrest, she probably was already aware of whose testimony was the basis for the case against her husband. "…he was such a dear friend to Daniil in some kind of spiritual kinship, however strange it might seem… I could only marvel at how they could understand one another with only a word, how they read poems to one another. It's like how they say, they 'found one another', as if two close people had finally met. I don't know whether that man was working for the secret police or whether they simply called on him to do so, but either way, he denounced us."

It seemed as if there were two sides to one and the same person. Light and darkness.

The most mysterious thing of all, however, is that Daniil Andreyev's *Wanderers of Night* contains a character that is very similar to Nikolai Stefanovich.

This was the mentally unstable Venedikt Lestovsky, the cousin of the main characters, the Gorbov brothers.

"However strange it might seem," Alla Andreyeva wrote, "it was this character, a partly negative one (though there are no completely negative characters in the novel), that the author endowed with his own qualities, which were furthermore caricatured… I don't remember where he had worked, what dull job he did for some miserable salary; by that time, he had already quit the job to dedicate himself fully to a strange and downright criminal idea. He lived in a small and empty little room in a communal apartment."

This character is passionately in love in the novel's main female character, Irina Glinskaya. He pursues her relentlessly. Eventually he discovers that the apartment she shares with her brother is used by a group of people that dream of changing the Soviet Union. After that, his warped mind gives rise to a series of thoughts. He gives Irina an ultimatum: either she spend one night with him, or he will go to Lubyanka and report their anti-Soviet group. Irina is appalled as she listens to him listing the names of people he would denounce. She tries to suppress her disgust and asks him for more time to decide. Venedikt loses hope, and this line of the novel's plot ultimately ends with him wandering through the dark streets of Moscow by night with a turbulent mind.

As we know from people close to the author, the novel had already been completed before the war, and then Daniil only put some finishing touches on it. It is thus all the most remarkable that Venedikt Lestovsky's story completely agrees with what had happened to Nikolai Stefanovich on the eve of World War II. It could have hardly been known to Daniil Andreyev – it was already too self-explanatory – but the facts remain.

For a long time, almost nothing was known about the odd and mysterious poet Nikolai Stefanovich. Years later, however, the fog around him began to clear.

On the site of the Sakharov Center, the memoirs of Alexander Borin were published. He had spent ten years in prison, and on the eve of the war he had been attending meetings of a poetry circle, meetings that Nikolai Stefanovich often came to.

Not long before a bomb destroyed the Vakhtangov Theatre and turned the odd poet then working there into a cripple, the summer of 1941 in Moscow saw numerous arrests made of participants of a poetry circle that met in an apartment in Vetoshny Lane, around October 25 Street (now Nikolskaya). The last member of this group to be arrested, already at the beginning of the war, on August 1, 1941, was the engineer and architect Alexander Borin, who was working in Antonov's design offices in Saratov at the time. Though his recollections of these events are somewhat chaotically arranged, many things became clear in this human tragedy that, like many others, had passed largely unnoticed.

While Alexander Borin was still a free man, he talked with the relatives of his arrested peers and already heard at that time that Nikolai Stefanovich might be implicated in their arrests. He didn't at all agree, however. Everyone in his circle considered Nikolai a brilliant poet. This esteem helped Stefanovich avoid any suspicion.

Then, when the investigator presented Borin with a typed-up report made by one of the visitors to their poetry circle, Borin clearly recognized in it the style and tone of Nikolai Stefanovich. "Not only conversations that had taken place particularly in his presence that were reported as quintessential anti-Soviet malice, but most importantly his handwriting, his soaring and strident voice, which could not be confused with anyone else's or faked."

There was one more proof however, the most devastating one: of the entire group, Stefanovich was the only person who was never arrested.

Once he found himself in prison, Alexander Borin began recalling step by step how Stefanovich had come to their circle. No one had known him before this period. He showed up among them as if out of nowhere.

Once Alexander Borin, as one of the group, was riding on a packed tram, and suddenly someone stepped on his foot. This person suddenly began to apologize in an ornate and old-fashioned style, which immediately won Borin over. This strange was clutching Nikolai Gumilev's *The Pillar of Fire* to his chest and this made for a mutual affinity between the two. A lively and highly interesting conversation ensued, and the young men left the tram and walked together for some time. After one of Borin's friends heard this story, he immediately felt that such a chance meeting in the street was highly suspicious. It was the late 1930s, and everyone was very careful. But Borin heatedly claimed that they wouldn't be able to resist his new acquaintance, and that all of their doubts would vanish by themselves.

As Borin recalled, "Nikolai soon appeared among our little band and charmed everyone, men and women alike, with the simplicity, his genuine intellectual quality, the magnificent way he recited poems, and most of all, his talent as a poet. The tension deep within his poems was combined with a freespirited quality, which was the mark of a true poet. The first poem of his that he recited so impressed me, that I learned it by heart."

His poems dazzled all. They couldn't hear the looming threat in the lines "Hiding from God behind corners..." or "Losing my human shape..." These were unusual lines that sounded like nothing else.

As he recited poems, Nikolai was completely transformed. His serious and low-key demeanor became unusually – though not exaggeratedly – distinguished, and his deep-set brown eyes gleamed strangely. I myself even found it unnatural, but it wasn't repellent. Rather, it was the opposite, it was attractive. Generally, like other people, I felt a strange pull towards him. Talking with him wasn't merely interesting, it was a real pleasure... He had thoughts that were insightful and often highly original, and he gave a friendly attention to whoever he was talking to. He even showed what I might call a strange charity... He would respond with a charming readiness, except for cases when his evenings were busy with rehearsals.

He was a small-time actor, playing minor roles at the Vakhtangov Theater.

"Do you trod the boards, Nikolai?" I asked.

"Yes, I trod the boards," he answered with an unfeigned sense of regret.

Perhaps Alexander Borin's belief that Stefanovich played a role in the arrest of his poetry circle, was a mistake or a coincidence?

As he sat in his cell, however, Borin remembered how his little group was coming back from celebrating New Year's, and then Tamara, the fiancée of a friend of his, began talking to him. She asked him if Nikolai Stefanovich seemed funny to him. Borin responded that he didn't understand why she was asking. Tamara then told him that Stefanovich was following her, walking behind her everywhere, and demanding that she reciprocate his feelings for her. When she refused, he suddenly threatened, "You'll all be sorry."

After Borin had heard this, he told Tamara that she shouldn't take his threats too seriously. It then came to him that the arrest of the whole group had been Stefanovich's revenge for this young lady's refusal. However, the more Borin thought about what his other arrested friends had said, the more he was inclined to think that this could hardly have been the motive for their arrest. Rather, the poet must have been sent to infiltrate their group, and he had found a way to rationalize his betrayal.

Thus, in 1942 when the war was at its height, nine members of the poetry circle were charged of organizing a counter-revolutionary terrorist cell not far from the Kremlin. The basis for this accusation were various conversations, including ones that Nikolai Stefanovich had reported. It wasn't only Borin who found a similarity to Stefanovich's style in the reports. Other members of the circle did as well when, on the eve of their closed trials, they could share their suspicions.

The sentences were barbaric: four members were sentenced to be shot, while the others got long sentences in the gulag.

If this story that entered the novel – Venedikt Lestovsky blackmailing Irina Glinskaya, directly corresponding to Tamara's story – is a coincidence, then it is clearly the result of Daniil Andreyev's mystical insight into the things going on around him.

The Dobrovs' home:
the arrest of Daniil Andreyev

The arrest of Daniil Andreyev took place in a very strange way. It happened in 1947, when Daniil was seemingly called to give a lecture in Kharkov, but in fact the car sent to pick him up took him to Lubyanka instead. Literally the day before, Nikolai Stefanovich had taken a bound manuscript of *Wanderers of Night* from Daniil Andreyev. Then, Stefanovich suddenly and unexpectedly returned to give it back.

As Alla Andreyeva wrote:

He called in a very agitated state:

"How is Daniil Leonidovich?"

I answered, "He's fine. A telegram came from Kharkov."

He sounded very happy. Perhaps he thought that everything wasn't so bad after all. He said that he wanted to bring the novel back. I told him not to worry:

"There's no rush. Daniil will be back in two days, bring it then."

"No, no, I'm going to bring it now."

He brought the book. He didn't even come in, he just passed it to me over the threshold. Daniil had bound the manuscript.

Stefanovich was never called in, never interrogated, and never arrested. The fact that no one was shot in connection to Andreyev's case is a real miracle. This was the lone year when capital punishment was unexpectedly replaced with a 25-year sentence to the gulag. In the following year, after the sentences in the "Andreyev affair" had already been passed, the shootings were resumed.

"Will I forget about the tender evening, / About someone's confusing address, / About how my whole life, / Has been crossed out by own hands?" Nikolai Stefanovich wrote these lines in 1948, not long after Andreyev's arrest.

Nonetheless, the question remains of how Stefanovich could go on living with this heavy burden, with a broken spirit and the lamentation of a Judas. He went on living, but he knew that he was already a dead man.

I think that the explanation lies in the fact that he saw himself as a special being, one of a higher order. Everywhere and always he stood at the center of the world. Though he called himself a dead man, he had almost a primordial fear of death.

"Some awful germ – / You lick a envelope / And right away there's coughing and shivering, / A suffocating pillow and death…"

The idea of an artist as an Übermensch appeared in the Silver Age tradition. The Soviet era that Stefanovich lived in, was a world in which "God was dead" and the world was left without HIs care.

"A gloomy era, / The stars reign as they want, / When there's no God, / What's wrong becomes right."

He did not resist these dark times. He did everything that this dark epoch demanded of him.

And although his life had indeed been crossed out, he continued to write poems. He sent them in the early 1950s to his favorite poet, Boris Pasternak, and received a reply expressing great admiration.

Those who managed to survive did not try to meet Stefanovich. However, in his letters to Alla Andreyeva from the Vladimir prison, Daniil Andreyev wrote that he had forgiven him. Only Alexander Borin tried once to visit him at home and to look in his eyes, but Stefanovich's loyal sister, who had spent her entire life at his side, said that her brother was seriously ill, and she did not allow Borin in.

Nikolai Stefanovich died in 1979.

Like many other poets, David Samoylov was extremely moved by Stefanovich's poems, which showed great talent but were known to almost no one. Samoylov decided to organize an evening event around Stefanovich's work. In his *Everyday Notes (Podennye zapisi)*, Samoylov describes the scandal that ensued:

I was presiding over an evening in memory of Stefano-vich, and five minutes before it was due to begin, an unknown young lady who resembled Gorbanevskaya handed me a letter from one Alexander Arkadyevich Borin. The letter stated that Stefanovich had sent nine men to prison before the war, and of them only Borin survived. I was requested to read this letter out loud.

The letter was no proof, of course, but I was at a loss as I opened the meeting, and I couldn't say everything that I had prepared beforehand.

I called Borin the next day. He was insistent that what he had written in the letter was true. Due to his health (he had already suffered six heart attacks), we could not meet.

As a result of my "investigations" into Stefanovich, both sides were upset with me: neither needed any proof.

When Borin later gave his story to a young man, a future poet, he would claim that on the day when Nikolai Stefanovich had denounced the others at Lubyanka, he had read Borin his poem "Judas": "…The apostle wordlessly swung / With his chin flung downward… / This is not difficult, it's simple, / Well, this isn't so terrible, is it?"

The Moscow–Kiev train

In the summer, when preparations for publishing Olga Bessarabova's diaries was already underway, Moscow was full of thick smoke from the forest fires raging around the city. At the time, I was proofreading the index of names. I soaked bedsheets and hung them over the window. An hour later, the bedsheets had already dried and turned yellow. The numbers and letters floated before my eyes like motes of dust. Moscow resembled a military area. Almost no one was out in the streets. Sometimes people emerged into view as if they were coming out of a cloud of steam. The metro was covered in the same smoke as the streets.

I started traveling to Kiev often. My son had recently moved there.

I knew that Kiev was Varvara Grigoryevna Malakhieva-Mirovich's city. The relics of St. Barbara, whom Varvara Grigoryevna and her mother had been named after, were also in Kiev. Every time I crossed the bridge over the Dnieper on the train and the domes of the Lavra came into view, I asked Varvara to help me get the diaries from Dmitri Mikhailovich. I told her that she, too, wanted at least some pages of her poems and even some of her diaries to be published. I asked her to make some effort as well.

In the train that I got on, only three hours after we had left Moscow did the acrid smoke finally stop burning my eyes. I felt that I was coming back to life. I now noticed a nice lady sitting before me. We started talking.

When I told her that I work in the museum, she happy to hear that for some reason, and she began to explain how she needed to look in the archives for the stories of her ancestors. She then started to tell me how her great-grandfather had been a priest, who was exiled to somewhere beyond the Urals and there lived with his family. One day her grandmother was raped by an NKVD man, who then proposed that they marry. Her grandmother got pregnant and was forced to agree to this. Her great-grandfather did not bless this marriage.

I asked her how she knew that her grandmother had been raped.

"She never hid the fact. My NKVD grandfather was 'lucky', he died in the war. My father, who was born from this rape, was terribly proud of my grandfather, and he couldn't forgive my grandmother for hating him."

I shuddered as I listened to what she was telling me. The simplicity with which this woman told her story made me feel uneasy. One could have talked in the same way about one's dacha or making pickles. This part of history sounded like some ordinary thing.

I turned my attention to my reading. Nonetheless, the woman continued to speak, and her tone lost its mundane quality. Now she started talking about what was going on with her now. She broke down and almost started crying. Her son-in-law was in prison, and her daughter had become pregnant after visiting him there. Now, her daughter had a little son who lived his father and she was going to wait for him. However, her son-in-law had committed a serious crime. She didn't want to say what he had done exactly, but her daughter wanted to be only with him.

I listened to this and could only answer, "You realize yourself that this story of how your father was born, is similar to what is happening now?"

"I realize that," she replied. "But what am I supposed to do with all this?"

Starosadsky Lane:
the fire at the Historical Library

When I was young and working at the Historical Library located behind Solyanka Street on the Ivanovskaya Gorka, we once received some issues of *Biblioteka dlya chteniya* ("Reading Library") for restoration. Among the pages, there were a few thin photographs.

A family was sitting in a field somewhere among the flowers: a boy, a girl, a lady in a white dress carrying a parasol, and a man with a mustache. Then, they were all walking together down a path. Then, the children were posing on a bench. The photographs had been taken before the revolution. Among the photos there was an amusing note addressed to a teacher – "kind sir" – from one of the parents and "your faithful servant", with a request that the son be excused from lessons "due to feeling poorly in the aftermath of a dog biting his left hand."

I laughed as I looked at the father in the photo, then the son. I repeated this odd phrase to myself again and again about a dog biting his left hand, and then I suddenly became unbearably sad. I thought how those issues bound in a colorful artificial leather (so nice and warm and even with that distinct smell of old books) had ended up in a state library. How the hands of a woman, leafing through the pages of some serialized novel, had placed these photographs here, and how this journal came to include the note that was somehow never delivered to the teacher. How the issues of the journal were tied together with string, and how later they were forgotten in the corner of an abandoned home, and how they were then loaded into a truck and thrown down in front of the library entrance... I didn't even want to think about what ultimately happened to the people in the photographs.

I was a young woman then, brought up in the Soviet tradition. Everything that surrounded me: factories, manufacturing plants, houses, theatres – I somehow automatically credited the Soviet regime for all of it. I seriously believed that history, just like the beginning of the counting of years in the Old Testament, had begun in 1917.

Only years later did I realize that the famous Stalin Factory, the Red October plant, and the TsUM department store had only been renamed, and they existed long before as Guzhon, Einem, and Muir & Mirrielees Co. I realized that the world around me belonged to others, and the Bolsheviks only took it and passed it off as their own. This completely destroyed something that I had been carrying in my head for a long time.

Books were something different, however. They always preserved the uninterruptedness of time. They had no relation to the Soviet regime, unless of course they were about the Soviet regime. Perhaps that is why my connection to Soviet life began to crack through books. This happened during the fire at the Historical Library.

Back when I was working in the Historical Library, the white church of St. Vladimir in Starye Sady, which stands on the hill opposite the Ivanov Monastery, consisted only of the remains of a bell tower and a structure that had been turned into a book depository. Next to it, a bomb shelter had been built during the war. The Ivanov Monastery itself hosted an NKVD prison in the Thirties, and then a police station. This twisting of the original purpose – making a church into a warehouse or NKVD branch, if it wasn't just destroyed outright – was a pastime of the Soviet regime from the very beginning.

In any event, what was kept in that warehouse was known only to higher-ups.

Once, when I was walking to work up Starosadsky Lane, I saw smoke and fire-suppression foam flowing down past people in the street. Little bubbles were flowing down to Staraya Square, where the building of the Central Committee of the Communist Party of the Soviet Union was located. It was probably the fact that the Central Committee was so near, that had caused the library officials to start panicking. In spite of the fact that for several days we were standing in a chain and passing to each other books that were half burnt, they told us to remember that there had never been a great conflagration, and only some wastepaper had burned.

So, it later happened that my colleagues and I were collecting all of this "wastepaper" in the bomb shelter remaining from the war next to the library. These were the remains of the Shchukin collection and – something that especially surprised me – the remains of libraries in the Third Reich. It was easy to recognize everything, as the books had *ex libris* stickers and stamps. At first, we discussed saving everything that had survived, but then... I realized that it was all in vain. Everything that we had saved after the fire was taken outside the city and destroyed.

The amount of lies that were told and this burned "wastepaper" gave me a powerful immunity against any illusions with regard to the Soviet regime. I realized that if we could see and grasp something from the past, then it was only happening by chance or the private efforts of individual people.

A metaphysical plan:
two civilizations

Preserving papers, diaries, and documents from the recent past was a noble calling. But when I would come across another keeper of the past, it was important to persuade him or her that the collection should live on, it should be opened up, like a box of treasure that has long been hidden from sight. It should be available to all who want to hear the voices addressed to them from the past. Sometimes I had a visceral feeling of being the guide for some person or another, and sometimes I realized that this particular history had nothing to do with me. Of course, looking from the perspective of great scholarship, it was just me following my own whims, but I constantly found myself somewhere where there was no crowd of researchers, nor was there any especial scholarly interest, and if there was, it was strictly a personal thing.

Finally, when it was already November, I received an invitation to visit a red house in Novogireevskaya Street that I knew well. It was already getting dark early. When I arrived, Dmitri Mikhailovich Shakhovskoy and his sisters were already sitting behind the old, round table. I had been invited at a late hour, and they were going to tell me what they had finally decided. I came into the house and sat on the chair that had been set out for me.

I noticed that Dmitri Mikhailovich was sad, but I could see the relief of someone who had finally made a decision. He suddenly said to me, "You know, we lived in a world parallel to the Soviet one. Faith gave us the feeling of a real family, a connection to everyone else who belonged to this world."

He told me how in the Seventies, he was looking for Maria Fyodorovna Mansurova in Borovsk, so that he could find the letters that his father Mikhail Shik had written to her husband, who had died back in the 1920s.

He simply arrived and went up to the boarded-up monastery. Women in black dresses with white scarves on their heads were standing next to it. He asked them if they knew where such and such a woman lived. They threw up their hands and said that she had left long ago, and no one with such a name lived here. They asked him sternly why he needed to find her. He started telling them about his mother and father, and their expressions suddenly turned softer and kinder. They began to say, "Ah, so you are Dmitri, Dmitri." They led him first to a wooden house, where Maria Fyodorovna Mansurovna came out of a tiny room. He told me that through these connections you could always find anyone, because this was community, understood as one large family.

As I listened to his story, I felt an enormous glass wall between us. In childhood, when we are at the same age, we each yet receive different lessons from our parents.

When I was five years old, it was summer, and I was at the kindergarten at our dacha outside Moscow in Petrishchevo, the teachers took us to the Zoya Kosmodemyanskaya memorial several times. They told us how and why she was hung, and why we absolutely had to follow her example. I sincerely did my best.

I saw myself as a sixteen-year-old girl: in front of me my father, was gaily and entertainingly revealing the picture of the world, with the dinosaurs, the first people, and slavery.

I was born when my father was in his early twenties. He was an educated and talented young man and had graduated from school with honors. He was then accepted into a military academy. All of his energy and desire to pass his knowledge on was poured out onto me. I was a kind of practice ground on which he developed his own view of the world, talking to me about books that he had just read. I was his one and only audience, although he didn't realize it: he was surrounded by friends that passed through his life like water through a sieve. Not only did I believe what he believed, I also tried to use them in life at every opportunity. With I was nine years old, I came to him with some religious question. He was writing then a dissertation on some topic of military engineering, but for some reason he was always interested in religion, especially as a family belonging to some small sect lived in the room next to ours. My father explained to me how through evolution, the world had been created from matter, how people had made up the idea of a god because of their fear of natural phenomenon and the struggles of life, and especially because of their fear of death, which was pointless because we live on in the good deeds we do. He retold me Engel's *Anti-Dühring* in an easily understandable form, and he explained how fooling the people only leads to savagery, and people should be liberated from such. He returned to his tasks, and I went out into the courtyard, and from that time I began to be aggressively anti-religion.

The majority of people on my block had come from the villages around Moscow, and therefore every boy or girl had godparents. They went to church and marked religious holidays. My self-assuredness had had its effect on them; I stood on a soapbox in the middle of the courtyard and made fervent speeches to expose the trickery of the clergy. In the end, two pregnant women pushed me into the driveway, literally pressing me with their bellies and forcing me to recant of my views. I held my ground, however. They spat and told me that I could believe whatever I wanted, but I should leave their children alone. I agreed to this, though without any enthusiasm.

Some time later, strange things started happening to me. During the day I was a true atheist and I followed in the path of my father. At night or in the moment between sleep and wakefulness, however, I started to experience strange fears.

After visiting the churches of the Kremlin, where the saints scrutinized me from the frescos that completely covered the walls, I began to sense a myriad of gazes on me, stern and grim. They haunted me for long after my visit, and they filled me with such fear that I came to be horrified by the faces depicted in those frescos. Sometimes at night, or between sleeping and wakefulness, the angels or even God himself would come to me. The more I drove them away, the more frequently they would pay me visits. I had a clear vision of how they stood on a cloud and looked at me with reproach. Usually they wouldn't say anything, they just looked at me with sadness. Their mute presence in my life created a mystery to my existence, and I didn't know what I should do. I could not admit to my father that the people against whom I fought so ardently, would come to me so routinely just like that. So, I would run to my mother and tell her that I was probably losing my mind…

But here, in the depths of Soviet life, as if contained in a nutshell, a different kind of civilization lived on.

The Shakhovskoy family once lived on Zubovsky Boulevard at number 15, where they took up the entire floor of the building in 1912. They not only had a bath, they had a gas boiler. Prince Dmitri Ivanovich Shakhovskoy was a leader of the Constitutional Democratic Party, and in 1917 he was appointed a minister in the Provisional Government. Later, space in their house was expropriated and the family was pushed into the large room that was then divided up into tiny cubicles. The children of Mikhail Shik and Natalya Dmitrievna Shakhovskaya, their old grandmother Sirotinina, and aunt Anya

Shakhovskaya, their mother's sister – their friends would call the whole swarm of people in the apartment the "Zubovsky anthill".

I first heard the story of their grandfather, Dmitri Ivanovich Shakhovskoy from Natan Eidelman already in the mid-1980s. He spoke ardently and painfully about how Dmitri Ivanovich, the great-grandson of the decembrist Shakhovskoy and the great-nephew of Chaadayev, had been imprisoned in 1938, and then, in spite of the begging and pleading of his close friend Vernadsky, he was shot.

Later I read a striking story about some young people in the 1880s who founded the "Brotherhood" and bought the Priyutino estate for their meetings. Besides Shakhovskoy and Vernadsky, this band also included I. M. Grevs, S. F. Oldenburg, and A. A. Kornilov, who would go on to become noted scholars and academicians. For them the Brotherhood was, in a way, meant to replace Christianity with the idea of a communality of consciousness.

They followed Tolstoy in claiming that they could no longer live the way they had before. "Work as hard as possible. Consume as little of oneself as possible. And see other people's needs as your own." Their children's generation did not share their fathers' ideas about creating a new religious faith, but rather the opposite: they immersed themselves deeply in traditional Orthodoxy.

After the assumed death of his friend in the torture chambers of Lubyanka, Vernadsky wrote, "Dmitri Ivanovich has been wiped out… However, his noble personality has left deep traces which will bear fruit. In our Brotherhood he played an exceptional role." It was Dmitri Ivanovich who had persuaded Vernadsky to return to Russia from abroad. Shakhovskoy himself had a vision of saving the economy in the 1920s through cooperatives and he even gave lectures at the State Planning Committee. He later took up local history in the hope that, by enlightening the people, he could save them from disaster. He was a romantic, but as 1938 approached he was increasingly overwhelmed by a feeling of impending doom. He hid in his corner behind the dividing partitions in the apartment, and he tried to avoid going out or talking to anyone. His family life was tragic: two of his four children committed suicide; his wife, in spite of their romantic youth that had been so full of lofty ideals, cared only about her own pursuits in the second half of her life. Nonetheless, both of their daughters, Natalya and Anna, proved to be extremely selfless and noble people.

Finally, Dmitri Mikhailovich Shakhovskoy told me that he had decided to give me Varvara Grigoryevna's diaries.

Boxes stood before me. I had brought them in a taxi to the Tsvetaeva museum. I looked at them and felt a great happiness at being able to open them and discover everything.

But soon my elation was replaced by desperation. After I opened the first notebook, I realized that Varvara Grigoryevna had made entries in a diary every day for many years. How was I supposed to read all this? I would have to spend a year on it or even more. And how could I choose what to publish and what to leave out?

Chapter 5.
The diaries of
Varvara Grigoryevna
Malakhieva-Mirovich

The Tsvetaeva museum: in a nutshell

A ship has gone down. But a tiny lifeboat
By some miracle has survived.
But will I hold on for long in this tiny boat
Without gear, without a paddle?
Oh, how fortunate are those, who in the ocean depths,
Have already found rescue and peace,
But here the last screams uninterruptedly
Echo over the silence of the sea...

—Varvara Malakhieva-Mirovich

Varvara Grigoryevna's diaries had come to the Veselovsky home while she was still alive. She was afraid that these notebooks would disappear, get lost. Olga stacked them, numbering each in turn.

I could see how she had worked on the notebooks and made notes. On each of these notebooks, Olga wrote a hundred and eighty times, "Varvara Grigoryevna Malakhieva-Mirovich. Born March 29, 1869, died August 16, 1954. 'About the fleeting and the eternal.'"

The diaries begin from July 23, 1930 and end on May 14, 1954.

The worn rust-colored, blue, or red covers, the children's school notebooks and drawing pads, thick and thin – they all looked at me as if asking: what, exactly, did I want to find out?

I wanted to see how Olga Bessarabova's life went on through the eyes of her older friend. I wanted to find out everything about the victims in the Dobrovs' home. I wanted to go through the war years with those who survived them. All of this history was contained within these notebooks.

I had never seen before how diaries, as if they were mirrors made to face each other, could reflect one another.

Throughout all the time spent reading Olga Bessarabova's notebooks, which were full of letters and poems by Varvara Grigoryevna, I constantly felt Varvara Grigoryevna's presence, and the question inevitably arose in my mind: who was she?

A poetess? A philosopher? A wanderer?

The doors of many homes in Saint-Petersburg opened before Varvara Grigoryevna when she was writing all kinds of criticism about famous writers and reviews of theatrical performances, and when she was the editor of the journal *Russkaya Mysl'* ("Russian Thought"), where she was succeeded by Valery Bryusov.

In the 1910s one noted female author in Saint-Petersburg told Varvara Grigoryevna that she would make a "real writer" out of her, which aroused such a protest from the latter that she fled from Saint-Petersburg.

She wrote poems constantly, but she never created a collection from them. Only after her death were they collected and copied by Olga Bessarabova, who gathered four thousand poems and preserved them for posterity.

Those who didn't like Varvara Grigoryevna called her a Theosophist, a "mystic". Florensky labeled her an "occult bog", and some spoke of her poems as "decadent bagatelles".

However, those who liked her – and there were many – considered her perceptive, intelligent, talented, and an exceptional person. She found unending esteem from the Dobrov family – from Filipp Alexandrovich, who called her "Vavochka", to little Daniil Andreyev who, even as an adult, wrote to her with a tenderness as if he were her own son: "…the feeling that now fills me is love for you. This love is rather strange and wonderful."

On a 1923 group photo of graduates from the school in Sergiev Posad, where Varvara Grigoryevna taught, she is standing in a loose dress, while Olga Bessarabova can be seen below her holding a lilac branch. Though Varvara Grigoryevna looks rather stern, she is still a significant presence, and in spite of being over fifty already, beautiful. Her deep and bright eyes look out from the photo with a demanding and strict gaze.

Varvara Grigoryevna tried death on almost as long as she lived. This was not due to a sense of pessimism, but rather because she believed that death is a new birth. She even sketched out her own "Mystery of Growing Old":

Act I: The horror of the approaching deterioration, the last outbursts of youth. An attempt to oppose it – fighting with the inevitable. Sorrow and bewilderment (age 45–55).

Act II: One grows tired of fighting. The pain of getting used to the way things now are. An elegy of remembrance. The difficulty of ascending a steep slope (age 55–60).

Act III: Initiation into old age. Yes, a new stage. An increased feeling of being alone. Increasing ailments. An increasing bravery. The first roots are laid into the hereafter.

Act IV: The first sounds of the requiem. A sadness of departing from Earth. One hears voices calling. The sound of the requiem grows. A new birth. Death. A lullaby.

She even spoke of "sister Death". She was always amazed how Death retreated further and further from her. She thought that the doors of the other world were already open, that Death was very close by, and therefore she had to bring the past to life and understand the meaning of the present. Nevertheless, in spite of her keen perception, she would err on the matter of how much time she still had before her.

The era in which she lived reaped an enormous harvest of death and general grief. The cruel forces of history turned her life into a fight for existence, into a constant pursuit of a bite of bread, of square meters of space. She wrote with horror of the suicides that were piling up around her. She took the loss of people close to her very hard, and she found it difficult to accept these things.

And yet the main idea that sustained her during all these years were her thoughts of immortality. Her friend Lev Shestov often wrote, "If it turned out that nothing awaits us after death, that God does not exist and there is no immortality of the soul – there would be no point living even a single minute further."

I looked through the notebooks that dated to the year of Daniil Andreyev's arrest and the persecutions in the

Dobrovs' home. I leafed through the entries from 1947, but I found no allusions to the events that entailed the arrest of every member of the Dobrov family. There were some mentions of meetings, complaints of how a retirement home wouldn't take her, some thoughts about the postwar food shortages and the loss of a few individual female friends. Nonetheless, the tragedy could still be heard in her tone, in her bitter recollections. It was extremely dangerous to write anything about arrests or the disappearances of one's friends.

The diary entries contain images of childhood and mystical revelations, descriptions of her dreams. Their main feature, however, is Varvara Grigoryevna's merciless evaluation of herself and her character.

"Old Mirovich", as she called herself, was sincerely searching in these diary pages for her "I". Not only in the present time, but also in the past and future. A desperate daring was alive in this woman already advanced in years, as well as an insight into very deep things that others simply could not see. She continually looked within herself and carefully described everything she found.

"Was it me or not me who has just now walked under the lindens with their wonderful scent of flowers and slowly (strangely slowly) walked up to the fifth floor? If it was me, then why am I old with a scarf tightly wrapped around my shoulders? I drag my feet to someone else's apartment. All this are only forms outside of time and space. The only form where all this has been recorded is in my poems. But they have embodied (and, generally, not in a satisfying way), some tiny part of my 'I', the 'I' that I don't even know myself, which I have been hunting for so unsuccessfully all over the world for over forty years now."

Can a person discover who he is and why he was born into this life? Why does suffering befall him and why has he come into this or that period of history?

Varvara Grigoryevna asked these questions and wanted to understand why.

I, in turn, was yet to understand what had been revealed to her and what steps her soul took in the past and present, before she left this world.

Homeless in Moscow

How cold it is, how damp and uncomfortable!
So ends my pathless path...

– Varvara Malakhieva-Mirovich

It was Varvara Grigoryevna Malakhieva-Mirovich's wanderings from one home to another, her routes going along Ostozhenka, Zubovsky and Smolensky boulevards, through the rooms and apartments of friends and loved ones, that allowed me to walk through time with Varvara's diaries as my guidebook.

Varvara Grigoryevna had no place of her own in Moscow, and therefore from time to time she would sleep at the homes of her former students or at friends', and she would call herself a "poor relation" who would be taken in.

All that was going on – the things she saw around herself – she noted with the observant gaze of a painter.

A line turns behind the corner
Like a long snake. A line for bread.

The low sky casts a sticky fog
Over the line.

Dirty, tough heels
Look out of the worn shoes,
Holes, patches — like wounds,
Like traces of evil poverty.

Grim skinny faces.
Complaining, quarreling, reproaches…
But maybe this is all an illusion
In this inevitably cruel hallucination?

– Moscow, November 27, 1932

She asked who among them actually believed in a brighter future, in the slogans that were fluttering all around, and she answered the question herself: "Almost no one."

She visited acquaintances in Sergiev Posad. Here a drunken youth with a harmonica was shouting and dancing in the Kukuyevsky cemetery, where Varvara had buried her mother not long before. She addressed him and told him that death and grief exist, but in the depths of her soul, she understood that they are the fruit of their time, where all links with life and death had been broken, and there is only a joyless Existence filling their new lives. This is how they – the new Soviet citizens – resisted that mundane existence.

She was ceaselessly tormented by the question of why a human being was incarnated in precisely this moment, why all of his thoughts revolved around food, drink, square meters of space, and clothes. She would observe herself for years, seeing if she wasn't giving up some part of her true self and surrendering to that mundane existence. She called all gluttonous eating "a madness of the throat". She saw how many people close to her, if they didn't perish in the torture chambers, would leave this life after burying themselves in this mundane existence to escape the inevitable grief that surrounded them.

And now Varvara Grigoryevna was staying the night at the Shakhovskoy house on Zubovsky Boulevard.

"It is enough to observe the morning routine of our little anthill (on Zubovsky Boulevard). The splashing in the bath, the noise of water flowing in the kitchen sink. In the hallway people with uncombed hair, and towels or coffeemakers in their hands, make a lively dance. In the entrance to the apartment, someone is bartering with the milkwoman. 'Will you take some herring for it? Some bread? Some cigarettes?' 'Well, for two liters of milk, give me two cups of salt...' At the gas stove there is a meeting of elbows, and a burning stick (used instead of matches to save money, and we take fire from the neighbors), people stepping on each other's feet, boiling, warming up, reheating. If people spent just one-tenth of this energy on spiritual exercises and the life of the soul, how life would be transformed (let people boil water, but let's keep things in perspective)."

The next night was spent at the Dobrovs'. Here she turned the conversation to spiritual growth.

Kovalensky was a fatalist. He said that everything had been predestined, that everyone walks the path laid out for them from above, and even the criminal on the cross was meant to say exactly what he said.

Filipp Alexandrovich and Varvara, on the other hand, said that when it came to the criminal who accepted Christ, this was an act of extreme freedom. His soul chose a path different from other people's.

When one knows what would happen to each of the people who spoke here, then a special meaning can be found in their words. Did Alexander Kovalensky believe in this predestination fifteen years later when he was arrested and sent to the camps? Did he believe in the inevitability of the death of Shurochka, whom he adored?

Now Varvara is walking through Neskuchny Garden and marveling at the busts of workers and farmers. She wrote, "Neskuchny Garden. Thirty years ago it was more thickly overgrown, more mysterious, more poetic. Now it is too well-trodden, too inhabited (there is a military camp, some stages are set up). In front of the museum palace, there are four terrible figure bearing flags. With the Park of Culture and Rest, one cannot speak of rest when every fifty steps there are hoarsely bellowing loudspeakers. And the risible tastelessness of the Alee Udarnikov with the huge busts... of the shock workers Zuyev, Salov, etc. Bisha [Kovalensky – N. G.] finds that although all this is anti-art, from a political perspective it is a great idea. Maybe so. But me personally, for the people, for the 'masses' who visit the park, I would wish them an aesthetically complete cultural and educational environment, and not the deafening rasp of the radio, the singers and reciters, and the bust of the shock worker Zuyev."

The Thirties marked a rupture in Moscow. The center of the city was turned into an enormous building site. Ostozhenka Street saw the buzzing construction of the metro. As Varvara Grigoryevna described in her diary, "The guts of that entire street are hanging out terribly. There is an infernal whine, whirring, and shuddering coming from drilling machines and an incessant hammering. At night, when human shades move along all this grating, it is a scene from Dante's hell."

In this same place, she witnessed a love scene, "…Over the belly of Ostozhenka Street that has been cut open. On one cold and unpleasant night, the lively sound of a harmonica was issuing from this wound, with boisterous lyrics about a 'young lady'. A young lady came out from under some scaffolding, brightly lit from below, in appalling padded-cotton pants and a red scarf over her head, and from the neighboring scaffolding the flirting voice of a worker with a wheelbarrow full of sand called to her. He offered her a cigarette, and she coquettishly adjusted her headscarf over her curls, done at the hairdresser's. She began walking towards him, stepping over beams, taking one step after another on legs wrapped in these padded trousers – her legs looked as if they were weighed down with sandbags. He put a hand on her shoulder, and she patted him on the back. His wheelbarrow came to a stop, they started puffing on their cigarettes. This lively flirting continued for some five minutes, accompanied by the plaintive whining of a drilling machine and the incessant screeching of metal inside the excavation. Really, 'life happens everywhere'."

The baptismal pool of Kiev

In the early 1930s, Varvara Grigoryevna would travel to Kiev, the city of her birth. Here she met some of the people who were dearest to her. As she looked at the hill behind the walls of the Lavra on her way back, she would see a portion of the Kiev riverfront, the embankment covered with building sites. As I read these pages from her diary, I found that every time I crossed the Dnieper on the train, I could see the changes that this place had undergone from nearly a century later. On both sides of the river there were huge embankments, bridges, the golden domes of the Lavra. It was curious how, even before I had read her diaries, I had addressed Varvara many times from this place that was so eternal and solemn for her. It was as if I sensed that in this particular place on earth, she was closest to me.

Here the young Varvara Malakhieva met the philosopher Lev Shestov, who would determine in many respects the future course of her life. She made the acquaintance of Leonilla Tarasova, the mother of the actress Alla Tarasova, and she would spend the last decades of her life in Tarasova's home.

Varvara was born in Percherye, one of the districts of Kiev and near the Kiev Pechersk Lavra, in a very unusual family. Varvara's father was a mystic and religious seeker, a self-taught philosopher, who was almost never at home and would wander throughout Russia and live wherever he was ordained to. Nevertheless, his every return home was accompanied by joy. Vava loved him madly. She dreamed of resembling her father in all things. She was jealous of her mother, to whom he wrote before he died, "…not in a dream, but in real life, on the shore of the sea, I saw 'a new heaven and a new earth'." Varvara that it was because of this vision that his face looked so happy and peaceful as he was lying in his coffin.

At the age of nine, the thought came into the girl's head that she was capable of awakening him from the dead. When her attempts did not meet with success, she felt a bitter disappointment.

Once a new girl with white braids came into her church-run school, and her classmates immediately took to her. They called her the "girl born out of wedlock". Varvara took the girl under her wing. She was Nilochka (Leonilla Nikolaevna) Chebotareva. A friendship emerged between them from the very start. Along with Leonilla, who was caught up in the ideas of the Narodnaya Volya ("The People's Will") party, Varvara turned away from the church and the faith; their main idols were now Zhelyabov and Petrovskaya, and their main topic of conversation was the suffering of the people and the "horror of tsarist rule". It turned out that this childhood friendship would determine Varvara's last years of wandering through Moscow homes.

When, in 1890, Varvara received a letter from Leonilla in Kiev saying that there was a job at the party, Varvara cast everything aside and came back from the small town where she was earning a living as a governess. She began working in this party that had broken off from a union of Narodnaya Volya adherents and terrorists in 1881. However, she chafed at the party discipline; she believed less and less in an imminent revolution, and she felt a sense of disappointment. A spiritual crisis began, marked by prolonged depression and thoughts of suicide. She sought treatment from various doctors. One doctor, who helped her recover from her illness, unexpectedly came to dominate her heart and mind. A period of long and fruitless love for the Kiev doctor Petrovsky began, but he was married with two children.

In a peculiar way, this falling in love turned Varvara Grigoryevna away from the revolutionary path that some of her close friends and acquaintances would follow. She would have romantic relationships with Anatoly Lunacharsky, who would go on to be the future People's Commissar for Education, but was then a young man in Kiev. She struck up friendships with the family of the revolutionaries Smidovich. By the time Varvara came back to have a look at her hometown, all of these people would be burned out from the revolution.

Her friend Leonilla managed to jump off the revolutionary train thanks to a fortunate marriage. She became the wife of a young doctor named Konstantin Prokofyevich Tarasov.

In the 1890s, the Tarasov family lived in the Kiev fortress at its northern tower, where a military hospital was located. Its walls were so thick that, Varvara recalled, one could sleep in the window niches and breathe in the scent of lilacs in bloom. By this time, the two friends had already become distant from one another, but the appearance of Konstantin Tarasov on the stage restored the friendship that had seemed to be fading.

He was a remarkable man, a fine doctor, and Varvara became a friend of his. She wrote that he was a person who truly treated everyone as a brother. He had a deep love for his wife and family, but his home life and family obligations served only as a background for his life.

In this military hospital, where Tarasov as a staff member at the psychiatric ward had an apartment, a number of prominent people in Kiev would gather at the end of the 19th century. "Leonilla's half-sister Talya (Natalya Nikolaevna Kulzhenko) shone and attracted people's attention on these evenings with her rare beauty. Both Minsky and Volynsky would visit the hospital when they came to Kiev to give talks at evening events. Often horsecarts would come bearing someone from the Balakovsky family, millionaires in the sugar trade. Shestov often came to see me (he was not yet a writer then, he was still known as Lelya Schwartzmann and worked in his father's manufacturing business – the 'spiritual seeker' always had his pocket New Testament with him). 'He was a person of great moral standards, Christ,' old Gerts Balakhovsky said about him once. Balakhovsky, his sister's father-in-law, stood equally far from Christ and from any moral standards."

The triangle

Hopelessness is the greatest hope.
So a friend told me once.
Although it was already vaguely known
To my soul being tempted in the desert.

– Varvara Malakhieva-Mirovich to Lev Shestov

If all people are children of God, then that means
that one does not have to fear or regret anything.

–Lev Shestov

Fate could not have helped but bring these unusual spirits together.

When Varvara was twenty-four years old, she was hired as a governess in the Balakhovsky family of sugar traders. The year was 1893. Balakhovsky's wife Sofia Isaakovna – the sister of Lev Schwartzmann (Shestov) brought Varvara in as her children's teacher. They lived in the Perevozovka estate outside Kiev, where the budding writer and philosopher Shestov began to visit often. In those days, he was contributing articles to leading Kiev newspapers. To his father's disappointment, Lev Isaakovich had no interest in manufacturing and would do everything possible to avoid taking up the family business. He could sing marvelously and he dreamed of a career in the opera.

An affinity soon arose between him and Varvara. One day Varvara wrote to him, "You have made me better than I was before… When you die someday, the fact that we have met will grant peace to your conscience, even if you had done nothing else in your life. How great it is that you have granted the ability to do this 'something else' almost everywhere you have made a path in life, a path not like the others." At one moment, their relationship became very deep and Shestov, as far as one can see, expected something reciprocal. However, Varvara had still not left behind her love for the doctor Petrovsky, and so she could not reciprocate his feelings.

Until Varvara's diaries were examined, the story of her relationship with the philosopher was completely unknown to anyone. Even Natalya Baranova-Shestova, who wrote the only biography of her noted father, knew only a few scattered facts from the past that could not add up to a whole.

"By the end of 1895," she wrote, "my father had a serious nervous breakdown… as a result of tragic events in his personal life."

What tragic events these were exactly, the biography left unexplained.

One can claim with all probability that the root of his nervous breakdown was his difficult and complicated relationship with Varvara.

Years later, she would bitterly admit, "And, if I had responded in my youth to L. Sh. in the only way that mattered to him, he would have not had that great experience that led him to his vast spiritual labors on the mystery of life and death."

For Shestov, an existentialist philosopher, the mystery of existence could only be revealed through a tragic event of his own experience.

When Varvara together with the Balakhovskys and their children went abroad, Shestov proposed to her younger sister. For Varvara, there was no one closer to her in those days than Anastasia. Since Anastasia was little, she had always heeded her older sister. Varvara read books for grownups to her and poems that she easily committed to memory. They both wrote poems and kept diaries. When Anastasia turned seventeen, and Varvara was twenty-two, they began to feel like equals.

This was the time when people in the offices of *Zhizn' i iskusstvo* ("Life and Art", a small-run journal in Kiev, where we both started publishing poetry and prose) called us Radika and Dodika, names of conjoined twin sisters who were shown in traveling freak shows.

If one of us had died at that time, the other would not have survived the loss. I remember with what horror, with what firm intention to take my own life should my sister die, I went to Odessa, where my sister was being treated for a bite from a rabid dog in Dr. Gamaleya's clinic. In those days, ordinary people didn't yet believe that his shots would work. I rushed from Kiev to Odessa tormented by the thought that my sister was no longer among the living.

Varvara described the conflict that broke out between the sisters as follows: "…my relationship to this person was so deep, and for my entire inner life it so incomparably important, that I thought it impossible to 'give him up' to my sister without a fight. A quarrel erupted, which was indescribably cruel because our two souls were like one soul, and that is why every blow struck against the other, was felt with the same pain as a blow suffered in return. In this battle my sister's mental strength was drained, strength that had already been worn down by losing my mother, her joining the party, and unbearable ideological burden she carried…"

We don't know what kind of fight this was, as Varvara's diaries do not provide any details. She only wrote that Shestov proposed to her sister, because he wanted to be related to Varvara. However, Lev Isaakovich's parents were categorically opposed to such a union, as they thought he should marry a Jewish girl.

As a result, Shestov suffered a nervous breakdown, descended into depression, and soon left to study in Switzerland.

"The person who led us to fight, was also suffering at this time – partly due to our quarrel – an enormous ideological crisis. In the sphere of life, he left it to us to decide who would marry him. He felt guilty in front of my sister like in front of a girl to whom he had 'given false hopes' with his overly tender and attentive relationship (I was abroad at the time and I left his sister to his moral care). From my side, this man was impacted and frightened by my incomplete response to the fullness of his feelings. All this turned into his philosophical investigations into the meaning of life and into a serious nervous condition, which led him into a foreign clinic and then, for years on end, living abroad. I finally 'gave him away' to my sister, but during a year he was living abroad, he met a woman who brought him into her bed with extreme ease and without any obligations from either side. She became his wife. He became a great writer. My sister had a nervous breakdown and her life ended in an insane asylum. By a stronger will to live that I'm embarrassed by, I lived on without her, without my sister, and 'without sail or rudder'."

Judging from everything, this story remained a secret kept even from the philosopher's circle of friends; he did not reveal these matters even to people close to him. Thus, Yevgeniya Gertsyk, a friend of the philosopher and the author of memoirs, offered her own views on Shestov's inner drama: "This person, so pure, bore on his conscience such a complex and not entirely ordinary responsibility, and from this, perhaps, his back was bent and those deep wrinkles made him old so early… This was the time of his inner catastrophe." Shestov himself, who had already emigrated by that time, noted on June 11, 1920 in his *Journal of Thoughts*: "This year is the twenty-fifth anniversary of when 'time fell out of joint', or rather, the anniversary will come at the beginning of the autumn, in early September. I am noting this down so that I won't forget: the major event of my life – and no one, besides you, knows anything about it – could be easily forgotten."

By counting backwards from the twenty-fifth anniversary, we reach a date of 1895. It was precisely at that time that he suffered his first nervous breakdown, which led him to go abroad in early 1896 for treatment. When Shestov made that entry in his diary, the unfortunate Anastasia had died from hunger in a mental institution outside Moscow. Varvara, whom Shestov tried to continually care for through the efforts of friends and acquaintances, was returning from Rostov to Moscow.

As Varvara wrote in her diary, "I have been going through old letters, with some intact pages and some half-preserved, from Lev Shetov. 1896, 1897. The 19th century. The letters came from Rome, Basel, Bern, Paris, and Berlin. Years of wandering and treatment after the cruel clashing of our lives: my life, my sister Anastasia's, and his, where everyone suffered an accident, one of those collisions from which one cannot recover in just a single lifetime… The only one who recovered, and who became a major, well-known writer and did not interrupt his life's work – philosophy – was Lev Shestov. Only one part of his soul recovered, however. The most important, intimate, deep part of his soul by which he was wedded to me, remained drained of life, without any sense or meaning."

Doubtlessly, his philosophy of hopelessness and desperation arose to a large extent out of this dramatic event. He and Varvara had in common a sense of compassion for those who suffered, a sense of grief for having no way out of the dead end of life on earth. But Varvara rose to ever-higher stages of consciousness through her constant attempts to understand Lev Shestov's personality.

This drama most likely became a sign that the two sisters reflected in their common pseudonym. Mirovich was the surname of a character in an early autobiographical prose work by Lev Schwartzmann (where he told of his unsuccessful tries at writing) that survives in manuscript.

Anastasia began to sign her poems "Mirovich", while Varvara became "Malakhieva-Mirovich". According to a clever guess by Tatyana Neshumova (who launched my adventures in exploring these diaries after I returned from Peredelkino), this surname might signal a truce (in Russian *mir* means 'peace') between the sisters. However, there is no mention of this in the diaries.

A new twist in Lev Shestov's relationship with Varvara came in 1911. She went to visit him in Switzerland, where he was renting a property in the town of Coppet. Varvara came to see Shestov's two little daughters. At that time his wife was away in Paris studying medicine. It was then that their souls were ready to understand each other and truly join together, but now it was too late for anything to be fixed.

The flight from Kiev

The last stage in Varvara and Lev Shestov's life together was the most dramatic. "Kiev. 1919. Autumn. There is talk of how in the winter we won't have a water supply, nor fuel, nor electricity. 'Every man for himself'. The families with whom I was bound with in my life and soul have left Kiev: the Tarasovs have left to Crimea (Alla is expecting a child). The Skryabins are in Novocherkassk. A group of friends and two or three people I didn't know managed to somehow get ahold of a heated train carriage. It had been attached to a hospital train that was being sent to the south. Mirovich was also a member of this bunch. Our heated train carriage might as well have been called a chilled train carriage. There was a night when in our half of the carriage, the passengers nearly froze to death. …On the other side of the carriage, which was plushly hung with carpets, the writer Shestov sat with his wife (who among the Skryabins' circle in Kiev was called 'Eleazaurus' because her name was Anna Eleazarovna) and two daughters. There was something in the thick armor around her soul, in her physical and spiritual simplicity, in her primitive mind and the bony strength in her being, something reminiscent of dinosaurs, ichthyosaurs, and plesiosaurs. She held the neurasthenic, weak-willed Shestov to herself with unbreakable bonds by bearing him two daughters and creating a home where he had a study where no one bothered him and he could think and write without interruption. In this train carriage Eleazaurus jealously watched to ensure that the two halves of the carriage would not mix in terms of food, because their family had larger and better provisions than we did. She also reacted with jealously to L.I.'s chatting with me, for which he had to step over the forbidden area. These chats soon ceased. On the night we were frozen stiff with cold, L.I. nevertheless decided to come closer to us, because he heard old Slonimskaya crying. He advised us to lie in a circle with our feet towards each other. I don't remember if we followed his advice. I remembered only that, in spite of the terrible cold, none of us got ill afterward." Varvara noted with regret how Shestov gave up certain opportunities to work and instead accepted a humiliating life according to his wife's rules.

Physically, their paths would split forever. Some time later, Varvara came to Moscow and he went with his family to Paris by way of Crimea.

On June 15, 1939 she wrote, "Today I happened to hear that the philosopher Shestov has died. 'I heard the notice of a death from indifferent lips, and I accepted it indifferently.' But there was once such a great and deep spiritual connection (it seemed) between us. And what they call love, from his side. On my part, there was a complete trust and a joy in having a companion. …The music during which I met his long gaze, I don't know where it came from and it was expressing the ineffable. Yes, there was that. I bow to him for all this, for the letters with friendship and care, for all our time together, although it was flawed and since it didn't take on a full significance, it could end the way it ended today, 'I heard the notice of a death from indifferent lips, and I accepted it indifferently.'"

Varvara Grigoryevna's inner bond with Shestov never disappeared, however. In life and faith she was strikingly free within herself, just like her friend who overcame old-fashioned ideas about morality and religion.

She would repeat all her life his musing from his book *The Apotheosis of Groundlessness* that she loved so much, changing it and citing it always and everywhere: "If we are all children of God, then that means that one does not have to fear or regret anything."

The year 1947 came. She was already seventy-eight years old. Again he seemed close to her. She was walking along the streets of Moscow and suddenly heard a piece of music she knew well. Everything came back to life once more:

In Coppet, on the day that I recall now thanks to that aria, he sang it there at my request, I recall it so well that the scent of those roses that bloomed around the villa, and the incredibly blue waters of the lake, and the stern landscape of Savoy, wrapped in fog – everything came to life and blanketed all of Moscow, the fate of my old age, the present day. And it fell over the thirty years we were apart, and over the knowledge that he has been gone for over a decade now. It was without doubt that, wherever he is now, he is more alive than any living person. At times his presence seemed so "hallucinatory-lucid" (as a psychiatrist would say), that it was impossible to doubt it.

On that evening in 1911 he sang for me alone. The girls had gone on a trip into the mountains. His wife was in Paris – she was busy with some kind of medical tasks (she was a doctor). He sang, looking straight at me and not taking his eyes from mine:

In questa tomba oscura
Lasciami riposar,
Quando viveo, ingrata,
Dovevi a me pensar

His divine voice rang with an awe-inspiring inspiration, with an unusual strength and power, as if it was a secret password for all of our meetings in the future in all of the ages to come, in all spaces of the world…

Moscow, Glinishchevsky Lane (Nemirovich-Danchenko Street): the Tarasovs' home and the end of the 1930s

On Nemirovich street
On the Mirovich lane behind
Behind a cracked screen
In a large family
My elderly twin
Hung his head,
Tired of the long fighting
(He has been defending from a terrible fate
His right to breathe,
His daily bread, pen and bed).

– V. G. Malakhieva-Mirovich

By the time her Kiev friend Lev Shestov passed away, it had been two years that Varvara Grigoryevna was living with the Tarasov family, where they remembered Lev Isaakovich very well. "I heard the notice of a death from indifferent lips…" This might have been from the lips of Alla Tarasova or someone in her circle, who might have gone to Paris on a tour and brought the sad news back.

In the late 1930s on Glinishchevsky Lane, an enormous house for actors of the Moscow Art Theatre was built. The Tarasovs settled here. But in spite of receiving a three-room apartment, the Tarasovs had a catastrophic lack of space. All of them – Alla, her son Alexei, her ex-husband Kuzmin, her mother Leonilla, her niece Galochka, and their housekeeper – lived in a large but densely packed apartment.

Varvara came to live in the Tarasovs' apartment as a result of an exchange with relatives. After her long wanderings, she was finally given a room in a communal apartment on Kirov Street. She lived there for a relatively short time, and her friend Leonilla Tarasova with her daughter Alla began to persuade Varvara to move to their place, because Varvara couldn't cope with everyday tasks alone. The room on Kirov Street was supposed to go to the granddaughter of Galya Kalinovskaya, a future actress at the Moscow Art Theatre, who was being raised by Leonilla in Alla's family. The Tarasovs ensured Varvara that they would take care of her and help her in anything she needed. Varvara found this offer an attractive one, especially since her life was closely linked with their family.

Varvara had known and cared for the Tarasovs' children from the time they were born. For little Alla, who was nicknamed Ay as a child, she wrote a few plays which the little girl performed in their home theatre. When Alla was grown up, a naval officer named Alexander Kuzmin fell in love with her, and they eventually married. Then Alla moved from Kiev to Moscow, where she began her theatrical career. During her entrance exam for the Art Theatre in 1913, Alla successfully recited the monologue of Joan of Arc and was accepted into the troupe by Stanislavsky himself.

Alla Tarasova lived in Moscow at Varvara Grigoryevna's place or at the home of a friend of hers. The first role to bring her great success was in Gippius's play *The Green Ring*. The play told of young men and young ladies who came together in a circle where they discussed complex issues of everyday life. This was a subject incredibly close to Alla Tarasova's own heart with her participation in the Joy circle, the meetings of which she attended with Olga Bessarabova. Alexander Stakhovich served as a mentor to the young people acting in the play and years later Marina Tsvetaeva would address a bitter epigraph to him.

Alla was apparently in love with Stakhovich; when she bore a son, she named him after her idol – Alexei. It must be said that at that time, Alla Tarasova had crossed Tsvetaeva's path many times. The actress's closest friends in those days were Sonya Holliday, who also played a role in *The Green Ring*, and Vera Redlikh, a future director, and then a close friend of the Efrons and Tsvetaeva from Koktebel.

Through Varvara Grigoryevna, Alla met a wide circle of her Moscow and Kiev friends.

Their paths would again cross in Moscow, where the so-called "Kachalov group", after years of wandering the world, were pardoned by the Soviet government and returned home to continue their work at the Moscow Art Theatre.

Varvara's move to the Tarasov home would have unexpectedly bitter consequences for her. She would call this a "dish of pottage" for which she had sold her freedom.

Finally I have something resembling "a corner of my own". They bought screens and divided three quarters of the space meant for me from the rest of the room. What got assigned to me were the bed, half of the writing desk, a chair, and a little bedside table…

There are people here who have no living space of their own (they are on a waiting list!). They live in kitchens, sheds, in closets, and wander through the homes of others (just like I lived for almost a year while I was waiting for a room on Kirov Street).

At the end of the Thirties, Alla Tarasova played the leading role in the play *Anna Karenina*, which Stalin highly appraised. All possible awards were heaped on her. People would line up for tickets, and such crowds would charge the theatre that mounted police were necessary to control them.

What was this? A passionate love for art? Rather, it was an attempt to see the bright life of the past on the stage, a time when men and women dressed nicely, there was a different way of behaving, a different world with different relationships between people.

It was then that Moskvin fell in love with Alla. After some time had passed, the elderly actor practically became a husband to this young actress who was quickly rising in status. Varvara always thought that Mosvkin, with his soft quality of being part of the intelligentsia, had a good influence on the entire family and Alla, too.

At the war's end, a new head of the household appeared: General Pronin. Fine dishes, clothes, and furniture came flying into the Tarasov home, borne on airplanes. And then a question imperceptibly arose for the family: since Varvara has been around on the earth for so long, couldn't she be moved to a retirement home? To avoid annoying the people who were once close to her, and to avoid discussing the subject any further, "old Mirovich" wrapped herself in an old cloak and walked out into the dark streets of Moscow to find herself another place to sleep.

For those passing through now and those who have already departed

Why, let the strucken deer go weep, the hart ungalled play.

—William Shakespeare, *Hamlet*

The central drama for Varvara Grigoryevna in the late 1930s was the frightening rift between the sorrow around them and the prosperity of the Tarasov family. Circumstances in the Dobrovs' home were very difficult. Filipp Alexandrovich was ill, he made little money, and the family had a hard life, constantly selling items.

But here, in Alla Tarasov's home, under the bright chandelier, the table was always nicely set: caviar, fine fish, fruit – everything that Varvara's other friends never saw.

"My God, my God! How our hearts have hardened!" Varvara Grigoryevna wrote. "One can marvel at sunsets, ensure that the table is placed closer to the bed, pick flowers, laugh with children, or read Bayle's biography, while the person who once loved you, who once gave you the better part of his youth, is suffering, dying, and horribly disappearing without people knowing anything... But after all, God has not and could not abandon the world.'If we are all children of God, then that means that one does not have to fear or regret anything.'"

She could always see the poverty and suffering of others, and for that reason it was very difficult for her to even leave her house in those years.

Anna [a friend of Varvara's – N. G.] and I, two old women living in comfortable conditions, both in warm clothes and clothes, carrying fresh Filippov bread rolls. Here in the tram, there is a very poorly dressed elderly woman with a worn and sad face, obviously a member of the intelligentsia. No gloves on her hands, and ragged felt shoes without rubber boots.

"Where is she going? What is she going to eat? Where is she going to sleep?"

We asked each other these questions and then went to have tea with a white bread roll and cheese. We were afraid to offer her a ruble lest we offend her.

In the spring of 1941, Filipp Dobrov died. People stood at their doors and windows to see their beloved doctor off. Later one of the investigators told Daniil, who was now under arrest, that Dr. Dobrov was secretly a monarchist, and he should have been imprisoned earlier. Thus Dobrov managed to escape arrest.

As Varvara Grigoryevna wrote several days after his death, "He was caught up by the writings of philosophers who lived on the heights of human thought, and by great poets. He wouldn't notice the patches on his suit jacket, how cramped the little room was where his bed stood, divided by a curtain from the bed of a relative [Yekaterina Mikhailovna – N. G.], and three steps away the housekeeper slept. He often wouldn't notice how his wife would scurry around, taking care of everyday tasks and chores, or how it was sometimes difficult for her to make ends meet with the tiny budget of a doctor in private practice (it is ridiculous and hard to believe how, after he had served for forty years as the head of the internist ward in the municipal hospital, he received a pension of only 200 rubles a month after retirement)."

Then, during the war, Elizaveta Mikhailovna Dobrova would follow her husband in passing away, though without great fanfare.

Nevertheless, ten long years had to pass from the time Andreyev began writing *Wanderers of Night* until its completion for the most terrible thing of all to happen. The Dobrovs' home was destroyed. It seemed as if Providence itself allowed Filipp Alexandrovich and Elizaveta Mikhailovna Dobrov to leave for the hereafter before the terrible arrests of their children.

For Daniil, the war was difficult, but he survived and returned home. At first he was on the front in Leningrad. Then, because he was deemed unsuitable for the fighting, he was sent to a burial squad. They buried not only their own soldiers but Germans as well. They would gather bodies that had been torn apart and sometimes were already half-decomposed. They would dig holes and carry the bodies off a horsecart into these graves. The name of the deceased would be written on his stomach with a marker. When the first flowers appeared, Andreyev tried to place a bouquet on each tomb.

At the end of the war, Alla Bruzhes came to the Dobrovs' home after leaving her husband Ivashov-Musatov. She was completely different from Tatyana Usova, who was believed to be Daniil's fiancée. In the Usov home, Andreyev had spent the years leading up to the war and the beginning of the war itself. Tatyana's sister Irina Usova was also secretly in love with Daniil. They would commit his poems to memory or copy them out, cook him meals, and take care of him as they could.

Alla, a beautiful woman with the profile of Botticelli's Venus, loved society life, and dreamed that Daniil would gain recognition as a writer. After the war she organized readings of *Wanderers of Night*, which was doubtlessly suicide.

Through a crack in time: an encounter with the Dobrovs' neighbors

A year after Varvara Grigoryevna Mirovich's diaries came to the museum, we commented on her prewar entry about a young neighbor of the Dobrovs: "She has this grandmotherly tenderness for children and adults, for young people (but certainly not for all the grandsons and granddaughters). In my case, apart from Sergei and his sisters and brothers, it is also for Alexei, for Boris (Olga's brother), and for Rinochka Mezhebovskaya. She is a child with big gray eyes (with a thousand years of sadness in those eyes), small and elegant hands, she speaks sincerely and intelligently, and she has a rare smile, one without joy but kind, that always draws out a great tenderness from me."

By some miracle I managed to find the phone number of this mysterious neighbor of the Dobrovs. Her name was Viktorina. I called her and asked about Varvara Grigoryevna. She remained silent until I mentioned the name Dobrov. Then it seemed as if she was crying.

I went to visit her at her apartment near the Voykovskaya metro station. I was met by a small, thin old woman with her headscarf askew and a simple dress for wearing in the home. Once we were under the light, I examined her face. It was clear that she had once been very beautiful, and at one point the same eyes with a "thousand years of sadness" looked at me that had looked at Varvara Grigoryevna.

But then she became embarrassed and again went back to being the old woman who seemed from another planet. Soon everything became clear. Many years before she had lost her adult daughter, whom she loved dearly, and since then she had deliberately killed everything within her that linked her with the past. She had once been a sculptor, painter, and a beautiful woman.

During her rambling monologue, I realized that after her tragedy she had found God, and now she only prayed and found consolation only in God. She didn't remember her works, which were probably in some museums somewhere. She didn't remember how she had been an artist. She only knew, loved, and remembered God. And the Dobrovs, too. For her they had been a shining light, a happy childhood, and the best time of her life. It was because of them that she became a sculptor. The very atmosphere of that wonderful home had made her love art.

She was born in their apartment, after the regime had settled other people in it, in 1926. Her father had been a doctor, while her mother was a teacher of Russian.

Varvara wrote to her, "…the spring flower that is Rinrinetta…" These were the first lines of a poem dedicated to her, to Rinochka, but the latter didn't remember it any more. She had forgotten everything. It is probably for that reason that she had written some things down before meeting me.

She handed me a sheet of paper.

Dr. Dobrov. A large room. A piano next to the entrance (I was often sitting under the piano, while Filipp Alexandrovich was at the piano). Opposite was the office of Filipp Alexandrovich (paintings, magazines). (Later Daniil and Alla A. lived there). When Filipp Alexandrovich took me to the theatre, I was very happy. Once I went with him to the cinema to see the film *The Great Waltz*. We were both so stunned by it that he got off the tram on Levshinsky Lane and forgot about me, and I kept going until Zubovskaya Square. He healed me. He once saved my life (I almost burned to death in a fire). He carried me, so heavy, in his arms. I was lying on the sofa and reading Dostoyevsky's *Humiliated and Insulted* breathlessly.

Before the war he suffered a stroke and died. At the funeral service, I couldn't manage to cry for some reason.

His daughter was married to Alexander Viktorovich Kovalensky (he made model airplanes and wrote poems). Alexandra Filippovna (Shurochka) loved me very much. When I went to school and went to morning assembly, she would dress me in Ukrainian national dress. The Dobrovs had a son, uncle Sasha (Alexander Filippovich). He and his wife had no children. He was a sickly person. During the war they sent me to a boarding school run by Mosgorzdravotdel. The war ended and we returned to Moscow.

And I remember the terrible day. People came from the MGB to arrest Daniil Andreyev and his wife Alla. They also took Alexander Viktorovich and Alexander Filippovich. Only Alexandra Filippovna was left. And then they took her, too. I heard a terrible cry: "What have you done with him?" and they took her away. The Rachmaninoff second concerto was playing on the radio.

After their release. Reading the diary of Alexander Viktorovich. He covered it with his hand so that Alla Andreyeva couldn't see (Alla Andreyeva died in a fire). I was at the funeral (she was buried in Daniil's grave) at the Novodevichye cemetery.

Each time, it seemed like this couldn't have happened. Now, a person from Back Then stood before me. The chasm was so deep and the connection so tenuous that it seemed that after another minute had passed, the person to whom I was speaking might disappear forever. It wasn't a question of her age – I had known many people older than she was. The difference lay in her belonging to a different civilization; she was from the Dobrov era and I was from the Soviet era.

She told me:

There was a study, and to the left of our corridor, there was a living room with a piano near the entrance. Filipp Alexandrovich was always at the piano. Then there was this large table, then one more room, and another one after that. Elizaveta Mikhailovna and Yekaterina Mikhailovna, I remember those two well... They all lived together. The kitchen was in the basement. What dishes they would make for Easter!

Shurochka Dobrova and Alexander Viktorovich lived in another room. The hallway was quite long. They had a lot of books in their room, and she had such a fantastic bed with a washbasin alongside. I remember well how I loved to lay on that bed with her when I was small. Alexander Viktorovich told me that at night, a little man would come out of the books and walk around the room. I naturally believed all of this. I remember how I would come home from school and say, "Alexander Viktorovich, the landed gentry would suppress the peasants so much!" He would answer, "On our estate we had very good relations with the peasants." He was telling the truth completely. When a plumber would come to their home, they would have him sit at the table, they would feed him, and they would treat him with great respect.

I remember Daniil. But when it comes to Alla, his wife, I don't have a very high opinion of her. After the war – I was already an adult and studying in Stroganovka – I remember how the secret police came. They came and took everyone. Only Alexandra Filippovna was left. I would visit her all the same. She would sit in the room that bordered on ours wearing a black dress. And then they came for her. I heard her in her room – and the walls were thick there, in that old building – shouting "What have you done with him!" savagely. And they took her away. I remember that shout to this day. Later some new tenants appeared. It was the Lomakin family, that family lived across from us. Two brothers. They were also sent to prison.

When those arrested began to be rehabilitated, Alexander Viktorovich was to be released. Alexandra Filippovna (Shurochka) called me and asked me to find a friend of hers. She asked me find out where this friend lived, so that I could help Alexander Viktorovich settle there. She had a son and a daughter, but Alexander Viktorovich didn't love them. Though they weren't little any more, he still didn't have any affection for them, and he complained about this to me. I would visit him, and he would lock us together in a separate room and kiss every one of my fingers and cry, not because he loved me, but because I reminded him of Shurochka, Alexander Filippovna Dobrova. He loved her very much. Alla Alexandrovna also went to prison. Maybe she couldn't stand those interrogations, you see, since a hundred people were sent to prison based on her confession. Alexander Viktorovich invited some literary people over, and at the table there was Alla and then me sitting on the other side. They read his diary, and he hid what was written from Alla Alexandrovna with his hand. I can see that now.

Then she started repeating everything from the beginning word for word. About the Dobrov home, about Alexandra Filippovna. I understood that it was time for me to leave.

The destruction of the Dobrovs

"After the Shipwreck"
I am floating on a rotten wooden plank
In the immensely vast ocean.
All who were saved are already far away —
Behind the wall of the night fog...

—Varvara Malakhieva-Mirovich,
July 5 – August 31, 1948

Varvara Grigoryevna loved Daniil Andreyev like a son, and she often called him "orangerie" or "mimosa". This was an apt label, because he was completely incapable of putting up any resistance to anything. The first time he was interrogated, he wrote up a long list of people who had not only read his novel, but who had heard it recited as well. Varvara Grigoryevna Malakhieva-Mirovich was number 11 in that list. Alla did the same under interrogation. They arrested not only her ex-husband Sergei Ivashov-Musatov, but also Daniil's former fiancée Tatyana Usov, who had been cast aside and had not seen Daniil for three years. And that's not to mention the Dobrovs: Shurochka with Alexander Kovalensky and Alexander Dobrov with his wife Galina. Strangely, of all the people in the list drawn up from the interrogations, only Varvara Grigoryevna and the parents of Daniil's wife were never brought in.

Several days later, Daniil was visited by the investigators at his home, and he showed them the place where the last copy of his novel *Wanderers of Night* was hidden

Before his arrest, or rather, a week before, Varvara Grigoryevna wrote:

"I have managed to restore the relationship with Daniil that sprung up between us thirty-six years ago. Now he is forty, but one would think he was already fifty – his body has been so worn down, burned out. The front, and his illness, and his plunge from Corbenic into Dante's *Inferno*, which he managed to break free of, as if leaping out of a flame, with burn marks and some kind of hellish pitch sticking to bits of his soul. Since I love him, and the fullness of his spirit is dear to me, I want to believe that he has managed to break free. His childlike smile (it is an angelic smile) tells me this. This is how he smiled since the first year we were acquainted, when he was four years old. After the front, for these last three years, that smile appeared only fleetingly, as if through smoked glass, during our rare meetings. Yesterday I saw it for the first time in all its charming clarity, in its otherworldly significance."

He would never meet Varvara Grigoryevna again. In his letters to Alla he would ask her how she died and where she was buried. In the Vladimir prison he suffered a severe heart attack. He went on to write his main work, *The Rose of the World*. Fortunately, he lived to see the death of Stalin and in *The Rose of the World* he described in detail the fall of the tyrant in Hell.

A feeling of guilt never left him, however. When Alla was the first to be released, from a labor camp in Mordovia, he asked her to find out what had happened to everyone who was sent to the camps because of him. Especially because she had ended up in the same place as Shurochka Dobrova, in Potma. (This was very strange, as usually people arrested in connection with the same case were never sent to the same camp). Alla found this request unpleasant, she did not have a good reputation among the prisoners. When Shurochka met her by chance in the camp one day, she refused to even speak with Alla.

Alexandra (Shurochka) Dobrova died from cancer in a hospital in the labor camp in 1956, without even the hope of being released one day. Her husband Alexander Kovalensky came to her to say his farewell. It was later discovered that Alexander had spent all of the reparations that he had received upon being rehabilitated to bring her body to Moscow and bury her in the Dobrov tomb in the Novodevichye cemetery.

"I am completely convinced," Alexander Kovalensky wrote to Daniil Andreyev in prison, "that no other feelings remained in her for you except for warmth. In everything that happened, she saw an untying of the knots that we ourselves and her had tied – but how and why this was, I'm not in a state to talk about it now… Yes, I saw something that is granted to very few people. In the Light of this vision, everything else starts looking bleak, without exception. I don't understand, and I probably never will, why this priceless gift was granted to me particularly, the way I was and still am. While I was trying to understand something, I was reading, studying, writing poems and prose, and she was walking the straightest and shortest path. She reached a place that I wouldn't have been able to crawl without her help for a thousand years. I know, I feel, that I've received this help…"

Alexander Dobrov would die in these same years in a nursing home in the camp. He had nowhere to come back to, for neither his building nor his apartment in Maly Levshinsky Lane existed any longer.

Daniil Andreyev would be released from prison, manage to write *The Rose of the World*, and he left this world in 1959. Alla Andreyeva would live for a good long time. She went on to publish Daniil Andreyev's works, she became blind, and in 2005 she died in the night when a fire broke out in her apartment.

Moscow: the return from the camps

When people bearing the same little bags were released from the labor camps and prisons and headed back to the big city, what awaited them in Moscow?

It wasn't their apartments or rooms – those had long since been reassigned. Rather, they could only find a corner for themselves at the homes of friends and relatives (but so many children, brothers, and sisters who had denounced their loved ones, couldn't even look them in the eye!). And that was only for a time, then it was off again to other refuges, but now outside of Moscow: cottages, sheds, dachas, a hundred miles away from where they had once lived.

In Moscow at that time, in 1962, the world of the Arbat had been wiped out. Those who returned could not find the past again.

Kitchens. Kitchens. The Moscow of the past was being ushered out. The darkness left Moscow, and the wanderers settled in the new developments on the outskirts of the city.

I saw the Arbat lanes being demolished. I was six years old, and I couldn't understand why Moscow was doomed to this. I had been repulsed by old things since childhood: from apartments and houses to smells... My father, still young, took me to the construction sites of the New Arbat and said: look how clean and nice it is. I looked at the remains of demolished houses and the shining glass-fronted buildings being erected next to them. My heart was filled with joy. I swelled with pride at the thought that I would be living close by to these, and I would be able to see this incredible beauty every day.

There was no one who could explain to my father and I, what we had lost.

Wandering through souls

When the war broke out, the Tarasovs were evacuated, which left Varvara essentially the caretaker of the apartment. However, she could not manage everyday tasks on her own with the bombardment of the city. Thus, in the autumn of 1941 she decided to move to Maloyaroslavets, to the home of Natalya Dmitrievna Shakhovskaya. The Germans entered this town in November 1941. They didn't live under German occupation for long, but everything was complicated by the fact that six old women had gathered under the roof of this one home. There was no source of food and the town became a battlefield. Children would go into the forest, searching for dead horses, which was considered a great find. Sometimes, however, this horse meat was already rancid, but people ate it nonetheless. Almost all of the old women died in that winter. They did not die alone, but rather along with their loved ones.

The diaries from this period were lost. The entries begin again only in early 1941, when the battle of Moscow had been fought and the Germans were driven away from the capital. Hunger, death, bombardment – the pages of her notebooks are full of these things, but above all, there is the incredible tenacity of Natalya Dmitrievna, who defended everyone that she had taken in under her roof.

Once, in 1917, Natalya Shakhovskaya had written to Varvara Grigoryevna: "Yesterday it became clear to me, that my life and the life of Mikhail Vladimirovich Shik are inseparable. For me, this happened without any fight or wavering on the point, because a readiness to admit and accept this had been growing in me for a long time. It had gone through such difficulties, it survived such trials, and it overcame my pride along the way... I didn't decide anything. It seems as if it is not us who decides. Somehow, I don't even have thoughts about the future, no joy, trepidation, or fear. There is only a readiness to follow this path to the same place that many paths lead to, which is essentially the only aim of life. I won't hesitate. But I don't know what would have happened to this readiness of mine and how it could have come true, had I not had your blessing, had I not felt it even before it came."

Natalya Shakhovskaya had the rare faith of the first Christians and martyrs. She believed in the idea of the Priyutino brotherhood, and she always shared the labors of her father, Prince D. I. Shakhovskoy, one of the founders of the Constitutional Democratic Party. In the religious sphere, she forged an independent path and followed it with incredible dedication. She supported her father in all his undertakings – their arrest and imprisonment by the Cheka was connected with their development of cooperatives. She was a good writer, but she could not produce many works because she had to take care of her family. Doctors had categorically warned her against having children. She gave birth to five. However, her forces were diminishing.

In June 1942 Natalya Shakhovskaya managed to enter a tuberculosis ward in Moscow, but it was already too late: her health was destroyed for good. As Varvara wrote:

An honest death before the Lord. Natalya is in the morgue. Since yesterday. And the day after tomorrow her dried body, destroyed by illness and hunger, will be given to the earth at the Vagankovsky cemetery. No one in this world will be able to see her clear eyes, through which her high spirit looked out, soaring with lofty aspirations and without a single stain on its white robes. No one will see her wonderful, life-giving smile (the light of which she partly shared with Sergei and Maria). With this smile and a tender handshake (and, before that, also a kiss on the hand) she bid farewell to me the day before she died.

And, like it always happens, she rises to her full stature, as if under the strange beam of a stage light, in the first days after her death, her inner self, the personality that we knew in different phases, refractions, and eclipses. Not only us, people close to her, but also the patients of the 38th Tuberculosis Ward, where she parted from her earthly form – everyone felt the hierarchic trembling: "A saint has lived among us."

One of Varvara's reminiscences of the war years, almost mundane in its observations.

Natalya returned after an entire day of wandering around the countryside, where she bartered for flour and frozen potatoes almost everything that she had around the house: linen, and pillows, and dresses. To feed twelve people – her family and the six old ladies that she took in during the war.

She stood with her back to the stove, trying in vain to warm up. When I stood next to her, she turned her face to me, pale and weary but lit from within.

"It's great, isn't it, *baba* Vava?" Natalya asked me.

"What's so great?" I answered.

"The fact that we're freezing and can't get warm, that we're hungry, there's rubble everywhere, and bombs flying over our heads."

After she had been silent for a time, she added:

"It's great to suffer with everyone. And for everyone."

The soul grew its wings back, and it could not satisfy its love for God and man in any other way.

Varvara later wrote, "For two days now, I keep seeing Dmitri's face as he used to look at his mother a long time ago, back in the winter. Before going to sleep, she stood with her back to the stove, her head back, her hands behind her back and pressed against the stove, and her eyes closed. She stood there for a long time, she didn't have the strength to walk away from it. It was as if she was crucified on the stove tiles, nailed to them and ready to give up the ghost. Dmitri looked at her from behind the table, where he was doing his homework. He looked at her for a long time, without taking his eyes off her, and he had such a suffering look, as if he was now being crucified, too."

Natalya Dmitrievna demonstrated such a level of spiritual effort that Varvara Grigoryevna saw it as an unattainable height.

A halo of martyrdom also appeared over the fates of Varvara's "adopted daughters", as she called her young friends. After the war, Daniil Andreyev's onetime fiancée, Tatyana Usova, was arrested, and Varvara had maintained a very close friendship with her. Then came the arrest of Yevgeniya Birukova, who had always helped her, gave her shelter, and had been a friend of V. G. since her youngest days.

Olga Bessarabova disappears

As I read Varvara Grigoryevna's diaries, and I saw how the people around her disappeared, I asked myself where Olga Bessarabova was in the last years of her life.

Olga had, after all, copied out four thousand of Varvara's poems that had been scattered about. Olga made transcriptions of her diary entries, put them in order, and numbered the pages.

As I wrote before, Olga married Stepan Borisovich Veselovsky in 1928. His relationship with Varvara Grigoryevna didn't go very well.

Olga practically became a secretary to her scholarly husband. For the first decade, she tried to break away and see Varvara Grigoryevna, in spite of the exceptionally difficult existence that Olga bore on her shoulders. During the war, Olga, her husband, and their daughter were evacuated to Tashkent. After the war, Veselovsky became a member of the academy, he received an apartment and a dacha. Nonetheless, Olga Bessarabova's life did not get any easier.

In 1947 she was summoned to the NKVD, where they held her for an entire day. Later she told her daughter that they demanded she testify against Favorsky and his circle. They didn't get anything from her, but she paid a great price for that one day of interrogation. Several days later she suffered a heart attack; she tried to conceal the true cause of it from everyone.

One might suppose that they questioned her about more than Favorsky. Otherwise, it would be hard to explain why she avoided talking to Varvara Grigoryevna for the next two years. Judging by the year in which this happened, they might have tormented her with questions about the Dobrov home, Daniil Andreyev, and, of course, Malakhieva-Mirovich.

One can see that the men in the MGB torture chambers tried to break Olga Bessarabova, who was such a bright personality and so resigned to her life and fate. It was not easy for her to withstand blackmail and threats. It is precisely out of fear for the people close to her that she blackened out in her diaries, and then in Varvara Grigoryevna's, the names of those who had been arrested: Daniil Andreyev, Alexander Kovalensky, and others. The secret police were probably trying to get information on these particular people out of her.

Nonetheless, in a letter from the hospital that she entered after all of her torments, one suddenly hears the same voice as in her diaries from her youth. It was Olga Bessarabova's true voice. They could not kill the life within her. As Olga wrote:

"...How many of our friends and loved ones are waiting for us, Vava. It cannot, it just cannot be that they are not there waiting for us and that we will not meet the ones who loved us and whom we loved. A person who has 'loved' (in general), and not just lived in this world – such a person cannot die. And only those who have never loved anyone, only those die, because they haven't lived at all. ...I haven't got the faintest idea about that world. Evening lights, sunrises, the air after the rain, the sun. My beloved earth... Dust, earth – for the nihilist Bazarov it is burdock. And why not burdock, and why not a 'handful of ash'? All is in me, and I am in all. There is no death. With every breath, every thought, every phenomenon of life, in all the world and in all our earthly human life, I know: there is no death. All-in-oneness... Life. They will be there always."

Once, in 1916, Varvara wrote to the 19-year-old Olga who was then lying in the hospital: "One shouldn't wish something hard on a loved one. But someone whose lot it is to face these things, is a chosen one... You sought from life, as its first and greatest gift, knowledge. Life responded to you in a well-disposed way by revealing an exceedingly short path that leads through a narrow gate, a path of pain and suffering... I believe that your path will lead you high and far, and that this gate was not opened to you in vain. I embrace you with love."

It was now possible to say that the true gates of Knowledge, which they could not even imagine, opened wide before their eyes. Both of them passed through such a grave experience of different losses and misfortunes that now they met with the true Reality. But nothing could be done to them any more, because they had already *survived* Death, they were outside of its bounds. "There is no death. All-in-oneness... Life. They will be there always."

The varieties of religious experience

A person from the pre-Soviet world knew a certain something that kept him alive even in times of the most terrible trials.

This was not only faith, but also an awareness that life has some higher meaning. Varvara Grigoryevna was a seeker from the moment her consciousness first awoke to her last hour. As a translator of and guide to William James' book *The Varieties of Religious Experience*, Varvara Grigoryevna explored, described, and studied the manifestations in our present world of the Other World.

"The other world. Invisible. I was happy to come across these words, this thought by James, during my time spent languishing in Zagorsk. With these words, this thinker, who was far from subscribing to mysticism, but who honestly and persistently aimed to understand through reason what faith is, he says what every person who is even slightly mystically gifted senses, feels, and knows without any argumentation. I am grateful to him for this book, for his wise company in the necropolis, where I have experienced the double loneliness of Mirovich from the tragic side: in the sphere of everyday life and in the spiritual sphere. On the physical level, thanks to some circumstances of my relocation, I have come to realize that the real-world, practical tool for detecting the value of human relationships, just like a hundred years ago and a thousand years ago, are blood ties, the law of the generations, the family. This is where *vae soli*[2] came from."

For her the religious life was a stream, a continuous movement. Everything that hardened, turned to stone,

---

2   Latin for 'the sorrow of the person who is alone'.

whether among the people or in the lives of individuals, was unacceptable to her.

She attend church and tried to grasp Hinduism and Buddhism. In her youth, she had twice met the noted occultist Annie Besant and recalled how she had experienced a transformation of consciousness. She was interested in the writings of Besant, who talked about bodily and spiritual coverings. Nonetheless, she wasn't at all a mystic or follower of esoteric thought, although Fr. Pavel Florensky who knew her in Sergiev Posad called her an "occult bog". She had an acute sense of all of the trends of this era, when people were passionately searching for a New Faith and a New God, which involved great danger for all these seekers.

She wrote, thinking of how they were all being tossed about in this ocean:

The decadent movement – not just literature, has its initial essence. Decadence is, first of all, willfulness, breaking away, self-determination, and lawlessness.

A poor-quality idea had triumphed, namely that "everything is permitted", that there is nothing sacred, no norms, no rules, no dogma, that one could transgress any boundaries.

It is hard for me to imagine now how a soul could withstand all these years of purgatory, and sometimes even one of the circles of hell. "The shadow of luciferian wings" doubtlessly hovered over me and over my sister in some acute moment of recklessness, willfulness, and desperation. Maybe I was able to withstand it because – as Geogri Ivanovich [Chulkov] has aptly described it – in decadence "light alternates with darkness". There were times when the soul was lit by a ray of light. We sang litanies to Satan (in French, a duet!), and some time later we went running towards the starets Barnabas in the hermitage at Chernigov, to some Varsonofy in New Jerusalem, who turned out to be such a drunkard that he couldn't put two words together.

The shadow of luciferian wings brushed not only Varvara, but also Sergei Durylin and Fr. Sergei Sidorov at one point when they were deep into occult techniques.

However, this experience only made their subsequent faith stronger.

Once Varvara Grigoryevna heard her close friend Konstantin Tarasov say, "Our spiritual seekers are looking for what nature and all our inner world tells us at every step…"

She wrote that these words were said by a "godless realist" shortly before he died, after he had experienced a sense of cosmic consciousness. He shared with her this experience when she was in a depressed state, and his account brought her back to life.

A firm belief in the possible existence of an "expanded consciousness" would not leave her for the rest of her life. She points out all possible cases in which she had such an experience, beginning from childhood.

This feeling, I first experienced it in my sixties on a mountain road overlooking the sea in Crimea. It involved my father's gleaming face, covered with tears of exaltation, as he held me in his arms. It involved my tears, my trepidation, the smell of dry and aromatic herbs (I had recognized this smell two years ago at the ruins of Chersonesus).

An expansion of the soul without limits, a state of being struck by the beauty of the world, a marriage with eternity, a Love for my father – and through him, for all things and for Him, Who is hidden within it. And a sweet, joyous fear that I would see Him one day, and I wouldn't be able to bear it…

At the age of twenty-six, at the St. Andrew church in Kiev with Lev Isaakovich – when I was telling him about Christ's temptation in the desert.

In later years – after a meeting with Mintslova – a transfigured Moscow, a feeling that all who died were alive…

The Optina Hermitage, the white halo around the starets' head. Transfigured nature (the forest, the paths leading through it, glowing in the darkness of the night). Joy, the disappearance of all desires, except for the desire for death. I cannot express in words this filial obedience.

The starets Fr. Anatoly, who would later be declared a saint, did not see any "occult bog" in her, and he blessed her tenderly for the trials she would face later.

"The face of my sister Anastasia during her period of mental illness that preceded her total breakdown, was full of light. It seemed almost transparent and enveloped with a white halo. During that time she called me from Moscow to say: 'The devil was in me. But now, God is in me.'"

Dr. Bekki, whom Varvara recalled in her diary, wrote at the end of the 19th century about expansion of consciousness, and he called "cosmic" the third stage, which was higher than a human being's ordinary consciousness. It is as if a human being is connected to the life of the universe, Along with an awareness of the universe, he claimed, an intellectual lucidity would come, transporting a person to a new means of existence that is connected with a feeling of elation, joy, and mental strength. Along with this, an awareness of eternal life would come. The most incredible thing of all is that this does not contradict traditional beliefs.

This was her own personal experience, which she did not impose on anyone, but those close to her felt it extremely necessary. She would peruse again and again the book that she had once translated.

After reading James's *The Varieties of Religious Experience.*

For the people close to me that have read this book, I want to add to the facts mentioned in that book about "phenomena involving light" some things that I have experienced personally. The most vivid example, which had a deep meaning for me (although I did not realize it right away in my heart and soul), happened at the Optina Hermitage more than thirty years ago.

When I stood among the other prayerful people under the blessing of Fr. Anatoly, I saw him surrounded by a sort of halo of bright white light and rays issuing forth that were unusually pleasant.

Several minutes later, when I had already left the reception area and gone to the entrance to the building, Fr. Anatoly sent an attendant to call me back. He invited me into his cell. There all of the objects, just like Fr. Anatoly himself, seemed as if they were illuminated from within themselves, but not with the same blinding light as the halo around his head when he was blessing the pilgrims.

Many times I have experienced these phenomena of light in the form of prismatic figures stretched out in ascending lines (or incomplete prisms and shining triangles).

Twice in my life they have merged into a single mass of prisms around me. Once they barred my way (when I was going up the stairs to Anna's apartment). I thought they were symptoms of some neurologically caused problem with my sight. But once, a person who was mystically gifted and well-versed in James's thought, told me authoritatively, "This is an entering into a sphere of perception, which is symbolically opened to you with prismatic light. Later you will understand what they meant. I know this phenomenon very well." I never managed to figure out what this all meant, but I stopped believing that it was a sign of illness.

It often happens that such thoughts are overgrown, as if covered in barnacles, with a large amount of speculation or the spiritualist revelations of not entirely sane people. One of her closest friends from the younger generation and a person she could talk to was Daniil Andreyev, who based his book *The Rose of the World* on such revelations.

He depicted in a remarkable way his experiences of his encounter with the Other World when he lived in Trubchevsk on the Nerussa river: "When the moon, noiselessly moving behind the finely patterned, leafy branches of the willow, entered the range of my vision, those hours that come close to being the most wonderful of my entire life began. Breathing softly, having laid back on a handful of hay, I heard the Nerussa flowing not behind me, a few paces back, but as if through my own soul. That was the first unusual thing I noticed. Everything on Earth and every-thing that must exist in the heavens poured exultantly and noiselessly through me in a single stream. In bliss barely supportable by the human heart, I felt as if slowly revolving, graceful spheres glided through me in a universal dance, and everything I could think of or imagine merged in a jubilant oneness."

Artistic creation would be impossible without such a feeling of oneness with the world. I felt something similar once as I was walking along the boulevard in Chistye Prudy, under a spring sun so blinding that it was hard to see any-thing. I only heard the squealing of children running by, the movements of people around me, and it suddenly I felt as if everyone was passing through me: the children, the people, and the sun. I became permeable and transparent – and this produced in me a strange sense of oneness with everything that exists in the world and in nature.

Personal experience

Not long before she died, Varvara wrote:

Recently, it is as I feel the movement of the globe, espe-cially if I close my eyes. Or on sleepless nights, in the darkness. If it happens during the day, then I can't sit on a chair, I have to lie down. I've forgotten which writer (perhaps it was Pascal) wrote about what he called *vertige d'infini* "the dizzying sense of infinity".

Any doctor would say, "It's simply nausea in your head from hypertension." I won't deny that, that's something I know very well. But I don't know if medicine has a way of proving that this so-called hypertension is an effect of the brain that causes a new feeling of movement (as well as time and space) in old age and on the threshold of death.

The most incredible thing of all is that Maria Iosifovna Belkina's account of her experience of joining with the universe was incredibly similar. She told me that her body trembled from every change in the weather, solar flares, and the movement of atmospheric fronts. She felt how clouds gathered in the sky, and how the sun sought to break through them. It was certainly because a person comes from the universe and returns to it.

Over the last ten years, I have met people who are not simply elderly, but who are very close to this Threshold between this world and the other one. Our conversations about the past or about literature inevitably turn to stories of experiencing "another kind of state". The older the person I talked to was, the more important such an experience was for them. Many of them were ashamed of it, because they thought, like Maria Iosifovna, that people would consider it a sign of dementia.

I have often thought that, if there was a way that we could record and then compile the various testimonies of our inner experiences, then we would be able to see connections and meanings that we normally cannot see.

Each person shows his or her own imprint of experiences, and if one could put them all together, we would get a big picture with the answers to many questions, including the role of Providence in the life of every person. This was actually what the psychologist William James set out to do in a systematic fashion in his book *The Varieties of Religious Experience*, shifting the boundaries of the invisible.

Of course, a lot of what Varvara experienced also seemed familiar to me, because I walked the same paths, and I was troubled by the same questions. Once, I felt that I could see this strange connection between life and what might come after it. It seemed a person should completely fulfill his purpose here, and only after that would he have a task to do in the other world, just like the stages of a rocket that fall away one after the other.

Why is it so hard to sense the Other World? Maybe it's because we are inside of Time, which moves, and over there is an absolute Eternity? We are located within different states of time. Only when some burst of energy happens, then a crossing of those worlds occurs. An artist can feel this otherness intuitively.

I stopped trying to see the future. I thought that several times I had managed to, though I might be wrong. This happens between sleep and wakefulness, when you close your eyes and try to distinguish certain images. Maybe it is all just my imagination.

The departed that I know, look like bundles of light. They are located in different places and not all of them cross each other's paths. They do something there, they are busy with something, they are creating something that I cannot fathom. This light resembles the light which is depicted in the halos of the saints.

When the difficult process of spiritual growth, of change, takes place, it is wearying, and it is accompanied by a fear of death, a fear of invisible threats. Everything becomes unstable and frightening. Spiritual strength, energy should be accompanied by humility, with destroying the fear in oneself and increasing the love. I have already seen how all true wisdom says literally one and the same thing, only in different words.

Varvara Grigoryevna Malakhieva-Mirovich passes away

In the early 1940s, one more remarkable thing took place in Varvara Grigoryevna's life. The actor Igor Ilyinski (his mother had once been a friend of Varvara Grigoryevna, and his sister had attended the Joy circle), at a time of a deep spiritual crisis linked to the death of his wife, read a book he had come across by chance: *The Varieties of Metaphysical Experience* in V. G. Malakhieva-Mirovich's translation. He began to look for Varvara so that he might seek her support. She was already hard of hearing by that time and she talked with everyone with the help of a rolled-up newspaper held to her ear.

Igor Ilyinski revealed to her not only a personal crisis, but a creative one as well.

Under the mask of a Soviet comic actor, there was a tragic actor hiding. He was not at all happy with his life on the stage and in films, he felt very alone, and he was secretly a believer. She gave him her support for several years, but when he gained a new family, he left to his new everyday routine, to his family obligations, and Varvara stopped caring for him. This happened very often in her life.

The worst thing of all was that with increasing age, she found it more and more difficult to find people to talk to; the war, arrests, and the deaths of her friends had taken away the people who thought about such matters and who asked themselves such questions as: "…the spiritual solitude of Mirovich… I've realized that I have no companions on the path of my faith, in its dynamic quality, in its creativity. And that if I shared with the people around me some stages on the path of developing my soul in its present incarnation, then the people closest and dearest to me would either think me a heretic, or a dreamer and madwoman. Or if, like in one of Chekhov's stories, or how it happened many times in the Tarasovs' home, I decided to share my thoughts, some experience of my soul, they would think: 'She just wants to show how educated she is, and she always talks about things no one understands.' This was what their contradictions were really about, the look on their faces. Actually, not always. Most often, it was simply incomprehension or indifference."

Varvara often imagined herself among homeless and poor elderly people, and she would always pinch herself: her fate could not be compared to the fates of those she saw come to the door of her friend's home on Ostozhenka Street when would stay there.

"…Early in the morning, poor people with crutches would shuffle in the semi-darkness towards the dark blue of the Ilya Obydenny church. There were hunchbacked old women with canes. The majority of them were dressed in rags, in threadbare clothes. Where do they spend their nights? In what filth, in what darkness, in what stench? In what cold? Among these poor, I am a privileged pauper, but sometimes it is a sad and difficult time for me, too. How is it for them, when begging before the church doors is their fate not in a metaphorical sense, like in my case, but in the most literal sense: getting up so early so that you don't miss matins; hurrying along on your crutches over the slippery cobblestones towards Ilya Obydenny; standing on your feet, worrying, and envying when someone else gets a ruble and you only get half. What can you buy for that?"

She turned out to me unlike anyone else.

The people around her were always moving towards some kind of goal, whether large or very narrow. They worked, raised children, established families, wrote books. For the entire first half of her life, Varvara Grigoryevna tried to do what everyone else was doing, but fate constantly pointed her in a different direction. While her companions, especially children and adolescents, listened to her and heard her, they took her lessons to their hearts, absorbed her experience, and they walked alongside her, but as soon as they grew up and began raising families, and began to solve their own problems, they abandoned her. The adults generally treated her with caution.

The closest to her of all were children. Newborns would reach towards her. Children and adolescents would, with her, explore a world that she discovered step by step together with them, and then they would fly away. She was a true spiritual mother to many children and even adults. It is remarkable how many people she helped to bring up, sometimes even by a single encounter with them. She was a continent inhabited by the most varied people. They lived, departed, and returned. But in her heart they lived on forever.

Her main trait was living and exploring the process of living itself.

For the entire second half of her life, Varvara Grigoryevna prepared herself for death. She feared it, but she awaited and even called it to her.

However, death took her unexpectedly. The diaries break off three months before she passed away. The last lines already float over the page, words run towards different directions on the paper. In these lines she thanks Alla for finding a possibility to get her into a hospital, for the fact that Tarasova was her adopted daughter again again.

To the Tarasovs' credit, it must be mentioned that they buried Varvara Grigoryevna in the Vvedenskoye cemetery, where they themselves would eventually lay beside her one after the other. Thus, after accepting her into their family, they kept her close forever.

The last notebook ends with a line written in Olga Bessarabova's hand: "Varvara Grigoryevna Malakhieva-Mirovich died on August 16, 1954."

Olga continued her dialog with Varvara after the latter's death by reading her diaries.

How painful it must have been for Olga Bessarabova to see these pages addressed to her with questions full of sadness and grief.

Every time I looked through the last pages of the diaries, I saw again and again the letters fleeing towards different directions on the page, and it hurt me so much, as if someone close to me was passing away. I couldn't understand why this was happening. Maybe it was because I had lived with Varvara day after day for twenty-four years of her life. She crossed my path completely unexpectedly, I didn't go looking for her, I didn't call her to me. It happened on its own. But it was as if she answered me:

"There are no coincidences on one's spiritual path, this is something I have already witnessed many times in my life and the life of those close to me. I have realized many times how along the paths of our souls, we encounter the people, books, and trials we should at the points we should – and that there is nothing accidental in the life of a person who is aware that he is moving where a higher Will leads him (even though it might involve delays or mistakes due to his insignificance – but everything is corrected in time). A knowledge of the ultimate meanings and goals of this movement is something we are not granted until the appointed time. But according to the feeling in the depths of one's consciousness, a person is granted a knowledge of what steps he took together with God, and which ones were against that greater plan, and for the sake of which he was appointed to pass through this incarnation."

It seemed to me that Varvara Grigoryevna created a common fabric of being for everyone that fate brought her together with, with all of her companions on life's path, and by weaving these fabric, she joined them together with one another. I seemed to have been woven into the same fabric and joined together with everyone else. This is mentioned in one of the entries in her diary, as if it were addressed to me personally: "If I had found somewhere in the attic a notebook with the honest imprint of the (inner) life of an unknown person, neither a poet nor a thinker, and if I knew that he was already dead, then for the sake of communicating with him after death I would read this notebook greedily, with sympathy, and with a sense of brotherhood, with a feeling of some kind of victory over death."

The Tsvetaeva museum took Olga Bessarabova and Varvara Grigoryevna's archives into its collection. Neither liked Tsvetaeva very much, and Tsvetaeva probably didn't even remember who they were, but in the end they all wound up together.

Who knows what turn one's life might take after one's death.

The Marina Tsvetaeva museum: ends and beginnings

We've carried our cross for everyone,
Walked a difficult path.
Oh, Lord, save the ones
Who will come after us!

—Yulia Panysheva

I needed to go along the furrows of memory. From the beginning to the end. And again from the end back to the beginning. Only then will we be able to remember what has happened. This remembrance brings back to life those who now look down at us from above.

Could I have imagined that, once I picked up the notebooks containing Olga Bessarabova's diaries, I would find myself at the beginning of a broken path, which would let me feel a completely different passage of time – their non-Soviet time and my Soviet time?

How distant I was from the map of the real Moscow, which, so I thought, I had known from childhood, but which now turned out to be only a mirage, a fantasy, a shroud thrown over the City that has gone away from us.

A rupture of our common memory occurred along some inner line, and Olga Bessarabova, Varvara Grigoryevna, and all the characters in their diaries ended up as if on the other bank of a river. They cry out to us, wave to us, but we can only make out scattered words and see their waving hands.

I had to not only read their diaries and books, but also try to find their reflection on the objects and buildings that no longer existed.

The work of history begun just before New Year's, came full circle, and reached the point that I had started out from. Tatyana Neshumova compiled and wrote a commentary for Varvara Grigoryevna's volume of poems *Chrysallis* (*Khrizalida*). When an evening dedicated to Varvara Grigoryevna Malakhieva-Mirovich was organized at the museum, I understood utterly clearly that great things can happen right before our eyes.

In the hall sat Maria Mikhailovna, Elizaveta Mikhailovna, and Dmitri Mikhailovich Shik-Shakhovskoy. They were from eighty-five years old to eighty-nine respectively. Three of the five children born to those parents that died so tragically, had miraculously survived to our time. They even said that they were now living the years that had been taken from their parents.

"We haven't repaid our debt to Varvara Grigoryevna," they said. "We are her children, after all."

Their parents had also been her children, in a sense, as were Tatyana and I. Their total openness spoke of something so serious that was happening right now: the fact that people were listening to them with such a hushed focus that spread throughout the room, rustling like a wave.

This story that had seemed a personal one, demanded its own ending. And one eventually came. All of the knots had been untied. Varvara found her first readers. Her "adopted children", who were already older than her, finally met with her. It was totally clear that those words addressed to Varvara Grigoryevna were necessary for them first of all, and infinitely important for us, too.

I walk out of the Biblioteka Imeni Lenina metro station. In front of me are the towers of the Kremlin, and further down the Novy Arbat. Daniil Andreyev had a vision that over the towers of the earthly Kremlin rose the Heavenly Kremlin. If such really exists, then it has long ago broken away from the one here and it is flying away somewhere over the earth in space.

A lady crosses herself as she stood in a trolleybus passing the church on Povarskaya Street. On the steps of the cathedral a couple of homeless are wrapping themselves in rags. No one invites them into the church, just like they never did before.

The Novy Arbat lies over Moscow like a tablecloth that has been cleared of everything. Cars jam-packed together in the lanes honk their horns, first timidly, and then louder and more insistently, as the vehicles of bigwigs fly by with sirens roaring. It's like that every week.

The hunger that persisted for many years through the 20th century has been replaced by the satiety of the 21st. The eternal fatigue of the past years has given way to drowsiness. Can the inhabitants of the City now consider themselves fortunate? Maybe they deserve this kind of life? Does the City preserve any memory of the catacomb churches, does it know about the secret house churches? Does it know about the wanderers of night? What does it remember about its life? Where does the soul of the city lie?

When I followed Varvara Grigoryevna's gaze, how she looked at the hills of Kiev, then I thought with sadness about Moscow's soul being plucked out of it, this city where the remaining wanderers of night gathered and where we dwell today. I think that there is no place which would join our gaze with theirs.

It may be, however, that they live in one of the narrow lanes where wooden fences and low windows have survived by chance. Or in the quiet backstreets of the Arbat, where sometimes we hear the echo of our footsteps.

There is a dark thread that connects that time with ours – an omnipresent fear under the surface. And there is a bright thread connecting the past and the present – this is love and compassion for the departed.

Spring brought the children of the Occupy movement onto the boulevards of Moscow. This was their Way of the Cross. In chorus, young men and women would repeat the words of the people giving speeches so that the back ranks could hear what was said. These choruses created an unusual atmosphere. The City, which didn't know itself, was becoming an Abode. It had long forgotten that it could accept people in, not into apartments behind iron doors and window slits, but into the palms of its streets, squares, and parks.

These children were hunted by men in uniforms. The young men and women would themselves become wanderers for several months, the Children of the City. They were thrown into the back of police vans. The entire brute machinery of the regime rose against them, but they would come at night to the boulevards so that the City would remember that it is alive.

Once in the dark streets of Moscow, in the spiderweb of lanes, individual wanderers of the night would walk around, enclosed in the deadly cauldron of the Thirties and Forties. Their grandchildren and great-grandchildren must now walk the same roads.

One thing comforted me, however: next to these children and wanderers stood the family of Dr. Dobrov, Olga Bessarabova, Varvara Grigoryevna Malakhieva-Mirovich, Lev Shestov, and many other martyrs, known and unknown, of our bitter history.

2010–2013

Chapter 6.
The House That Flew Away

A story

Whenever I had a fight with my parents, I would always imagine that I had been a foundling child. This started when I was around ten years old. Any reproach from my father was all it took for me to think: I probably wasn't their own child, they were concealing the truth from me, and somewhere out there my real parents were walking around, they would never raise their voices at me, and they certainly wouldn't cuff me on the nape. My tears would flow as I felt sorry for myself.

I would turn over these tragic, and, at the same time, sweet thoughts on our balcony. The balcony was small, with thick bars, and it hung over an enormous yard. The building consisted of communal apartments, though for some reason it was called "The Generals'", and it featured a silver-painted Lenin in the flower bed, a skating rink with gypsum figures of Pioneers at the entrance, and a green gazebo built from wooden boards, from which one would hear the squealing of girls or the twang of a guitar in the evenings.

The balcony became my place of solitude for a long time, and there I would meditate on the vanity of all things. I would look out from the heights of the ninth floor at the little shapes of people below: perhaps my real mother and father were there among them, and they couldn't even guess that I was watching them? The history I bore inside my head got increasingly intricate, someone turned out to be someone else, someone learned from someone else about my family's past, and, a miracle!, finally everything would be cleared up. My current parents would get down on their knees before me and beg me not to leave them. At the end of the play that was acted out before my inner gaze, I forgave everyone. Everyone would embrace.

When the first warm days came, the balcony served as my bed. I placed an old mattress on its concrete floor, covered it with my father's military cloak, and, when evening fell over the city, I would crawl into a sleeping bag. There, freezing, I would look through the bars at the endless space of the city lying under me. In the distance the Moscow River flowed on with little flames. Over it hung a metro bridge where shining metro carriages would run. I felt that I wasn't lying there, I was flying over the City, and my balcony was the basket of a hot-air balloon setting off straight into the sky.

We ended up in this building in a completely miraculous way: our family received the right to move from a communal apartment on the outskirts to a 12-floor building on Prospekt Kalinina, which furthermore stood right on the bank of the Moscow River. Back then my father had taken me, a nine-year-old girl with braids down to my shoulders, to look at the new apartment. It was on the ninth floor. We spent a long time going up in the elevator with its varnished wood and mirrors gleaming on both sides. It took our breath away.

On a light-colored door a nameplate shown, where "Colonel Malyshev" was written in cursive. I looked at my father with surprise.

"Those are the neighbors we'll have. Imagine, there is only one family living there now, and not ten like before."

A door was opened to us by a gray-haired military man, but this turned out to be not Colonel Malyshev but Major Kuzhelkov; he was frantically tying books and clothes up into bundles, and his movements had a strange haste to them, as if he was trying to escape from there as quickly as possible. It was precisely in these two rooms that Kuzelkov was now emptying, that we were going to live.

My father leaned over him and cheerfully asked:

"Well, how's life, comrade major, how are the neighbors?"

Kuzelkov shuddered. For a movement he froze over the boxes and, without lifting his gaze, he said:

Ah, yes… People are different. It didn't work out for us. Maybe things will be different for you…

My father only answered by nodding cheerfully. It was obvious how much he liked the two large and well-lit rooms after the one room where the four of us had been living, how he was joyously looking down on Prospekt Kalinina with people swarming like ants, on the old lanes of the Arbat that were being demolished ahead, and how he was happy to see a new Moscow being built. He grabbed me under my arms and set me before the enormous window, so that I would feel the same surge of happiness that he did.

Our neighbors turned out to be three women.

The mother was a woman already advanced in years with gray strands of hair covering her sharp eyes, and with a ceaseless grin that could change from obsequiousness to sarcasm – she was Colonel Malyshev's widow. The two unmarried daughters – Lyuda and Galya – worked at a secret military facility. At first, when they met us they would smile, but their faces really lit up when they saw men, and especially soldiers.

They resembled their mother to a degree, but this resemblance only became visible when their expressions grew dull. They considered themselves ladies of marriageable age, and they would organize birthday parties at their place with the married officers from their workplace. However, their coworkers, after raising toasts, kissing the ladies' hands in farewell, and eating and drinking up everything laid out on the table, would go home in the evening to their wives and children. Lyuda and Galya probably cried at night from the unfairness of life; I would sometimes hear sobbing sounds coming from under their door. In the morning, they would apply a thick layer of powder to their faces, put on long fringed skirts that resembled drapes, hang a lacquered handbag on their arms, and set off to work.

For some reason, at the very beginning of our life in the new apartment, Valentina Ivanovna – that was the name of the mother of the family – led me on an excursion through their rooms.

Two huge carved cupboards, reaching to the ceiling and covered with black varnish, gloomily looked at one another from opposite sides of the living room. In the near future these monsters, which could neither be disassembled nor taken out of the apartment, would in a way determine the fate of our family; all attempts to exchange apartments, to move out of one's present one, had been unsuccessful (so our neighbors said) because of those cursed cupboards. It was as if these fossils reared back so that no one could move them from their place.

In the meantime, however, I looked with amazement at these strange rooms, where semi-darkness reigned and there was a smell of naphthalene and dampness; I was amazed that on top of everything – the piano, armchairs, and even the table – white covers had been placed. To start with, Valentina Ivanovna brought me to the window; across from us the skeleton of an tall old building rose askance, and a wrecking ball was mutely smashing through it.

"That was the prison where Nadezhda Konstantinovna Krupskaya was sent!" she said triumphantly. I felt awkward, and not knowing how to answer this, I asked:

"Where is your husband, Colonel Malyshev?"

Valentina Ivanovna gave me a severe look, and I even thought she winced.

"What a curious little girl you are," she said, grabbing me roughly by the elbow and pushing me towards the next room. She opened a glass door covered with a white piece of fabric. I glanced around me: this was the bedroom, and in the center there was an enormous double bed with a bed cover over it. I shivered: for some reason, it seemed that now Colonel Malyshev himself would crawl out from under the white bedclothes.

I lifted my head. Over the bed, an enormous photograph hung in a heavy frame.

"That's him!" the window said triumphantly, and her obsequiously sarcastic smile distorted the expression on her face.

It was no portrait from waist up showing him with his medals. Instead, the photograph showed a coffin covered with flowers and wreaths, in which a man with a powdered face lay in parade dress. Over him Valentina Ivanovna towered stoically in a black hat, along with her two daughters, and behind them was a sea of epaulets flowing over the enormous hall with white columns.

I was still at the tender age when not only the dead, but even the mere sight of a coffin or cemeteries filled me with an inexplicable horror. Once, when I was going out the door of our apartment, I saw two men bringing a coffin down from the top floor. The elevator was too small for it, so they had to carry it down. I ran down the stairs as if death itself were chasing me. Furthermore, in "The Generals'", there was a village tradition, which I now know to be quite old, of placing a coffin on stools in front of the building entrance, so that all of the deceased's neighbors could say their farewells. I would try to walk past it without opening my eyes.

The photograph on my neighbor's wall always placed thoughts in my mind of how she wasn't entirely normal. However, I didn't try to share my conclusions with my parents.

They were young and naive; they were hardly into their thirties. They were enjoying the enormous size of the rooms, the large kitchen and some freedom in when they could use the toilet and bath. Meanwhile, I tried to get used to my new life.

Unfortunately, after some six months had passed, my parents' relationship with our neighbors broke down. Why that was, I cannot remember, but it happened suddenly, at once, and for good. Once, when I was going into the kitchen, I saw a huge dog chain and lock on the refrigerator door. I ran into our room saying that Valentina Ivanovna had probably got herself a dog that lived in the refrigerator. My parents only shook their heads sadly, and my father said obliquely:

"Remember what Kuzelkov said."

From my mother's nervous shout coming from the kitchen, I realized that our life in the apartment had changed. We could no longer go into the kitchen freely – Valentina Ivanovna would come out of nowhere, switch off the light that I had turned on, and stand next to the light switch like a statue wrought from stone, her eyes gleaming in the darkness like (as I would imagine) the piercing gaze of a wolf. Now our neighbors wouldn't talk to us any more. They would only *show* us with their bearing that there was no room for us in Colonel Malyshev's apartment.

This did not greatly bother me, however. I wanted to attract the attention of a girl that I liked very much. Her name was Anya Chizhikova. She had enormous green eyes with black eyelashes and a funny mouth that slightly resembled a frog's. I understood right away that she wasn't like everyone else. It wasn't only a matter of Anya knowing how to crack jokes without smiling; rather, it seemed that she lived in a different world that only a select group could enter.

Anya Chizhikova lived in the fourth stairwell, at the corner of the building, and the window of her kitchen could be seen from my balcony. This stairwell on the corner was crowned at the very top with a strange structure, which resembled a little house with little columns like an antique portico.

Although I entered the same class as her, Anya didn't notice me. She had her own friends from the seventh and ninth stairwells, friends she had made all the way back in kindergarten.

I suffered greatly, but I couldn't do anything. Once, when the girls had come back from school, and I walked at a certain distance from them, neither together with them nor apart, Chizhikova pensively stated:

"Did you know that a pilot lives in our stairwell? Every morning, he flies away from the 'little house' (that's what she called the columned portico) in a tiny plane."

The girls looked at Chizhikova with great curiosity, but did not seem inclined to believe her.

"That's nonsense!" one of them said.

Chizhikova looked towards me and suddenly said:

"Do you want to see for yourselves? Our building isn't like all the others. You just have no idea."

The girls nodded.

I gasped and asked, "And when does he fly off, this pilot?" For some reason, I felt that something important in my life was being decided.

"At six o'clock in the morning," Chizhikova said unflappably. "If you want, go see for yourself!"

I realized that I had no choice. I had to get to know our building better.

In the morning, after I told my parents that we had something important to do at school, I went to the fourth stairwell and begin going up to the twelfth floor. Doors were slamming and the inhabitants were trudging off to their jobs. I got out of the elevator. Before me there were two apartments, and next to them a little ladder led up. I began going up the ladder with some hesitation.

"What if the pilot isn't happy that I came here without permission? What if Chizhikova tricked me?" However, it was beyond my power to believe that she, who was so wonderful and special, had lied to me. I grabbed the knob on the little door at the end of the ladder. A lock hung on it, one similar to our neighbor's refrigerator. I tugged at it, but it wouldn't budge. I had probably come too late.

After the school day, when we came home dragging our knapsacks like barge-haulers of yore, I said loudly:

"I was up there today, on the twelfth floor, next to the little house, but it was locked. Something must have happened, and the pilot couldn't fly off today."

All of the girls turned to me at the same time, and their knapsacks suddenly fell from their hands. They started chortling with laughter.

"She went upstairs at six o'clock in the morning! What an idiot! You tricked her good!"

They were spinning around from laughing, and they laughed like they couldn't stop.

It wasn't just Chizhikova who was laughing. She looked me in the eye awfully seriously. And I looked at her.

Between us those giggling faces spun about. We said nothing to one another, but from that day forward we were friends.

Soon I became friends with each of the girls who made fun of me, and I started to visit their homes. This is how we called it, "visiting". I would go to the seventh, ninth, or tenth stairwells, take the elevator up to their door, and stand on the tips of my toes to ring the doorbell. Usually it was written on the doors: "For so-and-so, ring twice; for so-and-so, three times", and so on. Making a mistake was unacceptable. The doorbell would ring briefly and harshly. From behind the door I would hear:

"Hey, Skobeyevs, it's for you!"

Or:

Hey, Chebotarevs, open the door!

Our building had twelve stairwells, and each of them had a different smell. Of course, I loved the smell of ours, the first stairwell, most of all. Most importantly, I wasn't afraid of it. I started to be afraid of the others after one unpleasant episode. I went to the seventh stairwell to visit one girl that I played in the yard with. She lived on the seventh floor. Downstairs, also waiting for the elevator, a man with a narrow face and sharply chiseled features stood in a long leather coat. I didn't like the look of him from the start. The words "Never get into the elevator with a stranger!" came back into my head. When I would ask why I shouldn't, I would be answered with an odd sort of vagueness. Because that answer was so non-committal and unclear, every man in the elevator seemed to be a bad guy in disguise.

I hesitated as I stood next to the guy and then, breathing heavily and wrapped in a heavy black fur coat, I started to make my way up to the seventh floor on foot. The guy shouted something behind me, but I didn't understand anything of what he said. While I was walking up, I heard the doors of the elevator slam below, then I saw him rising up past the floors, and suddenly the elevator stopped on the very same floor that I was walking past up the stairs. A narrow head looked down at me, and I heard a wheedling voice, though maybe it only seemed that way because I was afraid. Nonetheless, he did say something like:

"Little girl, come here, come on."

It is hard for me to remember what happened after that. I can only say that I literally tumbled down the stairs. I leapt out into the street, ran like a bullet through the yard, and then flew up to our floor.

Maybe that guy just wanted to play a joke on a frightened little girl, but either way, I didn't go back to the seventh stairwell for an entire year.

When I became friends with Chizhikova, I literally fell straight into her strange world. The main feature of this was that people were strictly divided into children and adults. Adults were considered aliens from another planet, totally incapable of understanding children and their problems. For that reason, the most important thing was to always keep adults wrapped around your finger, so that they wouldn't get in your way and they would know their place. To a larger degree, this was true of grandmothers for some reason, and especially our friend Irina's grandmother, who lived in that haunted seventh stairwell. Irina's grandmother had been a heroic nurse during the Civil War, which was attested by the certificates of recognition and honors that hung abundantly on their walls. As it happened, this grandmother had raised Irina on her own.

It was in front of Irina's grandmother that Anya loved to act our her grand performance, namely showing how we were the best girls in our class, that we adored our Pioneer troop, and we loved doing homework. Chizhikova would perform this part as if with one breath. I had to play a supporting role, but I felt sorry for the old woman, who listened with amazement to our stories about the "good turns we did as Pioneers". My uneasiness probably showed on my face, and soon Chizhikova stopped putting on her act.

When the warm days of spring came, I returned to our balcony. I sat under the stairs and I thought incessantly about the pilot who would fly off in the morning from the little house under the columned portico. I thought that he must have felt the same wonderful feeling that I did. Chizhikova and I never spoke about the pilot. I sensed that if I said but a single word, something would break down between us in this world, too.

Anya and I had a rule: when I would leave the house, I would hang my bright red coat on the balcony. Chizhikova could see it from her kitchen window. This was one of the secret signs that we gave each other.

I lived my life, growing used to the fact that I had to enter the kitchen as seldom as possible, and that I, my parents, and my little brother would now eat in our room, but when the phone rang, I had to run full speed to the hallway so that I would be the first to grab the receiver.

Once on a Sunday morning, somewhere around six o'clock in the morning, my entire family was awoken by a strange and thundering sound. It sounded as if Indians were beating drums on the other side of our door. I leapt out of my bed and rushed to the door.

"Don't go out!" my mother cried, as if we really had been transported to the jungles of Africa, and a terrible danger threatened us. My father had gone away on a business trip, and my mother was now very afraid of something happening to me and my little brother. I was curious to know what Valentina Ivanovna had thought up this time, she was the director of our little home theatre. Not long before – in peacetime – we could see how she was getting bored with her retirement, and she didn't always have something to do. Now, when I would bump into her near the bath, I could see how her eyes gleamed with a certain energy, and what a joyful smile appeared on her face.

My mother locked us in the room and ran to fetch some lady from our neighborhood's burlaw court. This lady came to our place an hour later. The drums had already grown quiet by that time. Breathing heavily, this functionary asked us to set a chair for her in the middle of the hallway and to bring her a glass of water.

The neighbors stayed hidden and became quiet.

"Malyshevs," she insisted, "Come out right now!"

The elder daughter Lyudmila appeared out of the darkness in a long robe, with a pale but triumphant face.

"Well now, Malyshevs," this functionary addressed her alone, "Are you causing trouble again? How many neighbors have you driven away now? I've already lost count."

"That's a lie," Lyudmila shrieked and then disappeared into the darkly-lit entrance to the apartment.

What happened after that was no longer particularly interesting. A set of words and phrases was exchanged: "pressing charges", "court", "nothing is going to happen", "everyone has taken them to court", and then suddenly the word "exchange" was heard, immediately followed by "get out of here".

Now I could clearly see my House flying away from me. I was still living here, I could feel its warmth, but soon all this would disappear. Indeed, the events that came after that happened with incredible speed. My parents put all their energy into running away, escaping, not even looking where they where going, as long as we didn't have to see those neighbors any more. My pleading and crying had no effect. I was already thirteen, and I was in the seventh grade.

Several months before, something remarkable happened in Chizhikova's life and mine. We would often make fun of our classmate Sergei, but as we sat in the audience at a contest for marching and singing held at the Pioneer Palace on the Lenin Hills, Chizhikova suddenly saw Sergei in a new light. He was standing, as usual, under a red banner. Chizhikova suddenly turned red in spots, then she put her head in her hands and told me that she was in love with Sergei. At first, I thought that this was another example of her acting.

After she didn't come to class, however, I decided to find out what was going on with her. A nice neighbor of Anya's opened the door to me and pointed towards the kitchen with her chin. There, Chizhikova was roosting on a tall chair and looking out the window. She turned her head and, without shifting from her position, she indicated with her gaze the clothesline on which her handkerchiefs were neatly arranged.

"Well, what?" I asked, as I didn't yet understand the tragedy of what had befallen her.

"I've already cried through this many handkerchiefs," she answered gloomily.

From that time forward, we would mark that date. Some time later, Chizhikova got herself a scotch terrier, a little square-shaped dog, and she explained that the dog had the same brown eyes as Sergei. Nonetheless, the boy that Chizhikova had fallen in love with was still truly scared of us. Granted, this gave us strength and imagination. Every day we would come to his house from the direction of Konyushkovsky Lane, and next to a large stone Chizhikova would recite a monologue about her sad and unrequited love.

From the age of twelve, I constantly thought about how I should write memoirs about my childhood with Chizhikova. Now my parents were taking me away, tearing me away from all of the variety and colorfulness of that life! I was supposed to say goodbye to my childhood – to the pilot, the stone, and Chizhikova who would look out from her kitchen window at my balcony.

Thus we moved out. The people who we traded our rooms with were infinitely overjoyed that from the town of Babushkin, only recently incorporated into Moscow, they had now moved to Prospekt Kalinina. We set off to their Babushkin, to an apartment of our own that I never managed to get used to.

Time passed, and my mother, who worked not far from our former home, was walking in the street one day and ran into that same functionary who had come to us.

"So, we have our burlaw court," she noted sadly. "The new people who are living in your old place have been rushed to the hospital with acute poisoning. They think the neighbors did it. But, you know, they can't prove anything." She sighed heavily. "You might consider yourselves lucky."

At first, not so much time passed. At first Chizhikova and I would write to each other – we didn't even have a phone at our new apartment in the beginning. Then, everything just fell apart. We saw each other and talked on the phone less and less. Later, I found out that she was going to marry Sergei.

She became a completely different person – a homebody, a housewife with two children.

More time passed. It was 1993, and incredible things were happening across from the building I had once lived in. The deputies were sitting the White House, refusing to let the legislature be dissolved, and weapons were being handed out to the people.

Some snipers had gone crazy and were shooting here and there into the crowd. The storming of the White House began. All of this was shown on television. Like the rest of the country, I couldn't tear myself away from the screen. When the camera suddenly swept past our balcony, at the very top I saw, like on a tiny platform, right in the portico of my pilot's "little house", bystanders crowding and watching what was happening. There were so many of them that it seemed as if they would soon come pouring down like peas.

My heart was wrenched with pain. I realized that my pilot had flown away for ever.

Photographs*

* Courtesy of Natalia Gromova

Tatyana Lugovskaya, 1950.

Tashkent, the Lugovskoys' room, 1942. Drawing by Tatyana Lugovskaya.

Vladimir Lugovskoy,
1940.

Elena
Bulgakova,
1940.

Margarita Aliger and Daniil Danin, 1950.

View from a Lavrushinsky window.

*Maria Belkina,
1940.*

*Moscow,
Arbat Square,
1930.*

Lidia Libedinskaya, 2000.

Maria Belkina. Drawing by Dimitri Fyodorov

*Maria Belkina
and her cousin,
early 1920s.*

*Natalya
Shakhovskaya,
1910.*

Vladimir Lugovskoy, late 1930s.

*Maria Belkina and
Anatoly Tarasenkov,
1939.*

*Andrei Andreyev (brother of Leonid Andreyev), Filipp Dobrov
and Daniil Andreyev, 1912. Photograph by Leonid Andreyev.*

Alexandra Dobrova, 1920.

On the porch of the house in Sergiev Posad: Nyanya, little Sergei Shik, Natalya Shakhovskaya and Mikhail Shik, 1923.

Olga Bessarabova, 1919.

Boris Bessarabov, 1922.

*Olga Bessarabova,
1927.*

*Alexander Kovalensky,
1920.*

Olga Bessarabova and friends, Sergiev Posad, 1923.

Moscow, Sobachye Square, early 20th century.

Daniil Andreyev, 1930.

The Dobrovs' home on Maly Levshinsky Lane, 1960.

Lubyanka by night, 1930.

*Mikhail Shik and Varvara Grigoryevna Malakhieva-Mirovich
(second and third from left), Olga Bessarabova
(third from right, seated), Sergiev Posad, 1923.*

Alla Tarasova in the role of Finochka in the Moscow Art Theatre staging of The Green Ring, 1916.

Rinochka Mzhebrovskaya, 1930.

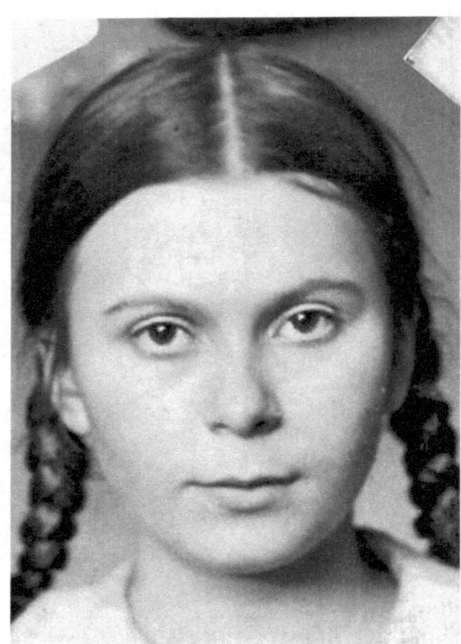

Varvara Grigoryevna Malakhieva-Mirovich, late 1940s.

Leo Tolstoy – Flight from Paradise

by Pavel Basinsky

Over a hundred years ago, something truly outrageous occurred at Yasnaya Polyana. Count Leo Tolstoy, a famous author aged eighty-two at the time, took off, destination unknown. Since then, the circumstances surrounding the writer's whereabouts during his final days and his eventual death have given rise to many myths and legends. In this book, popular Russian writer and reporter Pavel Basinsky delves into the archives and presents his interpretation of the situation prior to Leo Tolstoy's mysterious disappearance. Basinsky follows Leo Tolstoy throughout his life, right up to his final moments. Reconstructing the story from historical documents, he creates a visionary account of the events that led to the Tolstoys' family drama.

Flight from Paradise will be of particular interest to international researchers studying Leo Tolstoy's life and works, and is highly recommended to a broader audience worldwide.

Buy it > www.glagoslav.com

Glagoslav Publications Catalogue

- *The Time of Women* by Elena Chizhova
- *Sin* by Zakhar Prilepin
- *Hardly Ever Otherwise* by Maria Matios
- *Khatyn* by Ales Adamovich
- *Christened with Crosses* by Eduard Kochergin
- *The Vital Needs of the Dead* by Igor Sakhnovsky
- *A Poet and Bin Laden* by Hamid Ismailov
- *Kobzar* by Taras Shevchenko
- *White Shanghai* by Elvira Baryakina
- *The Stone Bridge* by Alexander Terekhov
- *King Stakh's Wild Hunt* by Uladzimir Karatkevich
- *Depeche Mode* by Serhii Zhadan
- *Herstories*, An Anthology of New Ukrainian Women Prose Writers
- *The Battle of the Sexes Russian Style* by Nadezhda Ptushkina
- *A Book Without Photographs* by Sergey Shargunov
- *Sankya* by Zakhar Prilepin
- *Wolf Messing - The True Story of Russia`s Greatest Psychic*
  by Tatiana Lungin
- *Good Stalin* by Victor Erofeyev
- *Solar Plexus* by Rustam Ibragimbekov
- *Don't Call me a Victim!* by Dina Yafasova
- *A History of Belarus* by Lubov Bazan
- *Children's Fashion of the Russian Empire* by Alexander Vasiliev
- *Empire of Corruption - The Russian National Pastime*
  by Vladimir Soloviev
- *Heroes of the 90s - People and Money. The Modern History of Russian Capitalism*
- *Boris Yeltsin - The Decade that Shook the World* by Boris Minaev
- *A Man Of Change - A study of the political life of Boris Yeltsin*
- *Gnedich* by Maria Rybakova
- *Marina Tsvetaeva - The Essential Poetry*
- *Multiple Personalities* by Tatyana Shcherbina
- *The Investigator* by Margarita Khemlin
- *Leo Tolstoy – Flight from paradise* by Pavel Basinsky
- *Prisoner* by Anna Nemzer

  More coming soon...